pop tart

pop tart

Kira Coplin and Julianne Kaye

AVON

An Imprint of HarperCollins*Publishers*

POP TART. Copyright © 2009 by Kira Coplin and Julianne Kaye. All rights reserved. Printed in the United States of America. No part of this book may be used or reproduced in any manner whatsoever without written permission except in the case of brief quotations embodied in critical articles and reviews. For information address HarperCollins Publishers, 10 East 53rd Street, New York, NY 10022.

HarperCollins books may be purchased for educational, business, or sales promotional use. For information please write: Special Markets Department, HarperCollins Publishers, 10 East 53rd Street, New York, NY 10022.

FIRST AVON PAPERBACK EDITION PUBLISHED 2009.

Interior text designed by Diahann Sturge

Library of Congress Cataloging-in-Publication Data
Coplin, Kira.
    Pop Tart / Kira Coplin and Julianne Kaye. — 1st Avon paperback ed.
        p. cm.
    ISBN 978-0-06-175694-8
    1. Women singers — Fiction. 2. Fame — Fiction. 3. Celebrities — California — Los Angeles — Fiction. 4. Hollywood (LosAngeles, Calif.) — Fiction. I. Kaye, Julianne. II. Title.
    PS3603.O6535P67   2009
    813'.6 — dc22   2009012852

09 10 11 12   OV/RRD   10 9 8 7 6 5 4 3 2 1

For Ruth Waller, my grandmother,
who always encouraged my silly dreams . . .
–K.C.

To my son, Jack, and my husband, Eddie,
for inspiring me every day . . .
–J.K.

Acknowledgments

Each friend represents a world in us, a world
possibly not born until they arrive, and it is only
by this meeting that a new world is born.
—Anais Nin

We would like to thank our editor May Chen, who believed in this project from the very beginning as well as our UK editor, Maxine Hitchcock. To our agent Mollie Glick, New School Media and our manager Brian Levy who fought for us and supported us through many sleepless nights and occasional tears, this book would not have been possible without you. Many thanks also to Matthew Hechinger and Jenifer K. Fischer whose support proved to be invaluable during this process.

And last but not least, thank you to an industry that has engrossed us, captivated us, infuriated us, and charmed us all the same—this landscape of the madcap and the marvelous that, most importantly, inspires us, is not one to be underestimated. Once in a while, our City of Angels lives up to its namesake, colliding the worlds of two complete strangers, forming unexpected and lasting friendships. On these rare occasions, you can truly believe in Hollywood endings.

pop tart

Prologue

> What can you say about a society that says
> God is dead and Elvis is alive?
> —Irv Kupcinet

A jolt of electricity runs from Crescent Heights Boulevard to Doheny Drive—a gleaming, vibrating stretch of asphalt and neon so notorious that Sin City named its "Strip" after it. It's there on Sunset Boulevard where the rich and famous play out their scandals for the world to see—where "It Girls" dance pantyless atop the oversized Monkeywood tables of Hollywood clubs, and where poolside catfights are veiled only by the thick foliage of the Marmont. And on one particular night in late November, just a stone's throw from the glittering lights and madness of the Sunset Strip, I inadvertently became a key player in one of the most shocking celebrity dramas of the past decade. No matter how I try to put the puzzle together, to coherently map out the timeline of events, pieces are still missing and holes will always remain.

There was an unnatural stiffness in the air that night as I raced down empty boulevards typically teeming with drivers blasting their radios, or assholes laying on their horns. Expressionless models from billboards stuccoed on the sides of shopping malls glared down on me; tonight they almost appeared menacing. The city itself felt like a ghost town at this hour, loosely woven and wrapped in nebulous unease. Waiting at a traffic light, anxiously drumming my fingers on the dashboard, I spot the only other living soul out on the street—a tall, muscular man with long brown hair falling past his shoulder blades, rollerblading in circles, wearing nothing but spandex shorts and laughing hysterically as if sending out a warning, "Proceed with caution, the crazies are out tonight."

I turned onto the tree-line street, lit up by the glow of a sign that read: Emergency Department. It was empty. Momentary relief washed over me. "Maybe it's okay. Maybe no one knows." But I knew this kind of thinking was premature. I'd been around long enough to know the percolating frenzy: chatter from police scanners had already alerted reporters and photographers, letting them know that something was amiss deep in the Valley. I screeched to a halt in the first parking garage I could find, almost forgetting to pull the keys from the ignition. "Fuck," I muttered under my breath, wondering if I could've parked any further from the hospital entrance. I moved fast— the gentle summer breeze mocking my distress—time was limited, that much I knew. Up ahead, a single police car with its sirens blaring flew up to the entrance of the E.R. That's where things get a little fuzzy. A wave of adrenaline washed over me, stimulating my heart rate and dilating my air passages, prompting me to break out into a sprint. Like an animal prepared for an attack, my footsteps echoed noisily along the pavement only to be masked by the drone of helicopters appearing suddenly overhead, circling like mosquitoes. "They've found her, this is it, get ready," I told myself, knowing that within mere seconds I would be submerged in complete pandemonium. I had hoped to make it inside before the throngs of people began to gather, but that hope was gone now.

By the time I made my way to the entrance, hospital workers had begun erecting screens in front of the doors to shield them from the hordes of paparazzi and news cameras on the sidewalk. No one quite knew what was going on.

"I just got pulled out of bed by my editor," a disheveled tabloid reporter, still in her pajamas, complained.

"Maybe she's dead!" one paparazzo yelled out, causing the crowd to erupt in laughter.

"That wouldn't be so bad. Then we'd finally be able to get some sleep," another reporter muttered to her coworker, who nodded sheepishly.

Our attention was soon directed to the motorcade that seemed to appear out of nowhere, more than a dozen lights and sounds spanning two blocks. As it moved in our direction, inhuman chaos broke out. Photographers leapt from cars stopped at red lights and swarmed the ambulance—hanging off of it as if it were a life raft—all elbows and shoulders, knuckles and dilated lenses, hoping for a snapshot of an American sweetheart in her state of distress. What had really gone on in the hours leading up to this moment, no one knew. Was she near death? Had she lost her mind? Would she emerge in a puff of stage smoke and dry ice, looking absolutely breathtaking and wave to the crowd as if the world were her stage? The only thing that was certain, not only to us outside the hospital, but to the millions of Americans tuning in to watch the drama unfold on live T.V., was that the girl who lived a life that dreams were made of, with a fistful of pop hits to boot—was being ambulanced to the emergency room, prompting people everywhere to ask, "How did this all happen?"

I didn't have to ask.

I knew exactly how it had happened. I had seen it all first hand.

To the rest of the world, Brooke Parker was an immovable force. To them, she was the girl that sang happy songs with childlike abandon, who gyrated with vampy sex appeal across glittering stages and who lived in a world of feelings instead of facts—a dream, all smoke and mirrors. It was that face they'd seen so many times before—her doe eyes turned toward the camera, radiating the screen as she smiles—a smile that made them wonder what it would truly be like, how it would really feel, to be the kind of girl who had it all.

Chapter 1

There are three sides to every story:
My side, your side and the truth. And no one is lying.
–Robert Evans

It was unusually warm for February in Beverly Hills.
Men in suits beckoned to take their lunch meetings outside while their wives trotted down to Rodeo Drive to
spend their hard-earned cash on things like diamond-
encrusted purse hangers. I sat at my desk facing the
window, watching groups of women saunter in and out
of pricey boutiques. Clean-cut boys in ties lounged outside of the Brighton Coffee Shop sipping vanilla lattes,
presumably conversing about their mailroom duties at
William Morris and favorite movies. As a pack of girls
zipped by, arms weighed down with shopping bags from
Ron Herman and Hermes, cell phone chimes peeled my
attention back to life inside the office.

"Jackie? It's your mother."

"Mom, I know it's you, it comes up on my caller I.D.," I said, rolling my eyes.

"How is everything going? How's the job?"

"It's great. Sheryl's just finishing up a cover shoot for a magazine and then on Sunday I'm assisting her for another job. Not sure yet what it is exactly, it's on a studio lot in the Valley," I told her, trying to sound as upbeat as possible.

"So, you're working on the weekends now too?" my mother asked.

"When I'm needed," I said quickly.

"Well, this doesn't sound like a job you had to quit school for . . . I mean, maybe next semester you could find one like it back in Boston," she said.

I inhaled deeply. "I didn't drop out of school for this job. I dropped out because I wanted to take my career in another direction."

"Oh honey, you are so close to graduating. You only have four more semesters left . . . it just seems like such a waste to quit now. Why don't you just finish and then if you still want to enroll in cosmetology school, do it then."

"I don't want to go to cosmetology school. I want to work on shoots . . . I don't need a degree for that, I can do it now and that's what I'm doing," I told her, eyeing the overly Botoxed blond entering the side door to the salon where we rented space. It was my boss, Sheryl.

"But you're just an assist—"

"Mom, I have to go," I said hastily.

"Your father will be home early tonight. I think it's a perfect time for the three of us to have a serious discussion."

"Sure, whatever you want—I have to *go*," I repeated before cutting her off and hanging up the phone.

Phone calls from my mother like that one had become routine during the last six months since I dropped out of Boston University, right before my junior year. Home for the summer and bored with books, I searched for a creative outlet to take my mind off of the grueling schedule that would be waiting for me once again at the end of August.

"I think I might want to try the whole acting thing again for a while," I said to my parents, who were poised on chaise lounges in our house, referring to my brief stint of commercial work at the age of three. My mother grabbed at bits of her graying hair and shook her head. My father just frowned. The endless dabblings of my childhood, which they once considered amusing, had long since grown tired.

Drawn to color and music at a very young age, I spent time experimenting with various artistic undertakings. "I am going to learn to play the flute!" I'd tell my parents at the dinner table, a typical outburst from me.

"Yesterday it was ballet lessons, and the day before that you were going to learn to play the trombone," my mother would laugh.

"You're a jack of all trades, kid," my father would say as I performed my latest masterpiece for him, perhaps a tap dance routine along the back patio.

The older I got, the more I disliked being good at many things: I wanted to be great at *some*thing. I wanted to leave my mark on the world, and somehow an art history degree earned in stuffy old classrooms in Cambridge didn't seem like step one. Although they had supported my creativity in little ways as a child, my parents were dead set on shipping me out East the day I had my high school diploma in hand. Both of them worked in Hollywood since as long as I could remember and always talked about how brutal "the industry" could be—they strived to keep me away, far away from it. So, when I announced my newly re-discovered acting career the summer after my sophomore year, the word "disappointed" is an understatement.

I spent weeks trying to make the right connections; I even tried to get back in touch with my old agent over at Gersh, only to find out that she was now retired and living in Santa Barbara with her family.

"Is there anyone you can refer me to?" I asked.

"Feel free to submit a resume and headshot and if they're interested someone will be in touch," she said, as if reading from a script.

I wasn't going to give up so easily. Instead of wielding a diverse but mediocre portfolio of skills, I wanted to shine in a more singular way. So, when a man from a generic company called Ultimate Casting responded to an email I had sent him, I was thrilled.

"I think I've got something for ya," he said. The tone of his voice revealed too much. He called me a knockout and assured me there was a demand for a "redhead" with "soft features" like mine. I could just picture him: hair combed over his balding scalp, Hawaiian shirt stretched snuggly around his protruding belly, short legs kicked up on top of a beat-up old desk, sitting in a miniscule makeshift office somewhere in the Valley, flipping through a roster of numbers and promising idiots like me that he had their "star" on the Hollywood walk.

"Here's the deal . . . we cast for every major network and every major production company in Los Angeles. We don't make money until you do. I repeat—we don't make a dime until you've booked your first job through us. When you do start working, our service fee kicks in—$69.95 a month . . . but really, when you think about it, that's nothing. You can make up to a hundred dollars a day working on movie sets." Was he selling me car insurance?

"Great, how do I get started?" I was a sucker, and I knew it, but these were desperate times . . . and I was desperate. If it got me out of the house two days a week it was better than nothing. At the very least it would prove to my parents that I was *on my way.*

Shelling out a portion of my "allowance," a mere $100 a week in exchange for picking up dry cleaning and odd chores around the house, I was relieved when Ultimate Casting booked me a job—and even more relieved to hear that the production was legitimate.

"It's a five-day shoot on the Warner Brothers lot," said the same supposed frump of a man who had called me the week before. "And it's a period piece, so they want you to sleep in rollers at night. Keep 'em in until you get to the set the next day. Call time is 7 AM each morning."

Making it to the Valley from Beverly Hills at the crack of dawn, my head covered in pink sponge curlers, was not quite my cup of tea. The seventy-five-dollar per day fee I was promised didn't quite average out to a fair amount once it was broken down by the long hours that seemed to drag on forever. My last morning on set, I sat groggily in the makeup chair, waiting to get powdered. The makeup artist who tended to the girl next to me, her brushstrokes creating a completely flawless look in seconds, struck me. She was an artist and her's was a real-life canvas, one that would be seen on film, by millions of people worldwide.

"I took a SPFX course over the summer a couple years ago—it was kind of cool—we did a lot of horror-movie–type stuff," I eagerly told her when it was my turn. I had hoped that would've impressed her, but she simply smiled and nodded.

"I think I would be good at makeup—I've always had a knack for it. But . . . how would I even start?" I asked.

"To get the good jobs—to be a *professional*," the woman said, "you would need to align yourself with a big company . . . one that will commission you to travel and to work on events all over the world."

"Umm . . . and how do I do that?" I asked confused.

"You'd be invited in for an interview with a makeup line and to do a demonstration for them . . . but before you could even *get* an interview you'd have to have a working portfolio and a video reel," she sniffed.

"Wow, okay. I mean, do you need to take classes someplace, or what?"

"Most lines offer advanced classes for artists who are already considered professionals, there's nothing for those that are aspiring." She stopped for a moment and then raised an eyebrow as if she was about to tell me a secret. "Your best bet would be to apprentice for an artist that's already established. That way you can get your feet wet right away. Look, I don't have anything right now, but I have a girlfriend who works for a line in Beverly Hills and she gets booked for entertainment and high-fashion jobs all the time. I'm sure she could use some help."

A week later I accepted an apprenticeship with Sheryl Lane, or as the slogan on her website read, "Sheryl Lane, Makeup Artist to the Stars!" I would be available to Sheryl five days a week, possibly more—starting at 8 AM and working as long as she needed me.

As I walked into the house, the smell of chicken roasting from the kitchen caught me off guard. My mother rarely cooked when I was in high school, and since I'd returned from Boston and settled back into the home I'd grown up in, it had become even more infrequent.

"Special occasion?" I asked, throwing my messenger bag clumsily on the floor near the back door. She looked up from the counter where she was preparing green beans to give me a disgusted look.

"I'm just cleaning up in here, do you really have to leave your mess all over the floor?"

"My mess?" I asked before pointing down toward my bag that I left in the same place every day. "You mean this?" Consumed with the green beans once again, she merely nodded. As I was scooping my belongings off of the floor, my father breezed through the back door, looking famished.

"It's almost done," my mother said seeing the look on his face. "Jackie, put out some silverware and get ready to eat."

We ate in silence for the first few minutes until my father loudly cleared his throat. "Since we're all here, we should probably talk."

"About?" Though I had tried to conceal it in my voice, the aggression with which I forked my food back and forth along my plate hinted at my annoyance.

"It didn't sound to me, when we spoke on the phone today, like you are too interested in going back to school," my mother said slowly. *Too interested?* The way she said it made me cringe, as if I had been stringing her along, forcing her to cling on to some sort of hope when in reality I'd been brutally honest with her for months.

"I'm not," I said.

"So working at that makeup store, which is perfectly fine if that's what you *want*, is the plan?" my father asked, raising an eyebrow.

"Yeah. For now, anyway." I didn't know if makeup was something I wanted to do for the rest of my life, but it was something I was good at, and something I could even be great at—something that would take me places. I could tell from their frowning faces, however, that this wasn't the answer they were looking for.

"Well, if this is going to be your career it's only fair that you start supporting yourself financially. A girl your age shouldn't be living rent free," my father said. I scowled. I could only imagine what most of the kids I'd grown up with in Beverly Hills were up to. I could just imagine them now, lounging in the private screening rooms of their statuesque homes, playing doubles on the adjacent tennis courts above Sunset, and guzzling out of $400 bottles plucked from the wine cellars of their parents who were vacationing in St. John for the next three months. For me, growing up here was far from fancy; in fact, I felt more ordinary here than I would've in Oklahoma City. I didn't return to my family's modest Spanish-style home on a square lot south of Wilshire to be pampered, I did it because I was unable to afford a place of my own.

"Fine. I'll start looking for apartments in Watts since that's the only place I'll be able to afford one," I joked.

"Don't be ridiculous, we're not pushing you out into the ghetto. You can stay in the garage apartment, you're just going to have to pay some rent."

"That's right." My father nodded in agreement with my mother. "And that goes for your car too. I think it's only fair that you take over insurance and maintenance."

In shock, I looked out the side window at the sad-looking Jeep Wagoneer that I had driven since high school. I couldn't believe what I was hearing. It wasn't the money that upset me . . . sure, a few skylights and a fireplace may have been the fanciest features of our home, but that didn't mean that we were poor. We were far from it. But we were also far from the type, like some I went to high school with, who took private jets and were driven around in limousines. These were the kinds of people my parents would complain about for hours . . . but they were also the ones that they gave their full attention to. As a kid I could never understand it. If these Hollywood folks were really so awful, why did my parents spend so much time tending to them instead of me? I wanted to know what it was like. I wanted to be a part of that world too, to be as fabulous as the creatures they cater to, and yet they found this to be unacceptable for me. And now I was being punished it seemed. Sometimes I wondered what I looked like through their eyes. *Goofy, clumsy, never-able-to-finish-anything Jackie—she doesn't have what it takes to work in entertainment.*

Interrupting my self-loathing, my mother piped up. "You had such a good thing going for you back East. I'd hate to see you ruin that. I don't want to see you get lost out here, like so many people do . . ."

"I don't want to live a life you've planned out for me," I said, the frustration rising in my voice and red flames burning up my cheeks. "Just because you've always been so miserable out here doesn't mean I'm destined to be!"

"That's enough," my father growled, but I was unable to stop myself.

". . . You always talk about people following their dreams . . . so why is it you want me to give up on mine?"

"Honey, it's not that I want you to give up on your dreams— I just don't understand what yours are?" The way she raised her eyebrows with mock concern normally drove me absolutely crazy, but as I listened to her speak a feeling of relief began to settle over me.

"Just because we don't have the same one doesn't make mine ridiculous," I said calmly before turning and walking out of the dining room. Cool winter engulfed me as I made my way up the rickety steps to the apartment over the garage. I had no plan, no idea as to how I was going to make extra money but at that moment I couldn't have cared less. I had never felt so free in my entire life. Starting immediately, I would pay rent like any other kid my age, and make sure to save enough money for things like car insurance, oil changes, and gas. Well it may have been the end of my social life, which was scarce these days anyway, it certainly wasn't the end of the world. Since the hourly wage that Sheryl paid me wasn't enough to cover even half of my newly incurred expenses, I was going to have to take on another job, and quick.

With Sheryl off in Santa Barbara shooting a local fashion spread, the store was in my hands. I was taking full advantage of this, using the time to surf the web for other part-time jobs, when our first customer, a rather big-boned woman, burst through the door around noon doused in shades of pink.

"Hi," I muttered, not looking up from pages of openings on myjobsearcher.com, "let me know if I can help you with anything." The way she clunked about—the heels of her strappy platform sandals resounding in thuds along the wood floor— roused my attention. Looking up, the annoyance on my face quickly morphed into confusion. Standing just a few feet away, testing shades of cream blush by swiping them on her forearm, was what most certainly was a man in drag. The flutter-sleeve chiffon top with a ruffled bodice and plunging keyhole neck-line tightly hugged what was supposed to be a cinch waist. A white cotton miniskirt with pink accents like rhinestones and piping was paired with the incredibly noisy six-inch wooden-heeled sandals to accentuate long, smooth legs. As I caught her eye, she lowered her chin, as if trying to hide the lump in her throat was an instinctual reaction. Then, thinking better of it, she turned and smiled at me, almost shyly at first.

"Are you finding everything you need?" I asked, trying to stifle my surprise. She made her way over to the counter, sling-ing along her pink-and-white purse—which featured a mish-mash of designs that included a Christian Dior signature logo, butterflies and flowers, and a bejeweled padlock at the zipper to top it off.

"I'm Rita," she said batting her eyelashes. "I need to find a good red lipstick, and a new shade of foundation. Something a little darker, I'm done doing Jayne . . . I'm on to Hayworth. She's got Spaniard in her like me, you know?"

Her warm and energetic demeanor rendered me completely comfortable, and I found myself giggling at almost everything she said. Periodically she'd say things like, "You can't rush glamour, honey!" Or "Every woman is a vamp until proven innocent," which would make me laugh even harder. We spent what seemed like an hour rifling through various shades of coverup, looking for the best products that would allow Rita to exaggerate her eyes in an attempt to play down at least a healthy portion of her masculine jaw, and me trying to convince her to give up lip liners that were darker than her lipstick. In the end, like any good transvestite would, she stuck to her guns and bought a deep plum shade to match with her classic red.

"What's all this?" Rita peered at my computer screen and then down to a list of names and contact numbers I'd compiled for job openings in everything from retail to government, none of which were too appealing.

"My parents are done supporting my creative endeavors," I told her. "So that means I need to find a second job."

She picked up my notebook, gingerly flipping the pages with her surprisingly feminine hands, before stopping to point out one of my leads. I tried not to stare when I noticed the exact pearlescent white Invicta watch I'd been drooling over for months on her dainty wrist. "You're not going to make the money you need serving up hash browns and waffles, I can tell you that right now." She was pointing to a listing for a deli just down the street.

"It's in Beverly Hills," I argued. "The patio there is always busy."

"Everyone knows, honey, that the real money is in cocktail waitressing." She raised a perfectly groomed eyebrow, and flashed a huge grin. "Today's your lucky day, girl." Reaching into her purse, she pulled out a business card and smacked it down on the desk in front of me.

"The Queen Victoria, huh?" I said picking it up. Beneath the embossed lettering were background images of cross-dressers that appeared as 1950s and Hollywood's screen legends. In smaller type was what I had guessed to be Rita's birth name, Jorge Vazquez.

"That's right, I'm the manager over there; we could probably use a little help. And a pretty thang like you. You'd do real well."

"Yeah—no thanks, I think I'll pass," I smiled, trying not to laugh.

"I know what you're thinking, but it really is a lot of fun. Plus . . . you can keep on doing makeup—some of the best makeup artists count drag queens as muses. Think about it." And with that, Jorge, er—Rita, scooped up her purchases and headed out the door.

Not heeding Rita's warning, I took the waitressing job at the deli down the street. Most days, like today, I started my shift there at 6 AM so that I could finish early enough to accompany Sheryl to bookings, watch over the store, and take the occasional odd job by myself.

It had only been two weeks but I was already hating my new schedule. Not only was I barely making any money, I was completely accident prone. I'd broken five glasses in the span of three days and in one morning alone I had forgotten two orders to boot. By the time I made it over to help Sheryl, I was already in a rotten mood. I could barely stand to listen to her as she shrieked into the phone.

"Oh my God! Is that not cool, cool, cool?! Totally, totally— we will be there honey and don't you worry about a thing—it's

on us, no absolutely, don't worry about a thing!" I became annoyed. Just listening to her I knew exactly what was happening
and I did all I could to stifle my frustration.

I had been working with Sheryl for almost six months by that
point and was always surprised, though I should've at some point
probably gotten used to it, at her sheer excitement for absolutely
everything and nothing. Just that morning she doubled over in
joy at a most recent purchase: a gift for a friend's baby shower.

"And, if you pull on that right there," she said, showing me
the glossy catalogue in her hand, "the diaper bag turns into a
backpack! How cool is that!" I had stopped trying to conceal my
boredom months ago after a half-hour rant concerning Candle
Belts, which are exactly as they sound—a decorative belt for
your candle.

Part of me pitied Sheryl, while my other, more sympathetic
half felt bad for feeling bad. She was, by all definitions, a very
in-demand makeup artist in Hollywood. From spreads in *Los
Angeles* magazine to booking the occasional job for a daytime
drama, she did it all. Though she had very kindly taken me
under her wing, I couldn't help but notice her enthusiasm
seemed to compensate for something, something I didn't know.
She had set up shop in one corner of a chic salon on Beverly
Drive, though we rarely worked out of there, instead using it
more for office space to schedule shoots, take meetings, and
market her services than anything else. When people did come
in for meetings, I was always blown away by her ability to make
eyeliner, makeup brushes, and lip gloss sound so wildly exciting, but was almost certain that the people who left would
never come back again. But shockingly enough, most did.

Here's the thing, Sheryl was a divorced forty-something who
left her cheating husband and McMansion in the Calabasas to
become a swinging-single career woman in Beverly Hills. This
was all, no less, inspired by an episode (her first, for the record)

of *Sex and the City* on TBS. I've heard her quote Kim Cattrall from that episode enough to make my ears bleed. Perhaps I was a pessimist, but no one in her right mind could be *that* excited all the time, and I was just sort of waiting for her to crack . . .

"I got you a gig!" Sheryl shouted in a singsongy voice as she hung up the phone. I braced myself . . . I knew exactly what she was going to say. "Okay, well, don't get mad at me . . . I told Nan Dressner we'd—well, *you*—would do her daughter's makeup tomorrow morning. She's walking in the 'Women in Holly-wood' fashion show. It's a favor, so we're not getting paid," she said, meaning *I* wasn't getting paid. "But, oh-my-God Jackie! I mean," she continued, "the Dressners! They would be great people to know!"

This was typical Sheryl, and this is what I mean about feeling bad for her. She was so desperate to be seen and liked, especially by the society types who lunched at the Polo Lounge, that she always did them favors to ingratiate herself to them. Although when I really thought about it, she adored attention from almost anyone willing to give it to her and was known to flirt with men half her age after no more than a single appletini. The Dressner job, however, was a definite step in the right direction for her as it was one more step up the social ladder. To me, it meant a wasted Saturday afternoon spent with a bratty teenager and her friends and no compensation in sight.

"Sure," I mumbled, feigning rapture with something on my computer screen, which I hoped would mask my annoyance.

"Fabulous! I would go—but I've got a hot date with a hotter man," she said before she leaned in closer to me. "And I prob-ably won't get out of bed 'til noon, if you know what I mean." Making a whispering voice without whispering, she said, "Ted Painter," and then sat there smiling, waiting for my reaction.

"Oh that's great—I was *supposed* to meet friends at one of his restaurants for brunch tomorrow . . ." I hinted. Standing up, I grabbed my coat as fast as I could in fear that she might start spouting more—where they were going, how they met, what he was like in bed. Just the thought of Sheryl and the sixty-year-old restaurateur holding hands made me gag.

"So, I have to go now, bye," I said as I practically ran toward the door.

"Oh—don't forget, we have a big job on Sunday," she called after me.

"We do?" I asked, halfway out the door.

"Come on, you remember, the music video shoot in the Valley," she said.

"Oh right, those dancing, singing boys from that Nickelodeon show, right? The ones with kind of spiky hair?" I asked nonchalantly.

"The Emerson Brothers!" she shrieked.

"Yeah, them." I shrugged. She looked at me like I was crazy, but I wasn't a twelve-year-old girl and I had no idea who they were.

"They're huge, Jackie, they just signed an endorsement deal with Street Cred!"

"Who is that? A rapper?" I asked, genuinely confused.

"Street Cred?!" she asked incredulously. "The energy drink? Well, anyway, we're not doing their makeup exactly . . ."

"Great," I thought, sure she was about to tell me we were doing their mother's makeup for her dinner reservation that night.

Much to my relief, she responded, "We're doing the makeup for this up-and-coming singer named Brooke Parker . . . a real cutie, she was Miss Teen Florida last year. She was discovered by some kind of talent manager or someone, doing her cute little song and dance in the pageant—anyway, she's their opening act and she's shooting her first video. I'll see you Sunday."

* * *

I was running late as usual the next day and hurried to put the finishing touches on the Dressner daughter's face while the Hollywood elite took their seats in the ballroom of the Regent Beverly Wilshire—soon to be filled with the amateur designs of local rich kids dabbling in the fashion world on their parents' dime. I giggled about this to myself as I spotted Delia Lutz, the *Queen of Gossip* and ruler of her own online domain, deliasdirt. com, sitting just a few seats away. She was snaky, sort of, in a very *Page Six* sort of way, but was even better because she sank her teeth into local personalities just as hard as international celebrities. And even though Delia could be cruel, I knew that she'd still write up the fashion show favorably since the proceeds were benefiting the Children's Hospital. She'd call the attendees *fashionistas* instead of fogies, and describe the clothing with supple adjectives like *sleek*, *flirty*, and *hip*, instead of boring, ugly, and uninspired. As I mused, her gaze unexpectedly met mine, and then the strangest thing happened. Delia cringed, either in a state of embarrassment or horror, or maybe it was a combination of both, and looked away immediately.

"That's strange," I said to Lauren, my longtime friend who had accompanied me to the show, "did you see the way that woman just looked at me?"

"It's not that surprising considering she just lit up your boss online," Lauren laughed.

"She what?" I asked.

"Don't tell me you didn't see it!" A look, similar to Delia's, spread across Lauren's face now. She punched a few keys on her Blackberry and flipped through a few entries—obviously having read Delia's Dirt more than once on the go—and handed it over to me. Squinting slightly, I read:

> Which well-known restaurateur currently going
> through a mid-life crisis was left waiting alone

at a table in his very own nightclub while his
recently separated, social-climbing date (who's
been known to do her fair share of both making out and "makeup" all over town) gave a little
"hand service" to a hard-rocking musician in the
next room over?

"This is bad," I said to Lauren, "I mean, everyone knows that
Sheryl's been seeing Ted Painter. . ."

"Who's the hard-rocking musician?" Lauren giggled.

"I'm surprised that *you* don't know!" I laughed though I was
still in sheer disbelief, unable to pry my eyes away from the
phone. If anyone knew the rock star's identity, I was sure it'd
be Lauren—because Lauren always seemed to know everyone's business everywhere. From celebrity blogs to the society
column in a tiny Beverly Hills newspaper, she was on it. We met
freshman year in high school and she was no different then—
always relaying the latest dramas that were unfolding in the
hallways as she twisted pieces of her unruly, strawberry-tinged
hair around her finger. And even though she somehow knew
everyone's secrets, gossip for Lauren had always been more of
a spectator sport. She worked at an art gallery and spent most
of her time between the door-chimes of incoming customers
compulsively hitting "refresh" on every gossip website and blog
in existence. Still, like me, she preferred to watch from the
safety of the sidelines, managing to never stick out.

By the time the sixth model strutted down the runway in
something that can only be described as "contemporary
culottes"—if there is such a thing—I had become completely
oblivious to the over-*oooh'd-and-aaah'd* crap being flaunted up
and down the runway. If Sheryl puts as much energy into her
anger as she puts into her enthusiasm, tomorrow was going to
be ugly, a sleek and inspired kind of ugly.

* * *

My ringing cell phone provided me with a rude awakening early Sunday morning, confirming my worst fear: Sheryl scorned was a force to be reckoned with.

"Hello?" I asked groggily.

"Jackie . . . it's Sheryl."

She was silent for a few seconds and I had momentarily forgotten all about the blind item in the newspaper as I looked sleepily around my garage apartment, which was basically attached to my parent's house. The sunlight leaking in from the blinds highlighted the disaster that had become my home—littered with unused chopsticks, empty Lean Cuisine containers, and invitations to showers, weddings, and graduation parties (and thank-you letters from showers, weddings, and graduation parties).

"Hi," I said, stepping over a pile of clothes that I meant to bring to the dry cleaner weeks ago.

"Listen, you're going solo to the gig today," she said slowly and grudgingly.

"Okay . . . yeah, sure. Is something wrong?" I asked, slightly wincing and wishing I could have taken it back the second I asked.

"I um—well, my right hand is in a splint," she said cautiously as if she was contemplating telling the truth. Then, unwavering, she burst out, "It was that stupid bitch Lunt or Klutz or whatever. Okay? Here's what happened . . ."

". . . It's fine, you don't have to explain, I can do the job—"

"She wrote this thing about me, which totally wasn't true—okay, so maybe it was kind of true—anyway, now Ted isn't speaking to me and I've been getting weird looks. . . ."

"Honestly Sheryl, it's fine. I can handle—"

". . . It's been awful, and I told myself, 'Sheryl, she is not going to get away with this, uh-uh.' And you know what? You're never going to believe this Jackie . . . never, never, never . . ."

"Okay . . ." I said knowing full well that she wasn't really waiting for my response.

"I go to Jubilee last night for dinner with my neighbor Dana, who by the way is the only one of my friends speaking to me right now, bless her heart . . . we go to dinner and you'll never believe who is sitting next to us! That bitch . . . Delila or whatever her name is . . ."

"Delia," I corrected her.

"Whatever—I recognized her from her stupid website . . . you know that picture next to her column—she's got the frizzy hair and looks like she doesn't pluck her eyebrows . . ." she took a breath before continuing, "well I saw her and you know, gave her a little piece of my mind and things sort of escalated from there."

My blood ran cold. I was scared to ask but knew I had to. "Escalated?"

Turns out sucking down one too many sugary sweet custom cocktails could not only influence Sheryl to bat her eyelashes at boys with fake IDs and give hickeys to her dates in public, but given the right antagonist, she could even throw a punch.

"You hit her?" I asked, feeling her embarrassment for her.

"Well, kinda. I mean, she went on and on about freedom of speech and then she started explaining 'blind item' to me in a very condescending way—I know what a blind item is for Christ sakes—but it wasn't very *blind* if you ask me, that's for sure . . ."

"What do you mean you *kinda* hit her?"

"Well, she was getting all sassy and in my face and she kind of raised up her hand—Dana later told me that she had started to wave her credit card to the waiter, like a 'get me the hell outta here' type of thing, but I just reacted instinctively and popped her right in the nose . . . I was trying to defend myself. But enough about me. Are you okay to go to the gig by yourself today? Can you represent?"

"Sure. Street Cred," I laughed.

"That's an energy drink! Remember that! If they ask you if you want one, say yes! Even if you're not thirsty!" And with that, she hung up the phone.

I was feeling a bit nervous by the time I reached the eastern end of the San Fernando Valley, where I quickly whipped into the studio's parking lot. I was my own worst enemy, obsessing over every little thing that could possibly go wrong all morning. Forgetting my makeup case had been one of those recurring nightmare scenarios and, because I had made a point to triple-check its contents beforehand, I was running steadily behind schedule.

Encompassing nearly 100,000 square feet, the studio loomed ahead. Adjacent production offices that looked unused for the past decade only complimented the mottled eighties signage out-side, making the facility look depressingly outdated. Once inside, however, its sound stages buzzed with life. Men in T-shirts and dirty jeans, who looked as if they'd been busy preparing the shoot for hours already, lugged cables back and forth and double-checked the PA systems.

"Hi." I smiled, approaching two men who were busy fussing with one of the cameras, "I'm looking for Steve Green?"

Not turning away from his work, one of the men simply shrugged before the other piped up, acting as if my question was a huge burden.

"Don't know 'em . . . you might want to ask someone back there," he said waving his hand to a small hallway lined with doors a short distance away. I maneuvered past the production assistants struggling to lug props and set pieces through the narrow space when a tall, slender man practically hissing into his cell phone caught me off guard.

"What a fucking bitch! I don't need to explain myself to a

Nickelodeon development exec—I can't even believe I even just spent time on the phone with her . . . She was like, 'blah, blah, blah . . .' and I'm like . . ." The man stopped as he noticed me staring at him and slowly pulled his phone away from his ear and frowned.

"Hi, I'm Jackie, I'm here for the job. . . ?" I said, more like a question than a statement.

"And what job would that be exactly?" he asked, raising an eyebrow.

"I'm, um, I'm here to do makeup for, uh . . ." I fumbled, grasping for the call sheet in my purse, "Brooke! Brooke Parker." I smiled at him weakly. Throwing the phone back up to his ear, he barked, "I have to call you back." He studied his phone for another second, and wrinkled his nose in disgust, presumably disturbed by another message that had just come in. He was a fairly attractive man in his late thirties with evenly tanned skin, though its texture was conspicuously, almost unnaturally, wrinkle-free. He had Tony Curtis hair, expertly shaping a curled coif on his forehead thick with pomade, while his sleep-deprived, wide-set eyes bore heavy, dark lids. He looked up at me suddenly, almost inquisitively, as if he had forgotten that I was still standing there.

"Now, what exactly are you looking for?" With his head cocked he acted as if I had just asked him when the next spaceship left for Mars.

"I'm doing Brooke Parker's makeup . . . Sheryl Lane, my boss—she was going to do it but she . . . well, she can't," I stammered, thinking fast. "So she sent me . . . I'm Jackie," I said extending my hand. In lieu of a handshake, he just kind of stared at my awaiting grasp, and then he spoke again.

"Robert. Robert Bernstein. I'm Brooke's stylist," he said. This took me by surprise, considering his style: a distressed long-sleeve rugby shirt fresh from an Abercrombie & Fitch catalogue, cheap-looking blue jeans, and Adidas tennis shoes. I then remembered that, for a makeup artist, I only wore makeup a couple days a week at best, though I'd managed to swipe some mascara on my lashes before taking off this morning.

"Well, nice to meet you, where should I set up?"

"The dressing room is down two. The dancers are taken care of, so we need you, obviously, to pay full attention to Brooke. And you'll do her hair as well I'm assuming?" he asked bitchily, raising an eyebrow.

"Yeah—yes, of course. Of course I know how to . . ." I stuttered, afraid he'd call someone else if he knew that the extent of my experience actually *doing* hair was limited to helping Lauren flatten her impossibly curly tresses before dates. But really, how hard could it be? Brushing, teasing, curling—I knew how to do all of that.

"Great," he cut me off, turning on his heel, off to his next drama.

As I located the dressing room, I nearly head-butted a boy bounding out of it. A bit shocked as I was, I jumped back, clutching my set bag as tightly as I could, but he smiled at me. Though I'd never seen their picture, I was able to peg him as one of the Emerson Brothers. From what little I knew about them, compliments of Sheryl, they were a pop sensation trio that had made it big with the 'tween crowd when their song, "Let Your Body Do the Talkin'," appeared on a Nickelodeon sitcom. Now they were traveling the country, much to the delight of twelve-year-old girls everywhere, performing songs like "Girlfy," and "Break-up Box." The boy standing directly in front of me appeared to be about eighteen years old and was dressed exceptionally trendy—a shrunken twill blazer over a v-neck T-shirt that accented a black-and-silver lariat necklace, skintight slub denim pants, and argyle-printed Vans—thanks to the styling of Robert, I guessed. He exchanged a knowing look with an older, heavyset Latina woman who was standing next to one of the makeup counters before taking off in the opposite direction.

"Boy! You are a troublemaker, I tell you that," she called out after him before letting out a gregarious laugh from deep inside.

Unzipping my rolling duffel, I timidly rifled through a mess of compacts, tweezers, and small spray cans of Evian mineral water as the woman turned to me and smiled.

"I'm Sasha," she laughed, placing a fleshy hand on her chest before nodding her head toward the door. "That one runnin' out the door there was Jesse, but you probably already knew that," she laughed.

"Yeah, I recognize him. He's one of the Emerson Brothers—quite a talented family, huh?" I mused as she wrinkled up her face as if she was puzzled. "Jesse and the others I mean . . ." She suddenly let out another boisterous laugh.

"They ain't brothers, at least not by blood . . . that's just what the band's called. The other two that ain't here, are Landon and Nolan. It's Jesse, you know, that's sweet on Brooke so that's why he's roaming around. Came to watch her shoot her first music video." She smiled.

"I'm Jackie, I'm here to do Brooke's makeup," I said, realizing I hadn't even introduced myself. "Do you work on the music videos?"

"Heck no," she said laughing again as if the question were unheard of. "I work for the label."

"Raindrop Records, right?" I asked nervously.

"Close—Rain Shine."

"Oh. I didn't—I didn't know. I was hired out of Steve Green's office." I muttered foolishly as the PDA that was clipped to Sasha's belt began to chime. Looking down at the waist of her jeans—first to the left as if she had forgotten just where exactly she had attached it—she seized it from the magnesium case on her right hip. "Damn things be clipped all over me," she told me with an exaggerated frown. "Hello?" she barked before quickly snapping, "uh-uh, no way. I told them they can schedule those little meetings another time. Folks in A&R be hustlin' me before we even got time to get the promos out the damn door." She put a chubby digit up to her other ear to drown out the background noise, listening to the person on the other end for a moment before continuing. "I told them I wasn't trying to rush, rush, rush all the time. Well, tell 'em, *please*." Flustered, Sasha hung up the phone, clipping it back into place on her belt.

"Sounds pretty intense," I said, breaking the silence.

"It *is*. Believe me." Shaking her head back and forth, she soon changed gears, cracking a smile once more. "I should probably tell you a little bit about myself—I'm one of the label's publicists—I work the younger musicians mainly. Basically, when the big guys give me a go 'head after decidin' a performer is ready I put the publicity wheels in action."

"Setting up interviews and things . . ." I offered.

"Yep, yep . . . that and a combination of marketing, helpin' to create an image for the musician that the label can use as a brand communication tool."

"To be honest, I wasn't really filled in too much about Brooke . . . or her image," I admitted. *Was that something I was supposed to know? And if so, why didn't Sheryl download me?*

"Don't you worry yourself, she's comin' right off this dinky little mall tour, so we haven't done much with her yet. They're adding her to the last leg of the Emersons tour now though, that's actually why I'm here . . . gotta start plannin' the press kits."

It was suddenly clear to me that Sasha—the label's "image maker"—had the power to make or break my career and many others like me. "Is there anything in particular you're looking for from me? You know—image-wise?"

Sasha started laughing uncontrollably again. "No pageant stuff—she likes all that sparkly, spangly garbage. Think fresh-faced—it's all about youth these days you know."

As if on cue, Brooke breezed through the door with a stocky man in his mid-forties following behind her. Because the only image I'd ever seen of Brooke was thanks to a quick Google search—which only led me to a few tiny thumbnails of a girl wearing a tiara—I fully expected her to be the quintessential pageant girl. And she was, to a degree. Platinum locks, toned and tan with green doe eyes and dressed in several shades of pink: she was the antithesis of a girl like me, a girl whose skin never saw the sun in order to keep freckles at bay, and who, if forced into a gym, wouldn't know the first thing to do there.

"Hi!" She grinned, looking around the makeup trailer, "I can't believe this is really happening—a real music video—sorry, I'm such a nerd." I watched as she chomped down on the wad of gum in her mouth before blowing a bubble that exploded on her face as she leapt into the makeup chair. "Oh my gawsh!" She laughed so hard that she made a faint snorting noise, which made her laugh even harder. *This was Miss Teen Florida?* I thought to myself, any predetermined stereotypes I had of her suddenly fading away.

"Brooke, love! You really need to lose the gum." A familiar-looking man with an even more familiar-sounding British accent behind her scrunched his face in mock disgust, as if he were trying to mask his amusement, before turning in my direction. "Hi, I'm Steve Green, Brooke's manager," he said, hooking a pair of sunglasses over the opening of his salmon-colored collar, before extending a hand to me. Grasping his palm with a firm shake I suddenly realized where I knew him from. He had been a longtime manager and constant companion of the heavily photo-graphed 80s music phenomenon Krizia. He had discovered her himself, spotting her on the dance floor at a London hot spot, Annabel's. This earned him a reputation in the business as a serious hustler, and before long both Steve and Krizia found themselves among L.A.'s glitterati. As time passed Krizia's star power dwindled, and though she was a pop culture legend, Steve knew she'd be unable to compete with the new generation of film, TV, and video game vixens. No longer pulling in the pay-checks that had made them both fabulously wealthy, they both disappeared from the public eye. And here he was now standing right in front of me with fresh blood—a girl he hoped to mold into the next big . . . star, paycheck, it was all the same. Clad in a crisp pair of Levi's that he wore with a sport coat and an out-dated haircut, he might've appeared "washed up" if it weren't for his pompous self-importance and busy charm.

"I'm Jackie O'Reilly, Brooke's makeup artist." I smiled, re-lieved by his seemingly affable nature.

"Great." He winked as his Blackberry buzzed abruptly. "Well, let's do this—go ahead and get her ready." Handing me a card from his wallet that read "Green Management" in embossed lettering, Steve motioned to the phone perched between his ear and shoulder. "It's a call from Paris, doing big things over there —closing some deals . . . I gotta take this."

Halfway through her makeup, Brooke handed me a bag stuffed with bits of hair, smiling sweetly as if I knew just ex-actly what to do with it.

"Here ya go, for my hair," she said taking her shoulder-length hair out of its ponytail holder. I was immediately dumbfounded. Makeup for me was a slam-dunk, but hairpieces? I had never even seen anyone put extensions in before!

"Oh, your hair is so beautiful already, you don't need these." I shrugged, trying to play it cool—I thought I had covered every possible disastrous scenario in my obsessing earlier on—but this was something I hadn't thought of. I didn't want her to think I was an amateur, because at twenty-two years old, I was *barely* her senior—I didn't want her to know that I had absolutely no idea what I was doing.

"No, I *have* to have them, they complete my whole—my whole, well you know, my 'Pillow Talk' vibe or whatever you want to call it," she said.

"Pillow talk?" I asked, forgetting to reference my call sheet once more.

"That's my first single—have you heard my album? It's the song about being best friends forever . . . do you know it?"

Ignoring her question I looked down at the bag of hair again. "Your hair has so much body the way it is, you really should try wearing it the way you have it now." I winced, hoping she would just go along and agree with me.

"I really *need* them . . . I can't shoot 'Pillow Talk' without them," she pleaded, wide-eyed. I imagined that any other girl in her position would've either thrown a fit or fired me by that point, but Brooke stared up at me like a child begging to stay up past her bedtime. In all honesty, it would've been easier if she wasn't so sweet, and I realized that there was no getting out of it.

"All right, you're the boss," I said, trying as hard as I could to appear upbeat as I plunged my hand into the bag full of hairy little extension pieces in disgust. *Here goes nothing*, I thought as I struggled with one of the snap clips.

"Oh here," Brooke, seeing my struggle, said. As I watched her miraculously pop the clip open by simply applying pressure to the ends with her fingers, I knew I had blown my cover—*I couldn't even open the damn things*. To my surprise, she handed it right back to me, thinking nothing of it.

"So, who usually does your hair?" I asked her sorting through weft pieces of varying widths, contemplating which ones to use.

"Oh, sometimes my ma does it, or my friend Hayley. I had been using this one lady from back home for a while. She was supposed to come up here with me today but she has . . . *arthritis* real bad?" She posed the bit of information to me as a question, as if she was suddenly scared she had confused *arthritis* with algorithm, or another word starting with the letter *a* that she didn't quite understand.

"Mmm-hmm," I answered, signaling that she had used the correct term.

"Yeah, I don't know much about it but her wrists and stuff swell up pretty bad—it's hard for her to grip things . . ."

"Oh man," I hummed unenthusiastically, hoping our conversation was distracting her from the disaster that was slowly becoming her head. To create a "fuller look," (or at least that's what I told myself I was doing), I had stacked the pieces on top of one another. Clipping in the last piece, I stepped back to survey my work, which to my horror resembled a stacked perm with hair of entirely uniform length.

"You did that fast! I've never had anyone put them in without straightening my hair first—it saves so much time," she squealed, the color draining from my face as I realized I skipped a vital step. She swiveled around in her chair and I braced myself for tears—hers following my own. Now, face-to-face with my new "head creation," she pondered her reflection in the mirror for a few seconds before erupting into a big smile.

"I look just like Cleopatra in that one movie!"

Chapter 2

Stardom isn't a profession; it's an accident.
—Lauren Bacall

"Oh my God! What did you do to her hair?" Robert screamed out, suddenly appearing out of nowhere, and not caring that everyone within a mile radius could hear him. I had to think fast and save face.

"It's a new look, everyone's doing it in Europe," I lied.

"I love it!" Brooke gleamed, still staring in the mirror and ignoring Robert. "It looks amazing!"

Now, I knew it didn't . . . and so did Robert, but time was running out and at this point I was just happy that Brooke liked anything I did. Scowling at me, Robert took Brooke's hand and yanked her out of the makeup trailer.

Though the fear of coming face-to-face with that awful hairdo again was almost more than I could bear, I was booked for the length of the shoot, which included touchups for all three scenes. I winced as Brooke emerged onto the set, waiting for gasps of shock from the crew as the dancers rushed to avert one another's eyes from the horror. But to my surprise there were no stunned silences or shrieks of terror—only the sound of giddy anticipation from those excited to finally begin filming. "Brooke!" A petite male, one of her dancers I assumed, called out. When I realized his attention was focused on the top of her head, I cringed. "That is so beat!"

I wasn't sure what "beat" meant, but from the smile on his face as well as the admiring looks from the others around him it didn't appear to be a bad thing. Happy to be the center of attention, Brooke cleared her throat as if she were about to make a speech.

"I've dreamt of filming a music video like this since I was just a little girl," she sighed sweetly to her dancers—who jumped up and down, playfully cheering her on—and members of the video production team that were within earshot. "Thank you all for making my dreams come true today. The fact that I'm just standing here . . . well it's all so serendipident." *Serendipident?* I cringed—she already looked so silly standing up there with that huge mop of misplaced extensions on her head—and now she's making up words! But no one seemed to notice. They were all completely charmed by her.

Like the "Pillow Talk" lyrics, the story idea for the shoot was pretty simple; therefore, the director spent an inordinate amount of time shooting what he kept calling "attention-grabbing angles" to make the most out of what little they had to work with. Despite the title of the song, the first scenes we worked on—like the one where Brooke dances up and down the aisle of a school bus with girlfriends—seemed innocent enough. After that day, "Pillow Talk" would be stuck in my head forever.

Looking up at the clock in the dressing room, I yawned. It had been a long day and I couldn't wait for shooting to begin on the final segment—the slumber party scene. I went to work, prepping Brooke and two of the actresses hired to play her "BFFs" while the production team set up. With a tiara in her hand, Brooke made her way across the set, where the director was busy testing out different filters and gels, asking those around him which gave off the most surreal look.

"Robert wanted me to give this to you—it's part of my costume," said Brooke, clad in a fluffy pink robe.

"A tiara, huh? That's very fitting." I smiled, struggling to nestle the rhinestone-encrusted tiara in between the stacked wefts. Suddenly, I became aware of a presence eyeing me from the doorway. Looking up, I caught the gaze of a man—who I guessed to be a little older than me, maybe in his late twenties—wearing a suit. He was handsome, I decided, in an almost unconventional way—with perfectly textured dark brown hair that looked almost black, and kind chocolate brown eyes.

"Hi." He moved towards me. "David Kagan, nice to meet you." As I introduced myself, I took note of his direct nature and air of extreme confidence.

"So how did you get roped into working with Green?" David asked.

"Green—oh, Steve?"

"Yeah," he smirked, patting Brooke's shoulder, "that guy's a real piece of work. Gotta love him."

"Are you—do you work together?" I asked.

"Yeah, I'm one of the lowly assistants at this firm," David joked. "So, a makeup artist—a creative girl, huh? I like it."

"And she's really good too . . ." Brooke half-whined before turning her attention to me. "I really want you to come on the tour with me . . . I love my makeup, and especially my hair." She looked back at David, batting her doe eyes like a little girl before saying softly, "Will you please tell Steve that Jackie's the one I want?"

"Anything you want, princess," he said as she stood from the chair. "Now get out there, they are waiting for you on set."

Wearing robes almost identical to Brooke's, the actresses commissioned to play her friends stood patiently inside the sound stage. There, three pink, candy-colored walls had been erected to create Brooke's bedroom, where a white shag rug, oversized queen bed, and window shades painted to look like a cloud-covered sky completed the set.

"Now remember ladies," the director yelled out before cueing the music, "the pillow fight is a sport *and* an art form, keep that in mind. And make it sexy!"

His comment caught me a little off-guard, considering that it was supposed to be a simple slumber party scene that featured BFFs doing things like eating pizza and making prank phone calls. But what really took me by surprise was when the girls dropped their robes, which I had naively assumed were costumes. *This has to be a joke—Brooke's so wholesome! So innocent!*

Clutching large white feather pillows, all three girls kneeled on the bed with Brooke positioned in the middle, facing the camera. The blond to her right, who looked way too old to be playing a high school student, was wearing a pink soft-cup bra with double ruffles and a magenta satin bow paired with matching bottoms. A double strand of fake pearls was draped around her neck and on her feet she wore pink bunny slippers. The girl to her left, who thanks to her dark skin appeared ageless, wore a retro-inspired lace-up halter camisole and garter skirt with scalloped lace edges and contrast piping. Brooke's ensemble, even though it covered more skin than the others, was perhaps the most shocking. Certain aspects of the two-piece outfit— the top's puffed sleeves and the lace ruffles that lined the boy shorts—looked very cutesy, almost childlike. And at the same time, accents like the bold leather trim and lacing screamed *seductress*. My eyes suddenly focused on her chest, which swelled beneath the sweetheart neckline of her top. Even though it made me feel like a creepy old man, I stared in shock, and so did everyone else. *What had Robert done to her?!*

"That top looks a little small," Steve barked from the sidelines.

"Well, it's the biggest size we have," Robert answered in a tone plagued with annoyance. Signaling toward Brooke's mysteriously perky chest, he scoffed, "Unfortunately there's not much I can do with those things *now*."

Before I even had time to mull over Robert's biting response, a production assistant whizzed my way, tossing a bottle of baby oil at me.

"She needs to glow! Make her look sweaty," he barked.

After drowning her in oil, I plopped down on a chair off set. David took a seat next to me, somehow able to ignore the fact that the shoot had turned into what looked like a soft-core porno flick.

"Be glad you're not on the business end of things . . . ugh," he said out of the blue, taking a sip of the bottle of water in his hand.

"That bad?" I asked.

"It has its ups and downs, just like everything in life, but out here it's nonstop. It wasn't this crazy in New York."

"Did you just move here?"

"When my old boss decided it was finally time to retire a few months back, he felt bad leaving me without a job so he called up a friend of his out here who was expanding his client list and the rest is history. It was pretty hectic at first. I'd never even been to L.A. before and there I was, moving across the country to work for a guy who really puts a lot of pressure on himself and his employees—I feel like I've gotten the hang of things now—but it's shown me that even a veteran like Steve has to continually prove himself out here. But, he's good at what he does . . ." David paused for a moment before turning back to me. "Oh yeah, the job is yours if you want it."

"What job?"

"Brooke's tour dates with the Emerson Brothers . . . you're interested, no?" David raised an eyebrow. "I talked to Steve about it—and when I say *talk*, I mean that he waved his hand at me and nodded while on his Blackberry." He laughed, waiting for my response.

"Oh really? Wow, I thought she was joking . . ." I said in disbelief as I watched Brooke break into song, the two other girls trailing her every move. She had seemingly morphed into a different being—one bursting full of energy and boasting an undeniable sex appeal.

"So . . . do you want it or not?" David asked again.

"Yeah. Of course, that would be great," I muttered. It wasn't that the job prospect didn't interest me, it did. But at that moment, I was fully intrigued by the anomaly performing in front of me. The young woman on the video monitors wasn't the same naive girl that had just been sitting in my makeup chair while I piled fistfuls of synthetic hair a mile high on her head. She wasn't the same girl who chomped her bubble gum obnoxiously or snorted when she laughed too hard. And she certainly wasn't a girl who would use a word (if you can call it that) like "seredipident." This was a girl with total power and control. Brooke flowed through each directed step—dancing for a few seconds before turning back to swing her pillow, which burst open with feathers on every take, at her girlfriends.

It was pretty late by the time the director finally called "cut!" As the lights went down, prompting a team of assistants to begin attacking the feather-filled stage with brooms, Brooke sprinted back to the dressing room, grinning from ear to ear. I began packing up my belongings, which were scattered everywhere, so that I could go home. I peered over at Brooke who, standing in the corner surrounded by dancers (her *besties*, as she called them), had erupted into a fit of giggles. I smiled as I scanned the mess of hair clinging to her scalp. It was a strange coincidence, I thought suddenly, recalling an old art history course I'd taken, that she had compared herself to Cleopatra earlier in the day. The Egyptian queen was known to use her melon-shaped hairstyles and wigged headdresses to enhance her power and fame. And maybe Brooke wasn't just the dumb gum-chewing, pageant princess she appeared to be. Tossing her head back with laughter, Brooke looked beautiful. She looked like a star. Maybe she wasn't as innocent as she would've liked everyone to believe.

Chapter 3

I don't know anything about music.
In my line you don't have to.
–Elvis Presley

Two weeks later, stuffed inside a snug North Face ski jacket, I boarded a flight to Albany, excited to join the tour with Brooke. Steve had booked the three of us on a later flight, first-class tickets for the both of them, coach for me. I didn't mind—in fact, I had expected as much—but as I boarded the plane, trudging toward the back with an armful of magazines and a large carry-on, I heard a voice cry out: "Where y'all going?" Turning my head, I spotted a cozy-looking Brooke, messy blond hair piled high atop her head.

"I'm back here," I yelled over to her.

"What?!" she shrieked, turning to Steve. Feeling the pressure of the line behind me, I headed toward my seat, unable to reply.

I wasn't sure if he was just trying to keep her happy or if the whining had finally gotten to him (probably both) but about ten minutes later, I felt a tap on my shoulder. It was Steve, who appeared slightly stressed and far less jovial than the first time we'd met. Swapping his reclining leather seat for mine, he left the free booze, personal T.V. screen, and aromatherapy oils behind. Since Brooke and I hadn't yet spent any time together outside of the makeup chair, it was the perfect opportunity to get to know one another a little better. Within seconds of being seated, Brooke whispered into my ear with a hushed giggle.

"I've never flown first class before!"

"That's okay." I smiled. "I haven't either."

As we flew across the country, talking nonstop the entire way, I was thoroughly amused by her wide-eyed wonderment. She was giddy, and seemed to be fascinated by everything. The truth was I felt equally awestruck by this new world.

"Aren't these so cute?" Brooke squealed with excitement every time she came across something new, pointing out ter-rycloth eye shades, tiny tins full of mints, pairs of blue cotton socks, or sticks of shea butter lip balm. It was all actually quite endearing. As Brooke navigated through hundreds of channels on the interactive screen in front of her, sliding her finger from one title to the next, she came across an old Disney film that caught her attention.

"I used to love this movie when I was a kid," I told her look-ing up. Going head-to-head on screen were two golden-topped twins in *The Parent Trap*.

"I have younger twin brothers, but I always wanted a twin sister of my own, didn't you?" She grabbed at a tuft of blond hair that was sprouting out of her messy bun and twirled it around her finger.

"Well, I'm an only child so I always thought that any brother or sister would be better than having none," I told her.

She ripped her hands away from her head and fluttered her arms up and down in excitement, not because I was an only child, but as if she hadn't been paying attention at all, she said, "Look, look—this is my favorite part!"

I shifted my attention back to the movie, watching as the twins served veal parmigiana to their recently reunited parents before a voice onscreen announced:

Well, without . . . further ado, ladies and gentlemen, I'd like to introduce you direct from Boston . . . playing Beethoven's "Fifth Symphony" on the piano . . .

"That's crazy . . ." I said, a strange déjà vu settling over me.

"What is?" Brooke replied, wide-eyed.

"Besides being direct from Boston," I laughed, "*this* movie, and more specifically, *this scene,* was the first time I saw the big black countertop in my parents' dining room as the grand piano it actually was . . . unfortunately for them."

"You play too?" Brooke was exasperated, nearly leaping out of her seat.

"Yeah, Beethoven's 'Fifth' was actually the first song I taught myself. I think it was the one time I truly amazed my father," I said whimsically. "Not looking to a Disney movie for profound insight or anything like that, but isn't it funny when you pull a bunch of things like that together in your head?" I asked her. "I know it doesn't mean anything," I said, chuckling.

"Do you believe that everything happens for a reason?" Brooke asked, now all of a sudden glassy-eyed and hanging from my every word. I didn't know exactly how to answer that question—*sometimes I did and sometimes I didn't.* Believing in fate had always sort of been a matter of convenience for me. If I'd gotten sick to death of harping on a single issue with my mother for hours, I'd find my way out with the words "what will be, will be." Watching a friend wail on in hysterics the sixth time her boyfriend had broken up with her, I found myself repeating "everything happens for a reason," because no one likes being told outright their boyfriend's a dick, no matter how true it is. I wouldn't play along with asinine explanations. (*He hasn't returned your calls because his phone's just dead; those gold earrings on his night table are his mother's, of course, not some other girl's . . .*) Fate was often the perfect scapegoat, always there to take the pressure off difficult discussions or decisions. So, I guess, I didn't *really* believe in it. Brooke, however, from the look on her face—expectant eyes, mouth hanging just slightly open—was dying to believe in something, and that something today was fate. She was ready, eager even, to find proof to support her theory through the most mundane events, and she looked like she needed my approval to cement her belief.

"Some of the things that happened over the past year, when I think about them, I figure there's just got to be a reason for them," she said. "I mean, look at how you and I met?"

"Through work . . ." I said. Excited as I was about this new job, I wasn't about to chalk it up to the stars aligning or anything like that.

"Not just through work," she said almost defensively, as if I were treating her like a silly little kid. "I mean, we both get along well and the fact that we have so much in common, like how we both love music and stuff . . ." While I didn't think anyone would be hard-pressed to find someone who could simultaneously find their way around a makeup chair *and* appreciate song, I had to admit the circumstances here were oddly fortuitous. I thought about the woman in Florida with arthritis-stricken hands who usually did Brooke's makeup, and Sheryl's very public disgrace. In a sad way, their misfortune was the best thing that had ever happened to me. If there is such a thing as fate, I took note that it could be very cruel as well.

Brooke sat there for a moment, making a nervous clicking

sound with her jaw, which I would later associate with Brooke being lost for words. "I get homesick real easily, but I'm gettin' to do what I love most—dancin' and singing my heart out—so I gotta believe that this is all happening for a reason." In a blink, that certain sense of seriousness that had prompted her to wax philosophical had disappeared and was replaced with a boisterous laugh she was unable to contain. She shrugged her shoulders and looked down at her fingers, coated in globby purple nail polish, before pausing entirely.

Then she was off to the next thing.

Although we'd been up since the crack of dawn, we were the last to arrive. Eyeing the snowflakes that danced on the wind as we exited the terminal, I zipped my coat up as far as it could go. I had almost forgotten how bitterly cold East Coast winters could be. Brooke, who hadn't traveled outside of Florida until this year, was excessively unprepared, underdressed, and consequently, unhappy. Standing next to me outside the airport, blue lips chattering, she clutched white-knuckled onto a cologne-drenched blazer Steve had draped around her shoulders.

"All right ladies, just two more minutes, I promise!" Steve said, struggling to compose a Blackberry email with his right thumb alone, while his left hand juggled a stack of papers that kept dropping one to four sheets at a time. Brooke's eyes darted back and forth in search of the town car that would whisk us away to safety.

"There it is!" I exclaimed, nudging her just a few seconds later.

"Thank goodness. I am fr-e-e-e-z-i-n-g!" Brooke squealed as it came to a stop and we leapt into the back seat. The heat blasting, it was nice and toasty inside. Without breaking his gaze from the screen of his Blackberry, Steve followed behind us.

Rows of pine trees freshly sprinkled with snow surrounded

us as we made our way to Saratoga Springs to join our tour mates. Shifting his attention from his inbox for the first time, Steve looked up at them while Brooke, head propped against the window on the opposite side, dozed off; a halo of condensation forming where the warmth of her face met the chill of the glass.

I felt miserable—my eyelids were heavy with exhaustion and my head throbbed—but even the worst aches and pains couldn't deter my anticipation. My first *real* job—one that actually came with a substantial paycheck—and I had gotten it myself! Even my mother, who at first appeared skeptical, *seemed* happy for me. She kept saying things like: "I don't get it . . . who are you working with?" or "You're doing pageant makeup? Oh right, she *was* in a pageant . . ." Sheryl, on the other hand, was not as enthusiastic about my little "break" as I imagined she would be. The Monday following the shoot, I'd met her in the salon at our usual time and told her the good news. I waited for her usual shrieks of excitement but none came. She just nodded her head in silence instead. Because her hand was still in a splint, we had been forced to cancel all of our bookings for the upcoming week anyway, so the fact that I was leaving her assistant-less for two weeks wasn't the problem. Her feigned nonchalance made it quite clear—*she wished she had booked the job instead*.

"Oh my gawd! It's so cute!" Brooke gushed suddenly, interrupting my thoughts. "Jackie, look! Isn't it adorable?" Rubbing the sleep from her eyes, she smiled sweetly, enchanted by the sprawling Victorian inn just outside our widow. While I nodded my head, I secretly hoped we were staying somewhere else. Maybe it was the Californian in me, but I preferred clean, modern spaces over nineteenth-century structures decorated with doilies and hand-painted stencils. Apparently, I was in the minority. Two of Brooke's dancers, as excited as she was, waited in the lobby to greet her.

"Look how pretty!" one shrieked, pointing to the large arrangement of fresh flowers on display near the front desk.

"So beat," the other agreed.

Even Sasha, who had complained to me about this trip for nearly an hour as we waited for the video shoot to wrap, genuinely seemed happy to be here. She trotted through the reception area with a big smile on her face, turning to me before laughing, apparently at my expression, which must have belied my distaste for the inn. As if on cue, Robert—hard to imagine ever *admitting* to having a good time—twirled through the lobby with another man on his arm. *Okay . . . so maybe it wasn't the hotel that had lifted his spirits overnight.*

"Oh, this place is *incredible*! How obsessed am I? No, seriously!" His shrill laugh caught me off-guard. I listened as Robert gushed to his boy toy about their room, talking breathlessly about the details he *loved* (the period brass chandeliers and the lace curtains) as opposed to the things he was *obsessed* with (the Victorian rose wallpaper and the hotel owner's personal collection of Boyd's Bears). I hoped that jolly Robert was here to stay.

By the time my room was ready, I had only ten minutes to change and make sure my set bag was in order. I left myself with only seven, however, after stashing the oh-so-creepy collection of porcelain dolls adorning my hotel bed into the closet. I pulled on an adorable Trina Turk tweed mini that Lauren had generously loaned to me after I'd called her on the verge of tears, distraught that I had nothing *cool* to wear. Only now did I realize I'd forgotten tights to go with it. With no time to waste worrying over *my own* appearance, I slipped on a pair of wedge heels and dashed out the door, making it downstairs just in time to jump in one of the buses to the venue. We pulled out onto Broadway, one of the busiest areas in Saratoga

Springs during the winter. People outside ducked in and out of the bustling bistros and funky boutiques housed in the Victorian storefronts that lined the streets. Turning off Broadway, the bus chugged towards the city's edge. The concert was set to take place at a brand new, state-of-the-art theater that had just been built on the campus of a small liberal arts college. The Emerson Brothers were one of the five big acts that had been booked to help kick off the venue's opening season with a bang.

Inside the sprawling performing arts center, decidedly out of place in comparison to the older buildings it neighbored, people buzzed back and forth excitedly. When I arrived, a group of volunteers, presumably college students, had just finished setting up so Brooke could do her sound check. I wandered backstage as they were leaving, pulling up a chair near the sound console to watch her in action. Save for the chatter of a prerecorded vocal track that Brooke relied on during her dance-heavy numbers—Gary, the sound engineer, was working on it now—the auditorium was strangely silent.

"What would happen if it gave out?" I blurted out as my curiosity got the best of me.

Gary, not looking up from his work, muttered back with certainty, "Wouldn't happen . . ."

"Really? How so?"

"There's a backup system, so ain't nothing ever gonna go wrong," he assured me in a way that also suggested that he no longer wished to make small talk.

I focused my attention on the stage. It was plastered with Emerson Brothers posters: three teenage faces, frosted tips and pearly whites and airbrushed to perfection. Additional signage peppered throughout showed a cartoon character wearing gold chains, baggy jeans, and a basketball jersey with *SC* printed on it, drinking a can of—you guessed it—Street Cred. Emerging from behind a large, cartoonish basketball shoe, standing there in her faded gray sweat suit, Brooke finally began performing.

"Out-rage-ous!" She belted into the microphone. The sound of her voice—the way it seemed to fill the big, empty space surrounding us with spirit—was invigorating. I was quickly reminded of the collage of sounds that had made up the musical moments of my life thus far. Between my grandmother, "Dodo" as we called her, and one of my father's famous clients, an actor/ musician who had opened up his own record company, my introduction to music came at a very young age. From six on, it seemed as if we were always around the recording studio. And during the days that we weren't, I'd hammer away on the keys of that baby grand I had discovered in one corner of our living room. Playing it was something that just came naturally to me. I can only explain it by saying that when I looked down at the keys, they just made sense to me. Listening to Brooke up on that stage, I was immediately aware of the rare opportunity I had stumbled upon. Just as Brooke was finishing, I could hear muffled voices gathering on the other side of the venue doors as people began to line up outside. *How many people would kill to be in my position?*

Past the gaudy décor, I made my way towards the cluster of private dressing rooms behind the upstage wall. The Emerson Brothers congregated beneath the harsh fluorescent lights in one of the large makeup areas, each waiting their turn. Their longtime artist ploughed through them, one by one, slathering concealer over the dark circles lining their eyes and coating their peach fuzz with layers of powder—not a beat missed; it reminded me of an assembly line. I paused for a moment to watch—there was nothing special about her technique—in fact, we were technically working the same job for the same amount of money. But there was a difference between her and me, and a very important one at that. She was a veteran, a true professional, and because she had paid her dues she had the job security that I did not. There were plenty of girls like me all over Los Angeles, working in cosmetic boutiques, salons, and small photo shoots—all eager to get their hands on an opportunity like this one. Continuing down the hall, I decided right then and there that I would do whatever it took to prove myself in this industry, and to never take a moment of this experience for granted.

I noticed a blue piece of paper that read *Brooke Parker* hanging from the door to the right of where I stood. Reaching for the doorknob, hoping to unload the heavy makeup bag I'd been toting around with me, a voice chimed sweetly from behind me, "It's awfully quiet in there." The voice belonged to a young blond leaning against an adjacent wall.

"Excuse me?" I asked, startled.

"I'm Hayley—I'm friends with Brooke. I go to school about two and half hours east of here."

Hayley was a classic beauty: thin and tall, almost the spitting image of Grace Kelly . . . from the neck up, that is. Her hair, long and stringy, fell limp around her shoulders, nearly blending into the textured yarn of the shapeless woven poncho she wore. Outdated Mudd jeans hung low on her hips, flaring at the ankle to reveal suede Birkenstock sandals paired with rainbow-striped socks, which encased each of her toes like a glove. Hayley went to Syracuse, she told me, with a classmate and fellow World Teach volunteer she'd met in Namibia. Just a hemp-necklace shy of hippie, Hayley was a freshman at Syracuse. We were so wrapped up in our conversation that we both nearly jumped out of our skin when the door to the dressing room swung open. Standing in front of us, Jesse looked strangely disheveled. He seemed out of breath and was fumbling with something below

his waist. Though I tried not to look, I couldn't help but stare
in shock, watching as he struggled with the fly of his pants.
Caught red-handed, an embarrassed grin spread across his face.
He nodded quickly in our direction before bounding past us.

"Well, well. What have we got here?" Hayley said slyly as we
entered the dressing room. Brooke, who was pulling a fluffy
white robe around her body, looked equally ruffled. With her
white-blond locks in disarray, mascara smudged, and skin glistening with a sheen that could have saved us three bottles of
baby oil during the "Pillow Talk" debacle, she was certainly up
to no good. Lowering herself onto the love seat, she exchanged
knowing looks with Hayley, pausing for a moment before leaping into the arms of her oldest friend like a giddy schoolgirl.

"Got you something." Hayley smiled. Reaching into the
patchwork purse slung loosely across her body, she pulled out
what looked like a green rock.

"What . . . is it?" Brooke asked, taking it in her hands.

"Chrysoprase," Hayley said casually. "I picked it up at this
trippy store right off Broadway. It protects against negative
energy, like a dream catcher except for when you're not sleeping . . . and it's particularly good for working with large groups
of people." She smiled, glancing down the hallway, where a
cluster of dancers had gathered to practice their steps.

"How does it do that?" Brooke wondered, propping one of
her honeyed legs up against the vanity table that was covered
with Kabuki brushes, stacks of palettes, and tubes of various
sizes and colors. My makeup bag disemboweled.

"Gemstones and crystals house spiritual properties that can
balance the energies around us," Hayley said, serious for the first
time. Dragging a stool across the room to where I was coating
Brooke's face in a light, lavender-tinted base, Hayley continued.
"But you have to keep it with you or it won't work . . . I mean,
you can set it down of course, but just make sure you put it

someplace close by . . . where you can still feel its healing vibrations, you know?"

Flipping the green rock, the Chrysler praise or something, in the palm of her hand, a look of curiosity bordering on fascination spread across her face.

"Jackie!" Brooke broke away from the rock. Squeezing Hayley's forearm, she enthusiastically made introductions. "This is my BFF Hayley. She's the sweetest person in the whole, wide world. She goes to school around here so I told her to drop on by. And Hayley, this is Jackie . . ."

"Oh, Jackie and I go way back," Hayley said warmly.

We playfully exchanged a handshake. "Nice to meet you again." I smiled at her, while attempting to reapply Brooke's mascara.

"Hey-y-y-y . . ." Robert sighed as he entered the room—I could tell from his tone that he was jolly no more. How could he run so hot and cold? I just didn't get him. Absorbed by the new-found powers that had been bestowed upon her, Brooke barely flinched as he heaved the large hockey bag full of the Emerson's rejects from his shoulder onto the floor with a big *BOOM!* Startled, I glanced up at him, quickly noticing the costumes draped over his arm. The first was a skintight race car jumpsuit offset with a sporty checkered stripe down one side. The second, a sparkly unitard adorned with iridescent flowers, wasn't much better. I couldn't understand why her look, Barbie doll meets circus performer, differed so greatly from the Emersons', who were always dressed so cool.

Robert had caught my stare. Gleaning my thoughts, he looked back at me, cocking his head in judgment. I scrambled for words, hoping to ease the situation with some kind of compliment. "I have the perfect eye shadow for that flowery one!" I smiled. Wrinkling his nose, he looked around for a place to hang Brooke's costumes.

"Oooohhh. . . . ain't those cute?" A throaty voice bellowed. Appearing out of nowhere, Sasha accosted the tiny pieces of clothing Robert was hanging onto. He looked as if he wanted to slap her hands away from the precious garments, but knowing where he stood in the pecking order, turned to her with a feigned smile on his face instead. Abruptly shifting her interest away from the bejeweled bodice in her grip, Sasha began rattling off a list of wardrobe concerns she had for Robert, who stood directly behind me with his arms crossed over his chest. Although they were engaged in a long-winded debate that seemed to be centered on Landon's new hairstyle, the close proximity of their conversation made me feel as if I, the newbie, were on display. Feeling as if my every move were up for criticism, my palm—wrapped tightly around a makeup brush—felt clammy as I swept midnight blue shadow across Brooke's lids. To my left, Hayley and Brooke were engrossed in their own tête-à-tête which, from what I could tell by only half-listening, had something to do with "negative energies" and "mean people." Trying hard to drown out the background noise around me, I focused my attention on Brooke's pout—disrupting her chatter by dotting a glob of pink gloss on her lips for the finishing touch.

Standing straight up, I breathed a quiet sigh of relief. With Robert behind me, I angled Brooke's chair off to the side so I could step back and survey my work. Reversing three paces, I was pleased to see that the way I'd dramatically lined her eyes had successfully transformed her from ingénue to glamour girl. And just as I was about to give myself a big pat on the back—it happened. Something on the floor behind me caused my body to lurch backward. Reaching out my hands, I instinctively tried to regain balance, betrayed by my legs, which were already unsteady in four-inch heels. The ground beneath my feet quickly disappeared. Flipping backwards, I landed on the hard concrete floor—legs up in the air—with a thud. I lay there for a moment wishing I could melt into the ground and disappear. Remembering that I was wearing a skirt, I jolted upward only to find four stunned pairs of eyes watching me in horror, unsure how to react. I narrowed my eyes toward the floor ahead, spotting the culprit: an overstuffed hockey bag of clothes. The increase of blood flowing to my face and ears as I blushed in embarrassment distracted from the throbbing of my tailbone and the rising hatred I felt for Robert. *So much for putting my best foot forward—err, backward.* Shrugging my shoulders, I flashed a nervous smile signaling that I was okay. *Okay, show's over, people* . . .

"Heh, heh, heh. . . ." Sasha guffawed, finally breaking the silence. "Have a nice trip—see you next fall!"

Soon the others were in stitches. Wiping tears from her eyes, Sasha chuckled, looking down at me with a goofy grin. "You okay, Calamity?"

"Just fine," I muttered sheepishly and turned my focus back to Brooke, hoping the others would also reoccupy themselves.

"Sup, my girl!" a gruff voice behind me barked just as I began to apply Brooke's finishing touches.

"T-Rooooc!" Brooke leapt from the chair, rushing toward the N.F.L. linebacker lookalike now barreling into the room.

"Gimme some love!" He threw his enormous arms around Brooke's tiny body.

Still buried in his chest and beaming, Brooke called out to me, "Jackie, this is my most favorite person in the whole wide world—Tariq. But we all call him T-Roc."

Erupting in sarcastic laughter, the man retorted, "You say e'rebody be your favorite in the whole wide world."

Brooke pouted playfully and whined, "But you know you're my favoritest, T-Roc." Brow furrowed, he nodded in mock doubt, as if to say *keep talking.*

"T-Roc's been working with the boys for*ever,*" she said waving a hand toward the hallway in the direction of the Emerson Brothers' dressing rooms. Her legs dangled, making her look like a child in his arms.

"Round the damn clock, kid!" He released Brooke from what amounted to an extremely long bear hug and stood straight up.

"So . . ." she said with a sly smile, "you finally get the courage to do it?"

"Do what?" He lumbered over Brooke, an almost comical pairing.

Delivering a light punch to his gut, she whined, "You k-n-o-w-w-w . . ."

T-Roc grabbed his stomach in sarcastic agony and laughed. "Alright, alright, alright." He laughed. "Take it easy killah. You will be happy to know that I *did* ask—even got down on my damn knee."

Brooke's eyes grew wider. "And?"

A sly grin spread across his face. "Shit, you think anybody gonna say no to this," he chuckled tossing his arms up to the side.

"T!" Brooke squealed, leaning in to embrace him again. "You're getting married!"

I cringed watching the eye makeup on the right side of her face smudge onto his shirt. T-Roc gave Brooke a little squeeze before looking up at me.

"'Sup?"

"'Sup?" T-Rock asked, extending a beefy arm my way. A massive diamond-encrusted watch, a gift from a former client, looked almost dainty on his wrist.

"He only pretends to be tough, but in reality he's a huge teddy bear." Brooke smiled adoringly.

Whipping back around to face her, he moaned sarcastically, "Why you always got to blow up my spot, girl?"

"Don't worry." I laughed and sized up his hulkish stature

once more. It was safe to say T-Roc could easily intimidate any of the Emerson Brothers' would-be attackers.

"I gotta get going . . ." he announced, swinging his arms up and back down again in an almost giddy gesture. Half-black, half-Samoan, he was as cheery as a six-foot-four, three-hundred-pound guy could be. "For real though, I cannot wait to see you turn this place inside out tonight!"

Chapter 4

From the outside, Hollywood is a
mass-market fantasy factory . . . it is the creator of our
collective imagination, and perhaps the lasting record
of what we are and believe and dream.
–Charles Fleming

And turn the place inside out she did. With pillars of
flame erupting from both sides of the stage, Brooke and
her dancers kicked off the night, arousing yelps from a
few unsuspecting preteens who stood a short distance
from their parents. Tackling six songs in a row, stopping briefly for a costume change, the crowd watched
breathlessly as Brooke morphed into a full-blown sex
kitten with each onstage gyration. Her dancers writhed
around her in unison as she strutted across the stage,
whipping her body back and forth as if it were a weapon.
Hair flying, she bumped, grinded, and crooned her way

through the short set with ease. Watching her from afar—cool and composed, ignoring the mixed reactions of the crowd waiting anxiously for the Emerson Brothers—I could tell she was in her element.

When the Emersons finally took the stage, the teenaged squeals from the audience erupted into ear-splitting shrieks. A robotic voice announced each "brother" one at a time: "Landon [poof!] . . . Nolan [poof!] . . . Jesse [poof!]," each boy appeared in a dramatic burst of smoke and sparks. Channeling Michael Jackson, Jesse moonwalked the length of the stage, much to the delight of the girls in the audience. Clutching T-shirts, tote bags, and posters bearing his likeness, they went wild.

I'd left the T.V. on overnight by accident, and when the chatter of the morning news woke me, my ears were still ringing from the blasts of pyrotechnics from the night before. Still groggy, I slid out of bed to turn it off when the voice of the Albany newscaster caught my attention.

If you caught the concert last night at the new performing arts theater in Saratoga Springs, you may have seen her . . .

Cutting to shots of both Brooke and the Emersons from last night's performance, a voiceover buzzed on while I darted down the hall to Brooke's room:

Honing her musical chops, former beauty queen Brooke Parker landed in Saratoga Springs last night. Just eighteen years old, she's the latest to join the Emerson Brothers on their national tour . . .

"Brooke!" I yelled. "You're on T.V.!"

"Huh?" She said, sticking her head out of the bathroom door.

"Look," I said, motioning to the footage taken at last night's concert. Seeing herself on screen, her eyes widened with shock. Like an excited child, she popped up on her tiptoes and threw her fists up and down. Toothbrush dangling from the corner of her mouth, Brooke sprinted across the room.

But her debut music video, "Pillow Talk," released just hours before yesterday's show, had some local parents concerned.

A clip of Brooke kneeling on satin sheets—feathers clinging to her toned, oiled body—flashed on the screen. Brooke actually gasped, staring at me in a stunned silence before ripping the toothbrush from her mouth. She was noticeably shocked, and I immediately felt sorry for her. I was just as surprised to see the way her sexuality had been trumped up tenfold in the editing room; I even felt slightly ashamed that I might somehow be at fault for contributing to it. She was just a small-town girl excited to be shooting her first music video. How could she know it would turn out like this!? How was she supposed to know that the pervy director was taking zoom shots of her midriff? She was dancing her butt off.

Brooke gulped a mouthful of toothpaste so that she could speak; I nearly gagged. "I can't believe we missed TRL yesterday!"

My jaw dropped. Concerned mothers all over upstate New York were eager to unload their two cents on local television. Brooke remained bafflingly unfazed during the series of public interviews, in which one woman called the video "repulsive," while another huffed on about the "pitiful, loathsome" message it sent to young girls. At first, I figured that Brooke was simply trying to make light of it, and I nearly laughed out loud. That is, until she added, "Man, I hope someone Tivo'd it!"

"This is no good," a voice grumbled. Standing in the doorway, arms crossed squarely over his chest, Steve narrowed his eyes at the T.V.. The polar opposite of Brooke, Steve was more than just fazed by the news. But none of us, not even Steve, knew just how out-of-control things were about to get.

"Pillow Talk" was the talk of the town—every town. You couldn't turn on the radio, pick up a newspaper, or turn on the television without hearing her name. She was suddenly linked to any of a bevy of issues up for discussion. Bible-belt parents and, apparently, anyone with an opinion anywhere somehow seemed to hold her singularly responsible for the moral decline in America. The buzz surrounding Brooke wasn't all bad, however. Not only did "Pillow Talk" soar to number one on M.T.V. overnight, but thanks to her "clever, Cleopatra-inspired bob," a new style icon was born. The direct result of my inexperience suddenly served as a model that was emulated by a slew of copycats all over America.

Despite the strict itinerary that required us to wait in the cold before loading onto the tour buses, I felt surprisingly refreshed. It was unusually sunny outside, which put me in good spirits and I couldn't wait to get on the road. We were set to drive overnight, which would allow us to make it to Florida by the next afternoon. Just as I was admiring the way the rays of the sun danced along the snow-covered roofs of the quaint shops across the street, I noticed that everyone else seemed slightly cranky. Landon and Nolan weren't speaking to each other, thanks to an argument over a video game earlier on. Already juggling the Emerson Brothers press, it was clear that Sasha hadn't planned on Brooke's profile rising anytime soon. The situation dampening her mood, she waited grumpily outside, complaining of back pains every so often as she leafed through a copy of *Vogue* with a frown on her face. Every few minutes or so, she'd look up in disgust and complain to anyone in earshot, "I'm too damn old for this shit." Up ahead I spotted David looking mildly annoyed as he paced back and forth outside the hotel with his cell phone to his ear.

"We either need it fixed in a timely manner or we need a replacement. Otherwise we'll be forced to cancel our remaining dates and I'm afraid that's not an option for us." Listening as David negotiated with the tour bus company, my stomach turned. Missing from the convoy in front of the hotel was Brooke's bus. *Oh God, please fix this—I'm not ready to go home yet!*

"That doesn't sound good," Hayley said wide-eyed as Steve zipped past us. He was already a wreck from the sudden media storm that had hit earlier that day—with every passing hour he had become increasingly stir crazy—even flipping through channels nearly gave him a heart attack—so he'd given up trying to watch completely. Now, pacing agitatedly and erupting in sporadic shouting fits directed at anyone within earshot, he looked as if he might explode.

"Looks like you're gonna need that chrysoprase today for sure." Hayley laughed quietly, studying the sour expressions on the faces around us.

"You're sure one is enough?" I joked along.

Reaching into her pocket, Brooke pulled out the green stone, clasping it tight in her fingers. Turning to me, she hummed excitedly, "Let's go!"

"I don't think we can . . . I mean, the bus could be here any minute," I hesitated.

"Good luck, I'll probably be back to Syracuse by the time it gets here. Repairs take forever," Hayley smirked. She reached into her patchwork purse, fishing out her keys. Turning towards Brooke, who looked on the verge of tears, she moaned loudly. "No crying . . . seriously." Nodding her head like a little girl, Brooke threw her arms around her friend without saying a word.

"I promise to come visit you over the summer when school lets out," Hayley continued. "Wherever you might be! Okay?" Brooke, still silent, nodded again. Spinning around, Hayley embraced me in what resembled a sort of bear hug, whispering in my ear, "Take good care of her. You seem to be the only sane one here . . . Calamity Jackie." Laughing, she made her way over to the adjacent parking lot before turning around to shout something at us. "Ankh! The store's called Ankh . . . it's pretty close by if you guys want to check it out."

She knew Steve wouldn't allow it—but Brooke remained adamant about sneaking off to go shopping—and she kept pestering me to go with her. I managed to keep her at bay for a little while and eventually she disappeared back inside the hotel, where a couple of the dancers—led by Jimmy, the one that always looked to me unusually muscular for his frame—had unrolled a mat to play Twister to pass the time. Sitting on a bench near the main entrance, I watched as Jimmy contorted his body in a painful position as he reached for one of the yellow dots with his right foot. Shaking my head, I returned to the ancient issue of *Guitar*—an iconic music magazine that I had collected and read religiously since I was a little girl—open on my lap.

Before I made it through the first sentence, T-Roc shouted his love to Brooke and sidled over to me. "Brooke! Girl, you blew the damn top off that place last night! Jackie, some show, huh? That girl's got er'one in New York talkin'."

"Yeah." I smiled. "It's pretty great."

"You gotta be worn out." T-Roc shook his shaved head, somehow sweating despite the chilly winter air. "Damn long drive ahead of us today. You hanging in there?"

I nodded, sighing, "This whole bus situation's crazy. I think it's starting to wear everyone a little thin." I looked toward Jesse— who was watching the dancers, limbs everywhere, contorting themselves every which way—his scowl growing more defined.

Following my glance, T-Roc shrugged. "Don't you worry 'bout them. Those boys are pros; they're used to it. E'erbody's staying strong—keeping busy. Haven't had a chance to shut my damn eyes yet, but it's all good."

I smirked, appreciative of T-Roc's unwavering optimism.

Here was this tough, larger-than life man you'd mistake for a thug until you spent twenty seconds in his glowing presence. A walking, talking, bodyguarding contradiction. Rocking back and forth on his heels, he stood contently, taking in the scene. I half expected him to start whistling.

"How you holding up?" David, freshly off the phone, asked as he stepped over to us.

"Depends on what's happening with the bus." Looking up at him I couldn't help but grin even though I knew my livelihood hung on his ability to get us to the next show on time.

"We've got some engine problems unfortunately. Our driver took it into a shop and it took forever for them to figure out what the problem was," David sighed. He looked messy and disheveled yet, unlike Steve, he was able to keep his cool—making him all the more attractive. "Anyway, they finally figured it out—bad fuel injectors. It's in the service garage now but it's going to take a few hours."

"So what does that mean for us?" I asked as David looked down at the oversized publication in my hands.

"Ric Craia?! No way, man." Grabbing the magazine from my hands, he studied it inquisitively. The image of a man in a vintage work shirt smiled up at him from the cover, with a wide grin beneath his drooping mustache that exaggerated the folds in his face. "1978? Where did you get this?"

"My dad had this huge pile of old issues in our basement and I just kind of started collecting them . . . I don't know, maybe it's weird but I love reading them."

"You a big Craia fan?" David smiled as he handed the magazine back to me.

"I am actually," I said as my cheeks turned pink. Though not necessarily "hip," I'd loved the blues rocker since I was a child because my father had taught me all the lyrics to his hits from the mid-seventies.

"Come on, no way." David laughed flirtatiously. "I didn't know you were into the whole 'blue-collar, plight of factory workers and truck drivers, modern day Romeo-and-Juliet-style tragedies set in New Jersey' thing."

"There's nothing wrong with making music for the everyman." I laughed. "He was arguably the best songwriter and guitarist of his time—nothing but an acoustic guitar and a microphone— that's impossible to beat today! No electric distortions, just plain old, good music."

"I hear he's making a comeback . . ." David said slyly. I rolled my eyes, now annoyed.

"Don't be a prick."

"I'm not kidding . . ." David said shaking his head. "A friend of mine out of New York, another manager, reps him—he's been looking for ways to revitalize his career for a while now. He may be a great songwriter, but my buddy's handpicking these tunes by pop artists for him to reinterpret. Seriously, Craia is into it."

"The world could always use a little more Rick Craia in it," I said, "but it'll be interesting to see what he makes of new pop music." I looked around, searching for something more intelligent to say, but I couldn't, for some reason, and so I tried to change the subject. "Anyway, back to the bus. . ." I said slowly in an attempt to change the subject. "Any idea how far this will set us back?"

"Well, we're going to rush like hell to meet everyone down there in time." He looked pained as he said this. "Usually, we'd all be on separate buses, but due to the circumstances we should probably ride down there with her together," he said, now flashing me a wry smile. "Good thing you brought yourself something to read . . . it's going to be a while."

Twister seemed to get the best of Brooke before long. Thinking fast, she kept confusing her left and right, but at least not hand and foot. She hunkered down in between David and me on the bench outside and called it quits. Resuming her quest to sneak off in search of voodoo charms, she whined to David sweetly.

"Can't y'all get Steve off our backs for just a few minutes? Puh-lease?"

David inhaled, looked over his shoulders, then patted me on the shoulder as if putting me in charge. "I've got your back for at least twenty-five minutes." He grinned at her. "Get out of here before anyone sees you guys."

As David walked away, T-Roc gave me a light nudge with his elbow. "Girl, I been watchin' you two." He smiled. "Mmmhmmm."

I cracked a smile, tucking *Guitar* back in my bag, "And what, exactly, have you seen?" I didn't think my little crush was *that* obvious.

"I see th' sparkle in those brown eyes of yours," He nudged me with a bulky elbow.

"Looks like Brooke's had enough Twister. We need to move on out while we have a shot."

"Want me to come along?"

"Nah," I said, but little did I know, I'd completely underestimated Brooke's rising star power. "I think we'll be just fine, but thank you."

A wave of patchouli incense stung my nostrils as we entered Ankh. The store was completely empty, save for an older woman, presumably the store's owner. Perched at one of the tables in the makeshift "tea room," she smiled at us as we moved about. Brooke adored and was obsessed with absolutely everything in the store. She'd stop to make a fuss over one thing, saying, "This is the coolest ever! Oh my gawd—look, look . . . I have to get it!" And two seconds later she'd be freaking out about whatever was sitting next to it. The storeowner, who must've known who she was, was getting a real kick out of her. I made a few laps around the store while Brooke loaded her arms with glittery candleholders shaped like winged angels and fairy-shaped pewter pendants whose labels promised to spur creativity. On my fourth lap around the store, I was just starting to get antsy when I noticed something strange outside the store window. Three girls, no older than fifteen, were pressed up against the glass. The one on the right had a camera in her hand and every so often nudged one of the other girls as if they were daring each other to snap a photo. I told myself I was being paranoid. I'd just spent an entire day traveling with Brooke and no one had recognized her, and if they did, they certainly didn't bother her. Even at the McDonald's in the airport, teeming with the types of kids who went crazy for the Emerson Brothers, no one knew who she was. I looked back at the front window, certain that the girls had gone on their way by now. Instead, I was shocked to see that not only had two more of their girlfriends joined them, but that now all types of people had stopped. Squinting their eyes, they peered inside to see what all the fuss was about.

"Hey Brooke," I said, suddenly worried. Growing up in Beverly Hills, I'd become accustomed to the flashing lights of the paparazzi. Never had I been on the other end of it. I watched as five became ten, and fifteen became a crowd. I knew it was time to get Brooke out of there. She was, well, oblivious and delightedly preoccupied.

"These, you know, could only be created during the correct moon phases," the storeowner was telling Brooke, who was wide-eyed and hung on her every word.

"Hey, sorry to cut this short, but we've got a problem," I said pointing to the front of the store.

"Oh my goodness." The storeowner smiled; obviously pleased it was her store that was causing all the commotion. Watching as anxiety spread across Brooke's face, she said, "Don't worry girls. I'm going to lock this door up here in front—nice and tight. And when you feel ready to go—you can slip out the back unnoticed."

"Thanks," I told her. Turning back to Brooke, I said, "We should go. Soon." I motioned towards the back of the store, reaching out for her hand.

"Wait!" she cried out. "I really, really want to get some of this stuff."

"All right, just hurry up," I told her, puzzling at the clutter of novelty charms, new age books, candles, and mythical figurines she'd set on top of the counter.

"I forgot my money," she sighed, looking at the crowd, still clamoring for a glimpse of her. "I guess we won't be able to come back, huh?"

"Here," I said, throwing my credit card on the counter. With every item the storeowner rang up, I cringed, but the only thing I really cared about at that moment was getting back to the tour bus in one piece. Too much money and more anxiety later, Brooke's new spiritual trinkets were bagged and we left out the back entrance.

Our footsteps echoed in the alley as we shuffled behind the rows of stores. We laughed under our breath, rehashing Brooke's first real celebrity moment, and our casual "escape." But we had spoken too soon. Suddenly, we heard something up ahead that made us stop in our tracks.

"Hey! Brooke! Hey!" The voice belonged to a teenage girl. We knew she was just a kid, but from where she stood in the shadow-filled alley, the way she addressed Brooke, she appeared almost menacing. Her scream alerted others, who rushed around the corner. I looked over at Brooke—her arms weighted down with two large shopping bags. She looked totally helpless.

"There she is!" we heard someone yell amid the chattering

voices. Erupting in spontaneous laughter, Brooke turned on her heel and began running down the alley. Following right behind her, I could hear footsteps chasing after us.

"I can't believe people are runnin' after me!" Brooke shrieked mid-gallop, still giggling, as if she didn't know what else to do. Sprinting as fast as my legs could carry me, the wind roaring in my ears and my long, loose hair flying behind me in waves, I felt like the Beatles in the opening scene of *A Hard Day's Night*. Overcome by a headlong rush, we raced down the alley. As we rounded a corner, up ahead we could still hear the voice of the girl who had first spotted Brooke in the alley. Her angry shout, fading in the distance, was the last thing we heard:

"BITCH!"

Chapter 5

The more I see, the less I know for sure.
–John Lennon

Nearly twenty hours later, after countless rest stops and highways, we stumbled off the dim tour bus and out onto the sidewalks of Pompano Beach, happy at last to be out of the snow and stretch our stiff joints. Our last two stops in South Florida—where the Emersons had more fans than anywhere else it seemed—were two nights apart, leaving a day in between to finish up press interviews, at venues just forty-five minutes from each other. Unloading the bus at our first destination took longer than we had expected, and before anyone could check into hotel rooms, the road crew found themselves right back on the buses en route to the concert venue just a few miles away.

Brooke, of course, was among the few that were able

to get into their rooms right away. At Steve's urging, I stuck close by so that I could be summoned immediately when needed. All smiles and giggles as we entered the hotel, Brooke moved like molasses, enjoying her own world and completely oblivious to many things, like the fact that we were in a serious time crunch, and that she was causing a sizeable commotion by showing off her pierced navel in that turquoise sports bra and old, skintight sweat pants.

"It feels s-o-o good to be home," she said loudly as we crossed the lobby. Flipping her hair from side to side as we passed the large splashing fountain in the lobby, we made our way to the front desk.

Brooke smiled sweetly. "Hey, can you tell me if my parents are here yet? They're meeting me for the show."

"Name please?" the clerk asked without looking up from her computer screen.

"It's uh—" Brooke paused, lowering her voice as she looked around to make sure that no one else was in earshot. "Magda Tropicana."

"Wait—what?" I erupted into laughter. "Magda—who?"

"It's an alias. Steve said I should start using one. Isn't it good? I made up plenty more, but I think this is my favorite."

"They have arrived and have gone into town to kill some time—would you like me to alert them for you when they return?" the woman asked as she placed two electronic room keys on the slab of marble in front of her.

"Yes, please! Tell them to come right up to my room," she squealed.

"Okay . . . Magda," I said, tousling her hair as we left the desk. "Let's hurry up and get changed. I'm dying to get out of these clothes." Tugging on the oversized sweatshirt stained purple from the grape soda I'd spilled on it somewhere between North and South Carolina, we made our way to her room.

The time crunch threw everything else out of whack. Keeping his cool, David wasted no time devising new schedules for both Brooke and the Emersons. I had to admit that it was pretty entertaining to watch David at work. He remained at an even keel throughout even the most turbulent times, turning off the goofy guy and stepping into the shoes of a serious business professional. Catching my eye as he flew past Brooke's room where I was calmly waiting outside, he broke out of character as a boyish grin spread across his face. "Hello hello," he said making his way over to me.

"Looks like you've got your work cut out for you," I yelled after him.

"No shit—the delay in Saratoga Springs didn't do us any favors, that's for sure." He tousled his hair, letting it fall in front of one eye. I had the sudden urge to throw my arms around him like a smitten schoolgirl when a voice quickly interrupted my thoughts.

"We're running out of time here. David, what's the latest they can do sound check?" Steve asked as he emerged from Brooke's room.

"Brooke should be fine to do it right after makeup," he said snapping back into work mode. He looked over at me, "You're slotted for your regular two hours, but if you can get it done sooner it would be a huge relief."

"No problem," I hummed, flashing him a killer smile, trying to turn on my professional demeanor to match David's. "Won't take me any longer than an hour-and-fifteen."

Steve, who had turned his attention towards me, motioned towards Brooke, who was sitting cross-legged on the floor of room. "Great! Let's get her into makeup now then so that—"

Cutting him off mid-sentence, a hearty laugh came from the doorway.

"Baby girl!" A noticeably handsome man, albeit a rugged one, rushed toward Brooke and spun her around in his arms. Drab clothing covered his somewhat bloated frame, though his chiseled facial features made it easy to imagine how attractive he might have been in his youth. Directly next to him, a woman in a seafoam green tracksuit, neck adorned with a silver necklace that read "Return to Tiffany's," smiled. She looked, I decided, watching her sip from a glass of iced tea in her hand, like an older version of Brooke—years spent under the blazing Florida sun had resulted in crow's feet around her eyes. Steve, whose surprise had given way to annoyance, mustered up what superficial charm he could. Greeting them both, he nodded his head in their direction.

"Mrs. Dianne . . . William, so glad—"

"Please Steve—call me Willy . . . and the pleasure's all ours," the man said, laughing sloppily once more.

"Certainly," Steve choked. "Hopefully the drive wasn't too long for you."

"Nah, 'bout twenty-four miles or so. Nothing at all. We'd drive just about any distance in the world to see our little girl sing, that's for sure." Noticing me standing there in confusion, Willy perked up. "Who we got o'er here?"

"I'm—" I started, but Steve quickly cut me off.

"This is Jackie, she's doing the makeup . . . we're *really* in a hurry here." Steve frowned as the Parkers failed to pick up on his urgency. Giving me a look as if stressing that I was indeed his last resort, he spoke sternly.

"I've got to head over to the venue and deal with the people over there, so I'm going to trust you to get her butt onto that bus as soon as humanly possible. Sound good?"

Scanning the room for appropriate lighting, I unloaded miniature bottles and pods from my makeup kit into my arms. Eyeing the bedside clock, before turning back towards Steve, I tried to sound as confident as possible.

"No problem." I shrugged coolly, turning around just in time for a high-pitched screeching noise to pierce my ears and fall into me. Before I knew what was happening, I heard a big crash, as everything in my arms fell to the tiled floor of the foyer. Ignoring the mess of broken powder, two identical eleven-year-old boys tore through the room. Grabbing a red bra Brooke had slung over a chair, one of the little monsters put it on over his sweatshirt while the other seized a pair of nylons and stuck them on his head. On cue, they both paused a short distance from their sister before singing out in taunting tones, "Oh! Baby! 'Pillow Talk!' Yeah . . . sexy!"

Brooke just rolled her eyes, yelling out to Steve and me. "My little brothers."

"Yep, yep—these here are the boys." Willy smiled. "That one there—" he said, pointing over to the green-and-mauve–striped couch where one of them was now jumping wildly up and down in a pair of dirty sneakers, "—is Chris." He threw an arm around the neck of the other, putting him in a gentle headlock the caused him to squirm wildly. "And o'er here we got Nick."

"I like to call 'em Tweedle Dee and Tweedle Dum," Brooke said, staring at them with a mock glare that soon turned into a grin she could no longer conceal. Looking as if he might lose it at any moment, Steve silently made his way to the door, stopping to gape at my mess on the floor.

"Sorry, I'll get this all cl—" I started.

Not making a sound, he narrowed his eyes, mouthing: "Just. Get. Her. There. ON TIME!"

By some miracle, I finished Brooke's makeup with time to spare. I didn't quite make the hour and fifteen minutes I'd so confidently promised, but early was still early, I figured. Just as I was about to give myself a pat on the back for a job well done, the shiny silver doors parted open on the first floor, revealing a curious scene outside. Standing between us and the waiting bus was an odd mix of revelers that had gathered near the front of the hotel. Some held up signs that said things like, "Music Videos Are Tools of Satan," "Dress As If Jesus Were Sitting Next To You," and paying tribute to the Beef Checkoff ad campaign, one that read in thick red letters: "Temptation: Its What's for Sinners." A handful of local news photographers and reporters lingered as well, ready to cover the developing story.

"What are we going to do?" Brooke asked in a weak voice.

"I think everyone is already over there." Though I didn't know much about how this kind of thing worked, I knew it was Sasha's cup of tea. But because she was consumed with the Emerson Brothers—as per usual—who were doing a handful of radio interviews at the venue, it looked as if we were left to our own devices. My eyes searched the crowd, looking for a familiar face—David or one of the crew members—even Robert would've been good at this point—*someone*. I did see men in hotel uniforms standing in front of the doors, trying to keep everyone at bay. T-Roc and the Emerson Brothers' three bodyguards, one for each brother, had left ahead of us. Because of the large turnout there was increased security presence both inside and outside the venue, though nobody, it seemed, had thought to prepare the hotel. Looking through the fogged glass at the flimsy staff they did have on hand, I waved toward the staffers, trying desperately to get the attention of at least one guard, but to no avail. Shrugging my shoulders, I shook my head slowly. The back of the hotel opened to the open pool area and patio, and from what I could tell there was no suitable escape route.

"I can ask the driver to pick you up at one of the side entrances," I offered.

"Won't everybody—when they see it pullin' up to the side—know that it's me?" she asked quietly.

"Yeah." I frowned, pointing to the front. "We go out there I guess . . . let me go first," I told her. "Maybe it will take some attention off you—maybe you can make a run for it."

All news cameras turned to me the minute the automatic doors slid open, their footage quickly interrupted by a couple of high school students that paraded past, chanting, "Down with aggressive media culture! Don't rob us of our childhoods!" To my right, a sweaty-looking man frantically seized his chance to impart his two cents—bellowing with rapid, pressured speech into the microphone of one newscaster, "A person like this promotes rebellion and sex by delivering evil messages to America's youth through risqué clothing, erotic body language, and suggestive sounds intended to arouse an audience. . ."

A well-groomed reporter with a finely combed back ponytail who had introduced herself on-camera as Nina Guagenti, looked over suddenly, the eyes of the crowd following her lead. Emerging from the hotel lobby like a frightened little girl, but to the amassed crowd something of an apocalyptic figure, Brooke seemed to both horrify and fascinate her accusers. The fading light fell on her messy blond tresses, framing her face with a faint glow, and they all watched her silently, squinting their eyes and craning their necks to see her.

First to break the silence, Nina Guagenti snapped her fingers aggressively to get the attention of her cameraman.

"Brooke, sweetheart," she called out, waving her hand daintily in the air. "Would you mind speaking to us for just one minute?"

Trapping Brooke at her side without waiting for a response, the reporter gazed into the camera. "Phillip, I'm standing here in front of the Haymarket Hotel with former Miss Teen Florida turned pop singer Brooke Parker, who is getting ready to take the stage in Pompano Beach tonight." The woman turned to

Brooke in one swift motion, jamming the microphone in between them.

"Departing your hotel just moments ago, you were met with some aggression here tonight . . . from Louisiana-based Christian group, The Tree of Knowledge. Isn't that right?"

"Uh, yeah—I guess. I don't really know what's going on." Brooke nervously smiled.

"Do you still consider yourself a Lutheran?" one of the protesters standing behind her screamed out.

"Of course I do," Brooke snapped, whipping her head around. "I say a prayer before every rehearsal *and* every show."

Without breaking eye contact with the lens, Nina smirked slightly, turning her body back towards Brooke to resume her interrogation.

"Mounting over the last month or so, your love life has fueled much speculation . . ." The phony enthusiasm Nina poured into the camera in front of her as she said this made me cringe, it was as if Brooke were just one of her girlfriends at a slumber party, belying the wolf in sheep's clothing licking her chops for an exclusive. Brooke stood awkwardly amidst the mob that hovered around her. From the naive expression of childish wonderment and confusion on her face, it was clear she hadn't been well-versed in how to handle press or how invasive they could be. I felt the sudden urge *to do something*—to pull my friend far out of harm's way—because where *I* came from, conversations with reporters that started out like this one never lead to anything good.

". . . Of a romantic relationship between yourself and Emerson Brothers' teen heartthrob, Jesse." Nina looked at Brooke in anticipation before continuing on. "Adding sparks to the flame were the photographs that surfaced recently in which the two of you appeared to be canoodling on the set of your music video in Los Angeles. Is there anything you guys are holding back from all your fans out there?"

"No, it's nothing." Brooke lied though the pink that tinged her cheeks was all too telling. "We're just friends."

I was just about to breathe a big sigh of relief as it seemed like the worst was over, but then another curve ball was tossed her way.

"What kind of role model are you for our children?!" It was the sweaty man again, vying for more air time.

Gesturing toward the crowd of protesting Christians behind her, Nina nodded. "That certainly is a question that's been on quite a few minds lately. The sexual innuendos of your lyrics, the provocative clothing—what do you feel your responsibilities, *if any*, are as a role model for America's youth?"

The microphone she shoved at Brooke met an awkward silence in the form of a deer-in-headlights stare. Brooke paused, twisting her face in confusion—as if pondering what to say—but I had had enough. Grabbing Brooke's arm, I pushed myself in between them. Stopping to glare at the reporter, I leaned into the microphone.

"I'd ask you the same question—murders, white collar crimes, the war overseas—what do you feel *your* responsibilities are, *if any*, in educating the public on its most pressing issues?" Lost for words, it was now Nina Guagenti's turn to be silent. "What kind of role model bombards and harasses an innocent young girl like this? Must be a slow news day."

Evading my questions, Nina clasped her trench coat around herself with one hand and smugly turned back to the camera. Leaving her chattering behind us, I pulled Brooke through the crowd, into the safety of the bus.

Notified of the situation just minutes before we arrived to the venue, Steve waited anxiously. Gripping the wheel, the driver turned into a private entrance that was far from where concertgoers lined up excitedly in front, dropping us off without any hassle. Valiantly throwing his arms around Brooke's shoulders, Steve escorted her inside, leaving me trailing after them.

"There were only a handful of them a little over an hour ago—no signs, no chanting—someone must've tipped them off," Steve, who had figured that the small gathering of people he saw were just the usual Emerson Brothers fanatics, grumbled. "Those news cameras must have just showed up—they probably brought all the commotion with them. Idiots . . ."

As we moved briskly down the hall behind him, our eyes fixed straight ahead towards the dressing rooms, I couldn't help but feel pleased with myself for stepping up to the plate and defending my friend in the heat of the moment. Certainly, I'd at least proven to Steve that there was more to me than meets the eye—*I was not only responsible, but someone who looked out for her client's best interest.*

"Calamity!" A voice called out. Wrapped up in my thoughts, I had fallen out of pace. Standing in a doorway just up ahead, I spotted Steve staring down at his wristwatch.

"You guys are really late . . . what took so long?"

Word of the madness swirling outside the hotel had spread and Brooke's dancers gathered in her dressing room to make sure she was okay. The sound of them all screaming at each other as they jumped up and down and threw their arms around her was deafening.

"That is so not *beat*," one of the girls, said, prompting the rest of them to nod their heads in agreement.

"You okay girl?" Jimmy asked as he placed his hand gently on her leg—his touch seeming to linger just a little too long.

"Yeah, thanks for being such great best friends," Brooke said smiling up at everyone.

I was still trying to process all of the things that had just occurred in the past fifteen minutes when I heard a bitchy voice out of nowhere.

"Where the fuck have you guys been?" Standing just a few feet away, a pile of sparkling spandex weighing down one arm, stood Robert. Though he was directing all of his attention toward me, the dancers took this as their sign to bail, running out of the room as they blew air kisses in Brooke's direction.

"We were mobbed by a group of crazies outside the hotel," I told him. "I did the best I could to fend the off—"

"Really?" Robert's face lit up in excitement, which he poorly attempted to hide by turning down the corners of his grin. Getting no answer from Steve, he turned to me as if I were his new best friend. "Oh my God, what happened?"

"Just these crazy people at the hotel—I think they belong to some kind of Christian teen life group. Something like that . . . and there were cameras too. I've never seen anything like *that*."

"How exciting!" Robert mused. I could tell what was going through his head—why he was so excited. The more buzz Brooke generated, the higher his stock rose. I suppose that the same went for me as well, but for some reason I didn't see it that way, this whole thing was very new for me, too. He stood there, just lingering, but finally left as I put the final touches on her hair.

"Oh my gawd, lock that door—I can't talk to anyone else right now," Brooke said, flustered. Spotting a window on the north wall, she gushed, "Does that open? I want to open it."

"I'll get it!" Afraid she was having some kind of panic attack, I lunged toward the window, thrusting it open with superhuman strength. I expected her to run over to it, gasp for some fresh air and collect herself, but instead, she casually moved toward it. Pulling a Marlboro to her mouth, fresh air clearly wasn't on her mind.

"Want one?"

I hadn't smoked since midterms when my stress level was at an all-time high, or, I should say, what I thought was an all-time high. I took a cigarette from the pack in her fingers, plopped down next to her by the window, hoping it would relieve some of the tension I was feeling.

"You okay?" I asked her.

She nodded slowly before leaning forward to flick the ash of her cigarette in an empty metal trashcan. "Thank Jesus I had you with me, I don't know what I would've done."

"What about Jesse? Is he going to be mad?"

"What do you mean?" She looked genuinely confused and I wondered for a moment if I had been mistaken about their relationship.

"He's your . . . boyfriend, right?"

"Mmm-hmmm . . ." She took a long drag of her cigarette.

"And he's not going to be hurt that you denied that to the entire world?" Brooke rolled her eyes as I asked this, blowing out a cloud of smoke like a sailor.

"Both Steve and Sasha think it's bad if people know that we're dating. They tell us not to be seen together."

"Really?"

"He's got all these crazy fans, you know? I think they'd be upset if he had a girlfriend." Brooke shrugged, looking down at the caller I.D. on her phone, which had suddenly buzzed to life. "Speak of the devil." Like a little girl—minus, of course, the Marlboro dangling between her fingers—she clasped her phone to her chest, cradling it like an infant. "I'm soooo in love with him!"

Ten seconds to show time and I hustled over to the security barricade at the front of the stage, trying to dodge the throngs of screaming fans that had assembled. A pair of bulky bouncers in matching red T-shirts chatting on their two-way radios nodded as I flashed them the tour pass hanging around my neck. "Sup?" a familiar voice asked.

"Hey T-Roc," I said cheerfully, turning around. His typical gentleness had gone, replaced with a definite no-nonsense vibe. He stood with his enormous frame between the concertgoers and the stage, eyes scanning the crowds. His dark clothing and stern expression made it clear: this was not a time to be congenial; every single person, every hysterical teenage girl, was a potential threat. How was I supposed to act toward him under these circumstances? "Quite a turnout, huh?"

"It's crazy, right?" he responded gruffly, not taking his eyes from the crowd for a second or even cracking a smile. "Jackie."

"Yeah?"

"I'm in Defcon Mode." I flashed him a grin, laughed to myself, and left him to his work.

Slipping past the wooden blockade into the pit—the closest you can actually be to the stage without being on *it*—a group of teenage girls congregating close by stared in my direction, except not really *at me*, but at the backstage pass dangling from neck. From their looks of longing and envy, this feeling of importance suddenly washed over me. For once in my life people were actually jealous of my good fortune and success.

They wished that they were me!

Wading past the handful of photographers, I found Brooke's mother and stepfather with ear-to-ear grins on their faces, excited to watch their girl in action. Sitting to their right, David had a half-pained and mildly amused expression on his face as "the Tweedles" clung to and hung from his back, shoulders, arms, neck. I chuckled. He looked like a human jungle gym. Catching my gaze, he winked at me and smiled, and, of course, I blushed. Before either of us could say anything the auditorium darkened and a computer-generated voice commanded the attention of the audience. It was routine—the *snap-crackle-pop* of the robotic voice as Brooke's silhouette appeared behind a screen onstage. But as I prepared myself for the high-octane introduction I noticed that the voice overhead didn't sound fuzzy like usual; in fact, it didn't sound like anything at all.

"Shi—" David looked down at the twins, rethinking his words. "Oh, crap . . ."

"What's happening?" I asked, concerned.

"I don't know," he said, staring in confusion. "The backing track must be out or something."

The screen rose to reveal a nervous Brooke unsure of what to do as her voice was drowned out by the precision-timed pyrotechnics. Without the layered, prerecorded vocals, she went through her regular high-athletic-style dance moves at a snail's pace, clashing achingly with the song's high tempo and throwing off all her backup dancers. She kept shooting looks offstage left toward the sound console in confusion. In the pit, we were one collective held breath (save for Brooke's parents who—still all smiles—didn't seem to notice anything was wrong).

It took two full songs: two agonizingly long songs, for those of us who knew better, to fix the problem. Brooke, it seemed, who had already been shaken from the press earlier in the day, couldn't fully recover. It was the end of the world as she knew it. After the final pyrotechnic flashes signaled the end of her set, we quickly navigated through security and followed the sound of sobs. We found her, elbows resting on her knees, hands covering her face, in a chair next to a boy in a tailored, scoop-necked vest and straight-leg chinos. Whispering in her ear, Jesse twirled locks of her hair around his fingers while passersby just stared. We all tried to find something to pretend required our attention, but I snuck glances, still upset by the sound failure but intrigued by the two lovebirds. They made a cute couple, I decided—with his tanned skin and shaggy, dark brown hair, loose curls, paired with Robert's trendy flourishes (the leather-tab elastic suspenders limp at his sides) he was handsome—seeing him for the first time as Brooke's boyfriend rather than as a *Tiger Beat* pinup.

No longer able to ignore the summons he was receiving to the stage, Jesse kissed her tear-stained face. Taking his place, Steve pulled a handkerchief out of his back pocket as Brooke rehashed the mishap.

"Jackie! It was horrible . . . it just went out, I didn't know what to do!" Brooke sprang from her chair, throwing her arms around me as I walked up to join them.

"But I thought Gary said that it couldn't happen?" I asked.

"Well, it obviously *did* happen, so I guess that would make Gary wrong, wouldn't it?" Steve snapped. Maybe it shouldn't have surprised me, but the iciness of his tone sapped what energy I had left right out of me. Not even an hour ago, covetous looks from high school girls had me on a temporary high. It was funny how Steve could put me in my place so quickly—how fast he could snap me back to reality.

By the time we made it back to the hotel, crowds of people were still outside, though thankfully there were far more fans now than sign–toting, Bible-belting protesters. Crowding both the front and side doors, they hoped to catch a glimpse of the teen stars. Under Sasha's instruction, the inexperienced hotel staffers on duty helped clear a path that allowed us to enter relatively unscathed. All of the fanfare excited Robert, who secretly dreamed of starting his own supermarket-checkout-lane tabloid, and here he found himself on the inside, snapped candidly alongside someone famous. He, of course, made sure to walk close to Brooke, though to his disappointment, all of the professional photographers had long since gone home.

Seeing that their daughter was upset, Brooke's parents had

sat with her on the ride back to the hotel. Mrs. Dianne (as *everyone*, I found, called her) followed her upstairs while Willy took the boys to the restaurant in the lobby for milkshakes—the reward that he promised them if they were able to sit still during the concert. I was a bit confused as to what the Parkers' definition of "sitting still" meant, as they hadn't stopped moving the entire time.

As I packed my set case—color-coordinating tubes of lipstick by their varying shades of pinks, reds, and berries—I half-listened as Mrs. Dianne attempted to boost Brooke's spirits with a little pep talk, though it didn't appear to be doing much good, while both Steve and Sasha argued over something petty in the corner.

"You know you can come home with us tonight darlin'," Brooke's mother, perched on the end of the bed in her room, cooed as a last attempt. "Might be nice to relax in your own bed."

"I don't know," Steve said, breaking away from Sasha and patting the opposite side of the mattress. "These pillow tops are pretty hard to beat."

Ignoring him, Mrs. Dianne continued on. "Don't you have tomorrow off?"

"She's scheduled to be on one of the morning radio shows along with the Emerson boys, actually . . ."

"Boyyyy, I dunno—you think that's a smart idea? Are you completely nuts!" Sasha bellowed. "After all that craziness, uh-uh, she's not going on."

"Steve," Brooke chimed in. "I want to go with my parents. I really need to go home." Her chin quivered and for a moment I thought she might cry. Regaining control, she flashed him a faint smile. "They can drop me off on Saturday. Pretty please?"

A *night*, Steve knew, was better than a couple of months. The original plan had been for Brooke to return home after finishing up the last leg of the tour, to wait and see how well her album did. But with the growing media buzz, everyone felt it necessary—after getting it under control, that is—to strike while the iron was hot. According to Steve and Sasha's ongoing discussions, it was no longer about a handful of songs. She was now a package, their newest singing, dancing commodity.

"It's all about her image—the Brooke Parker brand," I had heard him say. "I know I'm not the only one that feels that way." Back in Los Angeles there were additional music videos to be shot, magazine covers to grace, talent agents to meet, and a second album to record.

Knowing it was better to lose a battle and win the war, he smiled warmly at Brooke. "Whatever you want, princess. We can do the radio show without you. Get some rest and let me know if there's anything else I can do for you."

With my belongings slung over my shoulder, I tiptoed behind Steve's back towards the door, flashing Brooke a victory smile.

"Actually, there's just one more thing," she smirked. "I wanna take Jackie with me."

Chapter 6

You know, it's funny. As it gets closer and
more probable, being a star is losing its meaning.
–Janis Joplin

Brooke's family lived in a sun-bleached neighborhood of
single-family ranch-style homes just minutes from one
of the major highway exits. Their well-manicured yet
modest concrete stucco home was nestled at the end of
what would've been a relatively quiet cul-de-sac; quiet,
of course, if not for the Parkers. Aside from the nonstop
foot traffic of energetic kids who banged doors and rattled windows as they flowed in and out, a revolving door
of houseguests added to the liveliness. Friends, neighbors, and relatives came and went as they pleased without question throughout the day, kicking off their shoes
and helping themselves to leftovers in the refrigerator.
With this sort of hospitality, the twang in their accents

that seemed more "country" than Southern, and the kind of neighbors that sat in rocking chairs on their porches—Brooke and I were clearly from different galaxies.

By the time lunch had rolled around, several people had already come and gone from the Parker home and two visitors remained. An overly made-up woman with auburn hair wrapped tightly in a bun—one of Mrs. Dianne's girlfriends from the pageant board—busily blabbed on in the kitchen. Her quick visit to "see how Miss Teen Florida was holding up," had turned into a two-hour gossip session about a number of topics ranging from a disagreement she had had with one of the contestant recruiters a week ago, the disorganized ice cream social recently held by the elementary school, and a fellow pageant mother who, according to her sources, had allowed her twelve-year-old daughter to take diet pills. "Can you believe it?" the woman rasped loudly from the kitchen. "Now I hear she's got the youngest one on a diet too . . ."

"How old?" Mrs. Dianne coated a casserole dish with a sprinkling of handfuls of potato chips over a mixed bowl of chicken, rice, peas, and celery.

"She's ten."

It was Willy's brother Todd, however, who was the most animated. He had stopped over for beer and to see his "favorite, famous niece" around 9:30 AM. Since he frequently visited, the Parkers had given him a key to the kitchen door so he would no longer have to break in to recover things he'd left behind or to catch his favorite show on T.V. Loud and boisterous, Todd was where I placed the blame for our rude awakening that morning.

Stuffed into a bunk stacked three beds high, it had been nearly impossible to get any sleep on the tour bus the previous night. Passing through highway construction and over beat-up roads, the constant rocking motion was almost nauseating. By the time we actually arrived at the Parkers', it was pretty late and both Brooke and I shuffled into her bedroom like zombies. Even on solid ground, curled on a mattress on the floor next to Brooke's bed, I was still haunted by the sickening sensation from the night before. Tossing and turning for what seemed like hours, I finally began to drift to sleep just before sunrise.

"Z-z-z-z-z-z!" A loud noise tore me from my sleep just a couple of hours later. Groggy, my eyes darted around the room, struggling to focus for a few minutes. Centering on a pink-and-black argyle valance that matched the comforter wrapped around me, I let out a sigh of exhaustion. Feeling weighted down, I continued to scan the room, examining the mismatched dresser lined with old tubes of Lip Smackers, bottles of Sunflowers perfume, and half-used bottles of Oil of Olay that sat against the wall across from me.

"Z-z-z-z-z-z!" The loud noise seemed to move towards Brooke's bedroom, disappearing again suddenly. I looked up at Brooke on the black metal daybed. Snuggled beneath its scroll detailing and oak finished hardwood posts, she was still fast asleep. Unable to see anything out of the window in her bedroom, I dragged my feet down the Pergo floor of the hallway towards the living room, scanning the rows of photos housed inside gold metal frames of varying sizes. Aside from a couple of professional-looking family photos and the twins' most recent school pictures, the wall appeared to be a shrine to Brooke. The glossy images documented each stage of her life—pictures of her tenth birthday party at the local roller skating rink, in her high school cheerleading uniform, and posing in blue jeans and a cowboy hat at a country music concert with Willy. I smiled. As far as both he and Brooke were concerned, he was her real father—in fact, they were closer than most of the girls I knew were with their dads—you'd never know they didn't share the same genetics.

Kneeling on the overstuffed off-white leather sectional in front of the window, I peeked through the blinds to see what all the commotion was about. Appearing as two separate whirls of blond hair, the Tweedles zipped around the backyard in circles on motorized bikes. A man in a dirty Florida Gators cap, who looked like an emaciated version of Willy, stood in the middle of the fuss, cheering them on loudly.

"Guilty as charged," said a voice behind me, catching me off guard. I turned to find Willy grinning at me from the kitchen. "I admit, that Bozo out there is my own flesh and blood." He threw his head back laughing, as Mrs. Dianne peered from behind him.

"Good morning! You must be starving . . ."

"Not too bad," I said, as if it were an automatic response. "You don't have to go to any trouble—"

"Nonsense, she's always cooking up a storm in here," Willy smiled. "She makes the best French toast in the county; that there is a fact."

"Well that's an offer I can't refuse then," I smiled joining them in their newly remodeled kitchen—one of Mrs. Dianne's passion projects, which Willy had green-lighted as an anniversary present. "I just feel bad imposing."

"Ya hear that Di? Finally, a houseguest with some manners." Willy roared with laughter, glancing back at me. "Don't think a thing of it. The way Todd eats us out of house and home, we're gonna have to declare Chapter Eleven."

Scooting up to her husband at the kitchen table, Mrs. Dianne signed, "That wouldn't be anything new." She pretended to be annoyed, though her hand on her husband's leg indicated otherwise. Sinking into the plate she had set down in front of me, I gobbled up the thick slices of bread—which had, as Willy had assured me, been perfectly flavored. It with the first time I'd spent any alone time with Brooke's parents, and they wasted no time briefing me on their rollercoaster love affair. According to Mrs. Dianne, Willy—who was two years her senior—was a star basketball player for the Riviera Beach Hornets, her rival high school. Back then, it was his skills on the court *and* his classic good looks that routinely drew packed crowds.

"The moment I laid eyes on her, whew . . ." Willy laughed. "It was love at first sight."

"For him anyway . . ." Mrs. Dianne nudged him as she took a sip of her sweet tea.

Teasingly, he grumbled, "She had a boyfriend . . . some wimp she went to school with—"

"*Not* that he let that stop him," she interjected.

"I chased her damn near all over town—showed up at her parents' house with flowers, all romantic," Willy breathed as Mrs. Dianne uncrossed her legs and leaned back in her chair, over-exaggerating the winking of her eye and shooting me a sly smile.

"Never let a man know you're interested."

Interested or not, boyfriend or not, the Intracoastal Waterway divided her life from his in Riviera Beach, an area known for its high crime rates and levels of poverty. Her parents, as Mrs. Dianne put it, were "less than pleased" by the frequent and most times unexpected visits from the wrong side of the tracks.

"She was from another world. Her parents thought I was no good."

"Yeah, well it turned out that the jerk I was dating at the time was the one that was 'no good.'" She rolled her eyes and fell silent for a moment and I realized she was talking about Brooke's biological father. Willy grabbed her hand and let out a sigh.

"Said he was too young to handle the kind of responsibilities that come along with havin' a kid," she continued. "I'll never forget that day. I was just sittin' there crying on the porch of my parents' house when, lo and behold, Willy stops by . . . and I needed someone to talk to—told him all about it." She smiled warmly at him. "I'll never forget what he said to me that day . . . 'What kind of man would be crazy enough to leave a beautiful woman like you? Shit, and a baby on the way? It's like getting a two for one deal'. . ."

From that point on, no matter how much her parents resisted their union, Mrs. Dianne and Willy were inseparable and eventually eloped to Miami.

"And then during Desert Storm," he said, "I lost this damn thang." My eyes widened, as he held up his arm, revealing the "damn thang" to be his right hand. Almost more shocking than the stump itself was the fact that I'd spent the last day with the Parkers without even noticing. Then again, with all of the pressures and demands brought on by life on the road, I barely had time to sleep let alone pay any attention to Willy's extremities.

"Shrapnel?" I asked. Willy sat there stone faced for a second before erupting into a throaty laughter so boisterous that tears came to the corners of his eyes.

Answering calmly, as if it were her job to bring him back down to earth, Mrs. Dianne spoke up. "He never made it overseas."

"That's right, I was all ready to enlist—bein' that I come from a military family—then a damn gator bit the thing right off." Willy explaining that he'd "been trappin' gators" since he was a teenager, though he'd only been "state-certified" since '90. "Lookin' back, best thing that ever happened to me—my country needed me, but turns out my two-for-one needed me even more," he said, looking at his wife. Like the expression Willy was fond of saying—"you win some, you lose some"—in the very same week his dreams of being a war hero were chewed up and spit out, the couple received an unexpected addition, unexpected because she had arrived two months early.

"S'pose she knew I could use an extra hand around—I always say, 'The week I lost my hand, I gained two more . . .'"

With enough hands around, the Parkers settled into a modest home just outside of Boca Raton where he continued to work for the Statewide Nuisance Alligator Program, saving mountain bikers and teams of little leaguers from the vicious reptiles that emerged from the nearby lakes. Mrs. Dianne remained active with the Miss South Florida Fair Pageant; trading in the crown she'd won her senior year of high school and accepting the coveted position of pageant director.

"Wow, is it really that big of a problem down here?" I asked.

"What? Beauty queens?" Willy asked confused. I was so blindsided by the fact that gator trapping was a full-time profession, even more so that Brooke had failed to ever mention her father was a full-time gator trapper, that I had totally lost track of the conversation.

"Sorry, no . . . I meant the whole alligator thing."

"Oh hell yes," Willy said, his face suddenly turning serious. "The program gets about two hundred phone calls a day— sometimes double that—hell, just last week a woman was killed by one of those suckers damn near our house. The thing came right into her lanai and ate up her little poodle before coming at her. Damn tragedy, that's what it is."

Following Willy's gator story, the rest of my day was an insider's look at the Parker clan. Once we finished breakfast, Brooke gave me a full, fascinating tour of their home. Remnants of her pageant days were everywhere; every time I entered a room I noticed something I'd missed before: atop the entertainment center and down the hallways, even the side tables, which held the crown, photos, and newspaper clippings from her big win.

At one point Mrs. Dianne came through with a basketful

of laundry, but paused to admire the spoils. "We've sure done well for ourselves. I've been taking Brooke out for auditions since she was old enough to hold a microphone, and look at her now—just followin' in her mama's footsteps."

She looked at framed photo on the wall and pressed a long, red acrylic nail against the glass. "Now that one's at the Radisson in Tampa—named Miss Daisy Dot at six years of age." A tiny Brooke stared blankly at the camera as she struggled to juggle a trophy, an armful of flowers, and a cardboard check for $400, all while balancing a crown on her head.

Then she picked up a burgundy-colored album with the word *Memories* embossed in gold on the front. She sat on the couch and summoned us over to join her. Whisking through the pages, she stopped to comment every so often on a photo from a dance recital or Brooke and her teammates on the middle school cheer squad, but then she flipped to a page that rendered her breathless.

"Oh my. This is it—Miss Teen Florida! The day we took home the statewide crown. What a day!" She clucked her tongue. "Yup. I just kept sayin' to her, 'Baby, be the crown! You are the crown!'"

"One of my proudest moments, I tell you what! She got real serious about that one, she did. Di bought her this plastic crown and she wore it all the time." Willy smiled before speaking in a high-pitched girly voice. "Pop, I'm practicin' my evening gown walk."

At this, both Willy and his brother cracked up. "It was a trip, I'm tellin' you. I can remember sitting with her, going over these little flashcard things . . ."

"Interview questions," Mrs. Dianne corrected him before turning back to me. "You never know what the judges are gonna spring on you. Luckily, though, I've been around long enough to see most of 'em."

Willy sat on the recliner and hoisted one foot on his knee, then the other, taking off his shoes. Mrs. Dianne wrinkled her nose and playfully waved her hand in front of it. "Ohhhh, please keep those things on!"

"Wearing shoes is a hazard." Uncle Todd put his game face on and turned to her. "You know that."

His remark puzzled me, and I watched as he peeled off his flannel button-up before plopping down near the coffee table. He began sorting through a stiff, uncoated deck of cards and tossed the bent ones to the side.

"There were times when Di had to yank that girl outta bed by her hair—kickin' and hollerin' all the way to them pageant classes," Willy laughed.

"Oh, we really worked hard," Mrs. Dianne chuckled. "I remember I kept puttin' the Vaseline on her teeth, and she just hated the taste of it. I kept tellin' that child, 'Sweetheart, the only thing that ever sat its way to success was a hen.' I'd say it was worth it! We won all those trophies, and now it's all music videos and concerts."

"Don't hover," Todd scolded as Willy stood over his brother's house of cards.

"This kid's had a deck on him since he was nine years old. He tried to set the world record in high school. Got 'em pretty high, too, right in the family room!" As Willy boasted of his brother's talents, the twins raced by and wrestled each other to the ground. Todd winced as his masterpiece tumbled, then hollered at the boys as he chased them out of the room.

"You see why I couldn't waste her talent by keepin' her holed up in this house?" Just then, Brooke strolled into the room yawning widely and took a seat next to her mother. Mrs. Dianne patted Brooke on the knee as she got up. "Time to fold some clothes."

It hit me then that Brooke's pageants were Mrs. Dianne's

hobby. Healthy or otherwise, her supportive involvement helped form an intense mother-daughter bond between the two.

While my own mother seemed to enjoy living vicariously through me, as if I'm her one chance to do it all over again, it created dissonance. She was always trying to set my life up "the right way," meaning normal, or at least relatively so. Because she had a tendency to see things as black or white with no middle ground—right or wrong, good or bad, success or failure—my choice to leave school hit her harder than anyone. In her eyes, I was simply giving up, and by following in her footsteps, would be doomed to make all of the same mistakes that she had. She somehow failed to see that the unrestrained creative inclinations that I possessed had been inherited directly from her.

We finished the tour with their garage, which housed two identical red sport A.T.V.s—the cars got the driveway. Willy joined us, beaming proudly, as though presenting pimped-out Ferraris. "Brooke bought 'em for the family out of her very first paycheck. Did she tell you that?"

"No sir, this is the first I've seen of them."

Somehow, between those words and a single blink I was on one, gripping the handlebars so tight my knuckles lost color. Uncle Todd and Brooke rode the other one, giving me directions, explaining that going slower made it harder to steer due to the friction. I hit the gas, only to be pelted with a shower of rocks and wood chips.

"So that's why they call you 'Calamity'?" Todd was grinning from ear to ear.

After a day filled with the unexpected, I found myself sitting around their dining room table eating casserole topped with potato chips. The twins kept kicking each other under the table and launching balled-up wads of bread at one another. I grew increasingly annoyed, thinking, perhaps, that I hadn't missed out on having a brother or sister after all. As Mrs. Dianne and Brooke shared the inner workings of the pageant world, the boys continued goofing off without any consequences—not even a stern look. They were all too engrossed in Mrs. Dianne's tale about the time she and Brooke were almost scammed in Miami by a mall talent scout.

"Those people just take your money and run. We are so grateful that Steve's the real deal," she said with relief in her voice, although she it was fairly evident she knew very little about professional legitimacy beyond the pageant world. "Brooke's a lucky girl to have him lookin' out for her career."

"Just a year ago we had nothin'. Damn near lost the house after Todd took a gamble with a no-good investment opportunity. And now look at us! Living like kings and queens!" Willy threw his hands in the air.

"I took every last penny we had and flew Brooke to Hollywood, California, for Talent America, and she didn't win. But it did bring us to Steve, and he's made all our dreams come true. What an angel!" Mrs. Dianne gushed. And with that she began clearing the table.

"Yes, he is." I forced a grin and got up to help.

Soon the scraping and clanking subsided, and Mrs. Dianne plunged her hands into the soapy water to wash the dishes. Willy stood next to her, drying them one by one.

Brooke grabbed my arm and led me from the kitchen. "Wanna see something?"

In the midst of all the bric-a-brac the Parkers had amassed over a lifetime, sat an oak console piano. From its broken music book holder and bench with visible wear and tear, the instrument was clearly well loved.

"It was my granny Charlotte's piano," Brooke whispered as if she were divulging a family secret. "My granddaddy gave it to her as a wedding gift. It's so beautiful, isn't it?" she said, softly brushing her fingers across the yellowing ivory keys. "I wish I could do the dang thing some justice but I can't ever seem to finish any of the songs I start playin'," she said, twisting her face in frustration. "It's like, I have so much to say and I start playing and writing and then," she paused gazing down with an empty stare of disappointment, "nothing. I can't do it."

"Why don't you play me what you have so far?"

Beginning with simple chords, I was soon enveloped in the emotion of her song—watching in wonderment as she revealed this real talent. Hidden beneath the glittering nylon bodices she writhed in onstage, masked by the backing tracks that forced her to lip synch, where and why had this side of her been covered up. Suddenly pounding on the ancient keys with her fist in frustration, she stopped.

"This is where I get stuck every time . . . I start hearing all the parts of the song in my head, and it's like now that I actually have a chance to *record something*, I get stuck."

"What if you try this?" Sliding onto the bench next to her, I placed my hands on the keys, picking up where she left off, changing the melody with a rich, warm tone.

"Wow." Brooke smiled. "I didn't know you could play . . ."

"I didn't know *you* could play."

"I mean, I know we talked about messing around on the piano when we were younger— but that's, like, really good," Brooke said enthusiastically. "What else have you written?"

"Just stupid little things here and there—nothing that great," I said sheepishly. Here I was, showing off my musical talents while sitting next to a famous pop musician.

"I wanna hear!" she begged sweetly. "Please?"

"Um," I said looking down at the keys and shaking my head, "sure . . ." I contemplated for a few moments trying to decide which was suitable enough to play for her. "Well, here's something I guess."

Brooke watched with palpable anticipation, completely unaware of how uncomfortable I felt. She clasped her hands in her lap and raised her eyebrows as though begging me to begin. I inhaled deeply in an attempt to slow down my racing heart. *Relax and breathe*, I thought as I let my fingertips lightly brush the keys and then begin a song.

"No words, though," I quickly stopped myself and looked at Brooke. "I haven't done this in years. So, just the piano. No singing." My nerves couldn't handle both.

My hands felt slow at first, out of practice and almost waking from deep slumber. Then, it all began to flow from somewhere in my memory like a jolt of electricity running through my body to the tips of my fingers; I just played without thinking about playing.

A song just gets under your skin. I realize this as I play, examining the way my thoughts work their way into the act of playing. You use what you like, rewriting the notes as you wish to evoke the right emotion or memory. I begin to think back on the most important songs in my life; each is connected to an incident, a lover, a promise, a good time or a bad one, a kiss on the cheek or a stumble in the road. Music brings the most pivotal moments of our lives rushing back to us in a wave of nostalgia felt throughout every inch of our bodies. Before I realized it, the song bubbled up inside of me and its words spilled from my mouth. It felt like I played for hours. The final note drifted away, and then silence. As I drifted back down from wherever I'd floated off, I began to worry. It was *so* quiet. Maybe Brooke was trying to find something nice to say.

"That—is—so—*beat*!" she said, pronouncing each world overdramatically.

"Really? It is?" I asked, looking up at her skeptically.

"I love it!" she said, twisting a piece of blond hair around her index finger. "I want *that* on my next album."

Her reaction startled me. I enjoyed the piano, sitting at it and singing relaxed me and fueled my creativity. But I only thought of it as fun, never as something I worked at in hopes of recording and sharing.

"It would be so good for you!" Brooke urged, as though trying to convince me. "Do you know how much money you'd make?" Then she laughed, realizing even she didn't know. "Well, actually I don't even know the answer to that, probably a lot. A few hundred?"

It was cute, the way she encouraged me. She'd become a success, yet was so new to the business—and so completely unaware of how it all worked.

She looked at me with a gleam of excitement in her eye. "I'm ready for a smoke."

Brooke crossed the diagonal tile toward the French doors leading to the patio, pausing in front of the refrigerator to reach in and grab two ice-cold cans of beer. We sat on the deck inhaling our cigarettes and listening to the unfamiliar chirping of crickets in the backyard. Every time something creaked or cracked, Brooke's eyes darted nervously toward the window, hoping her mother wasn't watching. We cracked our beers and sat in silence, taking in the peace of the moment, until Brooke let out an enormous belch, which sent me into a fit of laughter.

"Brooke, why, of all people, did you bring me home with you?" I sighed, letting out a few trailing snickers.

"I just can be myself with you, I can be real." Brooke took another sip of beer. "Everyone else expects me to be something so important, but you don't care if I let loose or get goofy. I get to have my own 'calamity' moments when I'm around you, and I like that."

"Oh, well thank you. I enjoy your company, too. It must get difficult having so many people involved with who you are and what your image is."

"Yeah. It's all real cool and fun, but ya know, there are other things I want to do too," she said, taking a swig. "Like, I always wanted to open up a little bead store—right on the beach here— where people could come in and make all sorts of jewelry and key chains, and get their hair braided and stuff. I'd call it 'Just Bead It,' wouldn't that be cute?"

I laughed, wondering how she'd ever have a "normal" life after the events of the past few weeks. "What about you? You ever want to do anything more than makeup?" she asked. "You're real good on the piano! You could be a songwriter . . ."

"I don't know, I mean—I like playing, it comes kind of naturally to me. But I've never thought of really doing anything with it. I've never *tried* to create anything, I mean."

"Well you should. I love that song you played for me," Brooke said with a serious look spreading across her face. "I really am happy," Brooke sighed before perking up as if hit with a sudden idea. "You know something?" She turned to me, raising her beer as though to propose a toast. "I've got *thousands* of dollars in the bank!" The idea, which had obviously just dawned on her, caused her eyes to grow wide—she almost looked a little frightened by this revelation.

I smiled back, knowing it was probably much more than that now. When it came to the concept of numbers and the meaning of money, Brooke seemed clueless. Her success did something even more meaningful for her: it gave her a chance to give back to her family.

A smile resting on her face, she turned to look inside where her parents slept, the house appeared as a glowing fishbowl. "It just feels so good . . . there were times that my Mama had to work three jobs—my dad, overtime—just to help pay for all my dance lessons and gowns. Now I can help take care of them."

"That's really special." I smiled, realizing that beneath the newfound fame, Brooke was a girl who loved her family and wasn't embarrassed with anything about them. She loved what she loved without fear of judgment. She embraced tackiness and had no taste when it came to makeup, often shrieking things like, "Glitter! Oh, I love it! I want blue eye shadow and red lipstick," when I prepped her for a show. She'd get her nails done and would work on biting them off within an hour. I hoped to myself she'd hold on to that as long as possible.

The next evening, everyone was aflutter as we all prepared for the very last show on the tour. I watched the dancers practice in the hallway, showing off. They always tried to one-up each other, especially Jimmy, who practiced a dance style called "Krocha," which wasn't incorporated into their routine. Because it demanded a high level of fitness—one foot remained grounded while the other kicks about—it was perfect for Jimmy, who always seemed happy to do anything to show off his muscular prowess.

The Tweedles raced up and down the hallway, terrorizing the dancers and making fun of their profession. "Look, I'm a ballerina!" one of them would say in a high-pitched voice while twirling about, knowing full well that's not what the backup dancers were about. With the entire Parker family present, there were more characters than usual in the three-ring circus that was backstage.

"I wrestled that damn thing right into my trailer, I'll tell you what," I heard Willy say to an anxious Steve Green who simply answered with repetitive, "Mmm-hmmm's," to everything he said.

"Willy. Willy!" Mrs. Dianne unknowingly came to Steve's rescue. "I'm heading back to the bar. You want another drink?"

"Yes. Sorry Steve, we'll talk later," Willy said slamming the remainder of his bright red island drink before making his way to the bar for a refill. The Parkers swooned over the little oasis outside of section 116, and before the show even started, the bartenders knew Mrs. Dianne and Willy by name.

Such different worlds Brooke and I grew up in. For those of us who'd been around this lifestyle, whether we grew up in it or worked in it for any amount of time, it was easy to consider it "normal." Watching the Parkers experience everything as though they'd entered a mystical foreign land reminded me how far removed we actually were from the mainstream. My parents worked in Hollywood for as long as I could remember . . . my father, Alan O'Reilly, was a Harvard man who had studied linguistics in college and had become a highly sought-after voice coach in New York, where he met my mother. A young fashion designer, Alice O'Reilly was a woman with an impeccable pedigree whose pale skin was always perfectly powdered, her neck properly adorned, her chestnut hair flawlessly coiffed. Nearly a decade before I was born, she worked as the head designer for a popular juniors label in Manhattan, enjoying great success at a very young age. At her peak she received the prestigious Cody Award, putting her on the map, as the media called her, the "next big thing." Before long, more and more of my father's clients, many of whom happened to be the most famous celebrities of that time, requested his services in Los Angeles, my mother had to make a choice. In the end, she chose love, leaving her budding career and all of New York's opportunities behind to move to the West Coast, where work was sparse. Taking jobs to pass the time at department stores in Beverly Hills, my mother gradually let go of her own endeavors. Though she's never admitted that completely, I know it's something she still regrets. Today she works as a personal stylist, filling the closets of aging actresses with tweed suits, pastel pumps, and blouses from Saks. The more I thought about it I had to laugh. Maybe my parents' lives weren't so far removed from Willy and Mrs. Dianne's land of alligators and pageantry.

I shook my head and looked down at my laminated pass, newly anointed with a "special" sticker. This acquisition made me feel especially important because only one other person possessed the all-access pass to Brooke's room, Steve. Not even Jesse had one. The dancers and miscellaneous crew that flowed in and out while I tried to get Brooke ready made it increasingly more difficult to have her done by show time, so I had finally worked up the nerve to demand a "lockdown." It was a breath of fresh air to know I wouldn't have so many interruptions, which caused me to accidentally poke Brooke in the eye time after time and grab her chin towards me ten times a minute as she chatted with everyone. The dancers Brooke favored and hung out with in her spare time—her "besties"—were especially annoying and my biggest problem. They constantly wanted her attention. And, because they were responsible for their own makeup, they always bugged me to make them "look good, too" and to "please do my hair" or "please, just do my eyeliner!"

With the increased attention on Brooke for this show, there was no room for delays or mistakes. It all came down on me when Steve had an issue with Brooke's timeliness. When I approached him for help, he seemed almost happy to oblige in creating a situation that would alienate Brooke from her dancers.

"You little shit," a dancer screamed as one of the Parker twins flipped up her skirt.

"I saw your bu-ut," he taunted running away before she could grab him.

I wanted to get going, and Steve was getting antsy as well. "T-Roc, I need you to sit outside Brooke's room," he barked.

"Yeah, yeah—I'll be out here while you getch'er makeup done," T-Roc mumbled as he took his post in front of the dressing room door, sitting in silence except to tell a few big-name promoters that they weren't allowed to have glassware backstage.

"Thanks!" I called out after him, waving my own pass in the air. "And they have to have a sticker—one of the silver ones like this—to get in, remember!"

"Hey Jackie," T-Roc called out.

"Yeah?"

"Don't forget about Robert."

Dealing with so many distractions and frustrations, I was beginning to understand Sasha's edginess. I groaned. Unfortunately, we had to give one of the biggest distractions on our tour a sticker, too—Robert. He'd turned out to be one of the most difficult people to work with, and though I hated to admit it, there was something about him that also intimidated me. Perhaps it was the way he cocked his head, always appearing judgmental. No matter what came out of my mouth, whether it was a question as simple as, "Where's the bathroom?" to meaningless small talk like, "Wow, the sun is really shining today," he always looked at me as if I was a complete moron.

According to Sasha, he'd been a longtime friend of Steve's, having one thing in common with him: the desire to work with celebrities. This struck me as odd because he pretty much loathed all straight people. Robert had mastered the art of schmoozing in Hollywood by the time he was fifteen, and between his gift for gab and Steve's business savvy, their friendship proved to be a win-win situation.

He pranced past T-Roc while chatting manically on the phone, reveling in his fame association. The shrillness in his voice, combined with the metal hooks of the mess of wooden hangers screeching across his rolling rack, was worse than nails on a chalkboard.

"It was cuckoo crazy, there was all the autograph seekers, and when we were walking out of the side doors, we caught them all by surprise," Robert gaily recounted his very own Beatles moment the other night when we left the concert and were greeted by a mob. "No one actually expected her to just pop right out of the bus like that—and they start taking photos and videos. So, she signed a bunch of stuff, and I was like, 'We really have to go.'"

I had to admire the way Robert inserted this sense of fake annoyance into his story, because I had never seen him look happier than he did last night, being swarmed by noisy kids waving strips of paper and pens for signing in the air simultaneously.

Rifling through a mess of compacts, tweezers, and small spray cans of Evian mineral water that I had unloaded from my rolling duffel, I breathed a momentary sigh of relief. The only noise besides the two of us was the buzzing of the large vanity light bulbs ablaze at full power. Just as I began tracing her lash line in a cool mint-green color, a heavy knock came from the doorway, diverting her attention from the ceiling she'd been searching with her eyes.

The door opened, and there stood Jesse. T-Roc stood just behind him, shrugging his shoulders in mock surprise that someone had slipped past. The twinkle in his eye let on that he knew exactly what was up. Jesse poked his head back around the door frame, looking down the hallway in both directions to ensure the coast was clear. He whipped his right arm from behind his back to reveal a bright bouquet of long-stem red roses arranged with fresh green sprigs.

Greeting us both with his piercing hazel eyes, he sauntered into the dressing room. "I wanted to wish you luck."

"They're beautiful!" Brooke gushed, turning to me. "Jackie—we can break the rules just this once, right?"

"It's okay—rules are rules . . . I can bring these back by

later—" Jesse offered, beaming from Brooke's enthusiastic reception, which had also caused his cheeks to flush. He winked at Brooke and started toward the door.

"No, no, no—it's fine," I insisted, waving him inside. Jesse's stardom was clearly lost on his ego; respect and humility came naturally to him. "Just try not to let anyone see you or we'll have twenty people in here."

"Thanks," he laughed quickly closing the door behind him. Making his way over to her, Jesse wrapped his arms tight around Brooke, leaning in between me and my work. Burying his head in her neck, he became lost in the sea of hair extensions.

"Am I cramping your style yet?" Sitting up, he flashed me a megawatt and oh-so-innocent grin. Part of me wanted to throw him out immediately while the other half was so sincerely touched by the adorable display of young puppy love, you can guess which side of my thoughts I listened to. They were so cute the way they were always surprising each other on the road—and because their relationship was forbidden by management, it was like a secret agent operation in order for them to carry out each rendezvous. No matter how big or small the gesture, Brooke was always genuinely surprised and touched. She threw her arms around his neck and tousled his already-mussed, unstyled 'do.

After a few moments of hushed and giggle-filled conversation, Jesse kissed her on the cheek and stood to leave. "Well, I suppose." He turned to me before closing the door. "Thanks for letting me interrupt."

Brooke sighed a smitten sigh. "We met on tour. Our eyes locked, and it was love at first sight."

After finishing her off with a glowing pink lip, I looked up to examine her shadow-proof illumination in the mirror—bordered by light columns—in front of us. I stepped back to survey my work. Despite the disruption, I was pleased by the way I'd successfully transformed her into an ethereal beauty. She possessed a striking, delicate look, like a youthful warrior unafraid of her own power and magnificence. Until this very moment, I hadn't realized just how powerful her sexuality was, and she hadn't either. But it had always been there, in the way she walked down the hall—a pair of peach Juicy Couture sweats tightly hugging her curves, making her behind appear as two round globes—and in the way the old white cotton tank thrown on last-minute happened to fall perfectly short against her tanned, tight stomach. She seemed unaware that her outfit caused men of all ages to stop dead in their tracks to stare. And in just a few short minutes she would be on stage, sweat dripping down her bosom, moaning to the lyrics as if in ecstasy, much to the delight of the lust-craved boys in the audience. I scanned her reflection in the mirror and noticed the frown on her face. I looked at the roses sitting on top of the vanity.

"That was really nice." I smiled.

"Yeah. He tells me he loves me before every show. I can't get over how sweet he is." She swooned and then got quiet all of a sudden.

"What's wrong?"

She shook her head slowly and muffled a crooked smile before leaning closer to me. "You know," she said in a hushed voice, "it's supposed to be really bad luck to bring somebody flowers before they go out on stage."

"Really? Is that like . . . a thing . . . a saying or something?"

She nodded her head firmly before furrowing her brow. "There was this girl I knew a few years ago—we competed in this junior pageant together—and she had been 'favorite,' you know? She blew everybody away," Brooke said wide-eyed. "And then . . . right before the pageant—her papa brought her some carnations and a box of candies—and you'll never believe what happened next."

"What?" I immediately pictured the worst of the worst—becoming violently ill on stage in the middle of a tap dance routine, or a stage light suddenly dropping from the rafters, maiming the young beauty queen.

"She," Brooke began slowly, "only made it to first runner-up."

As I was trying to digest her rationale behind this she sighed, "I mean . . . Jesse didn't know. They are really pretty."

"I believe in that shit . . ." Listening from the doorway, T-Roc perked up, pulling a tacky yet expensive-looking long gold chain from his beefy neck. He thrust it over to Brooke. "Here, you better take this."

"What is it?" Brooke asked reaching for it.

"It's my good luck dragon." He put a thumb over the black jade pendant adorning the center that was decorated with diamonds.

As she reached out for it, he pulled his hand back—looking at her seriously. "But I better get it back from y'all . . . got it from a client out of China two years ago. The dragon is supposed to bring good luck and prosperity, and the jade, she told me, will bless the one who touches it." He immediately started laughing at himself, though I could see from his tight grip around his coveted lucky charm he believed every bit of it. "I been wearing it just 'cause it looks cool—but I'm telling you man, there is something freaky deaky about that thing because I've been havin' crazy luck!"

Just before show time the dancers stood by in their costumes, except for Jimmy, who was "half ready" and standing there conveniently shirtless as though he hadn't had time to put one on. Amongst the performers there was one person not in costume—Willy. All night he'd been haranguing people backstage, handing out business cards and telling them, "You ever get in a pinch with a gator, you give me a call."

By the time I had finished Brooke's makeup, I was pleased to find that Willy had successfully cornered his next victim out in the hallway.

"An eleven-footer, I tell you what . . ." Willy growled to a very constipated-looking Robert. "I caught that sucker on a metal hook—taped his damn mouth right shut too."

It brightened my mood to see how absolutely pissy and annoyed Robert looked as Willy shared his most thrilling and heroic gator tales.

"Oh she shot the darn thing too! But by the time we got there—oh man, you wouldn't believe it—sucker barely bled at all. Had to put the thing right back into the lake."

Willy roamed around backstage, excitedly sharing with everyone in earshot his penchant for working on automobiles and his dream of getting the "boys" back together (the "boys" being his high school pals who made up the short-lived rock band Screeeech!) to open for Brooke when she got a tour of her own. When someone would gaze over at his arms, which he flailed wildly when he told stories, he'd awkwardly ask them if they were looking at his hand—or absence thereof—and then explain, again, how he lost it during Vietnam. Without fail, Mrs. Dianne stood right behind him, stressing the word *during*.

As show time neared, the entire crew was abuzz about the size of the audience. For the first time, Brooke had become an attraction in and of herself, rather than simply the opening act. She'd always performed for a decent-sized crowd thanks to the overzealous Emerson Brothers' fans who always arrived early to stake their claim on the floor as close to stage as possible. Most of the time they chatted or mindlessly text-messaged on their cell phones as they waited. But tonight, for the first time, all of the seats were full and floor room was sparse. The 870,000 square-foot facility seated 20,000 for concerts, and she'd attracted a full house with all eyes on her. Clearly, the recent press only made her more of a spectacle.

She didn't disappoint—legs anchored to the stage, her curved arms stretched out tracing the air with elaborate circles—she lost herself in the performance. Each time I surveyed the crowd in amazement I took note of the increasing number of older men that seemed to appear out of nowhere. I had to admit, it was kind of strange considering that our fan base by far had capped at sixteen—and even the sixteen-year-olds looked slightly embarrassed at times for being there. Running into classmates from school, they'd exchange glances as if to say, "I won't tell if you don't." The young girls were the most fanatical of all. At one point I observed a pretty blond in her late teens strain to lean over the barricade—while perched upon a friend's shoulders. She begged Brooke to touch her hand and exploded into hysterical tears when she complied.

As the Emersons took the stage, I headed towards Brooke's dressing room to congratulate her on a job well done. Meeting the hand of a pimple-faced, venue-provided rent-a-cop who was motioning towards my badge, I rolled my eyes and flashed my laminated pass so he could see the sticker.

As I breezed in with my sense of entitlement, I saw that Brooke was not alone. With her stood a guy in red Nike Dunk hightops and a backwards baseball cap, which allowed his spiky gelled hair to poke out the front. It was Jimmy. He had his stage gear on, but had conveniently lost the puffy vest, revealing his much-too-muscular physique through a tight, cotton jersey beater tank. Then I caught a glance of Jimmy's hand—and the way he kept placing it over Brooke's as she gently glided across the washboard abs apparent through his tight shirt. I wasn't quite sure how he'd made it past the venue security genius, but

I figured Brooke's blithe approach to rules had something to do with it. She didn't seem to understand that making exceptions completely diminished the point of the special sticker and its exclusivity.

Neither of them so much as flinched as I approached, and if it weren't for the way Brooke compulsively twirled her hair, I never would have thought anything out of the ordinary was going on. Her schoolgirl giggles suggested she may be taking a little *too* much pleasure in his company.

"Hey," she said excitedly. "Jimmy was tellin' me how I could lose five pounds in two days if I just drink water with some kind of syrup?" She paused for a moment, looking back at him to make sure she had gotten it right. "And lemon and canyon peppers."

"Cayenne pepper," Jimmy corrected her, cocking his head flirtatiously.

"Ahhh . . . the Master Cleanse, huh?" I mused—though I'd never tried the famous Hollywood diet myself, I knew all about it thanks to Lauren, who always knew exactly which stars were doing it (all the time, according to her) and when (before any red carpet event). She'd even attempted the Master Cleanse herself a couple times, always facing defeat nearly six hours in when her blood-sugar would bottom out and send her into a Coffee Bean and Tea Leaf for some sweets.

"It's pretty beat," Jimmy piped up again before turning his attention to Brooke. "Gotta jam girl—I'll hit you up later . . ."

As he left, I was certain I'd detected a hint of a blush wash over her face. Catching my stare, she quickly wiped away the goofy, dreamy-eyed gaze she was shooting in his direction. Falling silent for a moment, I waited to see if she was going to confess something to me, if she'd gush on like a starry-eyed little girl in the same fashion she had hours earlier about Jesse . . .

but nothing. It was strange, but then again maybe I was making too much of it.

"So," I said, raising my eyebrows in disbelief. "Why would you want to lose five pounds in two days anyway? You have a rocking body."

"Well, I didn't think I looked bad but you know, Steve was talking about the stuff I'm going to be doing in L.A. and since the camera adds *twice* that . . ."

"So he wants you to lose weight?"

"Well, he didn't exactly say that—but you know, he kinda mentioned it, so I just figured maybe I should." She frowned for a moment before gazing up at me—her eyes suddenly like those of a sad puppy dog. "Do you think I'm *fat*?" she asked in a worried, hushed tone.

"You have got to be kidding me . . ." But I could tell from the look on her face that she wasn't. "I'm not even going to dignify that with a response."

I dismissed her irrational weight concerns. How could she constantly question her body that way? She was gorgeous. Surely she wasn't that naive; then again, maybe she was. She and Jimmy had been standing *really* close to one another. Replaying the scene in my head, I was a little surprised at the way she unveiled her indiscretion in a place where virtually anyone could walk in on them at any moment. But that was Brooke. She had this sweet, childlike innocence about her. You wondered if she ever considered others' misperceptions and ill intentions. Earlier when the reporters and protesters had cornered her, angry with their nasty signs, I instinctually wanted to put myself in between them to shield her from their ugliness. She was the one in need of protection.

Chapter 7

I love Los Angeles.
I love Hollywood. They're beautiful.
Everybody's plastic, but I love plastic.
I want to be plastic.
–Andy Warhol

Los Angeles is a city of salesmen, a place of relentless schmoozing and professional networking that are not only considered beneficial, but, in fact, vital for survival. In a town where every conversation starts out the same—"What do *you* do?"—standard etiquette need not apply. No place is sacred—the locker room at your gym, the checkout counter at the drug store, and even the playground where you brought your children to be kids—because any of these places could provide an opportunity to pitch ideas or sell screenplays. It doesn't matter where you're from—Paris, Ohio, even right there in Beverly Hills—if you're not a player in this industry of cool, you don't really matter. For those of us who operate below the town's radar, this was the ultimate shadow land—a region of unreality, a place where phantoms reside and we live in our own dreams unseen. And although, growing up, I wasn't fully conscious of it, I was nonetheless affected by it.

In the eye of a beholder, that is, in one's own mirror, everyone here is fabulous. Men with aviators and perfectly groomed hairdos stroll about atop the air of their own conceit; women in fabulous frocks air kiss on the streets. It's rarely a smooth landing for a person who arrives with dreams of "making it." And though she may have been a fresh face, Brooke wasn't trying to make it out here: she was already *it*.

When you're someone out here, life treats you a little bit kindly. And as I found myself hand-in-hand with one of the most famous women on the planet, I had become, in my own right, someone. Someone worth knowing in this land of lost souls, the ravaged dreams of good people who had fled their homes to express themselves. Suddenly, there were invitations to all of tomorrow's parties, freebies, and endless gifts. Brooke epitomized the rise from artist to superstar, all spun with the craft and foresight of managers and record executives. This was just the beginning of Brooke's career, which also meant the beginning of ours: for those of us around her, we weren't given a choice. But hey, if it were you, would you complain?

Everyone wanted to be in our circle because, to the outside world, *we* were the quintessential cool crowd. Think high school clique; now imagine your high school is the world. It turned out that even my parents thought I was "happening." This was particularly puzzling. It felt like they'd been discouraged with me for so long, I'd actually started to think I couldn't do anything right. Now just a month after they had basically kicked me out of the house and banished me to the garage, they stood in the kitchen, staring at me with large smiles on their faces, and patting me on the back.

"We saw that music video; what's it called again, honey?" my mother asked craning her neck back at my father.

"Oh yeah—that uh . . . 'The Pillow Fight,' I think it's called," he chirped in.

"'Pillow Talk,'" I corrected him.

Not even stopping to listen or let us finish a full thought, my mother buzzed on. "It came on at the department store the other day—you know, when you first told us about this Brooke Parker I had no idea who that was, did you honey?" My father was barely able to get in a "nope" as she continued to talk over him excitedly.

"And I just said, 'Oh my word, that's my daughter's handiwork!'"

"Practically everyone within earshot heard," my father laughed as he unfolded his newspaper. "She started telling all the other shoppers . . ."

"Well, I just couldn't help myself. It was so incredible!"

"Because she takes after her old man, working with musicians, that's why," my father said dryly, before abruptly laughing at his own cleverness.

This was the twilight zone. Not knowing how to react to their chipper moods or words of praise, I did the only thing I knew how to do with my parents, question them. Then, ultimately, find a way to disagree with whatever it was that they were talking about.

"Wait a minute," I said looking at both of them as I leaned against the stovetop island with my arms crossed. "I thought you both disapproved of me doing this, going into makeup. Working in the *industry*." I paused to unfold my arms, air-quoting the word "industry."

"Well, I was concerned, of course, at first . . ." my mother said, sounding flustered again. "There's just so many people who try to *make* it out here. Desperate people—*dirty people*," she said this almost whispering, and I knew she was referring to the people churning out pornos in the Valley. "They are *all* looking for the ultimate dream, I guess—searching for all the glitter and glitz of Hollywood. But you got lucky my dear."

Lucky? Why did I have to be lucky? Couldn't I have just been naturally *good* at something for once? I frowned. And yet, a little voice inside my head kept piping up: *You've made it; you're a tastemaker to the most rapidly rising young star on the planet right now.*

". . . And besides, I was just reading about that Kevyn Aucoin," my mother continued tirelessly, butchering the late makeup artist's last name. He was much too hip for his clientele. And, to this day, my mother still wouldn't have a clue who he was, except she'd recently mentioned my profession to a client, who then told her about Aucoin. "And that guy . . . what a mover and a shaker he was. He wrote all these books and even was on an episode of that *Sex and the City* show." Taking a sip of her tea, she furrowed her brow, turning on her serious face. "And he had to *really* struggle too."

Unbelievable, I thought to myself. There was no disputing that Mr. Aucoin's story was an amazing one. I read his biography, *A Beautiful Life*, more than once the autumn it came out. He'd been an accomplished saxophonist with the school band as a kid and I couldn't help but get teary-eyed reading about how his instrument was stolen and his family being unable to afford another one. It ended his music career for good. Because I, too, loved music so much, I could relate.

I couldn't pretend that I ever had to go through a fourth of what he did in his life; in that respect, my mother was right. I was *lucky*. But just when I thought it was my turn, now that I'd *made* it, she'd finally get to sing my praises. Every year when the Emmys rolled around she raved on endlessly about the awards her clients won, and she constantly boasted about my father's fancy business associates, who were all "names" in their own right. And once again, here we were talking about someone else's career—someone whose life interested her so much that she'd devoured 176 pages all about him. During our countless discussions about me returning to school, she never once listened or asked me about my profession. She only told me why it wouldn't work for me. I simply bit my lip because making a big fuss now wouldn't do any good. It's a funny thing—getting what you ask for—because you feel guilty if you dare to complain.

"It's so annoying," I screamed into my cell phone speaker as I zipped through a winding, terraced hillside. "She knows nothing about me—what I *really* do, or what I want to do. I don't think she is even *listening* seventy-five percent of the time I'm talking to her."

"Yeah, but she's always been like that . . . remember our final basketball game junior year? When she asked if you scored any home runs?" Lauren's laugh crackled from the speakerphone as I came to the end of my call sheet directions, arriving at a private, gate-guarded neighborhood that seemed to be completely canopied with lush trees and carpeted with flowering shrubs.

"Hold on one sec," I told her as I rolled down my window. "Hello," I smiled at the elderly guard outside my window, "I'm going to the Foxworth Estate—Jackie O'Reilly." Scanning the clipboard he held gingerly in his fingertips, he nodded when he located my name and stepped back inside the guardhouse. The chain of the freshly painted white iron gates ahead rattled ever so slightly as they opened inward, allowing me to pass.

"Where are you?" Lauren asked confused.

"Malibu. *Femme* is doing a piece on Brooke."

Every outlet was clamoring for Brooke, willing to bump covers they had shot *months* in advance in order to rush one with her to print. After much consideration, Sasha decided to do the story with *Femme*—a popular women's publication with a wide readership, covering everything from beauty and style to relationships and nutrition. Unlike its competitors, *Femme* maintained a perfect balance. Most magazines tried to differentiate themselves by honing in on certain areas of expertise, filling their pages with more fitness tips than necessary, or shamelessly continuing to push the envelope in order to upkeep a racy image.

"They've been working you like crazy, huh?"

"Day and night . . . and I don't see it letting up anytime soon."

"That's why you get the fancy car," she teased, referring to my first big splurge, the Porsche Cayenne GTS I had just leased. Sure, I could have moved out of my parents' garage apartment instead, but what would be the point? I barely had time to take advantage of a nicer place, or move into one for that matter. But at least I could enjoy my dream car.

"Well, I think that was her first clue I'd become a success," I complained, looping back to my mother. "Believe me, I'm not complaining. I can't believe this is all happening."

Brooke's intensifying recognition meant big money for those around her. Everyone—Steve, the record label, even Brooke's own mother—was tempted and started buying without stopping to ponder the implications. They just raced to her with open hands, all demanding more pay. I wasn't among them; even at my regular rate I was making a good income. For me, her success meant a lot more work and earned respect in the makeup industry. The look I'd developed for Brooke had helped "brand" her. Happily, I recreated it over, and over, and over again—tweaking it a little each time to suit the situation, such as when she needed a more durable look in order to withstand certain pitfalls of a particular shoot or performance. Like rain, wind, or the flashing cameras of red carpet events. Even a highly creative touch or two, such as exotic gold-highlighted eyes for a really *special* occasion, I was at her beck and call.

"I'm here, gotta go—I'll call you later tonight," I said, spying the address to my left, which belonged to a colossal, sun-drenched Mediterranean-style mansion spanning two lots with a commanding clifftop view of the Pacific. A collection of cars belonging to crew, assistants, and caterers lined the driveway, looking out of place in contrast to the regal dwelling. Two photographer's assistants in tattered blue jeans were unpacking equipment near the front door. As I approached, one of the young men abandoned the tripod and large reflector he was wrestling with and pointed me to the rear of the estate. The grounds dripped with opulence: an orchard of lush, mature fruit trees, a terraced walking trail, an English rose garden, a pool overlooking the ocean and a central courtyard into which many of the main rooms opened.

Making my way through the grandeur, inhaling the salty smell of sea air, I drifted back to my first tastes of freedom, beauty, and art. The one place I ever felt was truly *impressive* was my grandmother's home in the Hamptons. Although Dodo was somewhat of a society matron from Manhattan, she was quite unlike anyone that I'd ever met. Her eyelashes were heavily painted with mascara and resembled bat wings. Her hands were crowded with heavy cocktail rings on almost every finger, and she chain-smoked, sashaying around the house with one of those Cruella De Vil cigarette holders in her left hand. Once upon a time, she had been a relatively well-known fashion model and I was almost certain I had inherited my love of color and style and flair from her. At seventy she still took voice lessons and watercolor painting classes. Sometimes on Sunday afternoons she'd play the piano for hours on end and prompt me to ad-lib lyrics to songs that didn't have any. Thus, songwriting became another one of my favorite "trades," as my father typically called my talents.

Dodo, in spite of her Victorian elegance, was never hesitant to speak her mind, whether in contempt of all "the stuffy East Coast families," or simply as my grandmother whose compliments felt, to me, pithy and ageless: "My dear Jacqueline, with that effervescent light, you can be anything you want to be. Don't let anyone tell you otherwise." She was Miss Havisham without the crazy; Norma Desmond with her closeup.

My grandfather passed away when I was in grade school and my father, fearing that Dodo would grow lonely, arranged for me to stay at her rambling, festooned mansion nestled safely from the Atlantic amidst the sand dunes as often as I could, much to my delight. Dodo had left the home virtually unchanged since the passing of my grandfather. The old, yellowing newspapers that he last read were still scattered near an overstuffed leather chair in the Georgian paneled library. Mallard decoys, relics of his old days spent hunting in Maine, were draped thickly with dust, as was the half-empty matchbook he used to light his pipe. Dodo only entered this room to mix herself a drink in one of her highball glasses at the red leather bar stand. Because this was a special room—one seemingly unscathed by the hands of time—it was my favorite place in the house.

"Do what you like in there," Dodo would say sauntering in and out, stopping in occasionally to bring me cucumber sandwiches and Pepperidge Farm Chessman Cookies, or for a plastic swizzle stick from the bar to stir her Bloody Bull.

They sat in a stack, piled next to the chintz slip-covered sofa where I'd lounged many a warm summer's day, but for some reason had always overlooked. There had to be about a dozen. Leather-bound scrapbooks, covers engraved with my grandfather's initials, served as my passport to the glittering, grand old days once lived, but now gone, grayed as the pages they clung to. Christmases and graduations, society weddings and days spent lounging poolside with tastemakers and prominent social figures—all fully preserved through invitations and newspaper clippings, telegrams and shiny black-and-white photographs. There were pictures of my grandmother celebrating her birthday with girlfriends at El Morocco. Another photo—which later appeared in the New York *Times*— showed Dodo being dipped on the dance floor of some party by Truman Capote as my grandfather looked on laughing. There was even a telegram that read:

> *Mr. and Mrs. James O'Reilly, Will you join me for the gala reopening of the Chicago Theatre on September 10, at 8:00 PM. Black Tie.*
> *Looking forward to seeing you.*
>
>   *Frank Sinatra*

"You lived a very glamorous life," I told Dodo one day, living through the scrapbooks for the hundredth time.

"Yes, I did," she sighed, taking a moment between bites of her tapioca pudding.

"I want to have a life like that," I prayed.

"Oh, my dear." She smiled, getting up from the window where she was perched. She grabbed my chin, an armful of gaudy bangle bracelets clanging: "You will."

When I entered the detached guest suite where we'd be setting up, Robert and Sasha were already there and in true form. Checking the call sheet, I noticed that an A-list professional hairdresser had been hired for the shoot. This, I'd been told, was commonplace—I'd just never been on a shoot big enough to hire one. Over the weeks I had improved considerably on Brooke's hair, but it never really felt like my strong suit, so it was just as well. If I didn't already know, this kind of detail was indicative of just how important this shoot was.

I found that Robert's energy soared when he was on his own territory, and today was no exception. With an armful of vibrantly colored gowns in silk charmeuse and organza, he pranced about, tossing out sassy "heys" and giving everyone friendly air kisses. Everyone, of course, but me. Overemphasizing his every action, he busied himself getting everything just so for when Brooke arrived. I took it personally, the way he oozed charm in front of me at times, like he was doing it for my benefit to show how dialed into the scene he was and to establish that I, the outsider, was on his precious turf.

Shoving the rest of a poppy-seed bagel in her mouth before brushing the crumbs from her blouse to the floor, Sasha waved me over and stressed to me, for what must have been the tenth time, "Remember, we're going for a softer look here."

"So, very immaculate," Robert, buried behind a growing pile of colorful fluttery silks, chimed in from across the room. He couldn't dare let the newbie show him up. "*Angelic* even."

"I think I've got it under control," I said cheerfully. I had read enough copies of *Femme* in my life to know exactly what they wanted. Aside from the changing content within the magazine, the art directors at *Femme* had their covers down to a science. Featured beneath the magazine's iconic masthead—bright white against a rotating array of bright feminine colors—a different fresh-faced celebrity graced its cover each month. In real life, they were all women of varying ages, races, and talents—unique in their own right. But on the cover of *Femme*—these airbrushed beauties with their poreless skin and vivacious expressions somehow exemplified the same picture of healthy living, becoming the authorities on beauty, style, and fitness.

As I began to organize my station, Brooke arrived on set with Steve in tow. In a messy blond ponytail, unzipped hoodie, and a navy blue T-shirt that made the most of her midriff, she pranced into the guest suite and immediately kicked off her sandals, replacing them with a pair of furry pink slippers. The photographer and art director at *Femme* followed quickly behind her, anxious to greet her. It was entertaining to watch them in such awe of the little girl sitting cross-legged on the floor chewing on her fingernails.

Once everyone finished their adoring welcomes, I got her into the makeup chair. Stripped of the bronzing powder responsible for her famous faux glow, her young skin shone beneath a light base. "I feel, like . . . *really, really* pale," Brooke, unused to such a gentle look, pouted.

"Angelic, remember? And I don't think heaven has a tanning salon," I mumbled as I grabbed her chin to reposition her face toward me. Having my creamy white complexion would have been a real nightmare for Brooke, with her quest to look constantly sun-kissed. "Quit fidgeting! You're a moving target again today!" I said, exasperated.

"Oh! Sorry!" she gushed. Forcing herself to remain still, she appeared visibly uncomfortable, as if she were about to burst any moment. Blending an airy peach tone from her cheek to her temple, I took advantage of her brief immobility.

"So, I got invited to a party this weekend—Jesse and me were supposed to go together, but he's got a shoot early the next day so he can't go. You wanna come?" she asked, trying not to move her mouth, which caused her words to come out muffled.

"Really? Cool . . . yeah. Whose is it?"

"Alexis Young invited me . . ."

"How do you know Alexis?" I asked Brooke, slightly shocked and just a little annoyed.

"You know her?" Brooke perked up, failing to detect my blatantly unenthusiastic response to the mention of the starlet's name.

I nodded somberly. Know her, I did. *Everyone* knew her. Alexis, commonly referred to as "Rexy Lexy" in the tabloids due to her frequent bouts of anorexia, was the quintessential Hollywood "it girl." She'd also been the queen bee of my high school class, though I was certain she had no clue who I was. Lexy had always been so fully consumed with things like nail polish, her college boyfriend, and her childhood fame to ever venture outside of her social bubble. She came onto the scene in the early nineties as a child actress known for her role on the sitcom *Back to Boca*, in which she played a dimple-faced, bright-eyed child sent to live at her grandmother's retirement community when she lost her parents in a car accident. The show had made her something of a modern-day Shirley Temple, and she quickly became America's sweetheart, winning over audiences by delivering her signature line, "Cheese and rice!" in lieu of taking the Lord's name in vain. Her real notoriety, however, stemmed from her fabulously wealthy parents and her hard-partying ways. Though girls like that were a dime a dozen in Los Angeles, it was Lexy's certain kind of pizzazz—the kind that seems to focus a spotlight in almost any room—that set her apart from the other oh-so-trendy trust-fund babies. Hers was a mesmerizing tonic air of money and sexuality—but the effects were often times disastrous. Rehab, sex scandals, feuds with other starlets, you name it, Lexy had been there, done that. The last time I saw her was at high school graduation, though it had been pretty easy to keep track of her since. I couldn't escape images of her consistently sun-kissed face—accented by blue doe-eyes, perfectly groomed eyebrows, and overly injected pout—on the covers of countless tabloids lining the supermarket shelves.

"She's real good friends with Jesse," Brooke said. *How in the world was she friends with Jesse?* I wondered as Brooke went on. "I met her when I was in town doing that music video; right around the time I met you. She told me she was a huge fan of mine. Can you believe *that*?" she asked. I groaned inside. I could only imagine Lexy shamelessly hitting on Jesse in front of Brooke, trying to steal her boyfriend right in front of her face, and Brooke interpreting her fake "niceness" as genuine. "Anyway," she sighed, "Lexy's throwing it for Jessica Rader. It's her birthday."

"Jessica? Rader?" I asked. Now I was really confused. A pop sensation on the rise, Jessica had recently emerged after being discovered by an executive at Brooke's rival record label, Midnight Music. With long blond curls, curve-hugging attire, and a taut midriff that was rarely covered, Jessica was Midnight Music's answer to the Brooke Parker craze. A fellow Southern belle from Little Rock, her debut album with its Jamaican and West Indies influences, along with light splashes of punk and hip-hop thrown in, was designed to outshine Brooke's bubbly pop, and though it was released to rave reviews, Brooke continued to top the charts. In response, Jessica quickly began to shed her cutesy persona in an attempt to claw her way out of the shadow of Brooke's success. This, of course, sparked an imaginary war between the two singers in the press, though at the time the rumors began they'd never even met.

"Well, yeah—I think it would be nice—she's such a nice singer and I don't even understand why people make up all that crap anyway," Brooke complained, suddenly defensive.

"You're the boss." I smiled. *This was going to be interesting— and if Brooke didn't care, why should I?*

"I'll invite my friend Lauren, too; if that's okay. She knows Lexy." I smiled. There was no way I could go without her.

"Yea! I'm so excited!" Brooke gushed drumming her legs. "Now I just *need* to find something cute to wear . . ."

"Done. I've got just the place—I'll bring you."

"Jackie."

"Hmm?"

"You're so pretty. Why don't you have a boyfriend?"

"Well." Her question caught me completely off guard. "I did have a boyfriend back East."

"And . . . what happened?"

"It was complicated—or maybe it really wasn't. He just didn't 'get' me, I guess."

I hadn't though about "Trip" in so long. Randolph M. Puce, III, inherited the nickname as those with third-generation names often do in the blue-blood crowds. He was the son of old family friends; our grandfathers met in boarding school. And since the day I began wearing a training bra, our mothers plotted not-so-secretly that we'd fall in love and get married. Shortly after I'd been accepted at Boston University, his mother bombarded me with phone calls from the family's Connecticut estate.

"Well, darling, as your grandmother may have told you, Trip is in the School of Management undergraduate program," she hummed, pronouncing "program" icily as "pro-grum." "He's been interviewing for a position at Wendell Partners. They've got offices just off of Newbury, so fingers crossed, he'll be staying put in Boston for a while. Isn't that marvelous?" she said, not really waiting for a response. "Anyway, I've made dinner reservations at the Club for Thursday at six—I do hope you can make it," she said. And referring to the ultra-conservative staff at the exclusive Somerset Club, "They don't like it when we cancel reservations. Oh, it will be so nice for you two to catch up!"

That Thursday I prepared reluctantly for my dinner with Trip by running a lint roller over my black pencil skirt—well, the skirt I'd borrowed from another girl in my dorm to meet the club's business-casual dress-code requirements. I trotted over to Beacon Hill, and no sooner had I entered the white granite walls of the Somerset Club, than I felt the eyes of the hostess running me up and down, already judging me. Apparently "ladies that lunch," ones that leave big tips on tabs picked up by their husband's accounts, didn't dress in this kind of business attire. My Ann Taylor skirt told her loud and clear that I wasn't up to par with the desired clientele; the way her icy eyes scanned me made that perfectly clear.

"You can't dine here unless you are a member," the woman said haughtily.

"Right, I'm the guest of a member. Was I put on a list or something?"

"You cannot dine here if the member is not here," she said not bothering to look at the reservation log.

"Well, he is here, see . . ." I said, feeling inappropriately embarrassed.

"Jackie?" a male voice called out. Sauntering up from the bar was Trip, coming to my rescue. He tightened the grosgrain belt holding up his linen pants and set his empty rocks glass down on the hostess stand. "We have a reservation. Puce."

I'm not sure if it was Trip's odd resemblance to JFK Jr. or the three vodka martinis that got me into the mess, but that night, as we sat on the edge of Beacon Hill pretending to understand each other's careers, interests, and goals, I fell head over heels in what I thought was love. Never mind that he tried to explain his aspirations for a career as an investment banker to me as, "Remember Richard Gere's job in *Pretty Woman*? That's what I do." Or that he interjected with statements like, "You really ought to consider a managed market fund," when I expressed the excitement of someday having a salary. That night, as I looked into his blue eyes, framed by dark brown hair that was cut in a style more suitable for a sixty-year-old politician, was the beginning of a relationship that would continue on well past its expiration date. You see, Trip—being older than I and close to graduating—woke up one day and realized that his friends were all engaged or settling into serious relationships. Suddenly things like getting hammered before the Head of the Charles Regatta and getting arrested in Bermuda on spring break for streaking weren't so cool anymore. Both of which he often boasted he had done. I liked that he was smarter than me with things like finance and politics, and I liked the worn-out suede loafers that he wore—but good relationships take a little more than that. Trip was the kind of guy whose WASPY snobbery was somehow embedded in his genes. Yes, the Puces were that kind of family, but none of the other family members (even his mother with her brashness) seemed the type that would stick their noses up at you for pronouncing "aunt" as "ant," or requesting a doggie bag for leftovers. Trip, however, was another story—he was the type of guy who knew what thread count was acceptable (acceptable in his world of grandeur, of course) without ever being told. And because of his tremendous ego, he often became enraged when things didn't go his way—a waiter forgetting a side dish, a dry cleaner unable to remove a stain from his oxford dress shirt, me suggesting that we stop into Urban Outfitters (which, according to Trip was very "white trash" of me to even suggest). I just never knew what would upset Time-Bomb Trip and the relationship turned ugly, very fast.

I shared the sordid tale with Brooke, whose own world seemed a distant planet.

"That's too bad. You deserve someone nice." She looked heartbroken.

Suddenly I could hear Steve's voice. He was on the porch just outside talking loudly on the phone.

"Listen, Rain Shine has the option to pick up her second record without obligation to increase pay. It's in her contract, yes," he said coolly, pacing the length of the long wooden deck. "However, her price has gone up—she's worth a lot more now, which changes the game for us." Hearing his voice, Brooke—conscious not to move her head again—darted her eyes upward at me.

"So, I've been working on your song—the one you taught me . . ."

"Really?" I asked, suddenly flattered. "I'm glad you like it."

"I don't just like it, I *love* it," she signed breathlessly, "and you'll never guess what I did . . . I played it for Steve." Her face lit up so dramatically it forced me to grab at her chin again. Before I could react, Steve waltzed in with a handful of papers and set them down in front of Brooke. He pulled up a stool next to hers, ready to discuss business.

"Your star power is rising. We've got to renegotiate your contract with the label before moving onto the next album because you're worth a lot more money now, baby—and let me tell you, when you start getting big, *everyone* wants a piece of the pie."

I glanced up in time to catch a glimpse of something startling in his mouth. Revealed by a feigned smile were what looked like stark, white Chiclets, causing me to do a double take. He'd already taken a piece of that pie, it seemed, eaten it, then polished away the evidence. Her rising star power was clearly evident in the custom-made porcelain shells bonded to the front of his teeth.

"I told you how this happens—how everything can change pretty quickly, right?"

"You can say that again." I smiled, motioning to his mug with the end of the brush I was using to groom Brooke's eyebrows. The second it came out of my mouth, I wanted to take it back. It was a classic "calamity moment"—one that surely lowered his opinion of me. *What was I thinking? That we would all toss our heads back and laugh at my funny joke? Or, even better, that Steve would turn and thank me for the compliment—as if he'd been waiting all day for someone to notice his brand-new veneers?*

Breaking the uncomfortable silence, Brooke said, "Yeah, I guess. But what does that mean exactly?"

Peering at her through the mirror, he began rattling off a list a mile long. The contrast of their images in the mirror as he spoke, I had to admit, was pretty entertaining. Steve sat there very calmly, though the worry lines across his head were becoming more defined with each passing day. And then there was Brooke, who couldn't be any less serious, and who sat making faces at herself in the mirror by puffing out her cheeks or pushing up her nose to resemble a pig's snout.

"Well, it's time to pay attention because you're going to have to make some decisions here shortly," Steve said as if he were talking to a four-year-old child. He pointed to the stack of papers that were lying on the vanity. "The first of which are these babies right here."

Flipping through a small stack, Brooke looked at each piece of paper with sheer confusion. "What are these?"

"They are the contracts we put together for the dancers—and all the handlers, like Jackie right here, that you've been dealing with." The way he brought up my name, as if I were a fly on the wall mechanically applying lipstick and eyeliner, felt like a jab. My decision not to ask for a raise like the others had seemed even wiser now. "We need to take a close look at those you're willing to part with, and those who are indispensable."

A worrisome look registered on Brooke's face. Because she was so sweet, and equally naive, it troubled her to make such decisions, ones she called "being mean."

"Well, I like everybody."

"But you can't like everybody honey, that's what I'm trying to tell you. The dancers, for example, they *all* want more money. They've all got agents, and no one is willing to budge. For the amount of money that they're asking for we can get you the best of the best . . . think about it. Don't you want the most professional dancers out there?"

"But they're my best friends!" Brooke looked devastated at the thought of losing her counterparts.

"I know they're your friends, love, but that's not necessarily the point. We don't make smart business decisions based on friendships. The record label is going to be offering you more money, which means that you'll be able to afford the most incredible dancers the world has to offer! And if you're going to be as big of a star as I think you are, only the best will do." Seeing that Brooke wasn't yet totally convinced, Steve changed gears, playing up to her self-interest. Like he was making a sympathetic gesture, he lowered his voice and cocked his head as if to say "I understand you."

"Listen, I know you've been a little concerned about your weight—and hey, it's understandable—you're out there every night in these uncomfortable costumes. Look, I get it." I couldn't believe it. Just when I thought he was acting semi-decent, showing her some compassion, it occurred to me that he was actually the one feeding the flames of her weight issues. "But I think there's a simple solution for this . . . a quick fix . . . no tummy crunches or week training involved."

Brooke's eyes widened in excitement. "Really? What is it?"

Standing up, Steve stopped to rest his chin on his fist for a quick moment as if he were in deep thought. "Nah, it's just something Krizia did when she got really big," he muttered under his breath. "It probably won't work for you . . ."

"No, it-it-it could work for me too . . . what is it?" Her look of desperation, one that bordered on panic, was startling.

"Well . . . I don't know . . . I guess it could. We hired bigger dancers—taller, more muscular—to make her look smaller in comparison. But, if those guys are your *best* friends then obviously that's not at work here. We can just schedule some more time with the trainer." Thrusting the rest of the contracts back in Brooke's hands, he made his way towards the door.

"Steve . . ." Brooke piped up, causing him to turn around slowly.

"Yeah, love?" His new chops seemed to twinkle as if he were in a spearmint commercial. Here was a masterful manipulator.

"That's actually a great idea—I mean, just because they're not dancing for me doesn't mean we can't still be friends, right?"

At this, he paused briefly, flashing his perfect set of veneers once more. "That's the spirit! See, there is always a solution."

"Oh . . . and Steve?" Brooke called knowing full well she'd have to catch him before he was back on the phone for another round of endless negotiations.

"Tell Jackie what you thought about the *song*." She smiled.

"About what?" He looked annoyed at the thought of even engaging with me.

"You know, the one I played for you . . ."

"Ohhh, *that!*" His face lit up, causing me to relax a bit. *Did he actually like it?* "I thought it was fantastic—incredible—you're thinking big now . . . artists who write their own material make what they call 'mechanical royalties'—you benefit tremendously. I've already been hyping it up to the boys at the label—a great bargaining tactic—they think it adds to your credibility as a performer."

"That's the whole surprise," Brooke piped up, stopping him dead in his tracks again.

He raised an eyebrow. "Oh yeah? And what's the surprise?"

"Well . . ." she started slowly, giving me a devilish smile. "It's actually Jackie's song—she wrote it! Can you believe it? Isn't she so talented?"

"Hmmm . . ." Steve look bewildered for a second, and then held his index finger up in the air toward us. "Tell him you can't reach me—tell him I'm at a shoot . . ."

Brooke and I exchanged mystified glances before realizing he was yapping on his Bluetooth device once again. I continued applying the finishing touches, and Brooke remained perfectly still the entire time. By the time I was done with her, she possessed an all-American glamor that made even the harshest of critics—Robert—gasp. Everyone on-set *ohhed* and *ahhed*, pleased with the results.

"Good work, Calamity!" Sasha barked as we watched from the sidelines. *Calamity, huh? Still?* While on tour, I had wondered how long that nickname was going to stick and now, back in Los Angeles, I feared it was here to stay.

"Not too shabby. Not bad at all," Robert muttered with what seemed like genuine admiration.

Turning my attention to Brooke, I almost had to catch my breath—she did look stunning. Sprawled across an antique sofa with carved spindle legs that pierced the estate's manicured lawn, Brooke posed for the camera with a provocative pout. Draped in a yellow Grecian-style gown, a shoreline vista of pine trees and cliffs fading in the distance behind her, the down-home Southern girl morphed into a dewy poolside heiress. Bearing the chill of the shoot, she looked nothing like herself; she was ready for her formal introduction to the mass market.

Things were going perfectly. Stepping on the set to touch up Brooke's makeup, I noticed my cell phone buzzing in my pocket. I ignored it once, but then it started ringing again. My mom. Worried it was an emergency—she knew I'd be on the set all day—I grabbed for it, and then thought twice; obviously she hadn't paid attention.

"Jackie, just take it," Brooke urged. "You know I don't mind. It's your momma!"

I gave Brooke a half smile as I answered it. "Mom, I'm kind of busy right now." I held the phone against my shoulder with my cheek so I could keep working. The last thing I wanted was to hold up the show while Robert and Steve looked on.

Completely ignoring me as per usual, she babbled loudly into the receiver. "Oh, Jackie, this will only take a *second*. So your birthday is coming up and I was thinking, we'd love to have a dinner and invite Brooke . . ."

"Mom, it's a ways away—this really isn't the best time to talk about my birth—" I readjusted as the phone started to slip away from my ear. What on earth had her planning ahead?

She cut me off, suddenly sounding louder than before, "We figured Brooke wouldn't want to miss it—I could call the Ivy! Of course, I'd ask for a very private table because, you know, we'd have a celebrity with us—now I don't have to tell them who—" Things got really quiet around me. The speaker—I fumbled to click it off; the lump in my throat growing bigger as everyone stared. Shrugging goofily, I tried to disguise my embarrassment.

I could hear my mom cut through the silence. "Jackie? Or not—I mean, I guess we could let Lauren handle it again. She does a pretty good job every year."

Turning back to Brooke, I grinned ever so slightly, attempting to turn the whole ordeal into a joke. "Well *that* was awkward."

"Oh my gawd! You must try this!" A peppy blond saleswoman screamed at me from behind one of the boutique counters as I maneuvered through the racks of clothing with Brooke at my side. "They are so hot right now. Daily Candy is calling them the new Manolos! Can you believe it? The latest posting actually read, 'Move over Manolo!' What size are you? A six?"

"No, a nine," I said, knowing full well that they'd probably pulled an array of styles in a size six because that was Brooke's size.

What started off as a simple Saturday afternoon shopping excursion had turned into a major commotion. I was amazed the way the sales staff greeted us with exuberant attentiveness— all climbing over one another to give things away *for free*. I'd been shopping at Fred Segal for years and never once received treatment like this. And then again, they were used to such high-end clientele, the fashion cognoscenti and fashion victims alike. At each ultra-hip boutique in this breezy collection of ultra-hip boutiques, the sales staff greeted us in hordes, bringing Brooke everything from track jackets to leather purses with fringe, diet colas from large buckets of ice near the cash register, and each time saying, "Please . . . it's our gift." I scanned the jewelry, letting myself drift out of the flurry that Brooke's presence inspired.

"Wow, that's beautiful," I said out loud to myself as an antique gold locket caught my eye—it looked just like the one Dodo had worn in the New York *Times* photograph.

"Yikes," I said looking at the price tag, $625. I'd have to figure out how to channel granny another way. The sales girl fluttered about, pulling random pieces in Brooke's size from the racks and colorfully explaining why each of them was the latest and greatest. I made good use of my arms—coat racks for all of Brooke's goodies. I made eye contact with the manager responsible for taking care of us, and as I made my way towards the counter where she was leaning, I thanked her.

"It was really nice of you to take care of us like this," I said feeling slightly guilty and greedy, even though I wasn't on the receiving end.

"Are you allowed to accept gifts?" she asked, squinting behind her wire-rimmed glasses.

"Well, I . . ."

"Some of the girls aren't allowed to," she said, clearly mistaking me for a publicity assistant.

"I'm not in P.R., I'm . . ." I stopped. *What was I? Brooke's friend?* As I pondered the status of our relationship, one that had certainly—or so I thought—transitioned from mere handler to confidant, I nearly missed the pink satin pouch the woman had placed in my hand. "I want you to have this."

A gold shimmer caught my eye as I peered in. The locket.

"Oh, I couldn't possibly . . ." I said humbly, overwhelmed by her graciousness.

"You can't or you won't?" she asked briskly. "Take it; it's yours. I *insist*. It flatters that gorgeous copper hair." She smiled, her grin suggesting that she may know more about me than I knew I'd revealed. She'd seen my kind before, and she knew the locket would mean more to me than it would to her usual clientele who rushed through the boutique with armfuls of designer duds—all to be charged to the tabs of their wealthy fiancés and fathers.

The decadence of the morning could only be followed by lunch. I wanted Brooke to experience a place dear to me, a place she could blend in and fly under the radar. I decided to take her to the quaint little café tucked away behind the ivy-clad walls of Fred Segal—which was the entire reason we went there in the first place—protected from the buzz of Melrose. It attracted women adorned in oversize sunglasses, poodles at their sides, and men trying desperately to appear they weren't wearing overpriced workout clothes. Despite this, it had been one of my favorite restaurants in Los Angeles. Brooke, as physically fit as she was, was a huge fast-food junkie who constantly indulged in KFC and Burger King. Even so, she seemed to be enjoying herself.

"My friend Lauren—the one I'm bringing to the party with us—and me used to come here a few times a week in high school. We were obsessed." I smiled as we nestled into seats on the outside covered patio.

I enjoyed having this "girls' afternoon" with Brooke, showing her my favorite places to shop and eat. And yet it felt strange to be out in public with her. To my disappointment, I noticed people around us whispering and staring. It wasn't unusual to see a celeb or two basking in the sun on the patio, taking a long lunch or reading over a script with a manager or agent. So of all places, I thought this one would be safe. Here, stars were ogled discreetly and people were too cool to notice if the person sitting at the table next to them was famous. Nonetheless, Brooke seemed unconcerned with the gawking.

We chatted excitedly about her gorgeous new home in the Santa Monica mountains, discussing how the floor plan seamlessly flowed from its vast interior to the glorious outdoor view of thick pine trees, cherry blossoms, and a lush mountain pool. The server arrived, bearing two plates heaped with leafy greens and layered in avocado. As she set them in front of us, Brooke fished a wad of chewing gum from her mouth and pressed it on her plate with her thumb, all the while telling how thrilled she was that Steve found the oasis for her even though it wasn't necessarily the location he had originally wanted her in.

Just as we began digging in, we found ourselves surrounded by hushed whispers and gushing squeals of delight. I couldn't believe my eyes when I noticed a middle-aged woman standing inches from our table, screaming into her cell phone to tell someone who she was looking at "right this minute."

Brooke smiled briskly, brushing it off. But it didn't let up. Another gawker, followed by an autograph request, followed by a camera in her face. Each distraction seemed to weigh her further and further down.

"Did you see her? Did you see her?" a preteen girl asked loudly as she tugged on her mother's sleeve. "She's right there."

Every five minutes someone would approach our table with a pad of paper and a pen or a camera phone—mostly younger kids at first—who then paved the way for eager, nosy adults. Then, out of nowhere they descended—the paparazzi—we'd gone undetected the entire afternoon.

"Hey Brooke!" they yelled.

"I'll pose for some pictures but then please leave us alone after this," she said. It seemed to sate their appetite; they backed off momentarily.

"Thank you," she sighed, as the cameras kept on clicking.

"Okay, you got enough pictures; can we please eat in peace now?" She sighed. The clicking vigorously continued and she muttered, "Get a life."

This invasive behavior trailed us even as we closed the tab and left. We picked up the pace to my car, paparazzi hungrily pursuing us, shouting to get Brooke's attention. I was shocked at how shameless they were, moving in closer and thrusting their cameras literally two inches from her face.

"Brooke! You rule!" one yelled.

"Over here! To the left!" another screamed.

"Where's your boyfriend? Jesse or whatever," another piped up.

"You're a real gentleman." Brooke was becoming more and more aggravated by the second. It was exactly what they wanted.

"Brooke . . ." I asked slowly, totally freaked out by all the yelling and flashing. "Why do they keep saying this about Jesse? Don't you think that's weird?"

As if on cue, one called out to her tauntingly. "I'm a gentleman Brooke—can't I just get a hug? Or will your boyfriend get mad?"

"I dunno—I didn't say nothing about . . ." her voice trailed off as the voices got louder.

As we rushed into the safety of my car, gasping to catch our breath, I looked across the street and these guys were *still* taking pictures. Suddenly more approached in their own cars and on foot, desperately trying to photograph her in my car! My heart started beating out of my chest. Rather than frightened, Brooke appeared wounded and angry. She immediately lost it, sobbing,

"I just want to be normal. I wanted to shop some more." As I tried to gain composure and start the engine, it struck me that Brooke was only beginning to comprehend life's simple things would no longer, or ever again, be so simple.

The flashing of lights stung my retinas and I felt temporarily blinded. The adrenaline surged, mingling with the fear racing through my body. The voices got louder and louder, as the mob grew more and more out of control. Soon I heard nothing but the pounding inside my chest. Somehow I managed to focus back on Brooke, and some sort of motherly instinct kicked into high gear. I grabbed her hand, and when my eyes regained sight, I scanned for a gap through which to escape. Panic set in, despite my effort to remain calm for Brooke's sake, when I realized Range Rovers and Escalades, with tinted windows cracked ever so slightly to usher out long lenses, had completely trapped us. Then, through the swarm a man in a blue security jacket emerged. "Move! Move!" he yelled furiously at the snap-happy photogs. "Let them through!" He parted a path large enough for me to pull out.

As I maneuvered slowly, with the help of our lone security savior, a sudden, loud *smack* against the passenger window caused both Brooke and I to jump. Some paparazzo had thrust the latest edition of Hollywood's top tabloid against the window, and shouted at us, loud enough to be heard through the glass: "C'mon! You can't deny it! How's your boyfriend?"

The cover was simple; the implications, frightening. In the photo, just barely out of focus and apparently snapped from some hidden vantage, sat Brooke and Jesse backstage. She was leaning over, smiling—a real, genuine, and unmistakable fondness in her expression—and Jesse appeared to be whispering something in her ear. The angle made it look like he was kissing her neck. He had his hand in hers. Suddenly, the extra attention, the innumerable flashes, the invasive heckling: it all made sense in the most twisted and purely Hollywood fashion. Gossip swings between two extremes. Either you've overdosed or caused a fight—the negative extreme—or you've been spotted with a new, special someone—I guess you could call it positive. Regardless, the reaction was the same. This was that reaction.

I tore out of there, leaving the nightmare behind us. Once the tears subsided, we actually began to enjoy ourselves, making it a game to ditch the pests that mercilessly followed us. We drove up and down the small streets branching off of Melrose, laughing at how pathetic they were, but after a while Brooke sighed somberly, "Jackie, you're never gonna lose them."

"All right . . ."

"Don't worry about it. . ." The look on her face was sad, one of defeat.

One thing was certain (as if we hadn't taken note of it before): Brooke had arrived—a little disheveled, maybe, a little breathless for certain, but she had arrived. The days of being "just" a performer, a beauty queen, or a dancer with the ability to morph into any kind of being she fancied and then land, unrecognized, back into reality, were long gone. Los Angeles, I realized, was a shadowland for her as well—but it was much different from the one I had experienced in my early years. For her, it was a place where creativity and the underbelly of society collided, where she was separated from the world and even herself, and where spies lurked with lenses and opinions in every corner. This was the realm in which she had "arrived," like it or not, for better or worse.

The game had begun.

Chapter 8

> Without freedom of expression,
> good taste means nothing.
> –Neil Young

Our wild goose chase shook Brooke to the core. The very thought of spending the night alone in her spacious new house, tucked away at the end of a cul-de-sac with nothing but nature to the east, sent her into panic. Wide-eyed with fear, she asked if I would stay over. I figured my presence would calm her nerves, but every time the wind rustled the cherry blossom trees her eyes darted toward the window, searching for someone on the lawn. Finally, I closed the louvered blinds and suggested we make it an early night. And though there were three completely furnished bedrooms, I slept on the floor in Brooke's. Exhausted, she never woke once.

Late the next morning, we relaxed on the flagstone terrace by the pool, flipping through magazines and sunning ourselves.

"What should I wear tonight?" Brooke mused. She seemed less skittish after a good night's sleep, but you could tell she was working through a lot in her head. Thanks to the abrupt end of our Fred Segal shopping excursion, we found ourselves lacking *the* outfit for Lexy Young's latest bash. The childhood star turned Hollywood "It Girl," not to mention my former classmate, and her slacker boyfriend were often hosts of elaborate A-list parties, and tonight we planned to be among the guests.

"You do have that gorgeous pink . . ."

"Good morning!" A familiar voice boomed out of nowhere, startling Brooke, who jumped and nearly rolled off her chair. Steve came striding purposefully across the lawn with a big smile plastered on his face. "I've got a surprise for you!"

We quickly ditched our cigarettes, though it was too late to really hide them. As Steve came closer into focus, I wondered if the "surprise" might be his new look. He'd traded in his bad haircut, Dunhill business shirts, and traditional sports coats for quintessential L.A. style: True Religions, an Ed Hardy "Love Kills Slowly" tee emblazoned with a skull and heart, a studded gray camo Christian Audigier baseball cap, and a pair of retro-inspired Pumas.

I was suddenly aware of the heavy gold locket dangling around my own neck. *I guess the "freebie effect" trickles down to everyone*, I thought, as another loud voice interrupted.

"Lookitchu giiiirl! Damn! L.A.'s finest." Even T-Roc's ample bling looked mild compared to Steve's getup.

Waving back at him like a beauty queen, Brooke cooed sweetly, "How are y'all doin'?"

Crossing the lawn to the pool proved to be a mighty trek for T-Roc. He'd already broken a sweat by the time he reached us, which, I had to admit, made me question his effectiveness.

"That's my girl!" T-Roc belted out, throwing a thick arm around Brooke's little neck. "Stayin' strong . . . like you *do* . . . proud of you baby!"

Steve shot T-Roc a glare, urging him to tone it down.

"And even though we're *all* pleased that you've maintained good spirits through that whole mess, it's time you're protected for real." He paused while Brooke's eyes—squinting in the sun as she looked up at him—searched his face for answers, almost oblivious to the fact that the "answer" had his arm around her right then. "The Emersons have found a third guy to come work for them, and T-Roc's moving to you now."

Brooke let out a frustrated sigh, startling us all. I didn't see what the big deal was, even before he was technically working for her he had come to her aid a couple times a week. So many times, she would run up large tabs at nightclubs, buy armfuls of clothes, or test drive a new car, telling the dealer, "I'll take it!" and then notice she didn't have the money to pay for them. She never carried cash, much less a wallet. Taking advantage of T-Roc's soft spot for Brooke, Steve constantly pulled him out of bed, calling at all hours and telling him to "please make arrangements for Brooke."

Sounding like a used car salesman, Steve started, "You won't have to be scared like that ever again. He will be your own personal Secret Service, making sure you are out of harm's way twenty-four hours a day—fending off photographers so you can actually shop in peace."

Brooke looked up at T-Roc now like a child who didn't want to share her toys and felt *guilty* for sticking to her guns.

"T—you know I love you to lil pieces," Brooke said, trying to spare the gentle giant's feelings. T-Roc listened with his beefy arms crossed: he looked slightly wounded by her protest. "But don't y'all think it's gonna make me stand out even more? Like at the party tonight—it might look a little wei—"

Cutting her off, Steve shook his head with certainty. "Not tonight Brooke; I think you should lay low for a while. Nothing good is going to come out of you going to that party." Brooke began to open up her mouth in protest, but Steve squashed her with one glance. "Ab-so-lut-le-y not."

My heart sank—I'd been looking forward to this party for what seemed like an eternity, and, to make it worse, so had Lauren.

"That's a bummer," I muttered as Steve and T-Roc wandered inside to talk business. "I was so excited for you and Lauren to meet."

"We're still goin'," she said, closing her eyes and laying back on her lounge chair.

"But Steve just said—" I began to protest.

Without lifting an eyelid, she basked peacefully in the sun, shrugging. "I used to sneak out my room some nights on tour— for no other reason than to just hear silence. Not having to be anywhere, no one tellin' me what to do. It's easy." I now understood that Brooke never rebelled for the sake of rebelling. She did it in an attempt to grasp onto the remaining shreds of her anonymity, identity, and sovereignty before they slipped away completely.

"And you think you can get past T-Roc?"

"That's easy." She smiled, raising a hand to wipe away a puddle of sweat that had settled in the middle of her chest.

"Great," I said settling back in my chair next to her. Raising my chin to the sky, I shrugged too. "We'll see you at the same time tonight then."

"Cool," she squeaked. "I can't wait to let loose."

Security or no security, nothing was going to stop Brooke. She'd been complaining that she felt like a *slave* to Steve's rigorous demands and the round-the-clock schedule for the record label. Hoping we'd remain undetected in the darkness of night, Lauren and I veered up the twisty, mazelike avenues that snaked up the Hollywood Hills leading to Brooke's house. Once we reached the top of the hill, it lay just past a stretch of flimsy white guardrails in an area where the east side of the road dropped off sharply into the canyon, disappearing completely. I'd never ventured up there at night before and overwhelming vertigo washed over me as I gripped the steering wheel tight with my fingers. Loose gravel crunched beneath my tires as I pulled over a short distance from her driveway to an area partially hidden by cypress trees. I flipped off my headlights like a teenager sneaking out of her parents' house. Actually, it was exactly like that.

"You weren't kidding when you said this was going to be a blast to the past . . . I feel like a sophomore again," Lauren giggled next go me. I eyed the digital clock on the dashboard as it turned 11:29 . . . *one minute to go.* In all honesty, our top secret mission probably wasn't necessary because I knew Brooke could sweet talk her way past T-Roc easily, though there was a chance, knowing him, he'd still follow her so he could rest easy knowing she was safe. And besides, having a secret plan was fun for her and she always got a kick out of doing something sneaky.

Exactly one minute later, Brooke tiptoed across the lawn, a wide grin on her face, dressed in a delicate little vintage slip. I could see, as she got closer, that she had tried to experiment with a new look again. This time she had taken one of her skinny leather belts with beaded fringe and tied it around her forehead hippie-style, ruffling up the blond locks underneath. She could barely contain her excitement as she threw open the passenger side door.

"You like it?" she exclaimed, pointing to the speckled tones of her chemise. "I did it myself; I dyed it dark purple, even though it looks kinda gray," she smiled.

"Rad." Lauren smiled.

"Lauren, Brooke. Brooke, Lauren," I whispered, waving her in-side.

Lauren immediately went to work unloading her best Lexy-related gossip on Brooke.

"Well, I used to sit next to her in chemistry—when she was actually there—and she would go on and on about the movie stars she hooked up with and the wild parties she went to . . ." As Lauren gave her the dirty details, Brooke listened in silent awe. But every so often she'd interrupt with a question about what Lexy wore or drove or how she stayed so thin. It amused me how fascinated Brooke was by her.

"Oh my gosh!" Brooke gushed, suddenly interested in something else. As we turned onto the steep, canyon road, she pointed at the line of headlights winding up ahead of us. "This is insane! Where do they like, put all the cars?" she asked as we pulled up to the valet attendees standing outside.

"I'm not sure. There's probably a parking lot somewhere," I mumbled, suddenly aware of the looming mansion to our right. As I stepped out of the car I immediately noticed the almost eerie effect it had on me: here was one of those houses that was at risk of falling victim to the calamitous mudslides that plague the hillsides of Los Angeles. It was quite a sight.

"This is cool," Brooke cooed, enchanted by the Moroccan-style mansion where all the most fabulous people were playing just behind its walls. As we walked up the candlelit-paved motor courtyard, the only sounds that could be heard were music and the chatter of partygoers echoing in the otherwise silent canyon. A mix of beautiful people in their twenties and thirties had congregated in the two-story living room, and most of them stopped to stare and whisper as we entered. But Brooke, as always, was completely oblivious to the heads that were turning.

"I wonder if we're gonna see some big celebrities?" she whispered loudly to me, seeming to forget that she was a celebrity herself. I nodded slowly, suddenly feeling like a public spectacle.

"Where's the bar?" I asked, my eyes darting around the room.

"Brooke! You look fabulous!" a willowy brunette cried out from across the room. She was wearing a silk Geren Ford cami (which was certainly *not* a dress—though somehow she pulled it off as one), a pink and purple Eugenia Kim headscarf and white, knee-high Loeffler Randall leather boots. I immediately recognized her—Alexis Young. She set down the champagne glass she'd been sipping from and rushed across the room, abandoning her look-a-like friends all dancing and calling each other "be-atch," to greet Brooke.

"Hi, I'm Lexy," she said, confirming my insignificance.

"This is my friend Jackie," Brooke answered for me, giving me a look as if to say, *Can you believe she's talking to us?*

"Right . . . Alexis," Lauren piped in—playing the same game, she squinted one eye as if she were trying to recall something from ages ago, "Mr. Siegel's chem class, I remember now." Lexy looked confused, as if Lauren had just started speaking to her in Aramaic. She was not, it turned out, playing a game on her end.

"Tenth grade?" Lauren said, giving it one more shot.

"Hmmm . . ." was all Lexy mustered. She clearly couldn't be bothered with this kind of small talk.

The snub prompted Lauren to exaggerate the exasperated look on her face. She mouthed to me, "Okay . . . guess not."

Shifting her coked-out gaze and enthusiasm back to Brooke, Lexy gushed, "So, did you get the invite for tomorrow? I'm having people over early to nurse their hangovers. It's going to be at my parents' place in the 'Bu and it's going to be fucking amazing . . . everyone will be there–seriously, you better come, be-atch."

"Wow, that sounds cool," Brooke said, revealing her "I'm a simple girl from the South" persona.

"Fab, come have a drink with me after you make the rounds." She had barely finished talking to Brooke before she shouted out, basically *through* us, toward some guy wearing a rhine-stone-encrusted hoodie strolling in: "No way, no way! Now you are an asshole! Seriously, get over here and give me some love." And poof, just like that, she was gone with Brooke in tow to show her off to all of her fabulous friends.

But the birthday girl, it seemed, did not share Lexy's warm feelings for Brooke. In the hour before Jessica Rader's late arrival we mixed and mingled with the hot Hollywood crowd. There were inattentive agents and managers who seemed more consumed with their Blackberrys than with the actual conversations they were having. There were scantily clad models (or out-of-work actresses, depending on which one you were speaking to) scattered about, all looking painfully uncomfortable in their very own beautiful skin. There were the hipsters too, all with "complicated" hairstyles, skintight jeans, and scarves. Most of them sat there complaining about Hollywood, though fully reveling in their "cool" social status. One in particular was complaining about the Coffee Bean and Tea Leaf being "too corporate" before swigging heavily from a Grey Goose bottle. By the time Jessica did show up, around one-thirty, it was almost too late for anyone to care. Breezing through the doors in nothing but a navel-skimming shirred tweed vest and a pair of tiny shorts, she made a grand entrance, dainty as a Barbie doll.

"Well, look who we have here!" Jessica strutted over to Brooke, her tone sweetly dripping with venom. Looking her up and down, Jessica cast a critical eye over Brooke's self-designed ensemble before tugging at one of the straps. "Don't you look cute?"

"Thanks!" Brooke smiled sincerely. "Jessica, I want you to meet my friend Jackie."

Eyebrows raised, Jessica shot Brooke a look that said *and why should I care?* before pretending to notice someone she wanted to talk to near the stairs. With that she brushed past without saying another word.

"Is she mad at me?" Brooke asked, confused. She began to worry she'd said something wrong. For someone who barely hit five feet in height, Jessica certainly had big attitude.

"I wouldn't be too concerned," I said, though I didn't want to upset Brooke. I sensed Jessica had it out for her for any assortment of reasons.

"So which one is *David*?" Lauren asked in a singsong voice, flushing my Irish complexion in a shade of crimson. I hoped, for a moment, that Brooke wasn't paying attention.

"One of my managers? David Kagan?" Brooke asked, stopping to point across the room. "He's right over there."

"He's so cute!" Lauren said nudging me excitedly—I nudged her harder back even though I knew it was my fault, forgetting to mention that David was my "secret" crush.

Just clicking in her brain—Brooke whirled around to me with wide eyes. "Wait a minute—do you have a crush on David?" When I didn't answer, preoccupied by my cheeks stinging with embarrassment, she gave me a playful *I caught you!* grin. "You do! Awww . . . that is so precious!"

"He's like—the best guy in the entire world," she swooned to Lauren before her eyes fixated on someone across the room. She let out a sharp gasp and began to pat her heart as if she felt faint.

"Omigod! Omigod!" she squealed over and over.

"What's she doing?" Lauren mouthed to me. I shrugged, unfazed. This was typical Brooke.

"Look! Look! Over there," Brooke panted, pointing to a ruggedly handsome guy in his late twenties. "Is that who I think it is?!"

"Ben Hart," Lauren, chomping down on a carrot stick, said without missing a beat, "he's so hot, looks *so* much like his dad!"

When Ben Hart entered a room, it was common for people to stare. Most times they did double takes to see if their eyes were playing tricks on them. Son of Tinsel Town's "tough guy" and everyone's favorite old-time, megalomaniacal Academy Award-wining actor, Frankie Hart, Ben possessed features almost identical to his father's. And though his life thus far consisted mainly of surfing and suntanning, it was his famous surname and freakish genetics that cast him into the limelight. At first it was just photos of family outings, followed by occasional shutterbugs snapping him on the beach in Malibu pulling up his rubber wetsuit. From there it wasn't long before he was dating models, hanging out with Hollywood's elite, and generally causing havoc wherever he went. The offspring of a man notorious for his bad temper on the set, frequent cocaine binges, and nights on the town with Playboy bunnies, Ben was perfect rebel material—slightly on the short side, yes, but with a muscular physique and the attractive mix of recklessness and swagger he inherited from his father, he made up for it. Somewhere along the way though, Ben had decided he wanted to be taken "seriously" as an actor and, like everything else in his fast-paced life, quickly began making cameo appearances in almost everything broadcast on cable television.

"I'm gonna go talk to him!" Gaining composure, Brooke mustered up the nerve to approach him, but then chickened out before taking a second step. "I have the biggest crush on him . . ." she gushed, stopping suddenly as their eyes met. "Um . . . holy moley . . . I think he just looked over at us."

"He sure did," Lauren said without breaking her shameless stare. "And now he's heading over this way."

"Shut up!" Brooke gasped as she stared down at the floor awkwardly, "acting" like she hadn't noticed him.

"Cheers," Ben said, surprising us with a Scottish accent. Raising his beer, he took a swig before setting the empty bottle down on the table behind him. Patting the condensation off of his hands and onto his jeans, Ben took Brooke's in his.

"Its aboot time we met," he said, accent still intact.

"Why is he talking like that?" I whispered to Lauren who could barely contain her giggles.

"He's in method acting mode. I read online that he's been working with a voice coach for this movie he's doing."

"He's doing a movie?! I thought all he knew how to do was surf?"

"Yeah, me too. But . . . *Scottish Arms*? Something like that . . . set in the early 50s. He's playing a Glaswegian detective on a manhunt to catch these guys involved with a million-dollar horse betting coup. It's based on a true story, actually sounds pretty good."

"Ah've seen your werk . . ." Ben was now saying. "You alright? Gonnae get us a beer . . ."

"Sure, thanks," Brooke stammered, completely zoned into him. Flashing her a sultry smile, he dropped her hand gently, maintaining eye contact as he walked to the bar.

"Omigod . . ." Brooke said, turning to us excitedly and fanning herself with her right hand. "He is like, so cute!"

When he returned, Brooke had found her cool and managed to hold onto it when he handed her the beer, letting his fingers linger on hers.

"So you're really gonna be in a movie?" Her drawl seemed even stronger whenever she was nervous. They launched into a conversation that had Brooke smiling and nodding excitedly, though I was sure she only grasped a tenth of what he was saying, half was what she hadn't lost in the accented disarray, the other half was what was left for her to hear through the fog of being star struck.

Both Lauren and I began to drink faster so we could excuse ourselves and head back to the bar. By now, the party was in full effect, which was fine with me since a longer line at the bar meant more time away from Brooke's flirtatious giggles.

"What do you want?" Lauren asked as she leaned over the bar. Spotting David through the crowd once more, butterflies fluttered in my stomach. Clean-shaven, he looked more handsome than ever. Stopping every few inches, he fist bumped and half-hugged his way across the room.

"Hello?" Lauren belted out, startling me.

"Oh, um, vodka tonic please," I said.

"Hey Kevin, vodka tonic," she said, stuffing a twenty-dollar bill in the tip glass.

"Thanks," I said as she handed me the ice-old concoction. "Already on a first-name basis with the bartender, huh?"

"The best guys to know at a party like this one . . ." Lauren smiled.

"Oh shit . . ." I hummed under my breath as David walked in our direction. I couldn't understand why I was suddenly so nervous about being around him. Of course, we'd never encountered one another in a social setting like this.

"What?" Lauren asked.

"Shhh . . . he's coming over . . ." I tried to get the sentence out before he got to us but it was too late.

"According to my calculations, you guys shouldn't be here . . ." David smirked seductively, though I was too worried about getting caught to notice it. Sensing my despair, he quickly added, "Don't worry, I won't rat you out."

Like an idiot rendered speechless, I said nothing, relieved when Lauren jumped in, breaking the silence by introducing herself.

"It's nice to meet you Lauren," he said, taking her hand. We stood around watching the crowd, spotting an increasingly drunk Lexy as she danced seductively with some of her "beatches."

"Want to get some fresh air?" David asked pointing toward the manicured Italianate gardens just beyond the buzz of the pool terrace. Heat lamps lined the outskirts of the pool area and deck, the warm orange glow trailing off in points throughout the gardens and beyond. I looked over at Lauren, who glared back wide-eyed as if to say, *Go! What are you waiting for?* Realizing I needed a little push, she thought fast. "Kev and me need some alone time, scram."

Forced out on my own, it didn't take long until I warmed back up to David. We strolled the pathways of the extensive grounds punctuated with bright red roses and tinkling stone fountains, talking and losing track of time. As the real world, viewable beyond the mansion's perimeters, buzzed on by, we talked about our hometowns, our favorite books, and movies we loved to hate.

We wound our way past the waterfall cascading down a rocky grotto into the gently steaming, mosaic-tiled swimming pool and laughed at the colorful scene. A group of aspiring models—who'd finally drunk enough to become free-spirited—sat around the bubbling hot tub topless, smoking pot and soaking up the attention they were being paid. One of them shrieked playfully as a guy passed by and slapped her barely covered bottom. On the patio, Jessica Rader sat at a table with a pair of miserable-looking girlfriends while she sipped a dirty martini. They chattered amongst each other, exchanging plenty of eye rolls, yet the birthday girl's sour face let on that she was frustrated by all the people hanging out by the pool.

"What's it like to actually grow up here?" he asked, nodding his head in the direction of the party. "I gotta know . . ."

"It's not really *that* much different than anywhere else . . ."

"Oh come on, you can't say that—you've never grown up anywhere else . . . for example," David said, attempting to appear serious, "I don't think there was one person at my high school that drove a Ferrari; in fact, I don't think there were any European cars in the student lot period. Of course, there was that one guy who had a new Jeep Cherokee—which was like, the coolest thing—but it had one of those of obnoxious sound systems and those halogen headlight things? Anyway, we were all pretty sure that he sold drugs."

"Hmmm," I mused. "Sounds like Connecticut is a little wilder than you let on."

"Truly." He smiled, playing along. "But then 'huffing' went out of style, and he lost everything—it's really crazy to see someone fall apart like that."

"Yeah." I smiled, not having much to add, looking down as we roamed before coming to a small stone staircase near the far end of the property. Making our way to the top of the small hill, we stepped onto an expanse of lawn equipped with an octagon-shaped heliport. "But," I said in a singsong voice, feeling pretty tipsy, "not *everyone* in Los Angeles lives like this."

"They don't?" he said with mock seriousness. We both stood in silence for a moment—taking in the 360-degree views of the Hollywood Hills.

"So, what is this? House number three for the Youngs?" he asked.

"Ummm . . . yes, if you're counting just Los Angeles County."

I could never understand why the Youngs owned homes in Hollywood, Beverly Hills, *and* Malibu growing up. But as I got older I realized they weren't so much living spaces as backdrops for parties. "Otherwise, it's one of six—you're forgetting Honolulu, Swiss Alps, and their place on the Côte d'Azur."

"Must be tough," David guffawed.

"Right. I haven't exactly lived the high life; in fact, up until a few months ago I was making my rent serving up biscuits and eggs six days a week. But, this world," I said waving my arm back to the house where the party waged on, "was not the world I knew as a kid. I was kind of a dork I guess."

David laughed. "I can just see picture it now—kicking it at home on the weekends with your boy Ric Craia keeping you company." At this, I gave him a playful jab in the ribs, though in all honesty he wasn't far from the truth. "I'm messing with ya," David said, catching my hand in his. Not letting it go, he clasped it gently, turning to me in a sheepish manner. "Look, if it makes you feel any better—I played the viola in middle school, and thanks to my mother I was quite the dweeb too."

"Were you any good?"

"Nah . . . she was forced to come to terms with the fact that I don't have a musical bone in my body. Once she realized the only song I could play after a year and a half of lessons was 'Hot Cross Buns,' it was all over." I laughed, leaning into him— something I would never have done sober. "But I really do love music and so, that's why I do what I do . . ." David said wistfully. "If you can't beat 'em, join 'em, right? Even if joining them makes me this necessary evil that everyone has to deal with." He shrugged before turning towards me, pulling me in closer. "How about you? We all know you're a music fan."

"Actually, I've been playing whatever musical instrument I could get my hands on since I was a kid."

"Really? What can you play?" he asked. "A few more than some 'Hot Cross Buns,' I'm betting?"

"I don't know—on the piano I play different things, from classical to rock, sometimes I just make things up as I go. I like just hammering away—it gets my creativity flowing."

"That's pretty awesome . . . I'd love to hear you play sometime," he said as we descended the staircase back to the garden pathways.

"Well, I've only written a few stupid things. Brooke's obsessed with one of them; she keeps saying she wants to put it on her album, but it's pretty silly."

He stopped dead in his tracks, a dramatic gesture. "The new song she was playing the other day? No, wait . . . *You* wrote that? It's really, really good."

"Well, not good enough apparently," I sighed, describing the way Steve seemed to completely brush off the idea.

"What? That's weird, he was all about it last week—I think he even called it brilliant," David smiled jokingly, "and Steve's a harsh critic." Taking note of the long, heavy sigh that escaped my mouth, he quickly changed the subject.

"So, you're not used to any of this then, huh?"

"Yeah—I mean—I was away for two years, and, if Alexis Young was throwing parties like these in high school, *I* didn't know about them."

"All right, great—so you really are new to the scene, that's fantastic," he said taking a sip of his beer and nodding his head. "Well, you're going to need to know the places to avoid—you know, the obnoxious nightclubs full of cool people, hip parties with industry types, the restaurants that are plagued with paparazzi . . . and don't even get me started on the hotel pools frequented by all those rugged, foreign male models; I mean, who would want to go to those?" He laughed. "Maybe we should go to some of these places, you know, just so you can hate them and all."

"Sounds good to me," I said. I was smitten, maybe it was the moon up ahead, or the undivided attention (I had found that "undivided attention" in this industry was usually reserved for "important people," like Brooke), or maybe it was the fourth vodka tonic—still, you couldn't possibly paint a better backdrop in which to fall in . . . *like*.

When all of a sudden we were interrupted by a couple of bubbly, platinum blonds, practically Barbie-doll proportions in their skimpy minidresses, who looked like they had made a wrong turn on their way to the Playboy Mansion. All silicon and rubber-lipped, it was probably a bad idea for them to stand so close to our heat lamp in case they started melting.

"Hiiii David," chirped the duo in unison. Bimbo number one leaned in and suctioned her puckered collagen to David's left cheek, while number two greeted him with the inch-away Eurotrash: "*Muah, muah.*"

"Oh my gawd!" squealed bimbo number two. "We *so* had a blast last weekend! We have got to do that again!"

"Yeah, good times," said David without breaking stride—if he was unhappy with them being here, he certainly wasn't letting on. "Pamela, Sophia, this is my friend Jackie."

"It's nice to—"

"So do you think you can make it again this weekend?" Sophia said, completely ignoring me, without the slightest acknowledgement that I even *might* have been David's date. "We want you to come out and play with us again," she cooed.

"But you're not allowed to sing unless you do a duet with me," Pamela chimed in.

"Ahh, ladies, I hate to disappoint but I unfortunately have to decline," he said, almost a little too charmingly, but in a way only I seemed to pick up on his sarcasm. "Got plans already . . . but maybe next weekend?"

Are you kidding me? These were anything but the type of girls I imagined David hanging out with on the weekends, let alone going to karaoke hell with.

"What-everr, you suck!" said Sophia, as they both walked away blowing air kisses at David. "Toodles . . ."

"Nice—such a nice group of friends you have," I said jokingly to David.

"Do I detect a bit of sarcasm?" said David.

"I'm just surprised. Karaoke, eh?" I laughed.

"Pamela and Sophia are obsessed with going to Karaoke Heaven, they practically live there. I got dragged out last week. It was a major lapse in judgment."

Did David always surround himself with such plastic women? Oh God, I could only imagine what they thought seeing him with me.

Wandering back to the party, we were surprised by just how out of hand it had gotten in such a short time. Giving the performance of his lifetime, a shirtless Ben Hart continued to shout out to nobody in particular—his accent getting thicker and thicker with each beer he guzzled. "Everybody havin' a fookin' good time?"

Next to him, stumbled an obviously drunk Brooke who provoked death glares from nearby Jessica as she giggled uncontrollably every time he made even the most inappropriate move.

"A-nnoy-ing!" she called out in her best Valley girl tone, loud enough for Brooke to hear. Completely enamored and in her own little world, Brooke barely batted an eyelash, infuriating her further. Feeling upstaged once again, this time at her very own birthday party, Jessica gave her girlfriends an over exaggerated roll of the eyes. "This is lame—we're outta here," she snapped.

Wasting no time Jessica reached for her purse and began to make her way out of the party. As she passed, David caught Jessica's eye and she flashed him a sexy smirk and a wink.

Though dying to know what that was all about, I decided it was best not to even go there. After what happened with the bimbo twins earlier, I didn't want to start sounding like a jealous girlfriend—David and I weren't even dating!—so I kept my questions to myself.

As we tried to absorb the mess stretched out in front of us, I spotted Lauren near the back porch, sprawled out in one of the lounge chairs with a drink in-hand. I rushed over to her, feeling immediately guilty.

"Oh my God Lauren, I'm so sorry—I didn't think we we're gone that long," I hummed.

"I'm not upset—not in the least," she said with a devilish grin. Patting the cushioned seat next to her, she smirked. "I've got front row seats here, and—" she continued, motioning towards the pool behind me, "I'm thoroughly enjoying this whole scene."

I turned around in time to find Ben whirling around the pool, swigging beer and smoking cigarettes almost as rapidly as he hurled mouthfuls of expletives at innocent bystanders.

"Ah don't know wherr yerr fookin' purse is you crabbit auld bitch," he screamed as one of Jessica's minions, left in the wake of her friends, searched frantically for her clutch under the table next to him.

"Ew," Lauren said as we watched him stagger sloppily about. "Maybe he should slow down on the method acting. What'dya think? We need to get Brooke away from him stat."

"Looks like he's going inside to grab a drink," I told her, not wanting to go anywhere near the madness erupting a few feet away.

"Good idea, Hart—have another," Lauren laughed dryly. "Let's make a break for it."

Darting across the grass, I grabbed Brooke's elbow, and pulled her over to where we were sitting.

"Oh my gawd, Jackie!" Brooke, quite clearly on cloud nine, swooned the second she saw me. "I kissed Ben Hart!"

"Dude, you have a boyfriend," I said almost stopping dead in my tracks.

"It's okay, you know, I love Jesse," she quickly stammered to justify things. "Normally I never do that kind of thing—but you know, I had to kiss Ben Hart."

Suddenly, the mental image of Brooke and Jimmy in her dressing room flashed in my head, and for the first time, I didn't know if I believed her. Disrupting my thoughts, David—oblivious to the ensuing chaos—placed his hand on my shoulder.

"Hey . . . so, I had fun tonight . . . let's do this again sometime. Maybe next week?"

"Yeah, that sounds great," I smiled. At least something seemed to be going right.

"Good. What's your cell? I have it somewhere in the office, but not . . ." he muttered as he fumbled in his pocket for his PDA.

"Sure, it's 310-"

"'Ehy red! Wheryubeen?" A voice seemed to shout in my ear, before I could finish the rest of it, "Graaaahhh!!!!!" Without a clue what was happening, someone hoisted me off of the ground in a big bear hug. Encompassed in a beer and stale cigarette stench, it was easy to identify my captor—Ben Hart. Laughing like a mad man, he jerked me over to the edge of the pool.

"Okay, okay," I laughed. I was annoyed that he was touching

me, yes—but with all of my clothing intact, including my new leather boots and my oversized purse slung over my shoulder, I knew I was safe. "Seriously quit," I managed to blurt out between giggles. Then, just as he pulled me away from the pool, ready to release me into the wild—or so I thought—I felt his grip tighten and the bulk of my weight shift backwards onto him. Holy shit. . . .

Kerplunk!

Totally submerged under water, I raced to the top, grasping for breath.

"It's Baltic freezing in here, man—I thought the thing wiz heated," Ben said, still not dropping out of "character," as he sloppily hoisted himself out of the pool, leaving me behind bobbing like an apple. Besides Lauren and David who scrambled to help fetch me from the frigid water, everyone else stood still.

"Really fookin' cauld, man," he reiterated.

Crawling out of the side of the pool, both the left and right sides of my brain tugged my focus back and forth in between feeling deathly cold and completely embarrassed.

"Oh no," I gulped, suddenly bringing my hand to my neck.

"What's wrong?" Lauren asked concerned.

"My necklace—that gold locket from Fred Segal—the one I showed you? That reminded me of Dodo? It's gone."

Without hesitation, Lauren turned on her heel. "I'll get it!"

"No—Lauren, it's freezing . . . it's okay . . ." I called out, but she was already standing near the side, gazing down into the water.

"I don't see it, do you?" she asked a girl who also searched the bottom with her squinted eyes. She slowly shook her head no but continued to look, waving over a friend. After several minutes and no luck, I felt my lips turning blue.

"I need to go home," I said loudly so Lauren could hear me.

"Yerr nawt goin' hawm . . ."

Additional chills ran up my spine and I couldn't bring myself to even turn and look at him. I felt as if I might be ill at any moment.

"Come oan, get aff! I'm blootered drunk!"

"Let's go," Lauren said scrambling to my side and mouthing good-bye to David.

Grabbing Brooke with her other arm, she looked like a mother escorting two unruly children.

"No one's got to go hawm! Here yerr are," Ben howled after us, tossing a beach towel my way. "Just dry aff."

"I'm starting to realize why everyone calls you 'Calamity' . . ." David shouted out to me in an attempt to make me laugh. But with my hair matted to my forehead, the mascara streaking down my face, and my favorite purse looking as if it had sprung a leak from where it was perched on my shoulder, I shivered like a wet dog. I was still too embarrassed to laugh, let alone turn around, but I managed to shuffle my way toward the nearest heat lamp.

"I'll get your number from Brooke," David added, still unable to lift my spirits. "I'll call you later!"

The paparazzi had gotten wind of the party and were in full force as we crossed the street to retrieve our car from the valet.

"Shit," I muttered, spying them. As if the fact that I was completely bedraggled in my soaked clothes that hung heavily on my frame wasn't bad enough, now our cover would be blown too. But Brooke, drunk and giddy, gave them all a big smile before sticking out her middle finger and saying in her sweet, southern twang, "Have a good night." Lightbulbs flashed, the paparazzi loving every minute of it . . . I knew within a couple hours this image would be posted all over the Internet, that there'd be an irate call from Sasha or somebody at 8 AM, asking me why I didn't stop her. It would be the talk of the tabloids come Monday. But I didn't care—all I could think about at that moment was David, someone in this Babylon they call Hollywood, someone who finally got me.

Chapter 9

**Gossip is news running ahead of itself
in a red satin dress.**
–Liz Smith

I awoke to a raging hangover and the unpleasant noise of
my cell phone yet again, bright and early, eight o'clock
in the morning.

"How could you let her do that?!" growled an angry
voice.

"What?" I asked groggily without even looking at the
caller I.D.—I knew who was calling.

"That is you looking like a drowned rat in those pictures, isn't it?" sneered Steve. Apparently, nonstop calls
from every media outlet and their mother—all wanting
comments on Brooke's photo op—had roused him from
whatever aspiring actress/model/singer he had bagged
the night before. He wasn't too happy about it.

"Huh?" I rubbed my eyes, grasping to make sense of Steve's tirade. I rolled over and flipped open my laptop on the nightstand. Still on the screen from the night before thanks to Lauren, who checked the site religiously, was deliasdirt.com. Once the page updated, I saw the latest on Brooke, which offered a juicy photo montage "after the jump." Clicking forward to see the damage, I found Delia the Diva of Dish, true to form, remarking snidely on Brooke's "water-logged companion." There I was. Standing to the right of Brooke and Lauren—sans makeup and a drenched, squishy nightmare on display for the world to see. I scrolled down to see Lauren staring back at me, eyes fixed on the cameras like a deer in headlights, paralyzed by her first paparazzi ambush. I groaned.

"They're all over the Internet—CNN.com even ran something on 'America's newest Sweetheart gone wild.' It's a mess—a bloody mess for fuck's sake! Do you realize the hell you've thrown me into?" Steve screamed. "How could you be so stupid?"

"Steve, I couldn't stop her, I mean—she's a grown girl—I had no control over that."

"First of all, she's not even supposed to be fucking out at all—you know that—and you were in the car," he irately fired back, lecturing me like a child. "You obviously knew what kind of state she was in when you left. Now I've got people calling and asking, 'Is she acting out?' 'Was she drunk?' Did you not see the cameras? Did you not see the photographers outside?"

"No . . . I mean, I did, but not until it was too late."

"Did you not happen to notice Brooke was drunk?" Steve asked exasperatedly.

"I did, but . . ." I was cut off by the blare of a car horn from the other end.

"Yeah? Piss off!" Steve screamed angrily out his window. I could just picture him now—still wearing the same outfit from the night before, speeding through West Hollywood in his

Mercedes CLS 500 like a complete maniac, blowing stop signs all the way.

"David was there, Jackie! He could've gotten you guys out of the house and home without anyone ever catching a glimpse of her! Use your head," he cut me off. "And where the hell was her security? We assigned T-Roc to Brooke for a reason."

"I'm sorry. Okay? What do you want me to do about it?" I asked, massaging my throbbing temples.

"*Not* let my client look like a complete asshole when you're out with her!" he snapped back. "If you're going to play this little celebrity game you better start thinking with your head because this is a big fucking deal!"

With that he hung up. I rolled back on my pillow hoping to escape it all for a little longer. I fell in and out of a disturbed sleep when my phone chimed, signaling a text. "We made Delia's Dirt. How cool is that?" a delighted Lauren raved about her good fortune.

Closing my eyes, I might have slept, but after what felt like a blink my cell phone buzzed yet again. This time it was Brooke.

"What are you doing?" She sounded too giddy for the type of night we'd had before.

"What—what time is it?" I asked sitting up in bed, suddenly startled.

"It's noon-thirty." Brooke laughed. "Come over! It's mimosa time!"

"What?" I mumbled.

"Lexy's hangover brunch—she's having people out to her place in Malibu, remember?"

"Brooke, do you have any idea how pissed off everyone is right now? Steve called me at eight this morning . . ." I moaned.

"Oh, yeah. He's such a grouch," Brooke said nonchalantly. "Don't worry, he won't care. He just told me T-Roc needs to come with."

"Brooke. T-Roc's there for a reason. You don't need me, just take him," I suggested, hoping this incident wouldn't ruin my job.

"I'm not going alone with him. That's just embarrassing," Brooke whined. "You have to come."

We arrived at Lexy's pad on Billionaire Beach to find illegally parked cars everywhere. Apparently this wasn't the low-key gathering we'd expected. Crossing an arched stone bridge that distanced the estate from the rest of the world, we could hear the party chatter just beyond the stately palms and blossoming bougainvillea. Passing a pair of open French doors on the side of the estate, we stopped.

"Where's the party?" Brooke asked an older woman, presumably the Youngs' housekeeper, who was busy organizing a pile of mail in an antique-filled study as though oblivious to the raging party outside.

She pushed her glasses down on her nose as if examining us closely, giving T-Roc a good once-over and then another. After too much staring, she answered, "Follow the terracotta passageway down, you'll see a fifty-foot pink floss tree to your right before you hit the pool deck."

We made our way through the maze of tropical gardens to the oval-shaped pool and towards the crescendo of voices and party clatter to find nearly a hundred ridiculously beautiful people mingling, mimosas and well-garnished Bloody Marys in hand. Dozens of Lexy wannabes in skimpy string bikinis pranced about excitedly greeting one another with shrill "Hey beatches!"

"You're a total ass! Seriously quit!" We heard a girl laugh. The voice, I soon realized, belonged to none other than Lexy herself, who was grappling with the loose strings of her metallic pink bikini top as her oversized shades nearly fell from her head.

"Mm-hmm." T-Roc leaned over me, his voice as though divulging a secret. "I don't like that one. She's no good. Girl's bad news fo sho."

"Oh T." I smiled. He played the mother hen in an amusingly affectionate way, clucking to me about the people around Brooke that didn't jibe with him. His skepticism made me thankful I'd made the cut. "She's harmless T. Just a bit loopy, that's all."

"*Ser-ious-ly*, I hate you," she retorted to a boy in linen drawstring pants, presumably the one who had untied her top, before plunging her hand into a box of Lucky Charms. Pulling out a fistful of cereal, she began picking out the marshmallows one by one. Between mouthfuls, she looked up to see us arrive. "Hey bitches!"

"Whoa—what's going on here?" Brooke asked wide-eyed, soaking the seaside soiree in.

"Just a good old-fashioned pool party with a few friends." Lexy smiled before flouncing off to greet two more newcomers.

A team of attendants hired by Lexy's parents rushed about, cosseting guests with dry towels, frozen grapes, and neck pillows that matched the pink-and-white cabana-striped towels slug over the rows of lounge chairs on each side of the pool. There were all sorts of trendy types—some familiar faces, some complete strangers—congregating on the pool deck, all looking strangely out of place in the posh setting. A girl with a long blond ponytail in a bright James Scott sweater dress and pumps was sucking on a mini ginger popsicle, completely engaged in conversation with a boy that could've easily been mistaken for a criminal if not for the Evian spritzer in his hand. Their conversation was peppered with words like, "dope," "awesome," and "for real tho." Half-empty champagne glasses littered the patio since now, as it was mid-afternoon, the crowd had moved on to stiffer libations such as screwdrivers and Scotch on the rocks.

There was a skunky smell in the air, compliments of Osaka, a local fashion designer who was supplying partygoers with weed rolled like Marlboros from a silver cigarette case monogrammed with a large O.

Getting into the spirit of things, I grabbed a mimosa and guzzled down two aspirin. Brooke peeled off her sundress, and without any makeup her skin appeared broken out and dehydrated. Barely covered by a violet-purple bikini, her chiseled, perfect body saved her from looking like a total wreck as she curled up on one of the cushy chaise lounges next to the legendary Poppy Wexler, party-promoter extraordinaire. Her perfectly cropped dark hair, strikingly enormous blue eyes, and the TCB lightening bolt dangling from her neck further accentuated her confident air—here was a woman who made shit happen. I recognized her from my unhip days when Lauren came back for summer vacation or winter break and forced me to accompany her to the hot spot du jour. As far as I was concerned, Poppy was the most important person in L.A. She lorded over the red ropes at the hottest Hollywood nightspots. Wielding that kind of power, she could make any pro football player denounce his own team at her mercy and say the words "Brett Favre is the best quarterback in the N.F.L." just to gain access.

"'Sup," Poppy said, her husky voice oozed with a breathy sexiness. I stared at the initials on her wrist—E.A.P.—for Elvis Aaron Presley. Poppy's adoration of "The King" only added to her illustrious reputation. She glanced up at me, lifting a cigarette to her lips and sucking it down as though under extreme stress, perhaps to avoid the onset of a hangover.

"He's such a dick," Poppy muttered out of nowhere, her heavy-lidded eyes coming to life. I turned my head to see what she was staring at—Lexy and the boy she had yelled at earlier. He was somewhat handsome with a square jawline and dark hair, though slightly bloated—the swelling of his gut hung over his pants and suggested too many consecutive nights out on the town. He had a black sleep mask turned backwards around his head in an attempt to look chic.

"Who is that?" I asked.

"Med Johnson, Lexy's boyfriend," Poppy scowled.

"I don't think I know who that is," I said.

"Rich kid from Manhattan. Garrett Johnson? That's his dad."

"Who's Garrett Johnson?" Brooke inquired, still confused.

"Ew! Really?" I laughed aloud, recognizing him as a frequent guest on the cable program, *Crisis to Cougar*. On the makeover challenge show for middle-aged women that were stuck in a rut (though the casting directors seemed to favor the ones who were one Prozac short of a complete mental breakdown), Dr. Garrett Johnson made dreams come true one labia reduction at a time.

"He's on T.V.," I explained to Brooke between giggles.

"Specializes in labiaplasty." Poppy shrugged as if he were an accountant or an attorney.

"He what?" Brooke asked, responding to my laughter. "What's lab, lab . . . whatever you said?"

"Labiaplasty. It's like plastic surgery for your . . ." I motioned to her nether regions.

"What?! Gross! No way . . ." Brooke shrieked, her eyes widening, "people don't really do that, do they?"

"Yup. My friend Brandy's mom saw him once, said he's kind of a perv," Poppy declared unwavering. Shielding her eyes from the glaring sun, she looked up at a girl in a long, bed-sheet–like coverup that, slit up both sides, showed off her stick-thin pins as she approached us.

"We're talking about your ex," Poppy barked.

"Who? Oh, Med?" the girl asked as her six-foot-tall frame cast a shadow over our chairs. "Ugh, he's such a disgusting human being. I don't even know what he does all day? Drive his Lamborghini up and down Sunset, I guess." She peeled a pair of aviators from her face to reveal small but dramatic eyes offset with bags to rival Poppy's. Tossing them onto the empty chair next to me, her strawberry blond mane tumbled around her face as she shook her head.

"He's such a loser. Did you hear that he's calling himself a producer now?" Plopping down with outstretched arms, she arched her back and continued to rattle on. ". . . Which is such a joke because he's never had a job in his life. He's been going to clubs since he was in high school."

"Ladies, meet Alanna." Poppy smirked.

"Oh my God—sorry!" The hammered metal charms hanging from the cord wrap bracelet chimed quietly as she covered her mouth in embarrassment.

"I'm just so, like, whatever you know?"

Bemused, both Brooke and I gave her friendly smiles as Poppy picked back up to the conversation at hand.

"He *did* fuel funds into some indie film I guess. *Head Shop,* I think it's called . . . heard people talking about it the other night," she said of the stoner comedy a couple of Med's friends had written and directed.

"*Another* pathetic attempt to elevate his status quo," Alanna's pedicured toes—crammed into a pair of snake-embossed gladiator sandals—curled tensely as she watched Med flirtatiously wrestle Lexy into his arms.

"Awwww . . ." Brooke cooed, oblivious to Alanna's not-so-subtle implications, watching now as Lexy, whose face made it clear that she was enjoying every bit of Med's attention, squealed and wriggled herself teasingly from his grasp. "They're so *cute* together though."

"He's so *Hollywood* now," Poppy mused, trading her regular cigarettes for one of Osaka's.

"A total disaster—on a scale from one to ten of disgusting-

ness, I'd give him an eleven point five." Alanna whisked the
joint from Poppy's fingers and pressed it hard to her lips. Poppy
gave Alanna a look as if to say that her comment was a bit harsh.
"I just don't trust him."

In between deep coughs Poppy explained, "Guys out here—
they're only looking out for themselves Alanna—all tryin' to
get a piece of the pie, ya know?"

"Yeah but people change once they get out here, it's inevitable," Alanna huffed. Her comment made me think of David.
Would he really call me? He seemed unfazed by the typical
Hollywood male deal, but then again the girls always flocked
to him. That double dose of big-boobed bimbos, his karaoke
partners from last night, were just two out of who knows how
many. And he *had* taken Jessica Rader out on that date. I knew
all this about men out here, hell—I'd lived here my whole life.
David seemed different, but what did I possibly have to offer
that Jessica didn't? I was probably delusional to think I had a
prayer with him.

Poppy stopped to flash a peace sign to a girl in a flowered
sundress passing by. "Tomorrow night it's on—for sure . . ." she
called after her.

"Everyone has an agenda in this town," Alanna continued.
"They all want to climb to the fucking top—so they keep
climbing and fucking, climbing and fucking."

It was clear from Brooke's face that she *didn't* know and seeing
this. Poppy sat up from her chair to put things in plain English
for her. "I've been in the club business for a long time and I've
met some great people that turn to ugly people overnight. It's
like this—these guys, they sorta blind you, right? They'll tell
you anything you want to hear . . ."

"And the next thing you know *bam!*" Finishing Poppy's
thoughts, Alanna clapped her hands together loudly for effect.
"They get what they want from you and then it's time for an

upgrade—someone more powerful. Trust me. Love—even *money*—aren't even components in the real world that is Hollywood romance." She let out a long sigh, making it clear that her transition from New York model to California movie star wasn't going as smoothly as she had expected.

Contrary to what outsiders and newcomers thought, Hollywood is the easiest place to fall in love. There are many ways—with a handsome stranger, with opportunity, even with yourself. In this megalopolis of the culturally elite there are many beautiful, maladaptive people who use drugs, alcohol, or sex as crutches to maintain the grandiose visions they have of themselves. That's why they require excessive admiration and that's why there are so many seventy-two-hour marriages. All the beautiful backdrops, the beaches, the hills—they all aid the illusion of romance. Falling in love was impossible *not* to do here. The key is the nearly undetectable line between love and infatuation. Finding the real deal, amid so many inflated egos—that was the real challenge. I sensed my input wouldn't have added anything to the pity party, so I kept my mouth shut.

Now the occasional spinstress to the stars was silent as she eyed two guys trying to set up the deejay booth by the far end of the pool.

"Shit," Alanna said, springing from her chair. She looked back at take-charge Poppy for help. "It's not supposed to go there."

Pulling herself from her chair to save the day, Poppy trotted around the pool, waving her hands excitedly. Lagging just behind her, Alanna swerved to dodge T-Roc, who was ambling back over to us with a plateful from the barbeque.

I laughed as he saved himself from stumbling into the pool before Brooke piped up in a nervous voice.

Brooke lit a cigarette, her mind still on our conversation. "Wow. Well, I'm real glad Jesse is from Mississippi then!" Brooke exhaled, shifting her energy she called out to T-Roc, who was wiping the brown barbeque residue from his fingertips, "Hey T! Will you get me some?"

As the day turned to dusk, the party stayed hot. On the other hand, T-Roc, who wore heat-absorbing black from head to toe, was finally able to cool off.

Med had gone from teasing Lexy to downing Johnnie Walker Gold straight from a bottle on Osaka's table. He had replaced his headband with one of the Youngs' pink beach towels, wrapping it around his head like a turban. "Yo, Brooke!" Med suddenly yelled out as if he knew we were talking about him. "Get your ass over here."

Everyone wanted Brooke's company. She obliged and sat herself down at the table between Osaka and Med. Osaka, whose real name, as it turned out, was Kevin Brown, was a fashion school dropout who sported a faux hawk and dressed his friends in his eclectic signature pieces, which included tube dresses made from trash bags and track suits with ironic sayings in puffy paint. The line was total crap, but the good news for his fashion career was that he was a rich kid from Beverly Hills with famous friends—and that's all that matters in today's world of fashion—it's not who you're wearing anymore, it's who is wearing you.

"It's *Barber Shop* set in Hollywood man . . . with like bongs and shit . . . dopeness." Med talked up *Head Shop* while Osaka fumbled nearby, fishing something out of his pocket.

Turning the empty beer bottle he'd been drinking out of on its side, he rolled it over a tiny plastic bag on the table. A conspiratorial smile crept across Lexy's face as she joined the table. Apparently the opportunity to sponge recreational drugs off Osaka had somehow dissipated her annoyance with Med. She got right down to business, pulling her hair back into an uncompromising ponytail and laughing as Osaka fumbled over a magazine scattered with stark white powder. He tried unsuccessfully to arrange it into lines. Finally, he let Med take over. They watched as he snorted a line and passed it to Lexy. She fervently did her own line and gave her head a lofty toss before handing it to the other girl. Then, Med passed it to Brooke.

"It's your party." Med smiled at her, motioning to the fluffy white lines spread across the latest edition of Hollywood's top tabloid, *Scoop*. The cover's barely out-of-focus photo—taken from a hidden vantage—revealed a backstage shot of Brooke smiling fondly as she leaned over Jesse. He whispered something in her ear as he held her hand, but the angle made it look like he was kissing her neck.

"It's cool if you don't want—" I started, nervously looking for T-Roc, but before I could finish she was already bent over, vacuuming up the powder through a rolled-up hundred-dollar bill. She snorted the last droplets around her nostrils as if she'd done it a hundred times before. But when lifted her head, her senses began to spin; she tensed up a bit and a startled, almost-pained look crossed her face.

Nearly ten feet away, T-Roc had folded his muscular body into what now looked like a dainty pool chair. He hummed a song and turned a blind eye because, at the end of the day, he knew his place. I figured he'd been in this situation many times before with previous clients; this was the rock 'n' roll lifestyle after all. Everyone lived for the moment without yielding to consider the consequences.

Now my turn was up. I nearly choked as the powder burned and stung straight up my nose and down my throat. No one seemed to notice my lack of experience. Almost suddenly, I felt warm and everything—my heart, my breath—picked up speed as the sounds, faces, and moods in the room blurred into an electrifying collage.

* * *

Sliding just below the horizon, the setting sun cast brightly colored shades of orange and pink across the sky. As the temperature began to drop, the last of the beautiful creatures migrated to the beachfront to settle around a freshly ignited bonfire.

I stepped away from the action and made myself a spot to sit in the sand. Even though the intense burning in my throat left it numb and my nose was running like crazy, the afternoon sun blended everything together into a daydream-like haze. The hyperalertness faded into total relaxation. Chaos whirled around me, but the world seemed to drift away, as if it were merely twilight on Jupiter. Nobody seemed to mind the chill ocean air as the rollicking party sounds from earlier morphed into a low rumble of conversation and occasional bouts of echoing laughter as people moved along to the rhythm of the tides.

Drunk and coked out of his gourd, Osaka moved in and out of groups and conversations like he was on top of the world. Randomly standing up for no apparent reason at all, his loose-fitting pants would fall down around his ankles to reveal that he had nothing on underneath, prompting his friends around him to help lift them back up around his waist before sitting him back down. Every time it happened, Brooke's face turned beet-red with embarrassment. Her lips writhed in exaggerated movement as she talked to Med, whose inebriated head lolled back and forth. Free from the constraints of any "head gear," his mop of hair glistened like polished wood and lapped across his face. I couldn't begin to imagine what that conversation entailed.

Lexy, stroking her Maltese, emerged dressed in a yellow print camisole with matching velour sweatpants. "Hey beatch," she stopped to talk to a fellow brunette. "Did you see that chick throw up near the pool? What's her name? Alanna? Gro-oss."

"Stupid models. They can't keep anything down." The girl rolled her eyes in disgust before a skinny blond in billowy mock-vintage sweatshirt approached and whispered something in her ear. They both shrieked and giggled before running inside.

"H-e-e-e-y." Lexy slumped down in the sand next to me purring like a cat. "Having fun?"

"Sure." I dug my toes into the sand and watched as she pulled a dollar bill and a small baggie from a small pocket of her pants. She spilled white powder across a discarded magazine, which I recognized from our earlier round. With unexpected craftiness, she pulled out the subscription card and used it to straighten the coke into two neat lines.

"You want?" She snorted half the line and pushed the magazine and rolled-up dollar bill toward me. I held my hands up and shook my head *no*.

"I can't believe we went to high school together." She paused for a moment, snorting the remaining pearlescent powder loudly before throwing back her head. "It's like, so weird."

"Why is it weird?"

"How am I?" she asked, ignoring my question and tilting her head upwards so I could inspect the rim of her nose for any residue.

"You're fine." Not long ago Lexy couldn't recall ever meeting me; not even my name sounded slightly familiar. Like the others recently emerging from the woodwork, she knew that getting close to me meant possibly hanging out with Brooke, too. Even Poppy, the queen of the Sunset Strip, had told me—her voice completely sincere—to call her anytime and extended the most coveted invitation in L.A.—to visit one of her clubs.

Lexy's dilated pupils focused on the *Scoop* magazine she'd just cast to the ground. The wind gently fluffed her soft, light hair, and she leaned in warmly as though we were lifelong girlfriends. "Brooke and Jesse are so cute, right?

"You know," she said as if the thought had just occurred to her, "one of my girlfriends mentioned something interesting.

She was in a bathroom in one of the upstairs bedrooms last night, and when she came out she noticed something funny going on with Brooke and Ben Hart."

Hearing Ben Hart's name mentioned in the same sentence as Brooke's jolted my straying attention away from the rolling waves and back to Lexy.

"Really?" I sharply turned my head to look at her. I quickly wiped the eyebrow-raised expression from my voice and attempted to mask the telling tone of my first words. "I didn't hear *that*. She just said he was being very flirty and Brooke was, ya know, kinda responding to it . . ."

I stopped, then I feared my silence had confirmed everything. *She's no good* . . . T-Roc's warning rang in my ear. Picking up on my discomfort, Lexy changed the subject, gushing suddenly, "Oh my God! You *have* to meet my friend Zac. Totally hot and totally available."

I feigned a smile, while cringing inside. The cat was out of the bag—and I was to blame.

Chapter 10

Actually I don't know if honesty
is a strength or some kind of weakness.
–Ani DiFranco

From what little Brooke had told me, I knew Lexy had at least some sort of friendship with Jesse. Even so, I certainly didn't take it to mean he was in her gossip circle or that she told him *everything*. Two days had gone by since Lexy's soiree without a hiccup, in fact, earlier that afternoon Brooke had called me from her surprise date with Jesse at the zoo. The romantic he was, Jesse had arranged to have the whole park shut down for an hour so they could roam freely. As she clucked on and on about how all the animals were "sooo cute," I had just about convinced myself the storm had passed and I was in the clear. Later that evening, my phone rang.

"Hello?" I asked, unsure why I had suddenly broken

my own rule of not answering calls from unknown numbers.

"Hey Jackie, it's Jesse . . ."

I sucked in air and hoped he couldn't hear the anxiety he had just filled me with. I gulped loudly.

"H-h-h-i-i-i Jesse," I murmured, then, trying not to sound suspicious, added, "how was the zoo?" Only six words in, I was sure each one had given me away. *Strike one.*

"Listen, I know this is a little weird and I don't mean to just call you like this out of blue . . ."

Uh-oh . . .

". . . But I just needed to ask you something, to know something . . ."

"Mmmm . . ." I said nonchalantly though a pit was beginning to burn in my stomach. "It's just something I heard tonight . . . about Lexy's party . . ."

"It's too bad you missed it!" I said quickly trying to change the subject. "She's got such an incredible property right there on the beach!"

"Right . . ." he said.

Strike two.

"Actually, I'm talking about the one before that—Jessica's birthday party."

"Oh . . . *that* one." My heart raced. "I was so hammered that night, I barely remember a thin—"

Cutting me off, Jesse's voice turned serious. "I'm talking specifically about what you told Lexy. About Brooke and Ben Hart."

And—*strike three.* I was trapped—there was no way out of this one. I sat there in a silent storm as he started to speak again.

"Listen, I swear on my mother's life that I'll never tell a soul about this phone call," he pleaded. "Just please tell me the truth—for my own peace of mind—it's killing me."

There was a second of calm inside my head, when I guess inevitability caught up with my anxiety and cancelled each other out, if only for a moment. "Look, it was just a little kiss . . ." I pleaded, hating myself as I continued, "it didn't mean anything." I knew this would be the nail in the coffin for them. "I don't want this to affect anything for you two, she really cares about you . . ." I tried.

"Thanks for telling the truth," Jesse uttered, sounding defeated, though he had gotten exactly what he asked for. I would never be able to live down the fact that I had been the one to give it to him.

That night I didn't sleep.

Finding it impossible to relax, I woke up every time I thought I was close to being asleep—after a while I just gave up and stared at my ceiling fan. Seven o'clock rolled around and the sound of my father dragging the garbage cans out for the trash men made it impossible to consider trying any longer. The rest of the world was now awake.

Grabbing a plastic mug from the cupboard, I twisted the faucet to cold just as an odd, now pungent odor emanating from my kitchenette crept up on me. Nearly gagging, I stood there in shock as I realized just what a smelly, dirty mess my little apartment had become. Orange peels clogged the garbage disposal because, apparently, I couldn't take the time to turn it on. Weeks-old dishes sat crusted over in the sink. Dirty laundry had piled up in little mounds everywhere. But nothing was worse than my bathroom, where mold crept in the grout. Taking care of these things had become a challenge. I'd been so busy keeping up with Brooke's life, accompanying her to parties and tending to the multitude of photo shoots, that I put my own life on hold.

No small task lay ahead of me. I pulled out a roll of paper

towels and some cleaner, then started sorting through a stack of mail only to be interrupted by my phone. My heart stopped as I looked down at my cell: *Incoming call . . . Green*. The main line from Steve's office—this was it.

"H-h-hello?" I asked timidly.

"Jackie?" a voice asked on the other end. *Gulp. I was done for. Steve knew I'd told Jesse.*

"Yes. This is she."

"Hey! What's going on?" The voice asked again—it sounded strangely chipper.

"N-n-nothing much . . ."

"Okay . . . something wrong?" I suddenly recognized the voice, which had been masked by my growing fear. It was David. He *had* called!

"No," I gushed, suddenly elated. "Nothing at all. How are you?"

"Great—I'm about to walk into a meeting so I have to make this quick—you got anything this Saturday?"

"I'm supposed to do something with my friend Lauren for my birthday, but not until later that night," I said reluctantly, though the grin on my face was growing so wide it almost hurt.

"A day date, huh? No worries, I'll think of something good— text me your address. I'll pick you up at noon . . ."

Noon?

"Wear long pants."

"What? Where are we going?" I asked inquisitively.

"It's a surprise . . . just be ready and oh, no flip flops or sandals . . ." And with that he hung up the phone.

My cheeks felt warm as I set my phone down on the counter. *Maybe Alanna and Poppy were cynics?* There was only one other person who'd like to see them proven wrong more than I would. I couldn't wait to tell Brooke my news. Knowing she had the morning off, I abandoned my cleaning, deciding to surprise her instead with a couple of nonfat lattes.

* * *

Climbing to the very top of the hill, I arrived with the piping hot and sloshing cups of coffee. Bright morning sunlight flooded the expansive, well-manicured property—lush, leafy avocado trees shaded a little seating area out front. Spring had most certainly arrived, and although seasonal changes in Southern California aren't exactly *dramatic*, it was nice to feel that kind of refreshment. I stopped to appreciate the surroundings and the breathtaking view before making my way to the door. My wonderment was soon interrupted by a loud *slam*! Looking up, I spotted Jesse leaving with a perturbed (or was that pissed?) look instead of the charmingly handsome expression that beamed from his posters and music videos. Without stopping to acknowledge my presence, he booked it to the driver's side of his shiny silver Lexus convertible and peeled out. *Shit.*

I entered the house, walking into absolute quiet. Along with the stark white walls and vaulted ceilings, the silence made her place feel vast and empty. I wandered through the large, split-level living room, made my way to the French doors leading out to the deck where Brooke sat Buddha-style on the flagstone terrace surrounding the pool. Strangely, she applied glitter to her eyelids with a rollerball applicator.

"Hey Brooke," I tried to sound casual, afraid Jesse had ratted me out. "What's going on?"

She sniffed, not looking up. Was she fuming at Jesse or me?

"Jesse, uh, left rather abruptly," I tried to tread lightly. Did she know? I didn't want to press too hard, but my body couldn't take the suspense. My pulse was racing. "Is everything okay?"

She rubbed the tears pooling in the corners of her eyes and continued to apply the glitter as though it would somehow cover up her sorrow.

"He . . . he . . ." Her chin trembled. Once she regained control, she began again. "He knows Jackie. He knows about me 'n Ben . . . about our little . . . ya know."

"How?" I realized I was holding my breath as I nervously sat down next to her.

"I don't—" she sniffled loudly before bursting out. "I don't know! He said somebody told him."

"Who would—" I stopped myself. "I mean—did anyone *see* you together?"

"I dunno. I was in the shower and he must've gone through my phone or something." She scrunched her eyebrows together and took a deep, hard breath as she tried to gain composure. "There were texts from Ben. I knew I shouldn't have given him my number. You have to see what he sent."

Brooke thrust her phone into my palm. I could almost hear Ben's faux accent cooing seductively to her.

Aye sexy, when is yer man leavin' town? Ah wantae finish what we started the other night with that lil' snog.

"It was just a kiss," Brooke protested.

It did leave a certain impression. Before I could say anything, she continued her self-dialogue.

"He *knows* I have a boyfriend, so *why* would he do this to me?" You could practically see her mind cranking away, trying to find a remedy for her indiscretion. "I don't know why I gave him my number. I'm so, so stupid."

She momentarily sat in stunned silence before huffing, "This. Is. So. Unfair. I *loved* him, Jackie."

Stuck between my guilt and my relief, I tried to comfort her. I never wanted it to come out this way. It just happened. I sat down and listened—keeping my mouth shut about my own good news—putting it on hold—just like my dirty dishes and piles of smelly clothes—for a more convenient time.

Chapter 11

> If you come to fame not understanding
> who you are, it will define who you are.
> –Oprah Winfrey

Whispered among the paparazzi holding court on Los Angeles stretches and speculated on celebrity blogs outfitted with unflattering photos, word that pop music's golden couple had broken up spread like wildfire. As pressure from the media increased, Steve commanded everyone in Brooke's camp to remain tight-lipped until, as he put it, "We've got this thing figured out."

Sasha and her P.R. minions at the record label released a vague statement to the press on Brooke's behalf, hoping it would quell some of the heat. It ended up being so vague that it only redoubled the pressure, prompting a second onslaught of phone calls that ultimately went unreturned. Not one to sit paralyzed while his phones rang viciously off the hook, Steve began strategizing immediately—calling all of Brooke's handlers into his office one afternoon shortly after word had spread. Located in one of the few really tall buildings on the Sunset Strip beside a cluster of luxury hotels, couture boutiques, and trendy eateries, the energy inside Steve's office was dizzying as we all scrambled for ideas to amp up Brooke's image. This meant hair, makeup, clothing, of course—but there was much more involved in creating a revamped, overall public perception.

As I breezed in, David slipped away from Steve and sidled up to me with a sly grin. "Guess who got promoted to junior manager?"

"David, that's great!" I gave his shoulder a squeeze. "You move fast. Any plans to celebrate tonight?"

"Actually, I'm working on signing this girl I saw playing at Hotel Café the other night—twenty years old, cute brunette, very artsy—writes her own music—she's going to be huge. I'm meeting her tonight over dinner." The way his eyes lit up, I felt like a plain Jane in comparison. How could I possibly keep his interest now?

"Hey Davie. I heard the news. Congrats bro." Erik, another junior manager bounded over and slapped him on the back. "Oh man. This day's intense."

He thrust a finger in Steve's direction. "I would love nothing more than to sock you in your fat face you dumb fuck," he said before turning back to David. "Okay, so what about getting a hold of that publicist . . . you know, the one for that hot Canadian songbird? Nah, you're too busy. I'm on it bro." Having answered his own questions, his hyperactive, caffeine-or-cocaine–addled gaze fell on his reflection in the window behind me. Then, I shit you not, he nodded at himself and said, "Yep. I look awesome." With one more aggressive pat on David's back, he flew off.

"Seriously?" I turned to David, hoping that wasn't his future.

"Dude. Am I too A.D.D. right now? Am I? I am. Totally," David mocked. I laughed. "Honestly though—dude's intense, but he really gets shit done. Definitely got a bright future in this business."

"What the hell are you doing? We have a crisis on our hands." I overheard Steve bark at someone as I joined the huddle. Everyone was furiously shooting out possibilities for Brooke's "rebranding."

A few minutes into the day's Congress of Brooke, Steve interrupted the brainstorming and took a call from his office's speakerphone. The connection crackled as a caller from the record label patched through.

"Sasha is running a few minutes late," an assistant by the name of Kimmy told us. "She should be there any minute."

"Hey Kimmy—I just saw the *Times*—looks great, doesn't it?" Steve said in a voice loaded with sarcasm as he threw down the current copy of the *L.A. Times* in anger. As he paced back and forth, I could almost hear Sasha's innocent young assistant cowering on the other end.

"What have I discussed with you guys over there?" He paused in front of the speakerphone, staring at it angrily as if it were her face. When she didn't answer, he continued, "If you say 'no comment,' they are going to print 'no comment.' I don't want a peep from any individual that deals directly with my client. The release was one thing, but I don't want anyone talking to the press right now. Period." He picked the newspaper up off of his desk, just so he could slam it down again.

At that moment, Sasha sailed through the door in all her glory, talking a mile a minute on her cell phone. Steve, interrupted midseethe, waited without a trace of patience.

"So what happened with the *Times*?" he asked her when she hung up.

"Steve," Sasha shrieked as she rolled her eyes, "you are *some* piece of work. Now do you want me to share my notes? Or you just want to argue all day about some stupid reply in the *Times*?"

"By all means." Steve motioned to the front of the room as if it were a stage. "We'd love to hear your thoughts on how we're gonna crush this thing that should've never gotten so out of hand in the first place."

Discarding the large tote slung over her shoulder, Sasha nodded. "We've had countless meetings, lemme tell you, and many a suggestion—I think it comes down to this: everyone is focused on her love life right now. What we need is a distraction. Nothing crazy—just a new guy around so they quit trying to dig up dirt on Jesse and start digging on a new one. What we've come up with could be beneficial for all parties involved and would do wonders to deflect any more mentions of the breakup."

Sasha took a breath before continuing, "We've been thinking about Lou Jersey. He's just starting to blow up right now and since he's new to the label, it would be great exposure to get him in some shots with Brooke," she hummed, referring to the newest white rapper, Louis Winter—"the best since Eminem" reviewers touted—whose stage name paid homage to his Jersey Shore birthplace. "They'll take one look at the two of them— *voila!* . . . pictures everywhere—Jersey could end up doubling his fanbase, Brooke's bad press would be cut in half, and we're golden."

Steve needed only a moment to process the idea before everyone could see his shoulders slowly unclench. "This," he began dramatically, "could be *huge*. It could be a whole new thing for Brooke." Now Steve, obviously more than just intrigued, hung on Sasha's every word as she continued.

Every time she made a point he thought was particularly good, he peered down to the end of the table where David was furiously scribbling notes, asking him, "You got that?" Hardly having to look up from his notepad, David kept up with affirmative nods. He had a genius way of handling Steve, who was impossible to handle. David always listened to every word Steve said, never letting on that he was actually thinking for himself, even if he knew, in the end, he was going to get something done his own way.

Once Sasha finished, Steve rambled his thoughts back to her—though it seemed as if he were very much inside his own head. I have to say it was amazing, though equally disconcerting, to watch Steve plot out Brooke's life without her consent. "Hey—you never know, this could set her up as one-half a new, solid power couple. . . ." Thinking some more, he muttered, "It will give her versatility . . ." Finally looking up at Sasha, he smiled. "I like it—let's set up an introduction." And that was that, meeting adjourned. Once Steve latched on to the idea put forth by Sasha and Rain Shine, things moved quickly. Nearly a week later, Lou stopped by the recording studio to meet Brooke. Greeting her with a gangsta-esque handshake she fumbled trying to reciprocate, they chatted politely and listened to playbacks. Like an automatic reaction, the beats from the playbacks sent his legs into a frenzy—tapping loudly on the floor as he nodded his head to the beat. Even though Sasha had spent some time giving Brooke the rundown on Lou, she admittedly knew very little about him, not that he seemed to mind. Whipping out his iPhone, Lou gladly gave her a photo tour of his personal and professional history. Scrolling through pics of his "homeboys" in Jersey, carefully crafted promo shots that made him appear extra "shady," and a few self-snapped portraits that showcased the six-pack hutting from the low slung pants of his tracksuit—it was the perfect excuse to show off as far as Lou was concerned. Interacting with Brooke, a sly smile was plastered across his face—he hardly came across as the angry-faced menace to society that the record label portrayed him as. Afterwards, numbers were exchanged and arrangements were made for them to meet the following evening. Seated at a cozy table for two overlooking the ocean, they appeared more like friends catching up over a meal, more of a business dinner than a romantic first date. Although, for Brooke it involved more drinking than dining, she giggled a lot, trying to be cute, and spoke in a high, girlish voice while Lou politely listened. After two hours, Brooke was drunk and the conversation began to wane. Before parting ways they hugged; paparazzi photos were released showing them together, and soon the dating rumors began to spread. The plan was set in motion.

"So, you're taking me to see the Hollywood sign?" I'd been playing the guessing game with David since he'd picked me up for our mysterious date. While Brooke was in La Jolla for the weekend with the increasingly smitten Lou Jersey, I finally had some time off.

"Maybe. Maybe not." He shrugged as he turned onto Beachwood Canyon where the iconic sign came into view. Wearing an old pair of jeans, patched in several spots from years of use, and an old gray cotton neck tee bearing his alma mater in lieu of his usual business casual attire, David was slightly scruffy and incredibly handsome.

In front of us, a cluster of tourists and Los Angeles newbies alike stood beneath the palm trees, leaves like fingers radiating from an open hand soaring high over the street, welcoming them to live out their California dreams. With a couple more clicks of their cameras, they fled to the shoulder, allowing us to pass.

"Let me guess . . . you want to hike up there and touch it . . . to commemorate your big promotion. So you can know that you've really arrived," I chuckled.

"Oh believe me, I feel like I've arrived, that's for sure. Steve's put me through the ringer," he said, wide-eyed.

"I can believe that," I told him as I looked away to roll my eyes.

"Do you know that he used to make me climb two flights of stairs to fetch him a Coke out of the refrigerator . . . *that was next to his desk*?!" David laughed and shook his head. "And that's not even the worst of it . . . don't get me started on the paper shredder and the cooking oil."

"What?"

"Let's just say we used to have a lot of issues with people in our office who liked to jam too much paper into the shredders at once . . ."

"Well, it's nice to know you didn't sleep your way to the middle," I joked.

"Oh, that's so Hollywood, right? Eventually I can stop pimping myself out to get ahead," he teased. "Working for Steve, it's been a great start, or at least, a healthy learning experience, but I plan on breaking out on my own within a few years."

"You'll get there," I said, "then you'll be just like Steve." I stopped myself. Kidding or not, I didn't want to lump David in with him in any sense beyond professionally. His sarcastically angry smirk made me chuckle. "Well, you better not turn out like Steve."

"Ha—not planning on it, but say what you will about the man, he's good at what he does."

Not wanting to spend another second of the day think about Steve, I steered the subject back from the tangent. "So, are we here for a picture? Or are we going for the big hike?"

"Um, both. I mean neither—what?" he joked back. "I mean as a *man*, I would have to, of course, choose the hike . . ."

"So, you scared then? Are you chickening out?"

"No . . . it's just—these shoes I've got on—you know, they

just don't have the best arch support." He grinned, thinking he was pretty funny now. "They don't, how do I say it? They don't provide the kind of cushioning and stability I so desire while walking for miles up steep and rocky terrain."

"Good," I said gazing up at the big white letters in front of us. "Because it's illegal anyway."

I started to wonder if the feeling of having arrived applied less to David and more to myself. Like the palms that stood a close distance apart, their barrel-shaped trunks never meeting, my life, up until this point, had always run parallel to the glitz and glam of Hollywood. So separated from that world and by such a small gap, I was no different from those who stood outside my window, documenting the moment they stood at the cusp of their new adventure.

"I thought you were a risk taker—somewhat of a badass." He smiled.

"Really? What made you think that?" I said, wrinkling my nose.

"They do call you Calamity Jackie, don't they?"

"Ugh, I *hate* that," I huffed in disgust. "Okay. So what *are* we doing, then?"

"Chill, Calamity," he teased as we neared the upper reaches of Mt. Lee's rugged hillside. "You'll find out soon enough."

After passing through a set of gates at the end of the street, he pulled off to the right and parked. Directly under the Hollywood sign was a giant metal arch with a horseshoe that read: Sunset Ranch. Beyond it was a sprawl of land with barns and grazing horses.

"How did you find this?" I asked.

"I feel like I've *seen* this place before—don't you?" A devilish smirk spread across David's face as he turned off the engine and hoisted himself from the car.

I shook my head—of all the hobbies I'd taken my hand to

as a kid, horseback riding hadn't been one of them. "I've lived here my entire life and I've never—" Spotting an old red barn to my left I stopped short. Déjà vu washed over me. *I knew that barn—but from where?* Turning to David I searched his eyes suspiciously.

"I'll give you a little hint . . . it has something to do with arguably the best songwriter and guitarist—"

"Shut up!" I gasped, cutting him off. *The* Guitar *magazine cover shoot with Ric Craia—the issue I'd had with me in Saratoga Springs—he had remembered!* We stood in silence for a few seconds as I traced the precise framing of the cover and inside spread—picturing the horse with bold white head markings that stood slightly out of focus behind him. The guitar clutched in his work-toughened hands. The crinkly-eyed grin against his blue plaid print Levi's shirt with pearly snaps down the front.

"You are unbelievable . . . you know that?" I practically screamed with excitement after David, no longer forced to keep his little secret, burst into mischievous laughter.

I couldn't believe it. This was quite literally one of the most thoughtful things anyone had ever done for me. But just as I started to get all googly-eyed, a nagging voice reminding me of what both Alanna and Poppy had said about dating in L.A. brought me crashing back down to earth. I hated to believe David could be anything but the sweet guy who put so much thought into our outing. I quickly dismissed the thought as we made our way to the stable.

Any worries I had for my hair with the dusty riding helmet we'd been forced to wear had dissolved the second I lowered myself onto the horse. The white Appaloosa I found myself saddled on went by the name of Herbie, and the ranch hands had all sworn to me he was the most unlikely to cause any trouble. Surprisingly, he was even easier to control than expected.

With sloping shoulders, Herbie followed after the horse who led the way, his strong hindquarters colored in spots powered up the rocky terrain. But every time I started to feel comfortable, relaxing the muscles I'd held so stiff and tight, without fail Herbie would become a little gutsy, veering off to walk on the edge of the trail. Nervous we'd meet the company of a mountain lion at any minute, I'd have to drive him back on course.

We'd almost completed the first leg of our trek when the wrangler stopped just as we crested a ridge, allowing us to take in the panoramic views of the city. Over the hill, at the midpoint of the trip, lunch awaited us. Eager to hop off Herbie's back and get my feet planted firmly back on the ground, the nervousness in my stomach was replaced with growling hunger pains that reminded me just how famished I was.

Off in the distance, the Pacific glistened in the midday sun. Dismounting his horse, David held the reins in his hands as he ambled over to me.

"I never miss New York on days like this," David said, closing his eyes and breathing in the sweet, fresh scent of eucalyptus.

"Yeah, how is L.A. treating you by the way? You're so busy all the time. It's been a couple of years, but have you even had a chance to enjoy it?"

"Well." David grinned. "I'm enjoying the fact that my rent's now more affordable—so I guess that's a bonus."

"Yeah. That's it?" I found myself wanting to know more and more about him.

"Well, there's more space I guess. And I even get a little overhang thingy to park under, not to mention having a car." He paused as if trying hard to think of more. "You know, and the weather is a lot nicer too—I even have a swimming pool. Of course it's a little dilapidated, and the landlord never leaves, he's poolside all day with a parrot on his shoulder. No joke."

"Sounds nice," I said laughing. I suddenly felt his free hand grip my unsuspecting hand—his voice now serious.

"No. It is. There's a different vibe out here. Like, when I was a kid, my dad worked on Wall Street. He was never around, so I always felt the need to impress him when he was. He always thought I should and would follow in his footsteps and become a stock broker, but I didn't want that lifestyle." I nodded as we both peered out at the city spread out around us, at peace. Any concerns I had about dating in Hollywood or even mountain lions or horses with rearing legs faded away. For fifteen minutes of my crazy life, there was just the sound of the wind in my ears—no screams from fans, clicking of cameras, or wailing sound checks—just me and the earth. I had almost forgotten how moments like that could put things in perspective—I wanted more of those, I decided.

We'd just fastened our horses securely to the hitching posts in back of the lunch spot down in the Valley, perhaps the only restaurant in Los Angeles that accommodated such guests, when my cell phone sounded loudly. I scolded myself for not leaving it in the car as I plunged my hand into the pocket of my hoodie. *Incoming . . . Brooke.*

"David," I said, "it's Brooke, I gotta take this."

He nodded, understanding. "No worries." He shrugged. "I'll grab us some chairs."

"Hello?" I asked, stepping aside with one ear plugged. To my surprise, she didn't sound very happy.

"Jackie . . . you've got to come get me."

"What? Are you okay?" I asked, concerned.

"I can't deal with Lou anymore."

"Okay—well, has he—I mean, has he done something to you?"

Without answering she rambled on, "Please Jackie, please . . . you *have* to come soon," Brooke whined breathlessly.

"Sure . . . of course I will," I said worried that maybe Lou had really started to live up to his bad-boy image. "Tell me where you're at—I'll get there as soon as I can." As much as it pained me to disrupt my picture-perfect day, I was worried about her. As all the paranoid worst-case scenarios flooded my head, I just hoped that she was okay.

Chapter 12

Deep down, I'm pretty superficial.
 –Ava Gardner

On the way to La Jolla, I felt somewhat miffed by the fact that such a relaxing and uplifting afternoon had been cut short. On the other hand, I was actually kind of worried about Brooke—I mean, Lou seemed like a nice guy and all, but Brooke sounded pretty upset. I had to say, though, most of the vibe from the day hadn't left, due largely in part to the ruggedly handsome guy who decided to tag along for the ride with me.

This guy was amazing. "Don't worry about it," he'd said after I had taken the call from Brooke, "if anyone is used to their lives being interrupted by clients, it's me—I know how it goes." We actually did have a lot in common—we both worked our asses off behind the scenes, though I certainly had a little more "face" time.

"Just promise me," he said, "the next time I call you with a surprise, you'll say yes again—at least so we can have the pleasure of being interrupted again."

I had tried to play it cool. "I dunno, I'm a busy girl . . ."

"Well in that case," he had replied without hesitation, "you want some company?"

"That wouldn't be half bad." I flashed him a sly grin. "Seriously . . . you're pretty great."

Without giving it much thought, I leaned in to give him a friendly peck on the cheek, but he turned his head and our lips locked in a rather succulent kiss.

And so here he was, sitting next to me, on the road to La Jolla. What might have been extremely frustrating was now only mildly disconcerting. Actually, if possible, it was downright pleasant.

"So Mr. Hardcore from the Jersey Shore has a mansion in La Jolla, huh? Imagine what his fan base would think if they found out how he *really* spends his time—golfing and sipping cocktails with his sophisticated friends," David laughed as we headed south down the canyon.

"It's not *his*, it belongs to some loaded playboy type with deep pockets—he's got this sporting goods empire and a bunch of other things, apparently—I guess he's launching this line of low rider bicycles or something and he wants Lou to help design them."

"Just what the world needs—wanksters patrolling the streets on sets of Jersey-style chrome wheels," sighed David. "What kind of idiot would pump money into something like that."

"Some idiot named Richard Bernau," I replied.

"Richard Berneau?? You can't be serious," David said, suddenly shocked. I just shrugged; I had no idea who the guy was.

"Berneau is a self-made billionaire! He made a fortune after founding this private equity firm years ago . . . he's the guy behind all those over-the-top subdivisions with names like 'Whispering Pines' and 'Serenity Oaks' that started popping up all over Southern California." I just shrugged again.

"Oh man!" David laughed again as we merged onto the highway entrance ramp. "I can't believe we're going to Richard Berneau's house . . . this guy's notorious for banging Hollywood starlets, that's why he's always making pals with guys like Lou Jersey—offering them opportunities to 'brand themselves,' so he can get into cool parties and meet his next conquest."

Seeing a big-rig and cars clogging the southbound thoroughfare, his wide-eyed smile dissipated. "How long you think it will take us to get there?"

"I don't know," I muttered uncertainly. The last time I'd been to La Jolla was in the eleventh grade when Lauren, in her surfer-chick phase, would drag me down there on the weekends. "My friend Lauren used to bring me down there all the time for Alchemy Hour," I said wistfully.

"Alchemy Hour? I didn't know you were into wizardry?" David craned his neck backwards as he changed lanes.

"No . . . no . . ." I laughed.

"Mixing up elixirs and potions in your spare time? It's cool, you don't need to hide your true colors . . ." he continued on, elbowing me playfully.

"No, it's a surf thing . . . we used to go down to this beach where all the wannabe surfers hang out on the weekends— Lauren used to call the swell there magical." I laughed to myself at the absurdity of our teenage days. "We were *such* posers, but you know, we thought we were really cool. I could never get up on the board."

"You? But you've got such poise," David said with a sarcastic grin.

I started thinking of those carefree days—Lauren in her girly pink rashguard and me in baggy boardshorts as we navigated the ultra-crowded beach looking for cute boys and pretending we knew exactly what we were doing. A guilt-ridden feeling unexpectedly mushroomed in my gut. *Lauren*. She'd left me a few messages over the past week that I hadn't yet returned—along with the two emails that sat unopened in my inbox. Mid-terms, finals, new friends, new crushes—no matter what, we spoke every other day—sometimes more—even when I was away at college. But I'd been so crazed over the last week and anything that wasn't Brooke-related was just too much for me to handle.

Nothing I could do about it for the time being, I just needed to remember not to ignore her for too long. After a few miles of crawling traffic, the lanes finally cleared and we made it to La Jolla in no time.

The Berneau chateau sat high above the rugged, sandy coastline in northern La Jolla, in an exclusive, palm-lined neighborhood. I fished for the piece of paper where I'd scribbled down the address Brooke had given me.

"There it is, on your left," I said as the house came into view. Both David and I were quickly rendered speechless; neither of us had ever seen anything quite like it, not even Lexy's Malibu resort.

Bougainvillea sprawled up the walls of the Mediterranean-style mansion—in the natural light of the sun the papery shades of magenta, purple, and white almost looked like stained glass. A wall of floor-to-ceiling glass doors off the living room had been left open, allowing the salty ocean breeze to waft in. David turned back and looked at me like a little kid who was about to be scolded at any moment, mouthing *Oh my god*. Taking charge, I nodded towards the doors before making my way out to the multilevel limestone terrace overlooking the bluff. Directly in front of us was an L-shaped infinity pool that seemed to extend out into the horizon, creating a seamless border between water and land. Near the far right corner of the pool, two men sat at a rectangular rattan table beneath a cherry-red umbrella that shaded them from the sun. Brooke, clad in a tie-dye crochet bikini, lounged on a red-and-white–striped double chaise on the opposite side. Lathered in Hawaiian Tropic Dark Tanning Oil, she kicked a pair of dirty wedge flip-flops carelessly to the side, hoisting a knee to her chest. From where she sat, she looked bored; I could tell from the way she impassively puffed on the cigarette dangling between her lips. Without removing it from her mouth, she unscrewed the top off a bottle of nail polish and lazily began coating her toes in a metallic blue shade.

"Aw, look, she's multitasking her cancers," David sighed sardonically. I snickered and gave him a playful jab in the ribs. He grimaced, feigning injury. "Hey, that hurt."

"May I help you?" a regal voice called out suddenly, causing my heart to drop down to my gut. I spun around to find an older man who was unbuttoning the cuffs of his white linen tennis blazer, standing behind a bar.

"We're here to pick up Brooke," I said, pointing in her direction.

"Wonderful. Can I get you anything to drink?" he asked, dipping a cocktail shaker into the ice chest.

"I'm good . . ." I said, my voice trailing off as Brooke, who had just noticed us, waved happily before sprinting around the pool to greet us.

"Omigawd," she mouthed to me. Clearly, she wasn't expecting to see both of us together and the way she was awkwardly staring at us with her mouth gaping open was David's cue to turn the other cheek. "What is *he* doing here? Did you guys like go on a date or somethin'?"

I started to blush, reflecting on my day before snapping back to reality. Temporarily blinded by the mystique of Chateau Berneau—a mistake, I told myself, that could happen to anyone—I now looked every which way for signs of danger.

"Wait—wait—wait. Let's talk about *you*. What happened over the weekend?"

"Oh," she moaned, rolling her eyes for affect. "Nothing much. We went boating and drank a lot of wine. If it had been a little hotter I might have actually got some color." I grabbed the arm that Brooke was inspecting so closely.

"Who's that?" I asked, my attention drawn to the jet-black and tan minpin. Decked out in a purple angora sweater embellished with sequins, it stared intently at Brooke with its dark, ovular eyes and stood on its hind legs while pawing at her right knee.

"Oooh. This is Ginger," she beamed down, patting the dog on its head. "Lou helped me pick her out. Isn't she sooooooo cute."

"You got a dog?" I looked at her quizzically, but as if she hadn't heard me, she kept on petting Ginger. "Adorable." I needed to steer things back to the task at hand: our rescue mission. "Okay . . . so what happened to make you want to leave so urgently?"

Her eyes widened as a huge grin crossed her face. "I can't believe I almost *for-got* to tell you! Duh . . ." Making a fist, she playfully clobbered herself in the head. She tensed up in excitement, bobbing up and down on the balls of her feet, before leaning down to whisper in my ear.

"Ben called earlier. He wants to take *me* to his dad's red carpet movie premiere tonight! Can you believe it?" she asked, not pausing long enough for me to answer. "So that's why we need to leave as soon as possible."

I tried to digest this—more shocked than angry. Did David and I really abandon our lunch and practically abandon our horses, our day, for *this*? I couldn't be mad at her. The very idea of being invited to a movie premiere at all, let alone walk the red carpet with one of the world's sexiest men, was exciting in and of itself. Still, as I glanced over at the guys—relieved to find that David had been taken under the wing of Richard "Dick" Berneau himself—I thought of the absurdity of the situation too.

"You know that Lou is going to find out when you walk that carpet with Ben, right?" I said.

"Oh, I don't care—I already told him that we have a shoot tonight. Let's just grab David and—"

But it was too late. Strutting towards us in a pair of silk and tencel pants with golf tees sticking out of the right-hand pocket, a paisley medallion-print long-sleeve linen shirt, and croc-embossed driving moccasins on his feet, Dick had his sights set on making us a part of the party.

"Hello, you two. Please, have a drink," Dick insisted before hollering in his thick, Philly accent at the man in the white jacket, "Bring 'em both one, will ya? And I'd like some water actually."

His fitness clashed somewhat with his deeply weathered skin and full, wavy gray hair and eyebrows, belying his age as he grinned constantly, apparently energized by the youth surrounding him. He couldn't look more opposite of Lou, who remained seated to his right in baggy velour pants, short-sleeve shirt patterned with Gucci's signature double Gs, heavy platinum chain around his neck. He ran his fingers through the unruly dark hair on his head, and I noticed that a friendly, down-to-earth vibe had replaced the usual stoic yet restless persona he saved for his fans.

"Yo, you gotta try one of these!" Lou added almost quietly, motioning to his drink, as he rested his tattooed arms on the table. Before we could answer, Dick exclaimed, "It's a little concoction I discovered in Macau—aged tequila, Cointreau mixed with lemongrass, lime, and ginger—fantastic!"

Within minutes, martini glasses topped with a thick layer of whipped lemongrass cream were placed in front of us, along with a silver tray containing toast points and a seafood dish made with eggs, cayenne pepper, sherry, and cognac.

"Boy did you come at a good time, I love me some Lobster Newberg!" Dick said quickly, rubbing his hands together in exaggerated excitement.

David lifted his glass, "Cheers to Jackie; it's her birthday!"

My cheeks blushed as everyone raised their glasses and indulged me in the nicest round of the happy birthday song I'd ever heard.

While we nibbled away at the decadent snack, Lou entertained us with funny stories about his two-year stint as a grocery-store bag boy—his first job when he landed bright-faced and starry-eyed in Southern California. Dick gushed on and on about how completely smitten he was with Brooke. "That girl's the shot of adrenaline the pop scene's needed. I mean look atta way she's turned it around. Genius, I tell ya. Genius!"

"Absolutely," Lou concurred, "most pop music has always bored me, but Brooke," he said, looking over at her coyly, "you really have given a legit voice and gorgeous face to pop again. You're gonna be the new Madonna!"

I was blown away to hear Lou give Brooke such an incredible compliment, as I knew she adored Madge, but I must say I was equally blown away by how little she reacted to it. Hardly a smile, hardly an acknowledgement; another puff of her cigarette, and a sip of her Macau martini.

I kicked David under the table, but when Dick gave me a weird smile, I realized it had been him I kicked—and he got the wrong idea. In an effort to avoid any lingering eye contact, I looked over to Brooke who, after wriggling into a pair of Daisy

Duke jean shorts, sat at the table with us looking antsy and bored, and a little cold. She really wanted to leave, and from the look of it, the sooner the better.

"Hey Jackie, there's these mini houses on the property that are pretty sick," Lou said, pointing to a golf cart parked nearby; he seemed to have noticed Brooke, who was failing to conceal how much she wanted to go. "I can show 'em to you guys if you want. C'mon, it's your birthday. I want to show you some fun since you came all the way up here." Brooke gave me a look of death and cleared her throat loudly, causing me to wipe the smile off my face. Lou was really growing on me.

"Oh . . . that sounds cool, but we've got to get back to L.A.; we don't want to leave!" I said lightheartedly. *It was the truth!* I realized I had really started to like Lou Jersey. He seemed like a genuinely good guy.

"Yeah, Brooke told me," he sighed smiling at her sweetly. "Bummer."

"This is pretty damn good. Have you ever tried adding tequila to a Manhattan? You use an infused cognac with it—I'm not any kind of connoisseur but it's surprisingly good." David took all eyes off of us with this hell of a conversation starter. Confident and personable, I liked how he could engage in a chummy dialogue with anyone, even in the most awkward of situations. Watching him chat with Lou, I fell even more into *like* with him.

"Excuse us." I left David at the table while Brooke and I made our way inside. Once there, I pulled Brooke into one of the lavish marble bathrooms to try and talk some sense into her.

"Oh, Jackie. I'm like the worst friend *ever*! Your birthday? And I totally forgot." Brooke made a pouty face. "I promise I will make it up to you. I've just been stressing this Lou situation."

I stopped her right there.

"I really like Lou, he's cool. Why do you want to do this to him?" Brooke twisted her face in annoyance. "He called you the new Madonna!"

"We've only known each other for about a week now and he's sending me all these text messages talkin' about our *grandchildren . . .*"

"What?" I said, shaking my head in disbelief.

"Here—look at this." Brooke plunged her hand into the pocket of her mini shorts and pulled out her cell phone. Scrolling through it she pulled up a message and held it out to me eagerly.

> I know this is crazy n that we just met but
> I'm falling in < 3 wit u n we r gonna tell
> this story to r grandkids 1 day.

"Holy shit," I said, "you really made quite the impression on America's biggest badass."

"I just slept with him a couple times and he's real obsessed with me."

A couple times? It's been a week!

Looking stressed, she continued in an almost pleading voice. "I really gotta go, I can't handle this anymore. I really want to go out with Ben."

Sure Lou's message was a little intense, but he was so kind and friendly. You couldn't blame the guy for falling head over heels for a gorgeous girl like Brooke.

"Oh, don't mess this up." I shuddered as the mental image of Ben yelling drunkenly at partygoers he thought were messing around with him, *"An then yer arse fell aff!"*

"Just . . . think about it . . ." My voice trailed off as she turned toward the door. I knew it was useless because all of the things that Lou *pretended* to do, Ben really *did*—month-long benders, threesomes with strippers, drug-induced brawls. And

Brooke, always in search of the authentic in her manufactured and manipulated world, wanted a *real* bad boy. She wanted someone who defied all the rules and who could break her free of all the constraints that she felt so stifled by. America's reluctant sweetheart, Brooke Parker wanted someone who would take her along for the ride.

I realized I wouldn't make it in time to meet Lauren. I figured we could reschedule the dinner-movie date for another night. "Stuck in La Jolla. Drama with Brooke. So sorry." I sent her a text as we stepped out into the hallway, hoping to make a clean escape. My birthday, my date with David, like so many other things, they'd become all about Brooke. I mouthed to her, *I'll text David and he'll meet us at the getaway car*—but it was too late. Just as we rounded the corner, there was Lou, with a huge grin on his face. He was carrying an extravagant-looking little bed with sheer pink fabric draped across its iron canopy and tied in place by a large pink tassel. The bedding appeared to be real silk and even included a matching dust ruffle.

"What—" My jaw dropped.

"Don't forget Ginger's bed." Lou beamed as though he were a proud father. "I could always drop it off later, too. What shoot are you guys doing tonight?"

I looked at Brooke, who stared back at me, beckoning me with her eyes to come up with something fast. *Great. Now she's making me lie.*

"Oh, just this little PSA," I said, talking out of my ass. *I'm so going to run into Lou again, and when I do, it won't be pretty.*

Red carpets. Ben the badass. Brooke the sweetheart. Tabloids ate their hearts out.

As I predicted, when he found out about Brooke's little stunt, Lou went insane. Tabloid headlines screamed things like, "New Couple Alert!" and "Recently Single Brooke In Love Again."

The accompanying photos—Brooke bright and cheery; Ben, slightly scowling but cool as ever at her side—were plastered everywhere.

Lou wasted no time. He called a dozen times in the first day, leaving threatening messages about how he was going to ruin her career for making a public mockery out of him. The next day saw twice as many calls, but just after noon, Brooke couldn't stand the ringing anymore. And the messages, which at first had made her laugh, had lost their comic effect. Five minutes later he called again; this time, she answered.

"Lou, you have *got* to stop calling . . ."

"You bitch! You lying bitch!" His voice leapt out from the phone.

"I don't know what you're talking about . . ." I was rather shocked, impressed even, by her calmness. This guy was frothing mad jumping through the phone, and she had the placid audacity to be emotionless.

"I'm gonna ruin you," I heard him shout, "when I'm through, people are gonna be burning your CDs in the streets!"

If I hadn't been so focused on Lou's echoed shouts, I could have sworn I actually saw Brooke smile knowingly at his threats. Her response wasn't exactly vicious. But it made me think: Brooke was more aware of herself and her image than I ever gave her credit for. Here was a girl I had always watched others take advantage of—but now, in a single sentence, all those memories were reduced to second guesses.

"Listen, you can say whatever the hell you want about me," she hissed, "but *I'm* America's sweetheart and, in the end, I'm gonna come up smellin' like a *rose.*"

Chapter 13

It stirs up envy, fame does.
–Marilyn Monroe

Brooke was right. In spite of her romantic entanglements, things were looking rosier than ever. The first clear sign of her soaring fame came when we got word her first album had gone platinum only six weeks after its release. And thanks to the ever-ambitious Steve Green, Brooke was raking in the cash.

She'd become bona-fide, a brand name, and Steve was leveraging her clout for every dollar it was worth. Multimillion-dollar sponsorship deals made her the spokeswoman for teen skincare companies, trendy bootwear, clothing lines, and even an international fla-vored water brand. For Steve, the metric of celebrity was measured on a scale of money earned, and Brooke now banked the kind of revenue that proved her an outrageous success in his mind.

Nipping at her well-exposed heels, of course, was Jessica Rader. Jessica's management, doing their darnedest to break her out of Brooke's shadow, pretty much copycatted Steve's ambitious marketing tactics, following the same strategies, inking rival endorsement deals. These moves only fanned the flames of the already-sweltering competition that would culminate at the Industry of Music Awards. Head-to-head in the race for Best New Artist, in what was to each of them their first awards show, both were tapped to perform. The media frenzy and the tension mounted as the big night neared.

I arrived at Brooke's hilltop abode early that day to find Robert's red Mercedes SLK already in the driveway. As I gathered my makeup bags, it hit me that in mere hours we'd be at the biggest music event of the year along with hundreds of other famous, beautiful people. Instead of watching it play out on T.V., I'd be there as a part of the action. Brooke's appearance— my work—would be under a magnifying glass. Pulling it all off thrilled and terrified me.

Robert's gregarious voice led me through the house to Brooke's bedroom where she sat, looking cozy in a Juicy Couture tracksuit, her feet in oversized fuzzy yellow slippers resting at unusual angles off of her plush four-poster bed. She looked fidgety, I decided, as I moved closer, though I couldn't blame her.

"I'm just so excited . . ." she was telling Robert, as she reached over to light a vanilla-scented candle on her nightstand. Brooke closed her eyes, inhaling deeply as its aroma wafted throughout the room. "Mmmm, this smell always relaxes me."

"What do you think of *this*?" Robert asked as he unveiled a plum-colored chiffon cocktail dress.

He had spent the day prior digging through the couture frocks that had been offered up by designers at the I.O.M. Style Studio, where herds of fellow stylists and celebrities alike all clamored to find the perfect outfit to wear to the show.

"It's—" Brooke scrunched up her face as she tried to find the right wording, "kinda boring."

Robert pulled the plastic back down over the hanger abruptly before giving her a sassy smirk. "That's why I picked up a second option, my dear." Snatching a second hanger from the top of the chair next to him, he revealed a piece that could be described as anything but boring. Underneath the plastic garment bag was another one, or so it seemed. I stared at it for a moment, my eyes for some reason unable to fully grasp the construction in front of me. My confusion quickly turned to horror as I studied what appeared to be a pale green strappy dress crafted from a garbage bag. I turned quickly to Brooke, sure she'd hate it as much as I did, but *was that a smile on her face?*

It was.

Leaping off the bed in excitement she shouted out, "I loooooove it!"

I couldn't imagine what Robert was thinking. She would surely be lampooned if she were to strut her trash-bag-wrapped curves down the red carpet. It would be a travesty equal to former grunge queen Cloud Dour's 1993 I.O.M. appearance in a plaid flannel "gown." Her career careened into oblivion due to a single bad wardrobe selection.

"I didn't know Hefty started designing dresses," I joked unable to help myself.

Robert leered at me before snapping, "It's a Ceauê escu. All of his pieces are very high-concept. This new line is made almost entirely of Tyvek. He's got a huge following."

Brooke eagerly slipped it over her head to try it on as Robert rushed to fuss over her like a mother hen. Making sure it lay just so, he stepped back, allowing her to admire her reflection in the mirror.

"It's so fun! Maybe we could do some black fishnets under-neath it?" She twirled in a circle before gazing happily over at me. "You like it?"

I breathed deeply. The get-up looked like a something a mechanic might wear to shield his clothing from oil stains—a slutty mechanic, but a mechanic all the same.

"Well, you'll certainly be protected from any hazardous ma-terials." I smiled.

"Hello, hello, hello," Steve quickly called out as he rushed into the room. Wriggling into her tights, Brooke jumped up to greet him, letting the waistband snap against her skin. Jutting one hip to the side, she threw her hands in the air as if to sing out, "Ta-da!" We all looked at him, eagerly awaiting his reac-tion. "It's . . . *cool!* You look fabulous kiddo!"

Both Brooke and Robert squealed in delight, clasping each other's hands and jumping up and down. While they were oc-cupied by their own excitement, I darted over to Steve, speak-ing to him in a hushed voice.

"Oh, Steve. Can't we *do* something?" I didn't want Brooke to be the laughingstock of the I.O.M.s. Whatever she wore might be talked about for months, especially when the tabloids were eating up the tension between her and her fellow nominee, Jes-sica Rader. Everyone would scrutinize and compare every word they spoke, whomever they talked to, and whatever they wore. I could see the spread breaking it down now: who looked more fabulous, who performed better, who won more awards. A lot rode on her wardrobe selection. "I just don't want her to get any, you know, negative press for being *too crazy.*" I smiled as "too crazy" came out of my mouth almost song-like.

"Jackie. Are you nuts? Robert's a complete professional, he's been doing this for years—I think he might know a thing or two about red carpets at this point." Steve furrowed his eyebrows, looking at me as if I were a total lunatic. Feeling both Robert and Brooke's set of eyes upon me now, I blushed.

"I don't care what anyone thinks, I like this outfit," Brooke called out carelessly and Robert just scowled. "Dressing up is supposed to be fun!"

Okay, so maybe I was wrong. What did I know about couture fashion anyway? Before working with Brooke my wardrobe largely consisted of pieces from Forever 21 and Lauren's last season hand-me-downs.

"All right," Steve said breaking the silence. "Why don't we kill two birds with one stone here. While Jackie gets started on your makeup, we'll go over some things for the press interviews tonight." Steve took a seat at the edge of Brooke's bed, swinging one leg over the other. "You're gonna shine."

As Brooke settled into the makeup chair, Steve started firing questions at her.

"Brooke, what would you like to say to the young women who look up to you?"

"Make your dreams come true?" her response sounded like more of a question. Steve hovered over her as I worked. Every time I moved he let out a sort of sigh-grunt as though I were in *his* way, but he'd never directed so much as a syllable to me. No "excuse me" or "sorry." I was invisible.

"Okay. They're going to try to ask about your love life—Lou Jersey, Ben Hart—all that B.S. If one slips past Sasha while she's escorting you down the carpet, what do you tell them?"

"No. I'm not with anyone," Brooke answered flatly.

"Good. We don't want to answer those personal questions, but in general, you need to give up a little more. Everyone wants to get to know Brooke Parker." Steve kept a cool tone, but under it all he seethed with impatience.

He continued to play reporter, asking question after question with growing intensity. Brooke, meanwhile, seemed bored and offered up lackluster answers.

"Brooke. Sweetie. You are amazing. You are gorgeous. Say it to the world! Let them inside," Steve coaxed.

After more than an hour of pulling, combing, and spraying—while Steve prepped Brooke with all the intensity of a stage mom—I secured Brooke's hair into a sleek bun with silver bobby pins.

"I love it!" Brooke smiled, twisting her head from side to side as she took a long gaze in the mirror. "Steve, look how cool Jackie did my hair—oh! And my eyes too!"

Steve, checking his cell phone for the umpteenth time, pretended not to hear.

"Well, I've gotta go. Sasha will take good care of you at arrival." He winked as he stood to his feet. "See you inside babe."

"Oooh." Robert gasped wandering over to Brooke. "So pretty."

As Brooke slipped back into her dress, Robert emerged from her closet with a dark silk Fanchon hat and presented it to her as though he were presenting the crown jewels to the Queen of England. I half expected him to bow to her feet.

"It's vintage," he cooed as he gingerly fingered the trim of netting.

Humans, with our eyes set forward in our heads, are the number-one predator in the entire animal kingdom—and on the other side of the velvet ropes, tape recorders and cameras in hand, stood perhaps the most deadly, at least in Sasha's eyes. Geese know that predators tend to return if it's easy to get prey. So there she was, Mother Goose, standing her ground to let these predators know it wouldn't be easy and that they need not come back for more.

* * *

As Brooke stepped onto the five hundred intimidating feet of scarlet carpet, Sasha stood by her side. Her expressionless face and searching eyes made it clear that anyone who messed with Brooke had to get through her first. Their intrusive questions were unwelcome.

I froze. Everything buzzed and glittered. Bleachers packed with crazed fans lined one side. Every now and then they'd break out into the song of whichever artist happened to pass by and wave. Their eyes followed each star's entourage, and they asked themselves how we got so lucky. I'd been asking myself the same thing a lot recently.

"People be crazy out here!" T-Roc boomed out. Looking dapper in a dark suit and shades, he seemed to be more on the lookout for snipers than on guard for the press.

Camera bulbs flashed continuously as we passed the photographers, who nearly climbed on top of one another to get to Brooke. They shouted her name in unison. Up ahead I noticed a leggy country-pop singer with mountain-high chestnut-brown hair who was looking coolly over her shoulder as she posed. Just in front of her an even leggier brunette appeared to be giving someone off-camera bedroom eyes. And since there wasn't anyone in her eye line, I figured that she must be posing too. Apparently posing was the one base Steve hadn't covered with Brooke yet. Brooke stood there, her legs wide open and feet pointing out to the sides in stupefaction with a big grin plastered on her face, staring straight into the cameras. Sasha worked Brooke down the line, muttering, "They'd keep you there all night long if they could."

Reaching the print reporters, waiting enthusiastically in their sections for the chance to get a quote from Brooke, Sasha turned a skeptical eye towards the line of them. She pushed her glasses down on her nose to get a better look at the names of the outlet on their markers, hurrying Brooke past ones she found too unsavory or ones that had burnt her other clients in the past.

"Brooke! Brooke! Over here," a young, coiffed woman with a Dictaphone clamped tightly in her fingers called out. Behind her, dozens more reporters swarmed, pushing each other, desperate to be chosen.

Glancing over at her skeptically, Sasha barked, "Who you with?"

"Hi," she smiled, looking momentarily relieved as she stuck out her hand. "Kat Johnston with *Citizen Weekly* magazine."

Sasha narrowed her eyes before stepping aside. "No personal questions."

The reporter pursed her lips as she scanned her list of questions. The look on her face told Sasha they were probably all personal. She scrambled to think something up.

"Well," she said carefully, formulating the question as the words came out, "it's certainly been a whirlwind year for you. Has it been difficult to adjust to living in the spotlight?"

"Hmmm . . . well, I just sit back and let God do his work . . ." Her go-to answer for any thing she hadn't rehearsed with Steve.

Sasha's next chosen reporter came forward to gather his quote. "Brooke, who are you wearing tonight? You are just glowing!"

"Awwww, oh thank you. You're so sweet!" she answered, leaving him completely at a loss. She stood there smiling and waving at everyone as though she were in a parade, when I spotted Lou Jersey strutting past. Although he refused to stop for an interview he told reporters—in a voice loud and obnoxious enough that Brooke could hear—about an after party with a "hotel room full of women." He picked out hot fans from the sidelines and requested that they meet him at the Mondrian. Sasha glared at him and motioned to cut it out for the label's sake if not Brooke's. But Brooke, however, let his obnoxious comments roll right off her back. Not even giving him the satisfaction of acknowledgment, she kept her eyes focused straight ahead and flashed a grin at no one in particular.

As Sasha grew increasingly antsy and began to push Brooke onward, Kat—inspired by this passerby—came back with a juicy one.

"You and Lou Jersey are on the same label and you've been seen together recently, are there any plans to work together?" she yelled over her fellow reporters.

At this, Sasha grabbed Brooke's arm and started to tug her away.

"Hey! It's not *personal*!" The rest groaned as if she'd just ruined it for everybody.

Once we'd survived the treacherous journey down the red carpet, we made our way backstage. As if I weren't already breathless, this sucked the air right out of me. We went through layers of security. Pudgy men with ponytails scuttled about, directing everyone as the stars themselves checked one another out and frequently looked toward the entrance to see who might appear next.

In this gathering of stunning beauty was an equally impressive collection of microphones and stage equipment. T.V. cameras and video monitors were everywhere, ready to broadcast the event live and from all angles to the millions viewing from their homes. Between everyone's swag bags and the technical stuff, I wondered how many million dollars were present backstage alone.

Assistants were everywhere, checking up on artists to make sure they were taken care of and ensuring that every detail was accounted for. Dressing rooms lined the hallways, as did green rooms filled with televisions and food.

Accustomed to this bizarre land, Sasha led us toward the press room, where the more formal, televised interviews took place. Seated primly in front of the camera sat Jessica Rader.

"I'm wearing Collette Dinnigan tonight . . ." she sighed sweetly, running her fingers down the length of her demure watercolor-floral–printed dress. The delicate-looking television host sitting next to her thrust a slender finger at the six-inch rhinestone platforms on her feet and laughed.

"Well, let's thank God you're not dancing in those things on stage tonight!"

"Right?!" She laughed. Looking up, Brooke suddenly caught her attention. "No, I'm a serious singer," she added smugly. "I've got a talent and that's my voice. I don't need to dance around and show off like that onstage, you know?" Her words were caustic, and quite obviously meant for one person and one person only—Brooke. I glanced over to see Brooke's reaction and was surprised at just how well she seemed to be handling it.

"I think too many musicians try to bring all this attention to themselves, losing sight of their craft, which is really sad," Jessica hissed on. My ears started to burn as she said this and at that moment, I think I might've been even angrier than Brooke was. "And you can forget about scandalous affairs, I want the attention to be about my *music*, not the men I go through."

I wanted Brooke to shout something out at her, to stick up for herself. How many nasty, thinly veiled remarks could she hurl at Brooke before she fought back? How could Brooke ignore the fact that she was Jessica's punching bag, scapegoat, and nemesis? She didn't bat an eyelash. It took all my willpower not to ring her neck and shout, "Find someone else to take your aggressions out on!" I looked to Sasha now, helplessly. *Couldn't she stop it? Couldn't she say something?* But like Brooke, Sasha remained calm and professional. Jessica's blatant attempt to humiliate Brooke while she stood there watching made me hate her even more than I already did.

"Unbelievable." I nudged Brooke. "Doesn't that make you just want to kick her ass on stage tonight and bring home that award more now than ever?"

Brooke simply shrugged, quiet for a moment before she spoke.

"I used to worry about what people thought about me when I was younger, but I don't really care if she doesn't like me. I'm a nice person and if she can't see that, well, that's her problem, not mine."

"I like the way you think . . . *but* . . ."

"There are so many good things in my life—and why would I spend even a second of it caring about or worrying about someone who makes me feel bad?" Brooke asked. She placed one of her freshly manicured nails in her mouth, ready to chomp as I batted her hand away from her mouth. Without missing a beat, she kept right on going. ". . . who judges—who is constantly making problems? I've got better things to do."

I stood there for a moment in shock as I listened to her rationale. *Why couldn't I be that way?* Instead of thinking about Jessica—secretly hating her, constantly comparing myself to her, wondering if David still had feelings for her—I started to think that Brooke, half-chewed fingernails and all, was far wiser than I was.

After Brooke took her turn with the T.V. reporters, Robert joined us to prepare for the performance. Heading toward the dressing room, we heard someone loud blabbing down the hall, shrieking in excitement about what a wonderful job he'd done on whatever star he'd styled that night. The schmoozing and ego stroking never ended.

"Oh, we wanted a more subtle carpet look for Jess. Everyone is always so over the top at the I.O.M.s. Scaling it down is the very best way to make a statement these days. Don't you think?"

Realizing that the second loudmouth of the night happened to belong to Jessica Rader's stylist—*of course it did*—I sighed audibly first, surprised to hear Robert groan loudly right behind me.

"You know that guy?" I asked whipping around to face him.

"Case Nixon." He squinted his eyes.

"Not a big fan of Jessica's stylist, huh?"

"I despise him. I dated that little hyena years ago . . . when we broke up he left with my collection of Leif Garrett albums *and* my biggest client." He shuddered bitchily. The way he stressed the chain of events—making each sound equally drastic—I wasn't sure if it was the big client, the breakup itself, or the Leif Garrett collection that pained him the most.

I took a long look at Case as we passed him, in all his bragging glory. *Ah.* Brooke's garbage pail couture made more sense now. Case was risqué. His whole notorious reputation was built on getting his clients to take a chance—even if it landed them on the worst-dressed lists. They got attention for *attention's sake.* Robert wanted to outdo the lover who'd jilted him. Ironically, Case took an uncharacteristically conservative approach.

"Well . . . between the both of us, I think Brooke's going take home a haul tonight and have everyone talking tomorrow. Frankly, I think Jessica's schtick is a snooze-fest." I tried to encourage Robert, understanding his contempt.

To my surprise he looked over at me with a grin. "Totally. Brooke is going to look so fucking fabulous it will have that little tramp crying her tits off! Let's do this girl."

And fabulous *she was.* I brushed Brooke's lids with sparkly black powder while Robert put together the pieces of a showgirl-inspired costume—metallic fringe on the bottoms and rhinestones on the straps of the tank top. Long aubergine gloves elongated her arms. It wasn't hard to make Brooke look stunning, and now her big moment had arrived.

All eyes backstage were plastered on the monitors for her highly anticipated performance. As the house lights came down, the four huge light trusses that flanked the stage began to glow—softly at first before bursting into bright, blinding colors. Brooke dangled from the rafters, singing as she was slowly lowered to the stage. The tight gold outfits showed off the lean muscle mass of the dancers behind her as they moved in synchronized motions on the risers of various heights behind her. Her voice rang out, receiving gasps from impressed viewers. Her curves packed a punch with each power-infused move.

"Go baby girl!" T-Roc practically screamed out as he watched the monitors backstage—his voice nearly cracking like an adolescent. "I knew she was gonna tear it up like 'dis! It's the only way she knows how." Throwing an elbow into me—a light nudge if not for his massive stature—I nearly fell over into Robert and we both laughed as T-Roc fumbled to apologize for his excitement. It seemed like *we*, all of us behind her, were more excited about Brooke's talent than even she was sometimes. I continued to smile as I watched the rest of her performance.

It was unfortunate, I thought, as I watched her shimmy and shake. In the way that I never really connected with the sexpot on the stage, I knew the millions of viewers around the world that were watching her now would never be able to connect to the girl that *we knew*. They'd never see her giggling in hysterics with Robert, wrestling around with T-Roc on the living room floor, or watch her as she sat in my chair—making funny faces and musing about God, philosophy, and the psychics she often called. But she finished her number with a bang—rousing audience members to literally stand up and shout—I realized that Brooke touched people in a way Jessica Rader never could, no matter *what* she represented or *whom* she represented it to. She *was* America's sweetheart and no matter what Jessica or anybody else had to say about her, she really was going to come up smelling like a rose.

As Jessica prepared to take the stage, we were all in high spirits. Judging from the crowd, Brooke was the clear favorite. There wasn't a doubt in any of our minds that Jessica could top her now.

"Let's see this little bitch try to outdo Brooke," Robert chortled as we gathered around the monitors once again, ready to take delight in what was sure to be Jessica's flop of a performance.

"She might as well just git herself off the damn stage and take her ass home. What's the point? There ain't no damn statchu's with her name on 'em . . . our baby girl's takin' 'em all home with her," T-Roc howled.

"Shhhh! Guys! It's starting!" I pointed out excitedly.

The stage was recreated to look like the streets of Versailles, greatly contrasting with the uber-seductive publicity stills— used to shamelessly plug Jessica's upcoming album release—that flashed on the screens above the stage. One was cropped close to focus in on the thick feline curve of her black-lined eyes staring out intensely through a heap of tousled hair. In another, she stood looking at the camera through the glass of a window pane wearing a nude-paneled and cropped halter that made her look, well, nude. Palms placed on the window, her facial expression screamed sex, as if a moan were slipping past her pouted lips. As the music began in the background, Jessica glided across the stage—literally. In what could only be described as Marie Antoinette meets Mother Ginger, she sat atop steel frame casters, hidden by six feet of satin and tulle flared to the floor, making up her skirt. And with the help of the petite handlers hidden beneath it, Case's creation moved freely about as she prepared to belt out her number.

"Oh my God, Case! This dress *has* to be the highlight of the whole awards show this year!" called out a passerby.

"Thanks—it's definitely the biggest dress I've ever made," he responded with a chuckle, basking in all the compliments. "I took on the engineering duties myself."

"*Noooo!*" another admirer gushed.

"Oh yeah—though it took three wardrobe assistants to get her in the thing." With each cackle that rang out from his mouth, Robert looked ever closer to detonation.

"How pomp is this?" Robert asked, staring into the monitor testily. Pomp it was, but I could tell the real reason he was annoyed was for the simple fact that he couldn't make fun of it. Case had actually *constructed* an ensemble over six feet tall. Robert had been outdone; his trash bag outfit wasn't crazy enough and his showgirl outfit seemed bland in comparison. Once again, and fleetingly, I actually felt sorry for him.

"Well, I thought Brooke's costume looked fabulous," I smiled supportively.

"I don't *need* your pity Jackie." Once again, Robert jerked back into his normal crabby self. I had whiplash sometimes the way he switched on and off.

"Why the hell does she look like some kinda giant and shit?" T-Roc bellowed, adding some much-needed comic relief. But keeping in tune with her grand spectacle on stage, we were all silenced once Jessica opened her mouth.

Looking as if she may burst right out of her satin and lace corset as her chest heaved, soulful vocal riffs roared from deep within her tiny frame, catching everyone off guard. The powdered wig of tendrils decorated with ostrich plumes rollicked back and forth intensely as she went through what seemed like an entire range of emotions. She was a multioctave power-house.

Not really wanting to watch but unable to help myself, I scanned a second monitor to see if I could spot David, sitting in the crowd beside both Steve and Brooke. Feeling foolish, I was about to turn away when I caught a glimpse of them, immediately wishing I hadn't. Seeing him among the other revelers captivated by Jessica's knockout performance, my stomach dropped. *What was he supposed to do?* I scolded myself. *Look down at the floor?* Still, I couldn't help but feel incredibly inadequate as he watched the smoldering songstress dominate her audience with the confidence of a soaring deity.

The rest of the night was an emotional roller coaster as Jessica Rader ended up taking home three awards to Brooke's one. Both times her opponent's name was called, Brooke could be seen grinning sincerely in the audience and clapping graciously. Brooke seemed uninterested in the faceoff the press had built this night into, calling it the "Showdown of the Sirens." And later, when she collected her own gold-plated music note trophy engraved with "Best New Artist," she merely smiled daintily as she strolled backstage, swinging it like a dinner bell at her side.

Chapter 14

> Neither a lofty degree of intelligence
> nor imagination nor both together go to
> the making of a genius. Love, love, love,
> that is the soul of a genius.
> –Wolfgang Amadeus Mozart

"What do y'all want for dinner? Del Taco or KFC?"

Brooke was picking at her toenail polish as we sat in her living room, scattering tiny pink flecks of paint across her own face, which gleamed up from the latest issue of *Bank* magazine that she'd thrown haphazardly on the floor. It was their annual "Power Player" issue and Brooke had topped the list—something that surprised even Steve. He had stopped over to drop off the issue earlier in the evening, and from the wide grin on his face as he handed it over to Brooke, it was apparent that he counted this as one of his proudest accomplishments thus far. Since

Bank printed the only credible lists of net worth, veritably the *Bible Monthly* in the eyes of the world's most powerful business-men, Brooke's number-one ranking in the Power Players issue clinched it: Brooke was officially one of the most famous faces in the world.

But like her I.O.M. award and all of the lucrative promotional deals being thrown at her left and right—the accolade barely registered with Brooke, who was far more concerned with the roaring in her stomach and the specks of paint on her toes. I couldn't say that I was surprised—it was typical Brooke. She always remained blissfully oblivious to the aspects of her life that found their way onto tabloid covers and intrigued strangers worldwide. Power, for one reason or another, didn't appeal to her. Napping all day, watching T.V., or simply hanging out and doing nothing were sources of contentment for Brooke. And all of those, each and every one, were in increasingly short supply.

She may've been in the prime of her career, but sitting cross-legged in front of me on the floor now, Brooke looked completely forlorn. I knew that the whole Lou ordeal—no matter how tough she'd play it—probably wasn't helping her mental state at all. He harassed her relentlessly, but played the victim in public, telling everyone how she'd heartlessly strung him along. And now with only a week to go until they were supposed to "meet again" for a previously scheduled obligation, we hung in limbo, the future of the *Guitar* shoot uncertain.

"Why am I so depressed, Jackie?" The pleading look on her face made me think she expected an actual answer. "I mean, I even took a Prozac today."

"That's not really how it works. It's not like aspirin." I grabbed an almost-empty bottle of diet pills from the end table and shook it in the air. "Might these have something to do with it?"

"Jackie those are *diet* pills—not drugs." She released an exas-perated sigh to let me know I was the stupid one. I opened my mouth to suggest that some exercise might help reinvigorate her, but her phone rang. Gingerly picking it up, she peeked at the caller I.D.

"Hey—" Before she could finish Steve roared back at her with such unchecked fury that I heard every word clearly from my seat across the room.

"Damn it Brooke. How could you pull this shit? You're both on the same label—and they aren't pleased. He was producing your record! And the *Guitar* shoot? He refuses."

"Oh, Steve. You know I couldn't—" Brooke rolled her eyes.

"I don't care what you couldn't *stand*. Do you know—" Steve, collecting himself, stopped abruptly. He wanted to make the record label happy, sure. But making Brooke happy was beyond and above all, most important.

"Listen, I didn't mean to explode on you—I've just got a lot of people breathing down my goddamn neck right now . . ." Trying to play Mr. Nice Guy, Steve took another moment. "The good news is, you're still getting the *Guitar* shoot with or without Lou. That being said, they need some new direction—as in today. All right?" He didn't wait for any response from Brooke, but had one more thing to shout, apparently. "We need you up bright and early, first thing tomorrow, so you aren't going *an-y-where* tonight, no ifs, ands, or buts. Period. Good-bye." About to explode in frustration, Steve hung up. I imagined his face to be about the color of a pomegranate.

"Ugh." Brooke stretched her legs out and wiggled her freshly pedicured toes. "Like, did he expect me to *marry* him? Seriously. Like that wouldn't destroy my image."

Somehow I managed to dodge the bullet on this one. Not a single pissed-off call from Steve. To top everything off, David had invited me as his date to the "Pink Party," a V.I.P. launch event for a line of new T-shirts displaying the catchy pop lyrics lent by musicians. I'd already planned on going to the party with

Brooke—whose lyrics to her number-two hit, *Off The Hinges*, were among the proud few. But now that she'd promised to stay in for the night, I would officially have some more alone time with David—I couldn't say I wasn't excited.

Brooke let out a long deep groan as she rose to her feet. Dashing around the room now as she looked for matches, I could feel her nervous energy mounting.

"We gotta come up with a new cover now," she yelled, somewhat muffled by the junk drawer she'd just stuck her head into. After rummaging around for a bit she snapped straight up. "Aha!"

The buzzer at the gate interrupted her thought. We were surprised to find Sasha, who'd stopped by with a carload of gifts for Ginger. Photos of Brooke and her "first puppy" surfaced earlier in the week, spurring an onslaught of lavish doggy gifts from publicists and companies wishing to congratulate her on her "new arrival."

"Lookit! All. This. Stuff!" Brooke's eyes lit up for the first time in days as Sasha spread thousands of dollars' worth of doggy accessories across the coffee table. Brooke twirled around as she picked up a Ginger-sized velveteen formal dress adorned with a white maribou boa neck and hemline. I couldn't believe the sea of doggy T-shirts, gowns, and jewelry. There was even a set of chic houndstooth-patterned fabric bones and $198 snakeskin printed leashes in every color. I almost envied the little pooch, who seemed as excited as we were, circling the table and letting out an occasional yip.

"Yeah. Yeah. They just wanna get their stuff pictured in the magazines," Sasha scoffed as she plunked down an ornately designed carved wood puppy armoire perfect for housing all of Ginger's designer pieces.

I picked up the pink, gold-embossed card on top. "Couture Critterz," I read it aloud, amazed, as Brooke tore haphazardly through her gifts. All this, for a *dog*. "Dear Miss Parker, we hope you will enjoy this gift for Ginger . . . perfect for the pooch that has everything . . . protects her apparel and keeps her duds in convenient reach."

"Oh my gawd. I loooove it." Brooke lifted up a stainless-steel bowl with a hardwood base trimmed in "exotic multimedia" animal print fabric from Christian Audigier and custom-logo hardware. "Isn't it amazing?"

"Well, that's it." Sasha rolled her eyes and turned for the door. "Brings new meaning to the term 'lucky dog.' Anyway, my work here is done. Now that Lou's out of the picture, I suppose you two have some brainstorming to do before the shoot."

Right she was. We'd prepared the cover with them together: Brooke in pigtails with a yellow polka-dot bikini, and Lou pulling her bottoms down with his teeth like one of those vintage Coppertone ads. But clearly that was a no-go. We had no choice but to start from scratch now.

"Oh shit Jackie. What are we going to do?" Brooke asked. After little Ginger's "baby shower," she had picked up right where she left off and had successfully lit almost every candle in sight. Seeing that I had taken notice, she grinned, "For good luck."

I sat there thinking for a moment as the scent of freshly burning sage stung my nostrils.

Clink-clack! Clink-clack! Click-clack! Lost for words, there sat Brooke on the floor—make that clicking noise with her jaw again and, what appeared to be, oddly enough, counting the magazines in a stack near the edge of the coffee table.

"Just calm down. Let's think about this for a minute," I told her. "How about a retro pinup thing?"

No reaction.

"Or maybe we could do something mystical . . . like fairies?" Like a fog lifting to reveal a gorgeous day, a nerve struck, a switch flipped, Brooke went from worried to wide-eyed in a blink.

"I *loooove* fairies!"

"And . . ." I spouted off enthusiastically as I reached past her to grab a pen and a pad of paper from the coffee table, "what if we did the background like this? Oooh! And you've got to wear wings too! And for the . . ." I went on and on, further motivated by each look of approval that came across Brooke's face. Scribbling ferociously until every corner of the page—front and back—was completely full . . . and then turned another. *Crisis averted.*

It took me nearly two hours to get ready that night, for whatever reason. No matter how many outfits I tried on or how many times I fussed with my hair, I found myself changing, restyling, and generally second guessing everything. The fact that I was privy to every makeup trick in the book and armed with the most coveted products available in which to beautify still couldn't save me from the growing ball of nervous energy in my stomach. David had already been sitting outside of my house for nearly ten minutes by the time I finally threw my hair into a messy half-ponytail in defeat. As I ran out the door, I took one last look at my reflection and sighed. I didn't look *terrible*. In fact, I even looked cute. But *cute* wasn't quite what I was going for; I didn't want to look like a fresh-faced, doe-eyed college co-ed. I wanted to be smoldering sexy—the girl on David's arm that made his cohorts whisper things to him like, "How'd you land that hottie?" Doomed to go unrecognized in a sea of silicone and sex appeal, I frowned.

By the time we arrived I'd almost forgotten about my less-than-striking exterior by spying an even more less-than-striking one up ahead. On a sleepy corner in the flats of Hollywood stood an ominous building that stretched the length of one city block. With its windowless exterior and massive yellowing walls, the building looked like a sound stage forgotten by time. But as we got closer, my nerves were jarred once again as I spotted a line of shiny sports cars with names too difficult to pronounce and tricked-out S.U.V.s waiting in line for valet. I felt completely comfortable with David, and, more than that, I'd been to countless star-studded events like this one before with Brooke. *So why was I so nervous?*

After circling the block half a dozen times, we found a parking spot to avoid the long wait for valet just in case, as David put it, we wanted to make a fast getaway.

"I apologize in advance if this is lame." David's lips stretched into a subtle smile as we approached a narrow walkway flanked by large copper bowl torches. "But at the very least there's got to be a swag bag in it, right?"

"Thank God," I smirked exaggeratedly, "because I only attend events with swag bags."

"Oh, is that right?" He chuckled as we approached two clipboard-wielding women and a stern-looking man dressed in black near the entryway. "I did not know that about you. Good to know Miss O'Reilly, good to know."

After locating his name on the guest list, one of the women stepped aside, allowing us access to the mayhem within.

The large space opened up to a mass of bodies all bathed in a candy-colored hue from the lights above. Girls dressed as ballerinas served pink cocktails from trays as they struggled to maneuver in the pouf-pink tutus hugging their alarmingly petite waistlines.

"I need a drink!" I screamed, my senses now completely overwhelmed.

"What?!" The throbbing walls, compliments of the celebrity D.J. spinning beats from the silver platform suspended high above the crowd, rendered me inaudible.

"What?!" David struggled to make out what I was saying just as the lights went out, followed by the roaring sound of a lion

from high up above. When they came back on a second later—
this time followed by the intense pulsating of more music, he
reached out grabbed my hand.

"I can't hear any—let's go over here!"

David pulled me through the mix of tastemakers and hangers-
on over to a somewhat quieter spot near one end of the party.

"You wanna drink?" he asked, motioning to the swarm around
one of the bars.

"Please! Whatever you're having . . ."

"Who is this handsome mother fucker?" A boisterous voice
called out from the crowd. Nearly knocking David over as he
wrestled playfully into him, Erik slapped his back with a loud
thud!

"Hey buddy, what's going on?" David smiled.

"Nada," Erik replied, turning his back to the blond he'd been
talking to. She dangled a naked leg off to the side, hoping to
regain his attention and seeming downright angry as he continued talking to David. "There's a pretty good crowd going here,
man."

"I see," David laughed, gesturing to the girl. Glancing quickly
in her direction, Erik rolled his eyes.

"That bitch," Erik lowered his voice, "was blowing me off
until she found out what I did for a living. Now she's practically
begging for it."

As if on cue, the blond cooed out softly, "Hey Erik . . ."

Whipping around, he pointed to David in a frustrated
motion, as if scolding her and saying, *"Can't you see I'm busy?"*
Not picking up on his not-so-subtle message, she panted again.

"I wanted to—"

"Can't talk now babe, bigger fish," he told her throwing an
arm around David and leading him a safe distance away. "So
what's up with you tonight man?" Erik said, loosening the already loose tie around his neck as he came to a halt.

"Nothing much bro—just glad it's the weekend," David sighed though it appeared that Erik, now scrolling intensely through his Blackberry, was now already onto even bigger fish. Looking up from the screen as a dark-haired girl passed by— leaving the seductive scent of amber in her wake—he mumbled something that sounded like, "that's cool man . . ." though from the way his eyes followed her, it was apparent he hadn't actually heard David's response.

"Yo, see that girl?" Erik, snapping out of his momentary coma, asked as he lashed his fist playfully into David's chest. "That's that girl Ashleigh San Marco—dude, I'm telling you—I'm in love." Feeling Erik's eyes upon her, she swung her hips in an exaggerated motion—as if she just moved that way normally— and then smiled to herself knowingly. "She's an assistant over at Miller—all I gotta do is tell her I'll put in a good word with her boss, make her look good, etc. I'll tell her I'm bf with Jimmy Ivey at the label and—you watch—she'll be at my place in an hour."

"Wow . . ." David raised his eyebrows as he scanned the scene in palpable amazement. "She's something all right . . ."

Was I being ignored? Not that Erik seemed to me all that interesting, but was I even here? Or was I no different to David than the girl Erik had just snubbed?

Mostly stuck on his Blackberry, Erik exchanged a few more words with David, than wandered off with a pat on the back. David took a second before craning his neck around in search of me, and found me just behind him.

"Hey, where'd you run off to?" He grinned.

"I was right here . . ."

Smiling again, he took my arm and we wandered with our drinks back into the milieu.

Star-studded events in Los Angeles never ceased to amaze me. Just when you thought *this one* was craziest, or *that one* was the trendiest, you open your eyes to find tiptoeing ballerinas carrying trays, serving drinks, and . . . massaging feet? The event was extravagant, to say the least, catering to well over six hundred people—all the "talent" and executives this town had to offer, and all with their special V.I.P.s. Called the "Pink Party," after the T-shirt's designer, Jack Pinkerton, the place dripped in the color. Pink curtains, pink chandeliers, pink baskets, and pink Chopin martinis. Banquet tables with pink linens, plush "pink potion" chairs fit for pink queens, multilayer cakes with pink frosting and pink designs—and don't forget the pink tutus and the pink ballerinas inside them, some who curt-seyed and twirled through the crowd, others who offered hand and foot massages with pink lotion that smelled of cake batter and fudge. All of this to live up to the "transformational ex-perience" the invitations had touted. After a while, words like "swank," "luxury," "chic" or "eccentric" no longer apply out here. This was *Hollywood*, and that noun becomes the only adjective you can describe this kind of stuff with.

"You, uh, wanna get out of here?" David leaned into my ear.

"I thought you'd never ask." We both turned quickly on our heels to head towards the nearest exit—stopping briefly to scoop up two gift bags that were passed out at the door. As we stumbled onto the gritty Hollywood streets we were laughing so hard we could barely catch our breath.

"What was *that*?" I bellowed once we were a safe distance away.

"It was so weird, right?" David shook his head before reach-ing out for my hand—a casual gesture that made my heart beat just a little faster.

"I mean, ballerinas massaging feet! Really?"

"Yeah, I'm not sure which is weirder . . . that or the fairy princesses that were hand-feeding people glazed doughnut holes? It's pretty much as close to an acid trip as I hope to get." We both laughed again, suddenly falling silent as we approached the side street his car was parked on. The darkness of night swallowing the road ahead lit up for a moment as he hit the remote button to unlock the doors and we both shuffled towards it almost reluctantly—as if neither of us wanted the night to end. Sidling up to opposite sides of the car, David reached for his door handle before stopping.

"So . . ." He scrunched his eyes tightly shut as he spoke, like someone trying to muster up the courage to say what was on his mind. "You by chance like old horror films?"

A grin broke across my face as I looked up at him. "I think I've seen every Frankenstein movie ever made."

"Oh yeah?" He gave me a look, testing me. "Which was your favorite? *Revenge of Frankenstein? The Evil of Frankenstein?*"

"Neither. *Frankenstein Created Woman* was my go-to."

"Really? See, that's the second new thing I've learned about you tonight."

I started to chuckle. "Yep, what can I say? I'm a sucker for broad-shouldered monsters and gift bags full of—" I paused quickly as I looked down at the bag on my arm, my fingertips rustling the tissue paper within as I dug through it "—coupons and small bottles of hand lotion."

"Man," David moaned, pretending to care about the contents of his own bag. "We got the janky commoner swag, huh?"

"I get V.I.P. when I'm with Brooke," I teased.

"Well," he grinned, "let's just say I've got something Brooke doesn't . . ." he retorted as he reached into his back pocket for his wallet. Pulling a thin, plastic card from it, he tossed it across the hood to me. "That, my friend, is an all-access pass."

I swiped up the shiny card to examine it. "Kinetoscope Video . . ." I nodded my head, pretending to be extremely impressed as I scanned it over, looking up at him goofily.

"That's right, baby. Tell me Brooke doesn't have one of those bad boys?"

"I think you might just have her beat," I said sending the card sailing back toward him with a flick of my wrist. "Isn't Kinetoscope where all the really geeky film students work? You know, the ones that turn their noses down at you in disgust when you bring mainstream movies up to the counter?"

"They have mainstream movies there?"

"They're sparse, for sure, but if you wade through the Criterion Collection and rare indies, there are a few. I made the mistake of stopping in there and asking if they had a copy of *You've Got Mail* in and I thought I might be executed on the spot."

"*You've Got Mail*, huh? From a girl who loves Hammer Horror films?" David asked raising an eyebrow.

"Hey, it was a long time ago—I was renting it for a girls' night, if you must know," I said defensively before cracking a smile. "*And* they didn't even have it there anyway. So we got *Creature From the Black Lagoon* instead."

"Next best thing," David joked before looking down at his watch. "Well, if you really do love old horror movies as much as you say you do then you're in luck. It's only eleven-thirty and I have one of Kinetoscope's finest at home just waiting to be watched. You in the mood for a little *Dr. Jekyll and Mr. Hyde?*"

I'd have been in the mood for C-SPAN if it meant spending some alone time with David. Cuddled up on the couch, drinking wine, and making jokes, I couldn't have cared less about how all the fabulous people in their fabulous frocks and their fabulous friends were capping off their fabulous nights. For once I didn't care about missing out on all the night's parties, or even stop to worry about being smolderingly sexy (or not). At David's apartment there was no one to measure up against. It was just the two of us.

But just as I had, for the first time since I could remember, started to feel completely content just being myself, a little voice inside my head raided my thoughts, yanking me out of my state of bliss. Maybe it was the waves of giddy, girlish glee that were washing over me. Perhaps the silly smile that seemed to be permanently fixed to my face. Maybe it was both, probably, but regardless of which, I couldn't help but notice it, they, though foreign to me, seemed oddly familiar. Could I, Jackie O'Reilly, be perhaps . . . *falling in love?* Even though I'd dated Trip for almost two years, I was never in *love* with him. I wasn't really sure if I had the faintest idea of what being in love felt like—it was something I had only seen in movies or read about in books. According to those who had, love was something that was supposed to change you, sometimes even *save* you, though I wasn't exactly sure from what. Love was that thing that we were all led to believe promised a happy ever after. If that was true, then why did the voice inside my brain feel so . . . *nagging?* And then suddenly, I knew. Brooke.

Those feelings bubbling up inside my gut may have been new to *me* but I'd certainly experienced them, at least vicariously. The stupid grin, the all-encompassing glee . . . that was exactly how Brooke had been with Jesse. I was suddenly aware too, of the pain that love could bring—causing nervous thoughts to flash through my mind: Jessica, guys like Erik who leveraged their positions to get girls into bed, and everyone in Hollywood all scrambling to find the bigger and better deal. Brooke's heartache and unyielding loneliness felt all too alarmingly real at that moment—and suddenly I realized that the guy holding me tight in his arms, who had the power to make me feel so incredibly joyful, also had the power to break my heart completely. These thoughts danced around in my head—spinning like the grotesque whirl of faces that appeared onscreen as Dr. Jekyll downed the drug that transformed him into the vituperative Mr. Hyde—a man whose evil stemmed wholly from lust and a man capable of diminishing a once assertive and forthright woman into a trembling heap of anxiety and terror. In this industry of bigger and better deals—fame and power are just as addictive as any kind of drug—making it, too, the perfect recipe for heartache. I watched in horror now at the images on the screen in front of us as they began to take on a new meaning—appearing far less silly now.

With my mind back on my career (instead of boys), I woke up energetically to pack my things for the shoot. Driving with the windows down, I felt incredibly refreshed by the night with David. The anxiety I had had the night before seemed distant now—I was afraid of being just another girl to David, like Ashleigh to Erik, but I now found all those thoughts a waste of time.

Checking my phone, I saw that I had a missed call, but just as I was going to check it, another one came in.

"Hey Brooke."

"Jackie, I'm already on the way to the shoot and I just realized I left my fairy wand and wings at home." *For the love of God.*

"Brooke," I said with frustration, "when I gave those to you you promised you'd guard them with your life and *not leave them anywhere.*"

"I know, I'm sorry. Can you please, please, *please* go pick them up for me??"

Whether I could or not was not important: I *had* to. Who else would? As I pulled a u-turn, I glanced reluctantly at the time, rolling my eyes as I realized I would never make it on time. I had organized my morning perfectly, with *just* enough time to do everything *I* needed to do and make it to the studio on time. So much for well-made plans.

With the fairy accessories in tow now, I zipped into the parking lot at Fifth and Sunset Studios. I kept one hand on the wheel and the other elbow-deep in my bag on the passenger seat, nervously, compulsively shuffling around inside like Brooke lit candles. After all the brainstorming and prepping that had gone on for the *Guitar* cover, the day of the shoot had finally arrived. This, by far, was going to be my best work with Brooke yet. Not only was legendary photographer Jean Saint Jean on board (another bonus), but today, I'd be able to show everyone that I had a creative vision that extended far beyond foundation and mascara. It was time now to finally let that side of me shine!

Turning off the engine in the parking lot, I reminded myself to take a few deep breaths to settle my nerves. *The entire shoot had been landscaped in my head—I needed everything to be perfect!* A few breaths turned into ten before I finally got the courage to go inside. I could handle whatever calamities might be thrown my way, I told myself confidently. Besides, I laughed silently as I looked down at my emergency bag stuffed with every possible antidote I could think of, I'd come prepared for them all anyway.

"Hey Stu! Where are these things going?" Just steps ahead of me, a rail-thin man was struggling with an armful of polyurethane spotted rocks. Waltzing through the studio doors, I found myself in the middle of a lush forest. Banyan trees on wooden bases and in black cylinders with green underplantings stood twelve feet high, surrounded by rubber rope vine and flowering foliage that crept around wood. Barely looking up from the coffee mug he was sipping from, a man with a full head of graying hair looked on.

"They're supposed to keep the pump in place over there." He nodded toward a small water basin strategically hidden with silk ferns to appear like a small pond. About to drink the last of his coffee, he lowered his mug again. "Remember to change the settings—we don't want to set off the smoke detectors," he called out to another man tinkering with a fog machine.

It was just as I'd imagined it! Apparently, it was the way Jean Saint Jean had envisioned it as well. Standing there to take it all in for a moment, I nearly jumped out of my skin as he approached.

"Magnifique . . ."

Turning around, I nearly gasped. There he was. Powdery white complexion, shrewd eyes highlighted by flecks of blue and that unmistakable salt-and-pepper pompadour—all wrapped together in his signature rockabilly style. Jean Saint Jean.

"Everything good chief?" Stu asked, raising his coffee mug high in the air and fully alert.

"Eeez *great*," he affirmed, his tone dignified and carefully measured. He was still for a moment, looking around in an "I'm-tired-of-traveling" kind of hush and then just as quickly as he'd come in, he brushed past me in abrupt strides. *Magnifique! He liked it!*

Unable to hide the grin breaking across my face, I ambled over to the makeup station, my heels tapping loudly on the concrete floor. I could barely contain my excitement. To my surprise, Brooke was already in the chair, which was odd seeing as I usually had to *force* her into it. Pulling up the spaghetti straps of the tank top hanging limply off her shoulders, she sipped from a can of Street Cred. Spotting me, she simply muttered, "I'm so hot." My eye unexpectedly caught the sprawl of makeup on the counter—*not* my makeup—behind her. Just then, I heard a voice behind me through the clatter of hangers being raked across one of the rolling racks.

"We're doing an icy green on the lid and the lips nude—maybe a sheer gloss." I whipped around to meet a familiar-looking face—Pat Sherman. I'd recognized her right away having seen her in pictures from red carpet events. Pat had a reputation for being a shrewd and precise veteran in the industry. She was largely known outside of the business for her line of color-correcting products—mainly because she spent an inordinate amount of time on the phone trying to get "in" with beauty editors. But even with her $6,000-a-day rate and her countless years working with celebrities, her makeup didn't look a whole lot different from mine.

"Oh hi, are you one of Brooke's friends? I'm Pat." Oblivious to the makeup bag at my feet, she extended her hand. Just as I was about to do the same, not knowing what else to do, I was interrupted by a firm tap on the shoulder. I turned around to find Steve, clad in a crinkled denim jacket bearing the name of an ultratrendy Los Angeles–based designer. Curling the tip of his finger in a come-hither motion, he turned on his heel, prompting me to follow him.

"What's going on?"

"Well, maybe if you answered the bloody telephone you'd know," Steve said, stopping just a short distance away.

"What?" I asked.

"I called you and left a message—but surprise, surprise, looks like you didn't get it." *The missed call!* I had forgotten to check it after Brooke called! "To boil it all down," he said as he ran one hand through his hair and shoved the other in his pocket, "Jean Saint Jean just felt more comfortable using someone he already knows."

"But this whole thing—this was all my id—"

He cut me off, his face growing annoyed. "And besides, this shoot is a *big* deal . . . and let's face it, with your track record of tardiness, there was no way I was going to keep someone like Jean Saint Jean waiting."

This couldn't be happening . . .

But one look at Steve's smug expression told me that it was.

Just then, a wardrobe rack of distressed mini dresses whizzed by, adding insult to injury.

"I know there's been a couple times that I've been a little late, but I promise you, it won't happen again—I'm sorry." My face felt hot and I tried not to jumble my words. "I conceived this whole shoot myself. And I'm here, and I'm ready to go."

I searched Steve's face for a shred of sympathy but found none. Instead, he looked down at his watch and quickly snapped in return, "Even if you were still on this job—you're ten minutes late—look, I'm sorry but this is not negotiable."

I felt his cold glare on me—my chest now burning more intensely than my already crimson cheeks. I looked at my call log. When had he called? *Two in the morning.* What an asshole. I never even heard it ring.

I'd never felt so much disdain before—it was harsh, like someone had plunged a knife into my gut and just kept twisting. I felt paralyzed—should I run out of the room like a coward? Should I cry in the hopes that, baring my soul, I'd be able to evoke some sort of sympathy from Steve? Should I thicken my skin and become defensive instead? But I was too stunned to do anything—and so I sat there in a stunned silence.

"I just want to talk to Brooke about this. . ." I started to move toward her, but he stepped in my way.

"Sorry," Steve said thrusting his hand out to stop me. "You're off the job—we can't have people just hanging around—you gotta go."

I shot Steve the hardest glare I could muster, given my state of mind, and it probably came off equal parts loathing and defeat. But I sucked it up, if only for a moment, as I thrust the fairy wings and wand into Steve's hands: "This is why I was late." If his expression changed, I didn't notice. I took a reluctant step back and took in what I could of the scene around me.

Everyone from the makeup artist who'd replaced me to the

fog machine technician screamed one thing, and one thing alone: business. These were the dinosaurs of their entertainment fields, large or small, professionals with professional relationships. And it hit me, suddenly and entirely. Friendship and business were opposite poles in this town, if your job existed behind the scenes. My relationship with Brooke meant nothing to anyone except, I hoped, Brooke herself. I caught her eye.

"Sorry . . . I didn't know," Brooke mouthed over at me. My perspective in the room slipped through the first few stages of vertigo, and I felt weightless in my own bath of cold sweat.

Chapter 15

> What a heavy burden is a name
> that has become too famous too soon.
> –Voltaire

"You're on fire! Now we have to get you ready for Rio!" Manically pacing the length of his office, Steve looked as if someone had just lit a small bonfire underneath him. Brooke, instead, appeared as if she'd just been handcuffed to the outside of a moving vehicle. For a girl like herself, who might've given her I.O.M. and a few million dollars for her last shred of anonymity and a couple days on the beach, it was hell. The never-ending schedule Steve kept piling up for her on top of the constant trail of paparazzi lurking around every corner had begun to provoke more than just tears—they had started to provoke resentment. Steve, however, had no interest in slowing her down. Brooke was a shooting star, and everyone was jockeying for the best, most secure seat on board. Reflecting on what had happened at the *Guitar* shoot a few weeks ago, I wondered if she even had bothered to reserve a seat for me.

I suppose there are never any guarantees in a business like this. But still . . . *why didn't she stand up for me?* Just when I'd start to think about that too much, I'd remind myself just how great it was working for her. She'd single-handedly carved out a career for me. She had no control over what happened at the shoot . . . *it's not like she had planned it out that way*, I told myself. I knew the best thing I could do was to just come to terms with it all; my only hope was that I ranked a rung or two higher up the ladder than her original dancers had before Steve finessed them out of their jobs. They had been her friends too—her "besties." Once upon a time.

"Not only is it Sizzlin' South America, the biggest music festival on the continent," Steve bellowed, forcing me back into reality, "but it's also your first show after the big win: you're now an I.O.M.-winning-performer . . . it's going to be huge!"

Brooke broke into tears. "I don't want to do this show. I just don't want to do it . . ."

"You're not canceling. It's impossible; out of the question. You just don't cancel shows," Steve sternly reprimanded her, continuing on about what a big deal her next moves were because, now that the bar was even higher, there was no slacking off allowed.

Brooke's demeanor remained unchanged and Steve, who had whittled the art of persuasion down to a science, knew that if he was going to get a good performance out of her, he'd have to switch gears.

"Let me ask you something . . . you ever been to Brazil?" he asked, his voice suddenly calm and smooth.

"No . . ." she said, fidgeting on the couch across from him.

"Uhhhh! *Never been* . . ." Shaking his head sadly as if responding to an unexpected tragedy, he paused. "Well . . ." he said, picking up speed again, "then that right there should be more than reason enough to go! What's *not* to love about Brazil?"

Hmmm . . . the crime, the poverty, gang warfare . . . I stopped myself from blurting out. Brooke responded by shrugging her shoulders, but Steve, just warming up, inhaled deeply and answered his own question.

His nostrils flared in excitement as he rattled off a long list of things she *must* see. Using vivid, glorious details to describe the beaches and mountains—none of which she'd have time to see anyway—he played into her fantasies, mesmerizing her through the power of attraction. In just a few sentences he had turned Rio into Xanadu, and a virtually quarantined experience at Sizzlin' South America into a quest for the Holy Grail.

"Can I bring Pugslie?" Brooke sounded like a child asking permission to take her stuffed bear to the movies.

"Yeah. Fine." Steve waved his hand as he picked up his phone to make a call.

"What's Pugslie?" I hadn't heard her mention this before.

"My puppy," Brooke flopped onto her back, taking up the length of the couch. Seeing my confused expression, Brooke explained, "I sent Ginger to live with Momma in Florida."

I looked at her, still perplexed. Apparently a lot had changed since I got ousted from the shoot.

"Her skin got all dry and flaky. She smelled real bad. The vet said she needed medicine for some infection, and a special dog food. I dunno, but I don't have time for that kind of work." She sighed, then covered her mouth in a mix of disgust and laughter. "Besides she had the worst farts. Ew! The. Worst."

It was going to be a short trip, or as Steve had called it, "a fly in, fly out thingy"—which actually meant a two-flight, eighteen-hour excursion. It was clear that the show wasn't a top priority, but rather a smart marketing tactic executed by Steve. Proceeds from the weekend-long festival benefited well-known charity organizations and various community outreach programs, and for Steve, it was simply the best way for the stars to lend their support, and ultimately, bolster their images. Of course, the performers were still well paid, although because of Brooke's scheduling constraints, they had all flown down separately the night before, much to the chagrin of Steve and his checkbook—an extra night for just the *extras*. And much to my chagrin, David wasn't coming with us at all.

The most anticipated act of the weekend, despite Brooke's ever-increasing fame, was the Emerson Brothers, who were scheduled to take the stage after Brooke to cap off the festival. They were also, as Steve informed us, staying in the same hotel. You see, his sales pitch had also included: "I understand if you don't want to stay so close to Jesse . . ." knowing full well she'd like nothing more. And though she'd never admit it, my sneaking suspicions told me that this had something—a big something—to do with her decision.

After a few missteps and a two-hour delay taking off (just imagine the headache this gave Steve), we touched down on a tropical strip of land between the Mantiqueira Mountains and the coastline of the Atlantic Ocean. Carved by bays and lagoons, all greens and blues, Brooke was all smiles. A gust of thick air, heavy with humidity, hit us as we made our way outside to the driver, who would be waiting to ferry us toward the sun-drenched suburbs of Rio, where rock gods and bubble-gum pop acts alike would erupt with energy to delight the massive, crazed crowd all screaming and crying in Portuguese. Squinting our eyes beneath the bright, cloudless sky, however, no vehicle was in sight.

"We're late," Steve said, looking down at his wristwatch as he fished his Blackberry from his pocket. Scrolling through it rapidly, he looked for the driver's number. "That jackass better still be waiting for us," he said impatiently. I had to hand it to him, for as off-schedule as we were at that point—and a flight filled with Pugslie's snot-spraying sneezes—Steve was uncharacteristically relaxed. *Maybe this really was his Xanadu?*

"What if he left?" Brooke asked, twirling a large wad of purple Bubblicious around her index finger. In a quilted, pink camouflage carrier near Brooke's feet, Pugslie pressed his deeply wrinkled little pug face against the mesh screen. His dark, lustrous eyes looked around excitedly; he seemed more eager about Rio than Brooke.

"Well . . ." Steve shrugged, pointing across the way to where an overcrowded passenger bus screeched to a halt to allow more people on.

"Ew . . . I don't do buses," Robert said testily, not seeing the impish smile creeping across Steve's face. He whipped around dramatically, sighed with gusto and continued: "Me and public transportation are like Ivana Trump and K-Mart . . . we *don't* go."

At this, everyone belted out in laughter, even me, though I hated to give Robert validation of any kind. My reluctant chuckle quickly dissipated as an irritating thought came over me. I wondered how Robert's grumblings could be so endearing? And why, when my every move was solely to be as accommodating as possible, was I scrutinized so harshly? My nickname, which to my deepest dismay had stuck, was Calamity, for chrissake.

As if to rub this in, Steve gave Robert a friendly pat on the back. "Don't worry Robert." He grinned, the gleam of his new teeth now appearing like daggers to me. "Your chariot awaits."

A retro-style Volkswagen van with dark tinted windows barreled towards us, prompting Brooke to squeal, "It's so cute!"

"See?" Steve called out to Robert as he soldiered over to greet our driver. "It's cute." Robert raised an eyebrow, not entirely thrilled.

"We going to hit rush hour," our driver said cranking his head backward after we settled in and were on our way. To the trained eye—my eye—Steve worked hard to contain a reaction to this further addition to his tension.

"The hotel's on the way to the festival, let's pull up only to unload—we've gotta go straight there," Steve said nervously eyeing the remote stretch of road that lay in front of us. "Just try to get there as fast as humanly possible."

The driver replied with a wry, toothy smile in the rearview mirror. Aggressively approaching the road, he swerved wildly into, out from, and in between oncoming traffic. Curving up into the gloom of the inescapable hillside, he cut from the grass on the median into the middle to the shoulder. Veering back onto the road, we rounded a bend as rows of shantytowns came into view ahead.

Looking down again at his watch impatiently, Steve grumbled, "She's barely gonna have time to get ready." Twisting backwards from the passenger seat, he looked at both Robert and me. "Is there anything she can do on the way?"

"Well . . . it'd be pretty hard to start any make—" I was interrupted by a large thud as we recklessly sped over a pothole, sending everyone floating a foot off of their seats.

"She can start getting dressed," Robert sighed, taking the reigns. Turning to me in the backseat, he pointed a finger. "If you can reach my garment bag, Brooke's outfits are right on top—and *be gentle*," he warned me, "when you rescue her star-studded two-piece, remember that it costs more than your job . . ."

Of all the clever retorts I wanted to toss back at him—that I could've said, would've said, but alas, shouldn't and so couldn't say—I sufficed with an extended eye roll and sigh. Things had been frustrating enough today, on everyone, and to be honest, pleasing myself with a cut down wouldn't have done any of us any good.

"No peeking! Robert, I'm talking to you especially," Brooke laughed, pulling her tank top over her head.

"Please girl—I *dress* you . . . I've seen that ass a million times."

Tugging at her waistband, the bus jerked about, knocking us into one another in the backseat.

"Oh man. This isn't going to be easy."

"Here," I offered, gripping the lower part of her pant leg closest to me.

Please just keep on us the road, I prayed. As if my wish were granted, and then answered twofold in degree, the van stopped abruptly. Letting out a sigh of relief, I wrestled Brooke's legs from the grip of her tight jeans. She twisted her body to reach Pugslie's carrier, the source of some awful gurgling and hacking noises.

"Brooke. C'mon," I tried not to sound impatient, but this was hard enough.

Luckily Robert seemed to be on my side. He gave me an exaggerated eye roll and tried to coax her concentration back on the task at hand. "Brooke. Sweetie. Puh-lease work with Jackie, doll."

"One sec. Pugslie's got a hairball." She reached into the bag and rubbed his throat in a circular motion. He stretched his thick neck, adorned with a faux-diamond–encrusted gold-and-white leather collar, to let her come to his aid. It didn't seem like the time or place to inform Brooke that dogs don't get hairballs.

"Aw . . . *hell* no." T-Roc muttered nervously, suddenly noticing something to our right-hand side. A chill spiraled up my spine while each of us turned in unison to see what he was talking about. A lone militia guard had sidled up to the driver's side door; he was stern and his face was rough and etched deeply. Grabbing a handful of his thinning hair, the cabbie rolled down his window, quickly engaging in conversation. My eyes darted to the left and I gasped as I spied a pair of boys, not even teenagers, toting machine guns like guards on a nearby corner. Our only form of protection was T-Roc, who didn't carry a gun and, despite his intimidating size, was no match for AK-47s, even if they were in the hands of schoolchildren. *I'm going to die. Today. With Steve . . .*

Just as I was making a mental note to keep my fears quiet, Robert gasped out loud. "Oh my God! They're going to kidnap Brooke!"

His eyes, wide with fear, stared at three more men approaching from the right. Scouring the area around our vehicle, their guns were ready. With a quiet *thud!* Robert slumped down to the floor, prompting the rest of us to do the same as a chorus of *shhh's*! broke out among us. "Jackie," he whispered. "Don't move an inch. T-Roc will take care of Brooke. Just keep yourself safe." Curled up next to me, Brooke clung to my arm in fear as the voices outside rose louder. Obviously angry, the vigilantes began screaming in Portuguese as our driver tried unsuccessfully to calm them down.

"What are they saying? What are they saying?" Brooke frantically asked each one of us. Holding his breath, T-Roc hadn't flinched, clenching his teeth together in silence.

"What's happening, T?" Shivering, Brooke's eyes searched his face, trying to pick up the severity of the situation. He was always so cool, calm, and collected—and if T-Roc was worried, so were we.

"I'm sure uh—I'm sure it's— it's *nothing*," T-Roc choked out. He was scared but did his best to remain calm for Brooke's sake. "You know—something we're not used to, but I'm sure it's gonna be all good."

Rap! Rap! Rap!

With squinted eyes struggling to see inside, one of the militiamen tapped the passenger side windows with his gun. A car door opened, but from my crouched position I could only assume it was the driver's. Not a moment later, the sliding passenger door flew open and light flooded the inside of the van.

"Everybody git out . . ." our driver said. Brooke's eyes widened as she looked over at T-Roc who, after a moment to swallow his fear, turned to us.

"Stay behind me," he said, making the first move toward the open door.

"We—we—I mean she . . . can't," I blurted out. "Sir . . . how do you say 'no clothes,' er, 'undressed' in Portuguese?" Steve, stunned and silent, looked appreciative of my big mouth for once.

The driver, however, did not. Glaring with a force that said *How dare you?* he screamed, "Git! Git! Git! Everybody!"

Hoisting all 250 pounds of him up off seat, T-Roc emerged into the harsh tropical sun, seemingly ready and willing to take a bullet for Brooke. His face was carefully controlled, but I had faith in him, for what may have been no reason, but here, in this circumstance, Brooke and I (and yes, Robert and Steve, too) needed him. He stayed close to the door, but even in the shadow of this towering hulk, our aggressors refused to compromise.

The man who had originally approached the car leaned the barrel of his gun against T-Roc's formidable shoulder and nudged him aside, maintaining a dark, angry expression and unbroken eye contact. T-Roc raised his arms above his head, took just the slightest step to the side, and looked in at us while the man rapped his gun against the roof of the car. "Out!" he shouted.

We stepped out one by one—a nauseating stench hit our noses and we grimaced as two of the men heaved open the back door of the van and began rifling through our belongings. I looked upwards, my eyes meeting those of an elderly woman residing in a makeshift home nearby. Seeing me, she quickly pulled down her window shade. At my side stood Robert—head slung down to the ground—he appeared in a morose, fuguelike state, resigned to his impending doom. With nothing but a bra on, Brooke emerged behind us, embarrassed with her arms covering her chest and her blond hair swirling down around her shoulders.

Panicked, Steve pulled out the tour pass he'd put in his back pocket in an attempt to communicate our purpose of travel. My heart thudded in my chest as one of the men, his face dark in the shade of his military cap, pulled open his Hawaiian shirt. Our senses were now razor sharp as he drew out a two-foot-long sawed-off shotgun. *This is it—this is the end . . . good-bye cruel world*, I told myself morbidly.

My thoughts, my life, my doom, everything this situation had trenched deep into us were suddenly upended with an excited prepubescent squeal.

"Brooke! Brooke Parker!" Waving the large machine gun in his arms back and forth with joy from his curbside post was one of the young boys. The suspicious soldiers standing in front of us squinted their eyes to see what all the commotion was about before their faces erupted in laughter.

"Brooke Parker, ha, ha, ha!" laughed the gunman in the Hawaiian shirt, who immediately withdrew his gun. His comrades now came closer, abandoning their search of our belongings and setting down their weapons.

"I love your music!" one yelled in a thick accent while the others clamored for her attention in Portuguese. In a country where the most highly admired women are bronzed and toned and blond, Brooke, it turned out, was big in Rio.

"The 'Pillow Talk' you have make me feel real nice!" The guy in the Hawaiian shirt sang out butchered lyrics in between grunts to a man behind him who finally brought out a camera. "You take one? Just one . . ." He smiled.

Happy to be alive, Brooke responded with an overabundance of energy. Giving her adoring fans a sugary sweet smile, she gushed, "I, um, all right. I think I can do better than one, but just a few, okay?"

They clearly hadn't understood, as clearly they spoke Portuguese, but by the time she was finished, they had about five pictures, which is four more than Brooke ever felt comfortable posing for back home. The first two were slightly awkward as she modestly draped her tank top across her. By the end of the photo session, however, she seemed to be thoroughly enjoying herself, letting it fall to the ground as she flashed her megawatt smile, looking like a Playboy bunny, caramel skin accented by purple silk.

And just like that, the gun-toting crew that had us all signing our death warrants thanked Brooke, packed up, and left. We stood at the side of the road looking at one another, one at a time. No one dared to laugh it off or smile, except for Brooke, who was the first of us back in the van.

"Are we going or what?" she said. "That was craaaaazzyy!"

The tawdry street scene outside the concert gates did little to faze any of us—we were still reeling from our near-death experience. In the end, as the driver had translated for us, they had stopped us to inquire why we were going so fast. *If they did that for speeding violations in the states*, I thought, *we'd all be driving like grandmothers*.

Outside the venue, a few locals were resourcefully conning a trio of hung-over roadies while vendors shouted loudly in Portuguese, selling concoctions of iced tea and lemonade and cheap sunglasses. Slender cariocas fresh from the surf in their tiny string bikinis drew looks and occasional catcalls from men passing by. Backstage, it was a completely different world, one in which pampered rock stars tucked away in plastic cubicles sipped cocktails and held casual conversation while sounds of live music echoed all around.

By the time we arrived, we were already two hours late, yet the throng of fans with their feet planted firmly on the bladed grass beneath them waited patiently.

Rushing towards the stage, Brooke stopped dead in her tracks, putting her arm out to stop me. Up ahead stood Jesse, with his L.A. tan and tousled raven locks, and his team of handlers weighed down with giant duffle bags. Being the nice guy he was, Jesse smiled and waved at us, or just Brooke, probably. Taking this as a cue, Brooke ran to give him a hug. Wiggling uncomfortably out of her grasp, a feigned smile crept across his face. *Or was that amusement?* Nolan and I exchanged nervous looks. Their short conversation was painfully awkward to say the least.

"Oh my God, Jesse," she squealed, "you have no idea what we just went through!"

"Yeah," he nonchalantly replied, "what's that?"

As she gushed, it appeared to me that while her brush with death hadn't manifested an immediate reaction, in Jesse's presence she had suddenly decided to react. She clung to him as she recounted, in pretty accurate detail, what had happened. She wanted his sympathy; she wanted him to hold her. He was surprised to hear everything—I mean, who wouldn't be?—but as she rattled off the last few details, he started to pull away.

"Well, I'm glad you're all right," he offered. "Listen, it was good to see you," he said, "I gotta get going, but good luck out there."

As he walked off, Brooke looked confused. She shook it off

though and, following a promising native pop band, took to the stage in the twilight hours. A striking picture of sensuality, she passionately launched into her set beneath the spotlights of the cavernous stage. She transformed into a sexual provocateur adorned in a barely there sparkling bikini-like top and matching pants so tight they looked painted on. Shots of the sweat running down her tanned, toned midriff flashed up on the giant screens flanking the stage as she writhed back-and-forth, giggling, twirling, and groaning. Everyone in the crowd went nuts, shrieking and screaming. When she opened with an ear-splitting, high-octane version of "Pillow Talk," they absolutely freaked out.

As the opening number rumbled to a close, I felt my phone vibrate in my pocket. When I pulled it out and saw David's name on the screen, even I was surprised at how excited I got. I went flying behind the stage and picked it up at the last second—conveniently as soon as "Pillow Talk" had ended.

"David," I shouted into the phone, "hold on for a second while I try to find somewhere quiet so I can hear you." Ducking into one of the tents, I made my way past throngs of earlier performers and found a spot in the corner—but with Brooke's second number in full swing, I still had to stick a finger in my other ear to hear anything.

"Hey! Sorry about that, what's up?"

"No problem at all," he said, "I got a text from Steve about some sort of hostage situation or something crazy like that—are you okay? What happened?"

A smile from somewhere deep inside me rose up and stuck for the rest of the conversation. He was worried about me. "Oh, it was really nothing in the end, but for a minute there I think we all thought we were gonna die in Rio . . ." I started. "I think Robert pissed his pants."

He laughed and so did I. "Well tell me, you're okay . . ."

"I'm fine, really. A bunch of guys with machine guns pulled our van over on the way to the venue, two of them I think were actually fifth graders, but they were way scarier than my middle-school bully." He laughed again. "Anyway they pulled us all out of the van and were gonna strip search us or something before one of the kids recognized Brooke. Long, scary story short: some racy fan pictures and few autographs later and they left. Turns out they pulled us over for speeding!"

"That's insane," he said. "Not to make myself out to be a wimp or anything, but if I'd been there I don't think Robert would have been the only one with a mess to clean up." There was something in the way this conversation was going that made me feel for David a feeling much more direct than I ever had before—I didn't know exactly what to call it, not that I wanted to label it anyway, but it was, most certainly, more than just *like*. "Listen," he continued, "I'm glad to hear you're all right. Because if you weren't, well, I don't know who I'd get to work this Ric Craia shoot in a couple weeks."

A rumble of voices as clusters of people passed by drown out his voice on the other end—there was no way I'd heard him correctly. *Or did I?*

"Wait?" I asked, yelling into the receiver. "What did you say? It's loud here, I couldn't hear you." But from the mounting excitement in my voice, David knew that I'd heard him—muffled maybe, but heard him for sure.

"I said," he raised his voice slightly, "I know a guy who knows a guy, and I may or may not have booked you a job . . ." He trailed off. Another unbearable pause. "A shoot with Craia . . . promos for his big comeback . . . I told you he was making a comeback!"

Speechless. I was utterly speechless.

"Did I lose you?" he asked.

"No, no, I'm here I'm still here," I stammered. "Are—are you serious?"

"I can go cancel it if you don't want to—"

"NO!" I shouted. "I'm just totally and utterly blown away. You're serious? Ric Craia, *Guitar* magazine . . . *me*?"

"Yeah," he said, "you in?"

"You kidding me?" I practically choked into the phone. "That's maybe the single coolest thing anyone's ever said to me, ever, and, well, it's easily the coolest thing anyone's ever done for me."

"You're welcome," he said proudly, "well, sounds like Brooke's in full swing, so go get back there. And call me as soon as you get back so I can give you all the details."

"I will," I said, floating somewhere in between Brazil and a dreamland. "I can't thank you enough, David."

"Yes you can," he replied, "talk soon."

"Okay, good-bye."

As I closed my phone, the world around seemed to have just stopped spinning, like I'd been on a carousel with my eyes closed until it had slowed to a halt. I flowed back through the crowds in the tent, and up the back stairs of the stage.

By the time I got back to my post, the late flights, Robert's insults, even our hostage situation had become distant memories. I did remember how Robert almost seemed to soften on me during the day's many crises. Brooke had finished another high-energy dance performance, but unlike usual for this point in the show, her dancers, sweaty and out of breath, retreated behind the curtains. Brooke nodded to someone offstage who rolled a keyboard out to her. Sitting tenderly on a stool behind it, she placed her hands on the keys, pausing to address the crowd.

"You know, sometimes things happen to you that remind

you just how precious life really is—and I think you should live every day to the very fullest and make sure to let the ones you love know exactly how you feel about 'em," she cooed with heartbreaking sincerity.

"What is she doing?" Steve's face quickly became as red as flames.

". . . So, I'd like to dedicate this one to someone very special . . . and I think he knows who he is."

I cringed, unsure of what to expect. Then, in a voice somehow filled with sorrow, Brooke started singing—I mean, *really singing*. No backing track, no distracting dancers. The first word hadn't been fully formed yet I knew what I was hearing: this was *my song*.

> *I should have just told you what I wanted to say,*
> *But I was afraid you would walk away,*
> *Leaving me here with my heart in my hands*
> *And no chance of ever seeing you again . . .*

I was so startled to hear my own song performed for such a vast audience that it almost sounded foreign to me—and not only that, it hadn't been prerecorded—I was overwhelmed. She struggled to hit the high notes, but kept on singing, varying the words I had written just slightly so that it was clear, if only to me, she was singing this for Jesse.

> *I pulled out your picture today,*
> *It made me feel closer to you.*
> *You were like a pillar of strength*
> *And you left my world too soon . . .*

I could see in her face she meant every word she sung. She'd made them her own.

See this is what is wrong,
I've held on to you too long,
This is what I go through,
Trying to get over you . . .

I wondered if Jesse were even within earshot to hear this, and even if he was, would he recognize they were meant for him?

Sometimes I think you wanted to watch me bleed,
Or tell me it was all my fault.
Why couldn't we just let things be?
Instead I'm left to take the fall . . .

I looked out on the crowd: a thousand points of quivering light danced among the sea of people. Brooke Parker had garnered one of music's greatest honors.

See, this is what is wrong,
I've held on to you so long.
This is what I go through,
Try-y-y-y-in' to get over you . . .

As the song came to a close, cheers erupted from dead silence.

"Thank you, everyone!" Brooke's voiced echoed. "And thanks for being such awesome fans! I love Brazil!" The crowd roared.

After the show, Brooke wanted to wait to watch the Emerson Brothers perform. The Emerson Brothers unleashed their string of hits, bouncing into the spotlight. By the time the boys finished, they looked flushed from the enthusiasm of the crowd.

"Wait—I've got something special for you tonight," Jesse spoke into his microphone.

The crowd drew a hush—two special performances in one

night? They must have felt privileged. But I, I just felt worried.

"This is our new single," Jesse continued.

Not so bad . . .

"Has anyone out there ever been burned before? Or heart-broken—or whatever it is?"

Uh-oh.

"This goes out to all you out there that's been burned before." The lights dimmed.

A spotlight hit Jesse and the beat came in, though just slightly slower in tempo than most Emerson Brothers songs, it was hard to resist swaying along. It was a solo performance; the other brothers picked up harmonies but mostly stood near the back of the stage, making one thing clear: the words belonged to Jesse alone.

You weren't genuine and neither were your promises . . .

Light on his feet, the anger in his voice seemed to rise as he carried out the composed tune. The song was clearly less about romantic love than the soul-crushing feeling of deception.

You create a hopelessness in me . . .

Their whole relationship and breakup, while speculated, was a mystery—and here, on stage in Rio, it was all coming out—displayed on huge screens, Jesse was giving his fans the coveted pieces of the puzzle.

The air felt heavy as I worked up the courage to look over at Brooke. She stood stone still, peering from stage left, holding onto every lyric. Her face slipped sadder and sadder in slow motion, until it showed utter defeat. She'd just made a fool of herself, and in her eyes, there was no comfort to be had by anyone or anything. And thank God Steve spared her his "I-told-you-so" garbage, and put his arm around her.

I had to feel bad for her, and I did, but at the same time, sadly to say, a good part of me probably knew she had it coming.

Penthouses en el último piso!

The elevators lurched open only to meet the faces of two stern-looking bouncers. Their expressions had just started to bring back bad memories when, seeing Brooke, they blushed and grinned, nearly falling over one another as they tried to make way. Unfazed, Brooke charged down the hall ahead of the rest of us.

"I think she wanna be invisible or some shit. *Whoosh*! She's gone." T-Roc shook his head to me.

"I'm going to go see if she's all right. Sleep tight T," I told him, seeing that she'd left the door cracked for me.

"Brooke?" I called out, hoisting it open all the way.

"I'm over here," a voice replied.

Passing through the open double doors, I found her on the private terrace.

She sat on one of the built-in stone benches on one end, hunched over, depressed, and uncomfortably silent. She stroked Pugslie's smooth, fawn-colored fur as he sat beside her, wagging his curlicued piglet tail. Across from us, the moonlit, crescent-shaped beach had just starting buzzing to life. Throngs of bodies assembled outside of nightclubs, all shouting to be let in, and the already dreadful traffic worsened, clogging the streets below.

"Why did he have to be so mean to me?" she asked me, breaking the stillness. Pugslie tilted his head from side to side, listening to her woes. "What happened between me and Ben was nothin', really it was nothin' at all," she said, pleading to me as though her confession could ring down the hallway to Jesse's room and he'd suddenly forgive her. "I *know* that song was 'bout me and—" She stopped, grabbing another tissue from the box I was holding. "He," sobbing unable to catch her breath, "he hates *meeeeee!*" she whined and burst out in tears.

I threw my arms around her, hoping that I could comfort her, but it only made her cry more. I wanted so badly to tell her it was me, classic calamity Jackie, who couldn't keep her mouth shut. But what could that do? Jesse was going to find out one way or the other, through me or anyone else, that much was clear. Two celebrities making out at a crowded party? If I hadn't caved in to Jesse, wouldn't there have been a dozen more calls on his checklist right after me? For that matter, my slip-up to Lexy in the first place was hardly more than a whisper in, what I had to assume—knowing what I knew about her—a rock solid plan all along. I hated burdening the guilt, but now was not the time to give her someone to blame. The problem was, she'd never be able to blame herself.

"It'll be okay Brooke. I know this sounds cheesy, but everything happens for a reason. He's not the only boyfriend you'll ever have." I began to sound like my mother—*Oh God.* "Look, you are beautiful, talented, and one of the kindest-hearted people I know. If he can't see that then he's not worth having."

"But I love him and I don't want anybody else, I want him. I made a mistake, it's not like I killed somebody for Christ's sake! When you love somebody, you're supposed to work it out, not go sing a song in front of millions of people and make me look like a ho-bag!" Her voice suddenly started to get angrier. "You know what? *That* was low." She started to pipe up and throw the used-up tissues on the floor in a tirade. "Maybe he didn't love me at all. If he did, he wouldn't have done that!"

"But you did a song too."

"That was different. Mine was nice." She snipped back at me. "I'm over this, fuck him. Let's order mojitos."

I couldn't help but laugh. I just witnessed Brooke go from heartbroken to bitter bitch in under sixty seconds. She could be so naive, so innocent; the problem, I guess, was that her unfortunate naiveté sometimes manifested, especially in this instance, with vicious consequences. She made out with Ben Hart because he was a real-life badass, a crush, in much the same way you had to assume so many people throughout the world would have probably given anything to make out with Brooke. She just didn't understand that she had to keep one foot in the real world while she lived out the fantasy of pop stardom. Jesse was her boyfriend. And she cheated on him. Simple as that. But of course I felt bad for her, because she really did like Jesse, maybe even loved him—who knows—but mostly I felt bad because she was my friend.

But me? My night? I was on top of the world.

Chapter 16

In a way, we are magicians.
We are alchemists, sorcerers, and wizards.
We are a very strange bunch.
But there is great fun in being a wizard.
–Billy Joel

A few days later, stepping back into my house after the emotional rollercoaster of Rio de Janeiro, my mind was everywhere, it seemed, but here in Beverly Hills. As I dropped my bags in the foyer of the main house, I found it silent for a change. I just stood there for a minute, collecting my thoughts, trying to put the jumbled mass of my life and David, Brooke's floundering and Jesse, into some sort of perspective. Brooke's personal life was not mine. I felt good, I decided. I should've been exhausted; instead, I found myself full of energy, full of thoughts. Front and center was my song.

My. Song. The one I'd composed in the very living room I stood in now. Brooke had performed it in front of *thousands* of people. My words, or most of them, had been on stage, over loud speakers, in all those awaiting ears in the crowd. I felt inspired—a little restless maybe—but inspired all the same. I wandered through the living room, little waves of adrenaline pumping through me, when my eyes fell on the old piano in the corner. Unthinking, my legs carried me toward it.

Sitting on that bench—I'd sat there *countless* times in my life—I combed my fingers through my hair, inhaled deeply, then chuckled out loud. *Unbelievable.* I thought about the conversation Brooke and I had had all those months ago: *Jackie, do you believe in fate?* I don't know what I believed in, but all these successive, simultaneous intersections of chance and good fortune swelled up inside me, and all I could do? I kept laughing.

Running my fingers across the ivory keys, I felt I had so much I wanted to *say* now—things that were far more meaningful and deep than when I'd written before. I tried to let it all flow through me, but the more I tried to bridge my feelings into music, or describe in words the things I'd experienced, the harder it became.

David! Ric Craia! Brooke! Jesse! All of these things muddled around in my brain, and my only hope was that I could somehow funnel all the nervous energy into something constructive. I found myself focusing on the keys, not playing so much as staring at them—like a person willing them to life when suddenly, the sound of music unexpectedly filled the air . . . I whipped around to see where it was coming from and then frowned.

The futuristic resonance of my new *it* cell phone—compliments of the swag bag I'd received tagging after Brooke through the amazing phenomena that were celebrity gifting suites in Rio—was unrecognizable . . . and somewhat annoying. I reminded myself to switch it to something that actually sounded somewhat like a phone later on as I reached for it. As I did, I thought about the Invicta watch I'd coveted for so long. In Rio, an Invicta representative had offered it to Brooke and she turned it down because the band was the wrong color. It still hurt to think about it. But whatever, I'd made off with a sweet phone.

"Hey, hey . . . finally caught ya, what's been going on Miss M.I.A.?"

"Hi," I stuttered, recognizing Lauren's voice on the other end. *Shit*. It wasn't that I didn't want to talk to her—I just didn't want to talk to her *now*. I'd learned from my mother that the birthday date I cancelled with Lauren was actually a surprise party at Nic's in Beverly Hills. People from high school, who I hadn't seen in years, were there to celebrate—but I hadn't been. Everyone seemed understanding and acknowledged the unpredictable nature of my otherwise glamorous job, but I couldn't help but feel like a giant letdown. I knew only my impressive job rendered my mistake forgivable.

"I-I didn't recogn—did you get a new number?" I hoped my voice wouldn't reveal my annoyance but as soon as I said it, I wanted to take it back and try again.

"No . . ." she said slowly. "I'm at the gallery. Don't you have, I mean, you used to have this number saved?"

Awkward.

"Oh . . . right, the gallery!" I said enthusiastically—*almost too enthusiastically*, I decided. "I—uh, got the new Vivi and I haven't had a chance to put in all my old numbers." A feigned chuckle escaped my lips in an attempt to sound cheerful.

"The Vivi?!" At the mention of what all the blogs were calling "the newest celeb must-have," Lauren discarded her wariness. "No. F-ing. Way. They don't come out for another two weeks I thought! Oh my gawd! Did you get the purple one? Or the yellow? I like the metallic green, flashy I know, but that's just me. Can you really send a hologram of yourself through that thing?"

"I, uh, I don't think so? I think that's in the works for the second model or something," I said hastily, really wanting to get back to the piano and really *not* wanting to talk about cell phones.

"So, anyway," she began again. "What's up for tonight? You going out? I've been telling a couple new girls at work all about you and I really want you to meet them." Picturing Lauren at work all giggly and trying to impress some lame new hires— *"My best friend Jackie is like, really close with Brooke Parker. How awesome?"*—I rolled my eyes.

"I don't know," I replied, even though I did. Poppy had texted me earlier that week to invite both Brooke and me to the soft opening of the new Hollywood hot spot she was promoting, Siku. Getting in Poppy's good graces was no easy feat and now that I was, there was no way I was lugging dead weight with me to the party. "Listen, about my birthday party—"

"Jackie, I get it, this whole thing with Brooke, this whole Hollywood thing . . . it's cool. And you should be having fun and enjoying every second of it." She sounded sincere, but I detected a faint sadness. "I guess it just sucks for the rest of us that miss having you around."

I heard a chime on the other end that signaled a gallery customer had waltzed through the door.

"Gotta go—call me if you're going out. I would love to see you. I miss you."

I suddenly felt guilty for all the snobbish thoughts that had just circulated in my brain. It wasn't Lauren, I told myself, to ease my self-consciousness. I would've *absolutely* invited her along if she hadn't had plans with her co-workers.

"Absolutely," I hummed.

* * *

The sneaking feeling of guilt flared again. Co-workers or none, the truth was, I probably wouldn't have invited her. The eye of a social hurricane is a pretty good place to be. Best friends with the most famous girl in the world, I suddenly found my name on every guest list in town. Invited inside even the most hush-hush of celebrity after-parties that raged on until dawn in sprawling private homes dotting the hillside, I had become one of the lucky few who could breeze past velvet ropes practically any night of the week. Night after endless night, countless cocktail receptions and launch parties brought us together with the hottest names in entertainment, sports, and fashion. I had to admit that I thoroughly enjoyed my introduction to Hollywood's gilded inner circle.

I hadn't *planned* on letting any of it go to my head. Deep down I was still that awkward preteen who papered her bedroom walls with glossy images torn from the pages of *Vogue*. But as each new night presented us with a different glamorous adventure amongst the city's hottest young socialites who, draped in glittering baubles and one-of-a-kind ruby-in-diamond necklaces, tripped over themselves to befriend *us*, it's hard not feel, I don't know, *different*. As the fantasy world I had once crafted in the collages over my twin bed manifested before my very eyes, I no longer felt like an imposter among an ultraexclusive circle. Feted, the source of much hullabaloo—I had emerged a new social lion.

"Make a hole, make a hole! I said move it mutha fucka, I ain't playing!" T-Roc growled as the car doors opened, displaying madness just outside them. This wasn't exactly Brooke's idea of going out incognito, and especially on a night like this one; she was full of an unexplainable nervous energy.

"I have like this low life force energy that's causing me to feel, like—sick or something." It was the ninth time that Brooke had said this since we'd left the house.

"If you're not feeling well we don't *have* to go out." One half of me thought of the half-written song I'd left at the piano while the other half thought about David, who would also be trotting down to Hollywood tonight.

"I just need to get centered, you know?" Brooke had reasoned. So there we were, following T-Roc closely now past the banks of cameras outside Siku. "I just—I just really love Jesse. Lou, Ben, all those guys are fun, but they don't treat me like Jesse did. My momma always said that if you love something you set it free and if it comes back to you it's meant to be. I know he's gonna come back." I half listened as we weaved in and out of the wannabe superstars, who struck poses so natural I couldn't imagine how much time they'd spent perfecting them in their bedroom mirrors, it seemed the flash bulb waltz would never end. But it wasn't the endless stream of starlets continuing to sashay across the carpet, like little plastic dolls rolling off an assembly line, that anyone cared about. The one they really wanted to see flipping her hair, puckering her lips, and making love to the camera, was Brooke. Offstage, she was *not* an attention seeker, and so she silently paraded past the flashing cameras, making a point to ignore them by hurrying towards the tall pink doors, pulling down the brim of a boucle newsboy cap over her eyes and holding her purse like a shield to block her face. Offstage, she just wanted to be a normal girl. Sometimes I thought I was the only person in the world that really appreciated that about her.

As we made our way inside, Poppy was all over it—taking care of us immediately. She whisked us through the crowd, the thumping of the music getting progressively louder. The draw at Siku—Hollywood's answer to the hottest new thing in a long line of hot new things—was its ice bar. Separate from the rest of the club, for those brave enough to bear the crisp twenty-three-degrees–Fahrenheit temps inside, lay a bar—not

to mention walls, chairs, tables, and even the glasses too—
made completely out of ice. A small group of revelers cloaked
in sparkling silver capes trimmed with bright white faux fur
crowded past us, giggling loudly as they stepped into an air lock
and closed the door behind them.

"The ice bar is right through there, it's pretty dope," Poppy
nodded. "You guys wanna try it out?"

Looking down at her legs beneath a butt-grazing skirt, bare
save for a pair of black fishnets, Brooke clenched her crimson-
colored lips.

"That's what those capes are for," Poppy said, seeing Brooke's
expression. "They were designed to keep your body heat inside
them . . . Here ya go!" Poppy pointed towards the table she had
set up especially for us. "Have fun—I'll be back by in a bit—
text me if you work up the courage to try the ice bar. I'll grab
you mittens too."

We had barely made ourselves comfortable, let alone poured
ourselves drinks from the awaiting carafe of liquors and mixers
before us, when a piercing laugh jarred our attention. Throwing her head back in incontrollable laughter—or was that
sobbing?—at the booth next to ours, was Rexy Lexy. I hadn't
seen her since the dreaded phone call from Jesse, after she'd
completely thrown me under the bus, and if there was one
person I definitely did *not* want to see or spend time with, it was
her. Extending a long, tanned arm, she waved to us excitedly—
or was that crazily?

Just then, her beach-blanket-bimbo–looking friend plunked
down to the right of her, patted her back, and handed her a
tissue from her purse. Lexy was in the midst of a breakdown,
right beside us, and we shuffled silently in our seats.

"He was like, tripping on me for no reason. I told him, 'I know
I'm not crazy, don't make me out to be crazy.'" Lexy looked at
her friend as if she were trying to prove how gutsy she was. "And

then, the other day I was at his place getting ready in the bathroom, and I noticed that he left his phone in there . . ."

"Please tell me you didn't—" Blondie pleaded.

Lexy shot a cold glare in her direction. "I most certainly did! I get the phone and check it out, right? You have *no idea*! Text messages to all these . . . ugh, *whores*."

Brooke's face turned red, then white. I gave her a compassionate look. The topic hit a little too close to home.

"Guys in this town go through women like Kleenex. What did you expect Lex? Honestly?" asked Poppy, who stumbled over to check on her, firmly ignoring her sad doe eyes. "I'm giving you tough love, sister."

Lexy ignored this voice of reason, continuing on maniacally. "I couldn't even cry at that point because I was just so . . . *whatever*. You know, if another guy who's a *friend* even calls me he's always like, 'Who's that—why's he calling you?' "

"So," Blondie muttered, fully engaged in the story now, "did you confront him?"

"Of course she did . . ." Poppy piped up nonchalantly from the sidelines.

"Oh—you have no idea . . . he just started flipping out on me. And I just looked at him and started crying."

Overhearing everything, Brooke shook her head sympathetically as Lexy continued on. "And he like, wanted to talk—told me he erased all the numbers. But . . ." Lexy stammered before switching gears to anger. "You know what? He's got it *made*—he can go out whenever he wants to, wherever he wants to . . ."

"Yeah, what have I been telling you?" Poppy called out.

"I just told him, 'This is the last straw, you do not respect me.' " She blew her nose loudly into the tissue she'd been clinging onto. Holding it up in the air, as if she'd just sensed our presence, she looked over.

"Hi-yeeee . . . sorry. It's just, Med—we broke up."

"Aww. Lexy," Brooke looked sympathetically at her—another sister dissed by her man. *If she only knew.*

As Brooke took her turn to sympathize with Lexy, I scanned the room for David before sending him another text: "r u here?" He'd been dropping clues that I might run into him tonight, sending playful messages. Did I need to keep a safe distance? I knew all too well how guys in this town played the game. No one wanted to tie himself down and fade away into dullness . . . and why would they? Especially when fresh faces abound, many of them willing to shag their way to success.

"Where you going after this?" Lexy asked.

Someplace you aren't, you cold-hearted traitor.

"Not sure," Brooke cooed sweetly.

"Hey Rach!" Cutting Brooke off, Lexy yelled out to a familiar-looking brunette with carefully manicured, natural spiral curls. Just arriving, she looked painfully out of place, a.k.a. sober. She greeted each of her friends with half-hugs and wordy hellos—too wordy for Lexy, it seemed. Holding up a glass of champagne in one hand, she yelled out again. *"Rach-el!"*

Unable to hear her over the noise, Lexy's impatience grew. Pursing her lips for a whistle, she bellowed out once more.

"Whore Tits!"

Engaged in what appeared to be a rambling conversation with the beach-blanket bimbo, the brunette looked up from the other side of the table. Noticing Lexy for the first time, Rachel gave her a toothy grin and flashed her the "one minute" finger as she resumed her conversation.

"Rachel Horowitz?" I called out, forgetting my intent *not* to communicate with Lexy.

"Did she . . . get a nose job?" I accidentally asked aloud to no one in particular. The button nose, which had apparently replaced her perfectly fine original, mesmerized me.

"Yeah," Lexy said nonchalantly. "You know Rachel?"

How could I forget? It was the first day of ninth-grade gym class and we'd all just changed into our compulsory gym uniforms—which were actually just matching blue T-shirts with our last names stenciled in white on the back. Rachel and I had been assigned to a circuit-training group along with Kenny Jurgen and Matt Stein, the two biggest loudmouth jocks in our grade. One glance at the back of Rachel's T-shirt reading "Horo-witz," turned the virginal freshman—baby fat still intact—into "Whore Tits"—a name that stuck with her until graduation day. Suddenly, I didn't feel so bad about Calamity.

But I wasn't about to take a trip down memory lane with Lexy. Narrowing my eyes in her direction, I could feel my contempt for her flooding back. No matter how many times we'd hung out—or what conversations had taken place—Lexy's brain seemed incapable of actually grasping the most mundane details of my life. All of our social exchanges—flowing through her and never sticking—now seemed so phony. The way she routinely disregarded the existence of any living thing beyond her own established realm, it was a shock she even remembered the names and faces of anyone she'd ever met. The fact that she *had* remembered to completely ruin Brooke's relationship at my expense, however, proved that she was capable, and that made me hate her even more.

In a huff, though I tried to play it down—since the inner monologue I had just gone through was exactly that: *inner*—I walked to the bathroom. Pushing my way through the melee, I found myself in the back of a requisite ladies room line. It took forever.

Thankful to be out of there, and much more calm than before, I made my way back to find Brooke in what appeared to be deep conversation with three girls standing near our table.

"I've just been feeling so weird, ya know?"

Getting closer though, I saw that only one of them was really listening while the other two were busy showing each other pictures on their P.D.A.s.

"You totally have to go see this guy who works at the gallery with us." I gulped. *Gallery?* My eyes now honed in on the wild toss of curls possessed by the girl Brooke was talking to. "Ken. He's the best."

It was Lauren.

"Jackie!" Brooke called out—not sounding sick. "Look who I grabbed for you!"

"Thought you weren't going out tonight?" she chirped.

"Hey! How'd you get in?" *Yikes*—I sounded like a total bitch. I didn't *mean* to. I really was surprised to see her there, knowing that if it weren't for Brooke, I'd be at home with a pint of Ben and Jerry's. "Sorry," I apologized. "I didn't mean—"

"Hey—it's cool—I may not know any celebs personally, unless you count . . ." Lauren nodded to the side where Lexy was still carrying on, before giggling mischievously. "I'm so mean, I know. No, but—uh, Star's dad owns the place." To her right, a girl with hair parted sexily to the side fluttered her fingers and smiled warmly. Not waiting to be introduced, the girl accompanying them leaned towards me and gushed through lips bitten red, "I'm Leah—it's so good to finally meet the famous Jackie!"

"We've heard *all* about you—good things, of course," Star added.

"You *have* to come with us to coffee sometime when you're not working," Leah continued, "so we can validate all of Lauren's crazy stories. Just kidding!" She gave Lauren a sisterly smile.

"Sure, sounds fun," I told her.

"I need an alibi now?" Lauren roared as the three erupted in laughter. A sickening feeling washed over me now. I kept my eyes fixed on Lauren's new friends, testing them, almost certain that after they'd given me their song and dance they would try to snake their way into Brooke's comfort zone. But to my surprise, even when she'd started loudly complaining about her "low life force energy" and her need to get centered yet *again*, neither Leah nor Star so much as *glanced* in her direction. They actually seemed . . . nice. If they were as genuine as they appeared to be, I argued with myself, then where had this wave of nausea come from?

"I'm starving!" Lauren chimed suddenly, grabbing her stomach.

"You wanna go? I could use some Jerry's Deli," Leah told her.

"Me too—it's not like we *can't* come back whenever the mood strikes," Star laughed. "Besides, it's so crowded in here."

"You wanna come?" Lauren asked, though I could tell from her face she was just being nice, knowing we weren't actually going to.

"Nah," I waved my hand. "You guys go ahead."

"Okay, call me this week?" Lauren asked as she headed in the direction of the door. Before I could answer she whipped around faster than a bullet. "Oh my gawd! I forgot to tell you! I ran into David earlier!"

"You what?" I asked though I'd heard her loud and clear.

"David," she yelled—her voice muffled as partygoers crossed in front of her. "He's here . . . near the ba—" And with that, Lauren disappeared in the crowd without a trace. I glanced hurriedly down at my Vivi—nothing.

"I'll be right back," I told Brooke, before pushing through the masses to the far corner of the room. There he was—sitting at a table near the bar. That was weird. *Why hadn't he texted me to say he'd arrived? He knew we'd be here.*

I quickly found my answer. *Jessica.* A cascade of long bleached curls rolled down her back, spilling over to her heaving cleavage made even more visible by the deep red racerback dress. Teetering back and forth on a pair of sky-high black stilettos, she made a quick lap, barely saying hello to anyone before taking a seat at David's table. *Odd.* Tossing her head back with a laugh, she placed her hand on his shoulder before slowly running it down his bicep. *Was she flirting with him? Who else did David flirt with over text messages?* After all, he worked with Steve, the master manipulator. But Steve did the dirty work. Not David. David was authentic. But wasn't that part of the act with all the boys at the top, rubbing elbows at swinger parties and doing lines? They came off sincere to snare you in.

I glanced down at my phone again. Nothing. *Why was I stressing like this?* They were just talking . . . weren't they?

And there it was again—the same wave of nausea I had felt earlier with Lauren and her friends, and at that moment, I knew what it was. Jealousy. I wasn't an envious person by nature and yet here I was, sick to my stomach.

I stumbled back towards our table, feeling as if I'd just been stabbed in the heart. I arrived to find that Rexy Lexy's entourage had spilled over into our booth. Throwing her head back in uncontrollable laughter now, Lexy seemed to be in better spirits.

"There you are! We're just trying to figure out where to go after this," Brooke called out to me. "You okay? You look like—"

Just then Lexy leaned over from her booth, sticking her head in between ours. Earlier in the night I would've been compelled to wipe the devilish smirk now affixed to her face right off of it. But now, the searing feeling that plagued my midsection was slowly making its way up to my chest—hating Rexy Lexy was on the low end of my priorities.

"I need a shot," I decided, reaching past both of them and grabbing the bottle of vodka from the table.

"Me too!" both Lexy and Brooke called out.

One shot led to two and then four . . . huddled together in the booth with Brooke and Lexy, I relayed my sob story.

"You guys think she's prettier than me?" I asked.

"Nooooo! Not at *all*!" they lied. Despite the fact that *M.A.N.* magazine had just named her "Sexiest Woman of the Year," a title earned for her willingness to pose in next to nothing for almost *anyone*, I took comfort in this.

"Forget them all, ladies!" I raised my glass.

"Here's to you, here's to me, there's no better friend than me, so if by chance you disagree—well fuck you, here's to me!" we belted out in a drunken chorus as Lexy passed around some "party favors."

"Here," she whispered, putting her hand in Brooke's and then in mine, depositing small pink pills into each of our palms. "Bottoms up girls, here's to . . . us!"

I looked over at Brooke and shrugged and we all tossed them back.

"Lex—we're going to get outta here, okay?" Whore Tits called from the other end of the booth. "It's almost two; I'm heading home."

Lexy looked back at us with a look of annoyance. "Screw that, *we're* going out . . . I think I might know where to find David actually . . ."

I scowled, putting on my best "I don't give a shit" look when, in all honesty, I was raring to go. Call me a glutton for punishment, fine. But drunk out of my mind, all reason went out the window. Besides, I *had* to know . . . was he really with Jessica?

Chapter 17

You go through stages where you
wonder whether you are Christ,
or just looking for him.
—David Bowie

Its back nestled against the rocky cliffside, the Monte
Puchol Villa sat high above Hollywood. Just a quick
turn into the long lantern-lit driveway and the City of
Angels moving busily beneath completely disappeared
into the night. Looming ahead of us now, it sat in all
its weathered limestone glory—a growing number of
exotic cars jamming the path to the lime-colored, over-
scaled doors. The upper terraces, flanked by black-and-
white–striped exterior drapes, held small handfuls of
beautiful people drinking, laughing, and occasionally
calling down to their friends to ask what the holdup was
in the valet line. A true hillside hideaway, the snobby

chic hotel—where the parties never had to end—was a haven
for young Hollywood. I looked up at the digital display on the
dashboard as T-Roc brought the big, black-tinted S.U.V. to a
halt. 2:30 AM—we were early.

"You sure you this got under control?" he huffed over to me.

"Positive." Though in all honesty I had no idea what was in
store for us.

"Come on," Lexy, already out of the car and antsy, yelled to
us. "They're in one of the bungalows!"

"I'll be here!" T-Roc called out. "Call me if you need me . . .
for *anything*!"

Two steps behind her, we meandered over a small footbridge,
the collection of stones in the shallow water beneath it catching
the glimmer of the moonlight. Enveloped by a jungle of flowering vines and tall hedges screening out the world down below,
Brooke looked around in amazement.

"Where are we?"

"Haven't you ever been here before?" Lexy looked at her as
if she'd just asked what a hair dryer was. "Tell me you've been
here before Jackie?"

I was suddenly grateful for her frequent bouts of amnesia. The
Monte Puchol was one of those places I'd always *heard* about
growing up, a guests-and-members-only kind of place. Everyone knew *someone* who'd been there, a cousin's best friend's
older sister or a classmate who swore her mother had once been
a member. It may've been a home away from home for those
cut from the same cloth as Alexis Young, but like Alice, Brooke
and I had just come out the other end of the rabbit hole.

Our heels clicked along the interconnected weaving pathways as we passed red clay tennis courts, croquet lawns, and
walled gardens.

"They're over by the pool," Lexy said, breaking into a swift
stride. I could hear a roiling din of voices and the clanking of

glasses as the path gave way to an expanse of discreet dwellings. Snaked with ivy and surrounding an L-shaped stone pool glowing blue in the night, this place was not to be believed. Despite the fact that the party was just starting, I could see a cluster of bodies up ahead. Spilling out from the bungalow's white rolling shuttered doors, they lounged beneath the tasseled umbrellas on the matching fabric chaise lounges poolside.

Caught up in the moment, we totally lost Lexy, who had made an excited beeline *somewhere*. Maneuvering through the crowd, we retraced her footsteps, giving up almost as quickly as we started. Med's little bungalow, it turned out, wasn't as little as it appeared at first glance, it was more like a petite palace with four double bedrooms, a second-story balcony, and two separate private garden terraces.

"Wow." Brooke held her hand to her head. "I think I'm starting to feel it." I'd almost forgot, *the tablet Lexy had shoved down our throats*. Keenly alert, but still strangely calm—almost euphoric even—I suddenly felt . . . *invisible*.

"Me too . . ."

Just as I was grappling with the effects of my newfound mindset, the sound of a slightly familiar yet distorted voice came towards us.

"For sure brah . . . If you didn't get to see the dailies—you got to. Fucking hysterical . . ." The owner of the voice made his way towards the terrace, ambling through the shadows as if he were moving in slow motion. Just then, he came into view, yelling quickly to whomever it was he was talking to, though it felt like one of those moments you see in movies where everything screeches to a crawl, and the lines delivered by the actors on screen sound like demonic groans.

"I-i-i-t-t-t-t's-s-s-s l-l-i-i-i-k-k-k-e-e *B-b-b-a-a-a-r-r-r-b-b-b-e-e-r- S-s-s-h-h-h-hop* s-s-s-e-e-e-t-t-t i-i-i-n-n-n-n H-h-h-h-o-o-o-l-l-l-y-y-y-w-w-w-o-o-o-d."

Osaka.

"Where, um . . . where exactly did Lexy take us?" I wondered out loud but wasn't sure if I could even hear myself beyond the confines of my own head. It was as if I'd stepped out of time and into the stillness.

"'Sup ladies?" Answering my question, Osaka rushed over. *Apparently someone could hear me.*

"Glad you could make it. It's been *real* stressful puttin' all this shit together, ya know? I'm ready to fucking drink!"

"What shit?" Brooke asked.

"*Head Shop*. We just wrapped. This is our *wrap* party." Osaka looked mad now, and just as I thought he was ready to toss us out for crashing his fiesta, he flashed us both a toothy grin. "This place is tight, right?"

Whatever it was that Lexy had given us kicked into high gear, sending a warm rush through our bodies so rapid, the blood coursing through my veins stung. A stoned look spread across my face, and I began to walk aimlessly through the bungalow— paying close attention to the mixed pulsations vibrating beneath my feet. I felt like a creature disconnected from my environment until, through the crowd, I spotted her. Long hair swinging, Jessica moved back and forth, dancing to the music spun by one of Med's friends playing DJ. At one point, Med began cheering her on, requesting songs off her album. She played shy at first, before singing along with them. Dancing on the couch as if it were a stage at one of her concerts, Jessica gobbled up all the attention she was getting. The more people looked at her, the more they glanced to see who it was, the happier she seemed. At this Brooke and I giggled.

"I can't even *imagine* you doing something like that!"

"Never!" she sputtered.

A whole song had passed and still, David was nowhere to be found—I took it as a good sign.

"Phew." I whirled around to face Brooke, opening my mouth to relay the information. "I don't see him. He must've ditched he—"

"Look! There's David!" Brooke smiled sweetly, waving over at him just across the room.

"Hey *y'all*," Jessica, mocking Brooke's drawl, sauntered over before shooting her a "whatever" smile.

Panning from one to the other, I felt like my body was spinning—slowly at first and then picking up speed—blurring the details in between them. At that exact moment, Brooke spotted Maddi and Jesse, which worked her into a frenzy.

"Oh my God. Jackie, you don't think they're together? Are they?" Her voice barely cracked it out.

"No. No. She's waaay too old for him. I'm sure they're just friends," I tried to brush it off, since I needed to come up with a plan for the unavoidable encounter we were about to have.

"Jackie! I'm so glad you made it all the way up here," David called out as he crossed the room. At this, Jessica followed suit, flashing both Brooke and me another "whatever" smile. "Hey *y'all*," she taunted in a mocking voice. I quickly looked over at David to see if he seemed uncomfortable—caught, possibly—in action. Not batting so much as an eyelash in Jessica's direction, he spoke as if she weren't even there.

"I tried to text you back earlier but this Vivi or whatever it's called that Steve brought me back from Rio—"

"Hey. No biggie." I shrugged, cutting him off, as if to say I hadn't noticed.

He *tried to* my ass. I turned to face Brooke, ignoring him as he started to respond.

"Well, anyway—I wasn't sure if you got email on yours . . ." He stopped, noting the very awkward situation that had developed. Unable to avoid her any longer, David cleared his throat to get my attention.

"Jackie, this is my friend Jessica. I don't know if you two ever formally met?" Offering only a tight-lipped grin, Jessica ignored me, looking, instead, over at Brooke as if I weren't even there.

"And what does *she* do for you again?"

Proceeding from instinct rather than from reasoned thinking, I sputtered, "You're a bitch!" I grabbed Brooke's arm. Between my fury, my high, and my skyrocketing blood alcohol, everything blurred into a dazzling swirl as I stood. "Let's get out of here."

We passed Jesse and Maddi, and Brooke tried to stop as I heard her mutter, "It's a sign. We're both here."

"I know it's happening so fast, but you make me feel like I can be myself around you," we heard Jesse confess to the woman who wasn't Brooke. "I just—I've never dated a girl as cool as you before."

Fuck. Things kept getting worse. Now Brooke was the one pulling me. "We have got to go. *Now!*" I could feel her hands tremble.

David trailed us as we stormed to the door.

"Jackie," his voice firmly called out.

"What?" I asked, daring myself not to cry like a baby.

"What are you doing to yourself? Seriously? You two are way out of control. Everyone's talking about how *messed* up you both look. You're gaining a real reputation."

"Yeah? Good." First he tosses me aside, then he scolds me like he gives a shit? Where did he get off? "We've got places to go." I sharply turned away.

"Just pull it together."

Incited, I thrust my middle finger in the air and didn't look back. At that moment I could only hear Steve: holding something like that over my head to control my behavior was exactly the sort of thing Steve would do.

Making our way towards the door I gasped, seeing Lexy and

Med in a flirty embrace. *This had been her plan all along!* We were simply her wingmen.

"Med?! Really? But he cheated on you! What happened to Girl Power?" I blurted out before I could think about Brooke's situation, but Brooke didn't seem to make the connection. She kept peeking over her shoulder, trying to see what Jesse and Maddi did next.

Lexy and Med paused, looking at me awkwardly, at first, before Lexy shrugged carelessly. Middle finger still propped, I waved it under her nose too.

I was out of control? Screw them . . . *all* of them

Brooke fell asleep the moment we got back to her house. Beams of light cut through the dark and across her wall. Every passing car jolted me awake. So I lay there, eyes wide open, watching them. Whatever Lexy doled out at the club made for a wicked, paranoid comedown. My arms and fingers ticked as I watched the shadows pulsate and eventually give way to the sunrise. Sleepless, yet unable to motivate myself out of bed, I thought about David and our . . . was it a fight we'd had? I suppose I should have been upset. In reality, I felt nothing at all.

It'd been two days since our night on the town, and they passed slowly, but I suppose everything feels that way when your brain was in a sluggish, dazed state like mine. I dragged myself out of bed and into the shower around 2 PM. I *would* finish what I'd started the other day at the piano, I told myself, but somehow I'd found ways to be motivated by absolutely everything *but* that. It wasn't until nine that night, as the first hints of inspiration came over me, that I stopped color-coordinating the markers in my parents' junk drawer and actually sat down to work on my writing.

Sluggishly, I set my hands on the keys, tracing out the first steps in my head, when I was interrupted once again . . . my phone sounded like an alarm going off. *Hadn't I learned my lesson?*

Incoming . . . Brooke

"I need you to come see me," Brooke said as soon as I picked up the phone. "I really feel . . . weird."

"Weird, how?" I asked.

"You're not even going to believe me if I told you, just—can you come over?"

"Sure, later okay? I'm working on something right now." She'd been saying that for days—I figured a few more hours wouldn't kill her.

"No," Brooke said slowly. "I r-e-a-l-l-y need you to come now." Forget feeling weird, she sounded weird too—small and secretive almost.

"All right, well I can leave now and be at your house in about fifteen minutes," I said.

"I'm not at home. I'm at the Sunset Tower . . . under my usual name." And with that she hung up the phone before I even had the chance to ask why. Brooke had called me in a panic a few hours earlier, asking if I'd call Lauren to get a phone number for Ken, the Reiki healer. "I'll text you her number," I told Brooke lazily. "You can call her for it."

I wasn't surprised that she was a bit shaken up. After the past week's events, who wouldn't be? But it was the fact that she had holed herself up in a hotel room so suddenly that concerned me.

Briskly, I charged into Sunset Tower and made my way past the still-bustling Tower Bar. The place teemed with a sort of stale retro glamour. Vintage Hollywood starlets were immortalized in black-and-white photos adorned with gilded frames hanging from the mauve walls. Everything seemed draped in dark mahogany and my shoes click-clacked across the cold, marble floors. Before I could hurry to the narrow elevators that would take me to Brooke's suite, I stopped at reception.

"Um, I'm here to see Genesis, Guardian of the Rainforest."

Answering the door in dark pink sweat pants and an over-sized T-shirt, Brooke looked uneasy. Her long blond hair that hung wet around her shoulders coupled with the condensation on the hallway mirror suggested she had just gotten out of a hot shower, an attempt, I figured, to settle her nerves. But the moment I stepped foot into her hotel room she went off again, moving piles of clothes from one end of the room to the other before moving them back again, checking the lampshades to make sure they weren't cockeyed and stacking the magazines on the coffee table according to size.

"What's wrong? Why aren't you at home?" I asked her, unsure if I even wanted to know the answer. It was almost ten o'clock and here Brooke was for some reason, dusting off the already spotless end tables with a tissue she had found in the bathroom.

"You're gonna—you're gonna think I'm weird," she said suddenly looking up at me, her tissue-filled hand still resting on the walnut table. "I mean, you're gonna think I'm crazy. You wouldn't even believe me," she stammered, turning her attention back to the possible particles of dust that may be clinging to the furniture for dear life.

"Try me." I shrugged, plopping down on the bed. As soon as I did, Brooke tugged at the corners of the comforter as if by sitting down I'd disrupted the balance of the room. "Brooke! Quit your O.C.D. act for about five seconds and tell me what the hell is going on," I yelped, unable to contain my annoyance any longer. She stopped and looked at me, opening her mouth to speak, before she began pacing in front of the bed.

"So that guy Ken, the one Lauren knows, he came over and

did a spiritual cleansing—you know, to help me get centered. I *really needed* it, especially after that other night at Siku—bad energy there."

Bad energy? Or a bad reaction to whatever Lexy had slipped us? I was still in rough shape, and it had nothing to with bad energy . . . *or did it?*

". . . And it was fine—you know?" Brooke continued, her voice shaky. "But then after he left, I was sittin' in my house and I saw these two evil spirits—a man and a woman . . . and they were like, playing with my hair and then they started smacking me—and you know, pinching me and kicking me," she explained with freaked-out eyes.

"What?" I asked in disbelief. "You can't be serious—what did you take today?"

Becoming defensive, as if *I* were the ridiculous one for assuming that she was on some kind of freaky acid trip, she yelled back at me: "I didn't take anything today . . . this has nothing to do with the drugs! I know what I saw!"

I may not have known exactly what she was saying or why she was saying it, but I did know that it was no use to try to talk her out of her delusion, as batty as she was. "All right," I said as if I was speaking to a child who'd just awoken from a bad nightmare, "you're fine here tonight and when you go back home tomorrow I'm sure you'll see that the man and woman have gone on their way so that you can relax."

"Oh, I'm not going back there," Brooke said certainly. "I'm staying here."

"Right . . . fine . . . but I mean, you have to go back eventually," I sighed, walking over to one the room's large windows. When she didn't answer, I added, "You know—to get your things . . ."

"No, I can't—there's something evil there now. I can't go

back there." Brooke was now sitting cross-legged on one end of the bed, looking down at the floor as if in a trance. I wanted to shake some sense into her, but I knew the best thing was to just let it go and to play along with her crazy fantasies.

Snapping us both back to reality for a mere moment was a loud buzz, made even louder as it throbbed against the wood of the coffee table. Her cell phone. We both stared at it like a foreign object until it ceased. Now dead on the table, I peered over at it.

13 missed calls . . . read the display.

Oh no—who else had she called to tell about the evil spirits and her night as their punching bag? Seizing it from the table, I scrolled the list of missed calls. They were all from the same number—coming in every few minutes or so.

"Brooke—your parents have been trying to get a hold of you," I told her anxiously. She continued staring off in space without answering. "Don't you think you should call them back?" I asked slowly.

"No, it's okay." She finally shrugged. "I talked to them before I talked to you."

If that was the case, the Parkers were probably already on the line with the paramedics, police, and fire station all at once.

"Have you picked up *any* of their calls back?" I asked her, the phone still in my grip. She slowly shook her head. "Do you want to?"

The same response.

"Well, I'm going to let them know you're okay . . . at the very least," I said, bracing myself for her protest. "They're probably scared out of their minds." Still silent, I waited a few moments to see if she'd take my hint and call them back herself, but to my shock, she didn't move. *Okay, this was getting crazier and crazier by the minute.* Taking a deep breath, I pushed down on a green button near the screen.

"Yell-o," rasped the voice of a person who sounded as if they'd been falling in and out of sleep.

"Hi, Will—Mr. Parker, I mean?" I asked.

"Yeh, this is him." He groaned as he sat upright.

"Hi, it's Jackie," I said, remembering the absence of caller I.D. at the Parker's house. "I'm so sorry to wake—"

"Calamity! That you?" He laughed. The sound of his voice was surprisingly calming, though he was obviously stirred. "My baby okay? We've been tryin' to git her on the horn. She called and left some crazy message on the machine over here. Her mama and me were both as dead as doornails asleep. By the time we got to the phone, she was gone."

"I'm with her right now. Um," I looked back over to where she remained unmoved. "I'm, uh, not sure if she's doing so well. She's had a little scare, I guess."

"What? What's happened to 'er?" At this he was fully awake. He sounded far less calm now, which made me nervous once again. *How could I explain this to her parents?*

I covered the mouthpiece and motioned over to her, "Brooke—it's your dad."

"I—I—can't," she whispered, wide-eyed.

"Hold on, Mr. Parker," I said taking my hand away before walking over to Brooke. Holding it right in front of her I spoke gently. "You should take it . . ." Tossing my cell across the bed, she just looked at it sitting there—tears welling up in her eyes. Scooping it up, she slurred sweetly, trying as hard as she could to sound normal. "Hi, Daddy."

Willy was in a panic, so much so that I could hear him clear as day all the way across the room. "What kind of darn messages you leavin' this early in the damn mornin'? You all right? What happened to y'all?"

As Brooke rehashed the very same story she told me, I cringed. First only silence, followed by more bellowing from the other end. "Brooke Marie Barbara Parker, are you doing drugs? E'erbody knows there ain't such things as goblins comin' 'round your damn house."

Uh-oh. He was coming down on her hard.

"What's going on? What are you doing?"

"Daddy, you know I don't do that bad stuff," she lied.

Ripping the phone away from her husband, Brooke's mom came on, her voice as clear as day. "Oh my God baby, are you doing this stuff?"

"No mama, I swear. It's just—I got a lot on my plate . . . it's hard sometimes."

"I saw you smokin' in one of them magazines young lady . . ."

"Ma, that wasn't even *mine*! I was holding that for Jackie." Completely caught off guard, I was stunned. *Brooke* was the one that started smoking before me . . . and she certainly was *not* holding any cigarette of mine, ever. Taking deep breaths, I calmed myself down. I knew she'd place the blame on me for the simple fact that she didn't want to hurt her parents. *"My mama would murder me if she knew I was smokin,'"* she'd always say.

Wrestling the phone back from his wife, Willy got back on the phone, his voice calm once again. "Tell me the honest to God's truth, now kiddo. How ya holdin' up out there?"

Brooke was silent for a few moments. Taking a big gulp, she signed. "Fine, I get a little homesick sometimes, I guess."

"You know honey . . . you don't have to keep doing this . . . you can come home at any time," Willy said quietly.

"I know." Brooke fell silent once again.

"I'm gonna call you straight away in the mornin'. You oughta get some sleep—can Jackie stay there with ya?"

Brooke looked up at me and I nodded my head.

"She can stay."

"All right, pumpkin. And listen, do me a favor, will ya? Take that big piggy off the gas every once in a while, you hear?"

Chapter 18

Faster, faster, until the thrill of speed
overcomes the fear of death.
–Hunter S. Thompson

"Oh my gaaawd!" Brooke shrieked into my ear. "You will never believe it—Hayley just called, and she totally has the answer to our problems." I could still hear her loud and clear even with the phone held a few feet away.

"Oh yeah? What's that?" Knowing Brooke's tendency to flip out over things others wouldn't find all that incredible, I couldn't wait to hear exactly what it was.

"She's going to Vegas tomorrow, and we're going with!" she screamed.

Without any real objection—it was decided.

It was about time we had a chance to really unwind—to get out of town for reasons other than shows or publicity—and fortunately for us, neither Brooke nor

I needed to trick or sway Steve. We had an ace up our sleeve—at least Brooke did: a Southern-talkin', gator wrastlin' ace. Say what you want about Willy, he was a force to be reckoned with once he put his foot—er, big toe—down. Brooke would have this much-needed break, and no Svengali manager, testy publicist, or legally binding agreement could say otherwise. Shockingly enough, Steve actually seemed supportive . . . for once. Of course, his real motive quickly came to light. Always the opportunist, he managed to make Brooke's getaway beneficial to himself.

"I called in a favor—you girls are getting a high-roller suite totally comp'd, so at the very least you *must* pay those nice blokes some respect by having dinner with them Friday night," Steve explained to us in a fatherly tone. The "guys" he was referring to were Joe Warner and Ashur Khouri, joint owners of the casino.

Brooke grumbled and rolled her eyes at the same time that I piped up excitedly, "Of course! Wouldn't miss it . . ."

Steve turned an eye at a sulking Brooke and then back to me.

"Don't worry about Brooke, I'll handle it," I assured him. *Was I dreaming or was that a partial smile on Steve's face?* It wasn't. Turning to look at us head on, he revealed a toothpick sticking out the other end of his mouth. Even though my eagerness to "help" hadn't garnered a smile out of him, he did seem appreciative at least.

Hey, I was excited. Not only was I getting a free trip to Vegas on a private jet and hanging out with my best friend, but it's also not every day you get to have dinner with great-looking, casino-owning, mogul-liscious men. Joe and Ashur were the ultimate playboy businessmen, rip-roaring all over town in their expensive new "toys," including a yellow Lamborghini Murciélago. They started out flipping small-time casinos on the Old Strip and resold them for ten times their worth, reinvesting the profits into the high-profile, luxury casino-hotels like the one where we'd be staying. Steve wanted to assure himself VIP status in Vegas, and Brooke was his "in." And fortunately for Steve, Joe and Ashur wanted to expand their horizons to the entertainment industry, so the union proved truly lucrative for both parties.

Steve did have just one more piece to add, another non-negotiable term. "T-Roc is going with you guys. Don't even try say anything but 'yes, okay, or hooray.'"

Brooke went with a noticeable eyeroll and mocked: "Yes, okay, or hooray . . ."

When big ole T-Roc met us with the driver at Brooke's place the next morning, he looked even more excited than me. He really was good company, and I had no problem at all with him coming along. I mean, who knows, it was Las Vegas we were going to—anything could happen there, and a 250-pound personal protection, even at a distance, was comforting, at the very least. He was also handy helping with our luggage, which was plentiful—perhaps a little too plentiful. As we loaded the car, I noticed a rhinestone-studded pink dog carrier decorated with silver-plated hardware.

"So Pugslie's coming along? He's quite the world traveler," I quipped.

"Oh, that's Ruby." Brooke twirled her hair as she slid into the car. "I sent Pugslie to live with Hayley. He was real cute, but all that snorin'—I couldn't even keep him in my room. He was gettin' too big anyways."

As we headed for the airport, Brooke filled me in on her dog du jour: Pugslie's replacement, Ruby the Cairn terrier.

The thrill of flying to Vegas in a private jet didn't fully hit me until we pulled up alongside the plane. No metal detectors? No long lines? I decided I could get used to traveling like a star. I nearly pinched myself as we boarded our private jet, sent by

Joe and Ashur expressly to retrieve us and whisk us away for a glamorous weekend getaway at their hotel.

Entering the cabin, I immediately noticed a spread of food fit for royalty. The guys had set us up with Brooke's favorites—tuna fish, Pringles, imported Belgian chocolates, champagne. Magazines and newspapers fanned across the table ready to entertain us for the relatively quick flight. On the floor, a silver-plated tray offered up cinnamon-flavored doggie pretzels, dog treats shaped like burgers and fries, and sparkly pink doggie cupcakes with sesame seed sprinkles that looked good enough to eat. Thankfully they were on the floor, or I would have dug right in.

Brooke bee-lined for the treats. "Oooh. Lookit. Ruby! For you!"

I followed close behind, and before long we were popping the bubbly and tearing into the chocolates.

"Dat chocolate's like a hundred bucks a pop." T-Roc shook his head. He had Ruby's carrier slung over his shoulder; her head poked out through the front roll-up window. "Seen it before. Mm-mm."

Chomping on a mouthful, I managed to blurt out, "Whoa. Seriously?" I decided to slow down and savor it. T-Roc set the carrier down and opened the door. As she rose from the faux-fur bedding within, I noticed she'd dressed up for the occasion: polka-dotted pink ribbon hairpins, cream sandals with pink heart accents, satin ruffled puppy "training panties" and a satin bow around her tail. Despite the cute ensemble, her short, sturdy legs covered in hard hair and erect, wide-set ears made her look scrappy and ready for a tussle. I laughed as T-Roc reached in to change the carrier's mini pad, where Ruby'd had a little accident.

After gorging ourselves nearly to the point of illness, we

snuggled into our grand leather seats—basically La-Z-Boys with seatbelts. Before the wheels even left the ground, Brooke was sleeping like a baby. "Now she's got the right idea," T-Roc leaned over and said to me, "can't believe she's still a Vegas virgin. She knows she's in for a long weekend."

"Vegas virgin, eh, T-Roc? Would that make you a Vegas Casanova?" I quipped.

"That's funny," he laughed, "I like 'dat. You been to Vegas a lot?"

"A few times, but never like this," I said, indicating the decadence we were going to be arriving in. Sure, I'd grown up amidst such extravagance—but only as an onlooker. I never envisioned myself actually *being* part of it.

"Listen," he said, turning serious for a moment, lowering his voice, "now I know Brooke ain't exactly enjoy having me around all the time, so even though Steve wants me on you guys like flypaper, I'll do my best to keep outta your way most of the time. Just please, you know cause I like my job and all, just let me know where you guys are going and when—you don't even have let Brooke know you're telling me. A text message is all I ask, and I'll stick to the shadows—I'll be like a big black linebacker ninja—but it's just, you know, for Brooke's safety."

I smiled widely. "Sounds like a plan T, can't wait to see you in ninja mode . . ."

"You won't see me," he said ominously, waving his arms around like Bruce Lee, "that's the first rule of ninja." I couldn't help but laugh. "I'm staying two doors down from you guys, so if you need me for anything, you know where to find me."

"That is if I can see you at all, right?"

"That's right," he said, shifting his weight back into the center of his chair. "Time for this ninja to get some sleep." He reached in his pocket and pulled out a black eye mask, extra-large apparently, as it looked like it could have been a young girl's training bra.

So T-Roc and Brooke were out, but I couldn't sleep. Vegas was only an hour away.

As we touched down in the Mojave Desert, Brooke woke up and squealed with delight. Her first time, and she seemed ready to dive right into the experience. In true Vegas style, a bright purple Hummer with green trim was sent to pick us up outside the airport terminal. We were both restless as we settled in, and I couldn't understand why. What I did know was that the high-octane, hedonistic desert playground matched our moods perfectly. Strangely enough, the closer we got to the Strip, the more at peace I felt. Sitting there like an awaiting chalice, the Strip forever pulsating with several-billion megawatts and high rollers and all-night parties—we were ready.

It was safe to say that in Vegas, one's hotel room wouldn't be used for much more than sleeping—but then again, few people were given the kind of star treatment that Brooke received. High in one of the hotel's forty-story towers, our megasuite came equipped with a large aquarium and private hot tub. Once our feet hit that Nevada soil, though, all bets were off. You couldn't predict Vegas. Somehow, it's the only place in the world where it's totally acceptable for complete strangers to flash each other come-hither glances from across the breakfast buffet or undress fellow patrons with their eyes as they scoop up shot glasses and Vegas-themed casual wear in the casino shops to bring home to their loved ones.

From the moment the chiming of slot machines and the bustling energy hit me, I felt the anticipation of a fun weekend upon us. It was truly exhilarating—all the sounds and sights and people of all sorts—and I couldn't help but try to take it all in. Neither could Brooke. But she came back down to earth as we passed a small gift shop near the lobby; there, she paused to look in the window. We didn't have time for shopping.

"C'mon, we have to get ready for dinner," I reminded her.

"I want some magazines," Brooke whined, holding her gum between her two front teeth.

"Fine—but we *have* to hurry."

Ducking into the store, we parted ways. While I perused the candy rack, looking for something to satisfy my sweet tooth, I heard a gasp from Brooke who was standing behind me with an armful of magazines already weighing down her arms.

Front-and-center on the glossy cover of the popular weekly tabloid, *Scoop*, was a photograph of Jesse holding hands with a waifish blond, underneath a headline that read: **LOVE AT LAST!** Without taking another look, I recognized the blond as paparazzi favorite Maddi Danner, whose good looks and fashion savvy helped transition her from a struggling assistant working for a big time designer to a household name thanks to reality television. Now, the sassy smirk Maddi was famous for was splashed across three freshly stocked shelves of *Scoop*, rendering Brooke motionless.

"She's pretty," Brooke said sadly, flipping the pages.

"I heard she's a real bitch." I shrugged in an attempt to deflect any negative energy from infiltrating our first moments in Vegas.

Shoving the magazine in my face, Brooke pointed to a solo shot of Maddi–shopping bags in hand–walking down Canon. "She's so skinny–she's got the perfect body." Looking at the photo, I wrinkled my nose.

"Way *too* skinny," I scoffed, trying to change the subject by waving my hand over the ensemble she was pictured in—long denim shorts with unfinished edges, a tie-dyed drawstring top sans bra, and leather thong sandals that laced around the calves.

Paying no attention to attempts at distraction, Brooke continued to scrutinize the exposé.

Tracing the bead necklace of leather Jesse wore in circles with her finger, highlighted and magnified in its subsectioned photograph, she sighed. "He's really talented, huh?"

He really had grown into an extremely talented performer and singer; he was also her first true love. Coupled with the tremendous guilt she carried around with her, I knew Brooke would never be able to completely let him go. And even though he had clearly moved on, and wouldn't be giving her a second chance, I knew that Brooke would never give up hope that one day he would.

On the page opposite Maddi and Jesse's lovefest, another familiar face—or, figure—caught my eye. The buxom beauty flashing smoky bedroom eyes through disheveled blond locks was none other than Jessica Rader starring in an ad for Luci LeSar belts. Glittery silver and gold double-wrap mini belts adorned Jessica's taut, tanned tummy and framed her diamond heart-shaped belly button bauble. Butterflies swirled in my own stomach as David came to mind. I never considered myself unattractive, but seriously, how could I compete with her?

"Whoa, she looks amazing, huh?" Brooke sighed in breathy fascination as she misinterpreted my fixation on the ad.

"You know what?" I said, snatching the magazine out of her hand, opting for a more direct injunction. "Forget this. We're in Vegas, and we're gonna have a great time! You know what they say? What happens in Vegas, stays in Vegas!" Raising one eyebrow to her, I thought to myself, *I just hope I don't leave whatever I have left in my bank account here.* "Now, let's go! Dinner!" I playfully grabbed her shoulders and shoved her out towards the hallway before she whipped around to give me her best pout.

"Do we really have to go? Can't we just tell 'em I'm feeling sick or somethin'? . . . Or maybe Ruby needs me."

There was no way I could let Steve down now that he'd actually put some trust in me for once. *She was going.* Besides, it would be rude not to have a nice dinner with the guys taking care of us so generously.

I grabbed Brooke's hand. "Not a chance, young lady. I think T-Roc's taking good care of her. Look, it's just going to be an hour or so. After that we can do whatever we want, let's just do this okay?"

We took the elevator up to the room where Brooke plopped down on her king-size bed, sinking into a sea of Italian bedding, she continued to plead with me, "Please, Jackie. I mean we've never even met these guys."

I gazed out our enormous window, across the Strip's sparkling blur of colors where all things fantastic and unimaginable were happening. "Come on Brooke. It'll be fun," I coaxed, trying to mask my frustration. This dinner had to happen.

Despite Brooke's whining and excruciating, foot-dragging mope, she wouldn't snap out of, I managed to get us both ready in time to meet Joe and Ashur at Mince—what amounted to a super-hot, high-end, yet down-home steakhouse. Their dishes included decadent twists on the traditional southern fare— gourmet mac and cheese with expensive touches such as black truffles.

As we approached the table, Brooke ditched her attitude and at least seemed happy to join them. It began to feel like a blind date. What would we even have to talk about with men who were well into their forties? Hopefully not politics—not after Brooke recently spied an outdated Kerry/Edwards bumper sticker and asked me who "she" was. Spotting Joe Warner's familiar face—he was often in the tabloids, albeit not as much as Brooke—I flashed my most flattering "look." Not only was he extremely wealthy, he was great-looking, with dark, arresting features and intense cocoa-colored eyes that gleamed a little when he smiled.

"Hi . . ." she said, which through her girlish accent strained by smoke and the South, sounded more like, "Hi-yaaah . . ."

Joe, with his well-concealed awe, took her extended hand in his. After a brief and awkward silence—one highlighted by the crackles and snaps fired off by Brooke's gum (a sure sign she was getting antsy once again), I broke the silence by asking one of my favorite urban-legend questions.

"I just have to know. Do they really pump extra oxygen into the casinos so people gamble longer?"

Ashur grinned. "That's just a myth. Ever since Mario Puzo wrote about it in *Fools Die*, that chestnut's been going around for a while. Think about it, would you be able to light a ciga-rette in a room full of O_2?"

"Maybe you should try decreasing the oxygen in the casino to disorient the players," I laughed.

"What's oh-two?" asked Brooke, trying to keep up with the conversation. Thinking she was joking, the guys laughed even harder. They might've been the young princes of Las Vegas, but sitting at that table with us—ordering drink after drink, and then shot-after-shot—they could've been any of the starry-eyed guys hopelessly trying to work their magic on a girl like Brooke. Not only were we getting the full five-star treatment hanging out with these guys—but they were fun too.

Several jokes, stories, and lemon drops later—as the waitstaff nervously fluttered about our table, snatching half-eaten plates of food, dirty forks and knives, and empty glasses rimmed with sugar—everyone seemed to be enjoying themselves. Everyone, that is except for Brooke, who downed the rest of her liquid dessert before slanting over to me with a look of "is it over yet?" I felt disappointment creeping in. *I was having a good time!* But as much as I didn't want to ditch the guys, Brooke did, and so I knew I had to think of something quickly.

"Quickly" became about twenty minutes of careful consideration and inebriated brainstorming, and in the end, my genius excuse sounded something like, "Uh, I think we're just gonna gamble a bit. It's Brooke's first time in Vegas and I thought we'd play some blackjack, maybe some slots, who knows . . ."

Ashur's eye's lit up. "Well who better to show you around Vegas than us?"

Equally excited, Joe chimed in, "Let's go play some blackjack, girls!"

Brooke's eyes bulged in disbelief, as if I'd just handed them an invitation to ruin her first night in Vegas. I conceded what little I could: I shrugged my shoulders and offered her my best silent apology. After all, a few more free drinks and we could ditch them. We had already fulfilled our part of the bargain as far as Steve was concerned—what was to come was just icing on the cake.

As we strolled through the casino with its owners, I could only imagine what tomorrow's headline's would read, but it didn't matter because these were Steve's games at work, not Brooke's or mine for that matter. Following Joe, we made our way through the high-roller room, adorned with chandeliers, cigar-smoking cowboys and rich old Japanese ladies playing baccarat. Right behind us, Ashur stopped briefly to whisper into the ear of a pit boss that quickly scampered to his feet to lead the way to a very private room suited for the Rat Pack themselves.

Slipping into one of the seats, I felt a small twinge in my gut. I wasn't sure what they were expecting of us, but Brooke never carried cash and my life savings was barely over a hundred dollars, thanks to the absurdly expensive car payment that had just been debited from my account. High rollers we were not. Still, I never thought we were *actually* going to gamble—drinking and dancing the night away were the only things on Brooke's agenda. Nervously, I stuck my hand inside my purse and rifled for my wallet as if, by some miracle, my hand would stumble upon a wad of bills I'd long forgotten about.

"Oh no, don't do that," Ashur cooed, placing his hand over mine as the pit boss ambled over with two trays in his hand. *These guys were way ahead of us.* He placed them down on the table—on each, a thousand-dollars' worth of multicolored chips.

"Oh my gosh!" Brooke chirped. "You're so sweet!"

"Yeah, wow! Thank you guys!" I added as I eyed the little plastic discs suspiciously.

They couldn't be real. . .could they? If they were, I could certainly think of at least twenty different ways the money could be better spent in my bank account.

"How quick do you think we're gonna lose it all?" Brooke giggled before giving her full attention to Joe who was trying to—slowly—explain to both of us how blackjack worked. As Brooke nodded with an empty stare, I couldn't help but to wonder what would happen if one if us turned out to be Lady Luck? *Would they let us keep it?*

I knew card games weren't quite Brooke's cup of tea, but after a step-by-step tutorial from Joe, she looked ready to play.

My first hand left me at twenty; it was an encouraging start. Scanning over the two of clubs in front of her, Brooke quickly looked to Joe for guidance.

"Stay . . ." he said, motioning his hand across the cards.

Happy with the twenty in my hands, I pushed forth another two hundred dollars in chips. "Double down."

"Impressive . . ." Ashur raised an eyebrow in my direction

before leaning closer to Brooke on his right. He murmured, "Why don't you go ahead and do the same?"

"Wha—?" She belted out—her confusion adorable to the guys and the dealer alike.

"The chances of the dealer busting are pretty good," he explained. Still unsure, but ready to take action, Brooke bounced in her seat and clapped her hands.

"Me too! Double it!"

"Congrats—well played," said the dealer, tossing more chips onto our heaps.

"You know what they say?" Joe smiled. "Money won is twice as sweet as money earned." Ashur laughed in agreement. *We were off to a great start.*

Dealt two kings in our second hand, I was pleased to see my winning streak continue.

As Brooke flipped over her a queen and a six of hearts—both Joe and Ashur shook their heads sympathetically.

"Hit me!" she said quickly and confidently.

"Hit me?" she now asked in a small voice, unsure of what to do. We all held our breath as an eight of spades hit the felt.

Eyeing the dealer's five of diamonds, I exhaled confidently. "Stay." I started to ponder the things I could do in Vegas with all the money I was making as the dealer was showing a weak-handed five.

"Eleven," he exclaimed turning over his down card and revealing a six of hearts. Out of the corner of my eye, Joe bit down on one of his knuckles in suspense—or maybe terror?

Slowly, he flipped his last card over. Cocking a crooked smile in my direction, he stood over a ten of spades.

"Ouch!" Joe called out as Ashur cringed.

"Twenty-one—sorry. Everyone loses."

"Are you kidding me?" I shoved my cards back at the dealer

in disgust. The two hundred dollars I'd just won disappeared in a matter of seconds. I had hoped to be redeemed by the next hand, but half a dozen later, almost every last one of our chips were raked off the table.

Brooke squirmed in her chair as the stacks dwindled, clicking her heels together. She was dying to move on to the next adventure, and our hosts were quick to take notice.

With one lonely hundred-dollar chip left on the table and a perfect twenty-one showing, Brooke confidently said, "Hit."

The dealer furrowed his brow, looking down at her with a puzzled expression before he reluctantly hit again on Brooke's perfect twenty-one. An ace of spades appeared, giving Brooke twenty-two and a "bust" hand; however, before the dealer could say "too many"—Ashur gave the dealer a stern look in the eye and quickly shouted "Ace! Brooke wins!" This was followed by a wink at the dealer and "Let's give her another hundred dollars." I was astonished.

Then came another hand. Brooke had a ten of hearts and a three of hearts, with the dealer showing an ace of diamonds. "Oooh, they're both hearts! That's good. I'll stay!" Brooke shouted. Everyone around me sort of looked at each other, knowing full well what it was *we* all knew and Brooke clearly didn't. But sure enough, the dealer flipped over his down card, which was a nine of clubs, giving him a total of nineteen.

"This is where you bust," Ashur instructed. Brow still furrowed, the dealer continued to stare.

"At least, those are the rules," Joe piped in, as if trying to communicate telepathically with Ashur, "of Brooke Blackjack."

Ashur shouted, "Dealer busts!"

"You won! We certainly can't let 'losing' like this be a part of your very first Vegas experience," Ashur said with a smooth grin as Joe hooked his arm around Brooke's shoulders.

"Who's in for another round of Brooke Blackjack?" Joe laughed.

Several gin-and-pineapples and a heaping stack of colored chips later, Brooke was definitely in the mood to party. Having finally decided we'd taken just about enough of their money, the guys escorted us to a club on the opposite side of the hotel.

"It's the hottest place in Vegas right now," Ashur assured us as we made our way inside Terra Firma. Three security guards dressed head to toe in black, along with the casino's *mood manager*—a perky, metrosexual in tight white pants— ushered us past the heavy purple curtains into the V.I.P. lounge, where lingerie-clad dancers gyrated atop multilevel platforms nearby.

Shit! I'd almost forgotten about T-Roc.

Sliding into the one of the plush lounges, I held my cell phone under the table adorned with bottles of liquor and carafes of fruit juices, craning my neck downward to construct a message. Pressing send, I looked quickly back at Brooke, who was already being tended to by a voluptuous cocktail waitress in knee-high boots. From where we sat, elevated off the dance floor, it was the perfect vantage point to survey the madness below—I just hoped T-Roc's ninja skills were as up to par as he had bragged. Brooke, already puffing away on a blue Nat Sherman cigarette, danced to the pulsating beats along with the sweaty, scantily dressed masses thrashing below.

"Hey Jackie," a cheerful—and familiar—voice hollered. Looking over my shoulder, I saw club security escorting Hayley and a couple of her college girlfriends to our table. The room parted like the Red Sea to let them through.

"Hayley!" Brooke shrieked and embraced her so forcefully I thought they'd both go tumbling to the ground.

"Whoa. Someone's started the party already."

"I'm just so glad y'all could make it!"

"Brooke, these are my friends Mia and Renee," Hayley made her introductions, and the girls tried not to look too star struck.

"Nice to meet you," they both said enthusiastically. A round of shots arrived. Brooke wasted no time.

"Here's to y'all. And to one helluva night in Vegas!" Brooke let out a whoop and raised her shot glass, downed it in a second, and chased it with another before the rest of us had set our glasses down.

She grabbed my arm, and before I knew it Brooke and I were on top of a platform, go-go dancing. She was a wild woman, gyrating so seductively that even I, in my already far-too-drunk state, questioned the decency of it, especially when the slipping, plunging neckline of her dress constantly threatened to expose her boobs. Every now and then she'd wobble a bit—and I would freak out, momentarily, thinking she was going down—but then miraculously regain her balance and get right back into lascivious groove. T-Roc had responded to my text, but he hadn't arrived yet.

I had to take a break; there was no keeping up with Brooke on nights like this. Hayley and friends sat around the table drinking apple martinis as I breathlessly joined them.

"Jackie, she's wild. I've never seen her this way!" Hayley seemed astonished by her friend's transformation.

"Tell me about it . . ." I remarked. "Why aren't you guys dancin'?" Before any of them could answer, Brooke came prancing over to us barely panting, but as she was used to that kind of workout, I wasn't surprised. I noticed that her eyes twinkling with the all-too-familiar gleam: the one that sealed our fate for the wild night we had in store.

"Oh my gawd!" she shouted, then froze. All too late, I spotted what had captured her attention: Maddi Danner in the corner, laughing hysterically at something one of her friends said. Waiting to see what Brooke would do next, Hayley and I quickly exchanged concerned glances. But Brooke just shook it off, or so we thought.

"Let's get crazy! C'mon. I know exactly where we can go."

"Brooke," I said, glancing down at my watch. It was already 2 AM. "I *have to* be up by nine tomorrow to get on the plane. I have Ric's photo shoot at one," my speech already sounded slurred.

"Uh-uh." She grinned devilishly. "This is *my* night in Vegas, and this party ain't near to over."

More drinks, more dancing, and way too much drunken stumbling later, we found ourselves at Crazy Horse II. A sea of strippers thrashed about on stages around us. T-Roc had texted me from Terra Firma, wondering where we were, and I can't imagine he was pleased when I replied with where we had ended up. Somewhere in the past few minutes I had lost track of Brooke, but I nearly swallowed my tongue when I saw her emerge from the bathroom. My triple take managed to ooze into one long, blurry stare as she strutted out in nothing but her lacy pink bra and panties. Unflinching, she made her way to the nearest stage, hopped up, grabbed the pole and began gyrating against it. Though management typically frowned upon this behavior, approaching the stage with a half-astonished frown, with a little eyelash batting and sweet southern drawl, Brooke persuaded them to bend the rules. Hayley needed no convincing; she enjoyed this insanely wild version of Brooke, and sat there cheering her on, tossing dollar bills that had come from God knows where.

Somewhere in the intervening time, T-Roc had arrived. He stood near, but he remained silent. He hated this scene for the simple fact that if the future Mrs. T-Roc were to find out about him being here, there'd be hell to pay. And while we all ended up partying with the strippers late into the morning, T-Roc occasionally shook his head. To him, Brooke was spiraling out of control, and it tore him up inside. So he did the best he could, but he couldn't protect Brooke from herself.

My night had gone from worried to full-on carelessness, as I relinquished my anxiety in favor of succumbing to the . . . Vegas charm, I guess you could call it. As I headed to the bathroom, for some reason, I couldn't get David out of my mind. In my stupor, I decided it would be a good idea to send him a racy text message when, pulling out my phone, my eyes uncrossed and I noticed it was already 5 AM. *Shit.* In perhaps my only good decision of the night, I packed away my texting plans for another day.

Returning to the girls—Brooke, Hayley and friends, and a half-dozen strippers—I had made up my mind. At 5 AM, it was too late for sleep anyway, and when our newfound friends offered us some coke, I took a few bumps, figuring that since the day had already arrived, I could stay up until we had to jet out.

"Brooke," I could barely form my words at this point. "Brooke, I godda be on the plane and back by one." She nodded. My head was throbbing with the incessant beat of the strip club music. The entire place was still a packed and sweaty, noisy mob.

"I wanna go with you, I'll be your assistant!" She lit up. "Yay!! It'll be soooo much fun!" Wide-eyed and clapping her hands, Brooke insisted she tag along to the Ric Craia shoot. She gushed about arriving under the assistant-alias of "Melinda," because no one would realize that she was indeed, the one and only Brooke Parker.

Hands down this was one of the stupidest things that ever slipped out of her mouth, and I spewed out my Ketel One and soda before collapsing to the floor in laughter. As a very recognizable celebrity, the fact that she thought for a moment that she could pass as my assistant—while cute—was about as likely as a monkey flying out of my butt.

"You—you're joking, right?" I said, reaching up for her hands to help me back up to my seat, all the while wiping the spillage off my mouth.

"No, I'm totally serious. I'll just wear my reading glasses—oh!—and maybe I'll wear a wig too! No one will have a clue, and since my name will be Melinda, it'll be totally fool-proof!"

"Okay. Genius," I balked. "That may have worked for Clark Kent, young lady, but you're Brooke-fucking-Parker. My neighbor's goldfish probably knows who you are, but you're right, no one who *works in this industry* will be able to perceive your real identity when you show up as Melinda, assistant extraordinaire."

"C'mon! It'll be fun, Please?" she said with the classic puppy dog eyes.

At this point, I was so fucked up I actually thought to myself that maybe the glasses could work. If anything, I'd look like a rock star bringing Brooke with me to my photo shoot. What's the downside? I might look like a codependent lesbian needing my friend/assistant with me, but at least it would be her. "Melinda, you're fucking crazy. Let's dance!" Another round of shots, and we danced the rest of the night—er, morning—away.

Somehow, miraculously, and with no shortage of oversight and assistance from T-Roc, we ended up back at the hotel. A faint *cling-cling* from somewhere aroused my consciousness, yet another miracle, though the heavy lids of my eyes took longer to control. As the room slowly came into focus, I was able to identify the source of the *clinging* as Brooke, who was moving about the communal bathroom, arranged her belongings along one of the neon lit washbasins. The blood rushed to my head as I climbed out of bed, and I looked down in disgust at the disheveled outfit I was still wearing from the night before.

"I feel like death," I said groggily as I made my way to one of the bathroom sinks. I felt woozy, as if I might fall over, and was surprised to see Brooke so alert and concentrated. I looked over at her and realized she looked frantic. Reaching into her toiletry bag, she lined up things like bobby pins, tubes of toothpaste, and deodorant in concentric rows before grabbing them all suddenly and tossing them back in her bag.

"What are you doing?" I asked—my head pounding so viciously I almost didn't want to hear the answer.

"I don't want to leave anything behind," she said without stopping to look at me. "I might need this stuff on the way to the airport or somethin'." Watching her frenzied state, a sudden fear washed over me followed by a lightheadedness. Bits and pieces bubbled sluggishly to the surface.

"Oh my God," I gasped, feeling like I could vomit at any second. At this, Brooke stopped what she was doing and looked over at me. "You . . . ah . . . you remember anything about last night?" I asked her fearfully. My mind raced, as I tried to recount the night's debauchery. We were screwed. "What time is it, anyway?"

It was 10:00. We were completely fucked. Both of us.

Hoisting ourselves into the backseat of a big, black Hummer waiting in the back of the hotel for us, we'd only had two hours of sleep in the span of forty-eight hours. The faint tinkling of Ruby's nickel-plated dog collar sounded like a gong banging in my ear. T-Roc had delivered her to our door dressed in a faux-fur leopard print coat that morning, per Brooke's request, and now the little diva sat and tortured me from Brooke's lap. I felt weak, nauseous, and suddenly the bright desert sun felt like my worst enemy. To make things worse, the severity of last night's actions became increasingly clear with every passing second.

"What are we going to do? Say? This is just going to be bad . . ." I muttered.

"What is?" Brooke's confusion was so startling I began to laugh.

"Well . . ." I started sarcastically. "You were dancing around with the strippers last night, and I'm pretty sure you showed off a hell of a lot more than you should have. And I'm going to miss the shoot."

"But not like, for real *real*," she smiled.

"Um, yeah—for real *real*."

"But I thought that's why they said that thing . . . you know, something like 'what you do here, doesn't leave here?'"

"What happens in Vegas stays in Vegas," I corrected her. "Untrue." Just ask the guy who gambles away his home or the girl sitting next to you on the plane itching uh, *down there*, in a suspicious manner. Yep, what happens in Vegas, surely *does not* always stay there. And when you were there with Brooke Parker—when you *were* Brooke Parker, that certainly wasn't the case.

This was dawning on Brooke. She took a deep breath.

"It'll be fine," she said aloud, as if trying to convince herself.

As all the sights and sounds of the Strip began to fade in the distance, I had the strange urge to scream out, "Stop! Turn this car around . . . leave me behind, I'm not going back." Every few minutes or so, one of our cell phones would ring, and each time Brooke and I would exchange worried glances, looking at them as if they were ticking time bombs. More waves of nausea kept washing ashore and I couldn't even begin to digest the repercussions that were in store once we returned home. As if reading my mind, our driver peered at us through the rearview mirror and smiled—I was sure he'd seen this kind of post-Vegas look many times before.

"Where's home for you? L.A.?"

"Yep. Good ole' Los Angeles, California," I said unenthusiastically.

"I've got something for you," he smiled as he turned up the radio, filling the car with the sounds of the swinger of the Sunset Strip himself, Sinatra.

"*. . . The only town like a this town. This town is a make-you town. Or a break-you-town . . .*"

"I never seen it confirmed or anything, but I always heard it was about L.A. You ever heard that? Being from there and all . . ." I noticed a small picture of Old Blue Eyes taped to the dash, and I imagined him as the kind of guy whose obsession with all things Frank prompted him to leave whatever small town he was from and head to Las Vegas, dreaming about nights spent in the Copa Room only to find himself working in transportation instead.

"No, I haven't heard that . . ." I said as we pulled into the terminal. Spotting a cluster of men—cameras in hand—awaiting our arrival in anticipation, I realized that we were going to have to contend with our consequences sooner than we had expected. You would think, by now, this was something I should've expected—these sweaty, frenzied guys who, after being tipped off somehow, had driven ninety miles an hour all the way from Los Angeles in an attempt to get what they all called "the money shot." I watched as they morphed from merely anxious to completely chaotic. The way they yelled, shoving innocent bystanders out of their way in fits of desperation, always shook me. No matter how many times it happens, it's an experience you never really get used to.

"*This town is a quiet town. Or a riot town like this town. This town is a love-you town. And a shove-you-down and push-you-'round town . . .*"

It was all the above. And all I could do was grit my teeth and hope that, somehow, I'd remain afloat.

Chapter 19

Chaos is a friend of mine.
–Bob Dylan

The obligatory Lincoln town car greeted us at Van Nuys airport and chauffeured us back to Brooke's temporary home. Quite dazed, very tired, and still plenty drunk, I wondered what I would have blown on a breathalyzer test as we stumbled in to the bustling lobby of the Sunset Tower. To my astonishment, I came to find that Brooke had stuck to her word. She never returned to her Hollywood Hills home; it was put on the market almost immediately. Brooke, apparently, had made it quite clear that this was to be her homestead until she found herself another place. Steve, who knew more about her finances than she ever did, would usually interject in these situations. There would be lofty explanations followed by simple sketches of pie charts or even stick figures to show her the difference between everything from impulsive decisions to good investments. Even I had to agree with him 98 percent of the time—Brooke had no concept of money—$1,000,000 or $100, it was all the same to her. And though she could usually be persuaded into making the smarter decision, most of the time, this was one thing she refused to budge on. When it came to asking for time off or sticking up for herself (or her *friends*), Brooke was a pushover. But when it came to evil spirits, she was a stone wall. Snuggled away in her plush—not to mention pricey—two-story suite, which Steve had pointed out would be way more expensive than just renting another house in the interim, she refused to budge. At the end of the day, her earnings were *hers* to spend any way she saw fit.

"No!" I heard her tell him on the phone one day. "I can't move into any ole' house—I've got to feel out the energies first and make sure it's cleansed."

Whether this was a bad after effect of too much partying or a brief but serious mental collapse, I couldn't be sure. The one thing I did know, however, was that whatever *did* happen that night on the hill scared her silly.

After running through the lobby to escape the hustle and bustle, we shut ourselves inside her private oasis. "I'm still fucked up," I told her, letting out a shrill *hiccup!* "I've got to get this under control."

"I still wanna go to your shoot—I'm Melinda, remember?" she chirped.

"Jesus Christ, Brooke, I thought you were kidding."

"Jack-ie—" she huffed, "it'll be fun, I promise. No one will know it's me."

"Everyone will know it's you Brooke, but I'm in too much pain to argue rationality with you anymore."

"Yay!"

Ugh. "But we have to hurry. You *must* be ready when I leave."

Highly doubting the likelihood of that, I shut the bathroom door. The warm cascade that greeted me upon entering the shower couldn't have come any sooner as I sluggishly soaped off the stripper pole scent I was sure had clung to me.

No longer smelling like someone fresh off of Skid Row, I felt myself sobering up. Throwing a towel over my tangled mess of hair, I headed towards the stairs. Standing at the top of them I paused—maybe I hadn't sobered up as much as I thought— looking at them now, they might as well have been Mt. Everest. *It's only one flight—okay, you can do this* . . . I told myself, dropping to the floor. Fearing falling and breaking my neck, I scooted down each one on my backside with great caution. Maybe the nickname Calamity had worked its way in far enough that I actually believed it—or maybe I was still that smashed. On my feet again, I wobbled my way into Brooke's bathroom, not the least bit pleased to see her casually blow drying her hair and juggling a lipstick tube when she knew I was in a hurry.

"We don't have time for this Brooke! We have to leave *now!* It's twelve-thirty and I have to be in Culver City by one. Ugh! This is not good, I'm so out of it. I had to wash my hair at least four times to get out the brothel stench," I said, clasping my face in my hands. Of course, the brothel smell was the least of my concerns at this point. I felt like a wet cat and who knows what I looked like—I had made it a point to steer clear of all reflective surfaces.

"Okay, okay I'm done; let's go. We'll have to leave the top down in my car to blow-dry our hair," she said, mindlessly rearranging the lipstick on the counter in order of shade.

"Great—I just want to get this over with. Let's go." I felt too awful to feel guilty about it, though the nagging wave that flushed through me made it quite clear. The man I'd admired since I was a little girl—whose songs told stories that had profound meanings I'd taken with me throughout the years—

awaited. I not only got to *meet* him, I got to spend *time* with him—trapped in my chair with nowhere to escape, this was my chance to pick his brain. *Who had I become all of a sudden?* An opportunity like this should be the highlight of my life . . . but the only things I could think of in my current state were sleep, an abundance of water, and how I would make it all the way to Culver City without barfing on my lap.

"Just *one* second! I want to make a drink first," said Brooke.

A drink? Reaching into the mini bar, Brooke pulled out a can of V8 and she mixed six parts Grey Goose from a bottle she had stowed in one of the drawers. I could feel the chunks rising and I immediately started to gag as if a horse pill was lodged in my throat.

"I'm gonna grab my stuff," I yelled, turning away, afraid I was about to lose it any second. I grabbed the makeup cases I had left in the entryway before sidling up to her white Mercedes 500 SL convertible pulled up outside.

"You drive," she said, taking her keys from the valet and flinging them in my direction as I groaned. Just because I didn't have a cocktail in my hand didn't mean I was any better off than she was. She ducked into the passenger seat quickly—I was so far gone, I'd almost forgotten to look out for any pesky paps lurking nearby.

"Great," I mumbled under my breath, thinking I may've spotted one across the street. The last thing I needed was to be trapped in a pack of bloodthirsty, camera-clutching scavengers. If we were lucky, however, no one had seen us and then *maybe*, if I covered one eye just so, I'd only see two lanes instead of four. And *maybe*, just maybe, I'd be able to stay in the right lane. Coasting out onto Sunset, I decided to stick to side roads—no highways!—leaving the fast lanes to those physically and mentally capable of operating things like staircases.

Smashbox Studios was the crème de la crème when it came

to studios nestled on Hayden Place. As I pulled into the parking lot, I noticed that most of the crew was congregated outside
having cigarettes and enjoying craft services.

"Oh shit. Everyone's looking at us," I said to Brooke. This
wasn't exactly how I envisioned my entrance. I imagined I would
be able to slink in undetected, find out who the publicist was
and head over to the makeup room with Brooke in tow. That
would have been wonderful, if it hadn't been a fantasy. Everybody stared. The crew, the photographer, and at least the people
who looked pretty important.

"Just keep your sunglasses on and smile a lot," I said under my
breath. "You can do this." I just didn't know if I was talking to
Brooke or giving myself the best pep talk I could muster. Probably both. I shut the engine off and prayed away my increasingly
famous Calamity Jackie persona, hoping I wouldn't trip and fall
over myself getting out of the car.

I headed toward the back of the Mercedes to grab my gear
while Brooke, forgetting that she was my assistant, stood
chomping on her gum and hugging the V8 two-liter she had
made a makeshift flask of, just watching me struggle with my
fifty-pound makeup cases. Predisposed with gathering my
belongings, I could hear people muttering Brooke's name in
somewhat hushed tones, ignoring the fact that we were clearly
within earshot. A familiar voice emerged from the pack in the
distance and called out my name. As it drew closer, I could tell
it was David. With Steve in New York working on a very important deal for Brooke, I didn't think he was actually going to be
here. I had always been under the assumption that David was
Steve's American Express card. He never seemed to leave home
without him, so I didn't figure him into this equation.

"Why the hell is Brooke with you?" he said in a condescending tone—the kind you use when your dog just peed on a new
carpet. "Good God, you reek of booze." Since I had already

cringed when I realized he was even here, I can't even describe the feeling that was coursing its way through me. Some terrible amalgam of embarrassment, confusion, and not a little bit of shame. "This is so bad Jackie—*so* bad. What were you thinking? That you were just going to show up here with Brooke, who is clearly trashed, and nobody would notice a thing?"

"I'm totally fiiine," I slurred, trying to keep my composure. "Where's the bathroom?" I blurted out, hoping against hope that I could quickly change the subject and divert some of the shame and attention.

"I put my ass on the line for you, Jackie, so you need to get it together for me. Not soon. Not quickly. *Now*. What have you guys been doing?" he said, scolding us like bad schoolgirls. "Have you *even* slept?"

"Oh David," Brooke said putting her arms over his shoulder, more as a crutch than as an act of contrition. "I'm Jackie's *assistant* today," she said with a long emphasis on *ass*. And I thought this feeling couldn't get any worse. But this, despite my deepest, most heartfelt wishes and prayers, was reality. And reality kinda sucked.

"Jackie, we have to—" I completely tuned David out when I noticed, out on the lot, a striking man with wildly curly hair and a long face. Wearing one of his signature plaid work shirts and faded Levi's, he leaned up against a wall and watched everyone around him with a wry, reflective smile. I recognized that smile. It was Ric Craia. Then, I became acutely aware that Brooke had wandered off.

"David, where'd Brooke go?" My headache raged on, and this panic wasn't helping. Then I heard a crash, followed by gasps.

"Will someone get this woman out of here?" the photographer growled.

"Jeeze. I was just helpin' out. I'm Jackie's assistant y'all."

Brooke stood near thousands of dollars' worth of camera equipment, nervously arranging things in neat rows. She'd spilled her V8 all over. I closed my eyes, hoping it was all some horrible drug-induced nightmare. But it wasn't. I wanted to crawl under something and die.

"Brooke. Please," I pleaded, interrupted by a hiccup.

"Jackie! I don't know what's going on with you," David gave me a look half furious and half pitying, "but I worked my ass off to get you this job. I can't believe you'd treat me this way. I'm done. You two need to go, now."

He turned around and coolly walked away. His chilly demeanor further perturbed me. I knew following him and offering my apologies would be pointless. People, I learned, were going to do the things they wanted to do whether we like them or not. I looked around, longingly at what might've been, should've been, but because of *me*, couldn't and so wasn't. And there was Ric Craia, watching the whole grand mess unfold. I didn't deserve this shoot, and while every childhood memory begged me to walk over and at least introduce myself, I pulled down my shades and turned away.

"Brooke!" I wanted to scream her name, but in my defeat only said it sternly. "*Now.*"

Marching back to the car, my day couldn't get any worse, right? *Wrong.* Once it began, I knew it wouldn't be going away.

"Brooke! Hey Brooke!" one voice shouted.

"Wild weekend in Vegas, huh? Care to comment?"

The paps found us. My phone rang. I ignored it.

"Brooke. What about the strip club? I hear you ran into Maddi Danner. Care to comment on that?"

"Maddi who? Never heard of her." Brooke almost enjoyed her little cat-and-mouse game with the paparazzi now. She flipped up her middle finger. "Peace guys."

Cameras clicked as they swarmed around us with every step. Once we'd entered the car Brooke grew worried.

"Jackie. Don't run them over. Be careful." She closed her eyes and started to pray inaudibly as I pulled out. Already rushing to their cars, they followed after—ready and waiting—always waiting—for our next move.

Chapter 20

Rather than love, than money, than fame,
give me truth.
–Henry David Thoreau

Even the faintest gusts on a hot and dry summer night like this one can stoke the anxiety of those with multi-million-dollar homes dotting the hillsides; the threat of fire season, where flames can rise and spread seemingly out of nowhere, caused unrest in the surrounding canyons as seasonal winds spread to the north and west rims of the steep ravines. And below the base of Benedict Canyon, I'd just shut the headlights off in my driveway, home from my late-night trip for takeout, when my cell buzzed to life in my pocket. Some silly, girlish part of me was hopeful, for a split second, that it was David calling to tell me he was no longer mad . . . and of course, that he couldn't live without me.

Just before killing the engine, the radio blared a quartet of familiar voices singing lyrics that cut through me like a knife.

> *You weren't genuine and neither were your promises . . .*
> *You create a hopelessness in me . . .*

"Back in the spotlight again, that was the Emerson Brothers with the first single from their upcoming . . ." the D.J. announced.

The display of my Vivi bathed the darkness in my car with an eerie bluish glow. *Incoming . . . Brooke.*

"Hello?" I asked breathlessly, wondering why she would be calling at such an hour.

"Jackie?" the voice on the other end sweetly purred.

"Yeah, hi—what's going on?" I sat hovering in my car in anticipation.

"You asleep?" she asked.

"No, I—uh, I'm actually still in my car. You?" I asked, feeling suddenly foolish. *You? She had called me!*

"No, I'm awake," she said unfazed. I let out an uncomfortable laugh before she spoke again. "I can't sleep. I hate being up in this new house all alone. You wanna come up?"

"Um . . . sure. Why not? What's the address?" I scribbled it down on the back of a leftover fast-food napkin. Brooke had finally ditched her stigmatized digs and had just settled into her new place over the past week—I couldn't wait to check it out. We had a 7 AM call time the next day for a big interview on Celebrity Central's *Hollywood Junket*. Between that and her usual skittishness, I figured she was a bundle of sleepless nerves.

Turning off of Sunset Boulevard, I made my way up the narrow tree-lined roads to Brooke's estate—her sanctuary amid the chaparral and lupine. More disturbing, now, than the very real danger of fire season was the life beyond its walls. Within the sprawling home, hugged by a sparkling blue-tiled pool and outfitted with sand-blasted green-glass walls, Brooke hid herself away in a self-contained world like a recluse, imprisoned in her last shred of anonymity.

I slowed the car to a crawl, squinting to find an address, *any address*, on the ivy-covered gates of the manses on both sides of me. Just as I began berating myself for not getting a GPS with my car (forgetting, for the moment, that I didn't even have enough money in my bank account to cover one of its *hub caps*), I spotted twin S.U.V.s—one white, one black—lined up on the right-hand side of the road. *Paparazzi.* I could now spot them anywhere. Staked out with only their dome lights gleaming, they took a breather from the gyros they were inhaling to watch me like hawks. To my surprise, it turned out that on a night like this one, when I found myself completely lost in the hills, they were actually good for something, if only this once. I could only imagine what a nightmare it must be to have Brooke suddenly pop up as your new neighbor though. Sure, there were only two now—but in the morning there would be five, and the next week ten. I couldn't help but wonder if those surrounding neighbors, high up there on that promontory in their beautiful houses designed to sit in perfect harmony with nature—knew the kind of discord that would soon befall their little enclave. Before long, Brooke would become so paranoid that she would be forced to flee once again. The crowds enveloping the streets, the racing cars and the clashing of voices that all screamed at once—this is the kind of welcome wagon Brooke Parker brought to town.

"Brooke?" My voice echoed in the empty space of the foyer as I stepped inside. The home was far larger than they one she'd just moved out of, and it didn't look as if she'd had time to fill the space in between. Silence was my only response.

"Brooke!" I now yelled as I wandered through what looked

like it would've been a formal living room if not for the one lonely armchair and the empty dog bed that inhabited it. Apparently Ruby got her walking papers after one too many accidents on the new carpet. I shook my head at the pink tennis ball sitting in the middle of the room; it was too big for the dog's mouth and now she wouldn't be around to grow into it.

I heard a tinny octave strumming from somewhere in a distance. Following the faint sound down the hallway, past miles of Rojo Alicante marble counters, I paused briefly to notice an open bottle of red table wine sitting atop the long narrow island. A sad straggle of cork sat haphazardly to the side, its broken half bobbed ever so slightly in the half-drank bottle. The clanking of the piano keys got louder as I made my way to the farthest reaches of the house. About fifteen feet from where I stood, there was Brooke.

Perched on the bench of a baby grand in the expanse of her den, the serene water of the swimming pool twinkled behind her. Sensing I was near, her delicate fingers eased up on the ivory keys.

"It needs to be tuned I think." She smiled sheepishly.

"No, it sounds good . . ." I chuckled, sauntering down the split-level stairs.

"That wa-as fuuun," she slurred. "I—had—a—guuuddee—t-y-m-e."

I stopped short. She looked horrible—*red all over*—the alcohol sloshing through her system bringing out the ruddiness in her skin. I noticed another empty wine bottle sitting atop the piano. The tears that stung her eyes turned them a light shade of pink. And there was *something else too*. I first saw it out of the corner of my eye—hardly realizing just what it was as she started to play once again.

Red all over—smearing the keys in crimson. Her hands gliding over them.

"Brooke, what's going on?" Noticing my startled reaction she guffawed, pulling her hands back down to her sides, where they hung loosely from her wrists.

Discarded on the floor, near the piano bench, lay a worn copy of *Scoop*—the one Brooke came across in Vegas. I remembered the remorseful tone in her voice when she'd said: *I don't want to be alone anymore—Jesse was a good guy, huh?*

"Oh my gawd, I am so stupid." She shrugged with a smirk, then became serious. "Don't tell anybody." She glanced down at her hands, running her right index finger over her left wrist as though unsure the blood was real.

Adrenaline surged through my veins and despite the aching pit in my stomach, I tried to play it cool as I went to call for help.

In the weeks following the breakup, especially since Jesse'd been spotted with Maddi, Brooke found overindulgence—food, partying, popping pills like candy, work, sleep, and, of course, sex—was the best way to deal with her heartache. But I knew long before this Brooke carried a sense of sadness wherever she went. But now with the Emersons' newly released single, "Betrayal," climbing the music charts, she had something to fixate on. The thinly veiled lyrics created a media frenzy that kept Brooke captive in her own home. Everyone wanted her reaction: "Brooke! Brooke! What do you want to say to Jesse?" Others wanted to torment her: "How could you be so heartless. You deserve everything you get, you cruel bitch."

"Come on, come on," Brooke stammered as I picked up the telephone, her eyes frantic. "Can't we just sit down and play, and sing . . . and, you know—like we used to?" She was trying desperately now to gloss over the panic in her voice. I barely looked her in the eyes. This wasn't real. It couldn't be.

Seeing that I was unwavering, she tried to play down the situation. "I didn't do it. I didn't—" She sprung from the piano bench and raced to her room, coming back at me with something pink clutched in her hand.

"See?" Uncurling her fingers she revealed a pink Daisy Gillette razor that'd clearly been used one too many times. She looked at me hopeful that I'd drop the whole thing but I wouldn't. Whether it was done deliberately or for attention—the reason didn't really matter. I looked down at the dull, germ-collecting Daisy and shuddered.

Brooke kept chattering on and though I watched her mouth moving I couldn't hear the words. Or that fact that I couldn't get the mental check list of tetanus symptoms out of my head. *Was her jaw looking a little stiff? Would she soon break out in uncontrollable spasms?* I doubted it. My plaguing fear and confusion went back to Brooke and what had compelled her to this extreme. It was as loud a cry as silent suffering could make—as far as I was concerned, that pink Daisy Gillette may have as well been a loaded gun. It scared me—and I began to wonder what else she was capable of. Conflicting thoughts started racing through my head: *What if the cuts are deeper than they appear? I can't believe she's doing this for the attention! What would happen if I hadn't come? She's so selfish!* The one thing I *did* know was that she wasn't going to harm herself any longer—not on my watch.

"This is so messed up," I told her walking back and forth nervously. "This isn't a small thing Brooke . . . this is a big deal you're making here whether you know it or not . . ."

"It's fine . . . it's fine . . . see?" She wiped her finger over her wrist as if she were magically healing her wounds.

"We've got to call someone—we've got to get you in to see a doctor," I said, suddenly feeling like her mother. I grabbed one of her hands to examine it closer. Ugly, long, and red—jagged but not life-threatening. I just wanted to get her in good hands, and there wasn't a second to waste. I'd never forgive myself if I let anything happen to her.

"Brooke, you have no idea if it's fine or not . . . you need someone to look at it. What if it gets infected?" I tried explaining the repercussions in the simplest way possible—when all I wanted was take her by the shoulders, shake her violently and scream, *This not okay! You are not okay!*

But I knew how Brooke operated. Not being able to grip a microphone again was scarier to her than losing her mind completely.

"What if you weren't able to use that hand properly? You may have severed something—a tendon or nerves—that we can't see right now. Brooke—you *have* to see someone." I started to dial the phone when she stopped me.

"Jackie," she put her hand on my arm and looked up at me with her big brown eyes, motioning toward the gates where the vultures awaited her in their S.U.V.s. "Please, don't." Her eyes contained so much pain now—pain that I'd never be able to fully understand. And still I knew that she could, in the strangest way, suddenly turn off the tears and those eyes would be cold and vacant once more. I knew the drill all too well—I knew that this was all an act—one that would make you love her, consuming you in her personal, manufactured tragedy before turning back into an automaton leaving you spent, cold, and alone. And it was this empty feeling that kept everyone coming back like masochists. Perhaps it was the reason I was here now.

And like Brooke, I also knew what placing an emergency call would do, the chaos that it would provoke. I went back and forth in my head, trying to make a sound decision. *Maybe she's fine . . . it's probably nothing . . . maybe she's just drunk.* Still, I'd been drunk plenty of times, and it had never send me running to the razors. With T-Roc in Tennessee visiting his "mama," there was only one person at this point left to call, and I really, really didn't want to call him.

Within forty minutes Steve stormed in, David trailing behind, both looking particularly dapper since they'd come from some fundraising gala or another. Hoping he didn't notice, I let my gaze linger on David. Rather than his typical collected self, he looked absolutely horrified as he shuffled off to the side. *This* part of the business was uncharted water, and he let Steve take the reigns.

Steve put both his hands on Brooke's shoulders, looking her squarely in the face. Her eyes half open, she seemed elsewhere, humming something that was barely audible. She had hit her peak and the only place she could go was down. Everything was getting fuzzy now.

"Shhhhh," Steve coaxed. "You just need some sleep. Let's get you to bed."

"I c-c-c-a-a-a-n-n-'t *slllllleeeeepppp!*" She howled and whined deliriously—though in body, she was too lethargic to do much else.

"Aren't you going to call a doctor or something?" Steve pretended not to hear me, prompting me to pipe up again. "She needs help . . ."

"No, she'll be over it—she's fine . . ." He stood by and watched as she chugged yet another half a glass of wine on autopilot.

Watch it Jackie. I warned myself.

No.

No. Not this time.

I knew what was right. I had to muster the strength. Brooke needed me.

"Steve! She. Is. *Not. Fine!*" I brazenly spoke back.

He ignored me. "Here—take one of your Valium. You need to get some rest. You have the big *Hollywood Junket* interview tomorrow and you've got to get your beauty rest . . . you want to look good, don't you?"

Was Steve out of his fucking mind? The *Hollywood Junket* was long out of the picture—was this guy delusional? Brooke was crashing hard, far from good, far from okay, and a few hours of sleep would hardly be enough to refresh her. Muddled up together—the bottle and a half of wine, eleven-hour-a-day schedules, Valium—it was a lethal combination. I wanted no part in this sick situation.

"Well, you're going to need to find yourself another makeup artist then because I won't support this," the words flew out of my mouth so fast that I felt like someone else was saying them. "This disgusts me. You disgust me, Steve."

Brooke became dead weight in Steve's arms and he half-dragged, half-carried her to the armchair in the dim-lit living room before striding back to me.

"Look, Jackie. We've been meaning to talk with you about this, and I guess now is as good a time as any. I'm just going to tell it like it is. You've become a liability, and to be quite honest, after your latest stunt your services are no longer needed anyway."

Before, I would've cowered, paralyzed. But after all I'd been through, my skin had thickened.

"You're right about the Ric Craia shoot. Okay? I fucked up, and I'm sorry. You have no idea what that meant to me, and if I could do it all over again I would, but I can't." I tried to keep my voice stern without screaming or pleading. I felt David's eyes on me and realized my outburst was as much for him as it was Steve. Ever since we met, Steve had waited for an opportunity to say something like this to me. Anyone who got in his way, who had Brooke's ear, was considered a threat that must be squashed.

"Brooke's a human being, Steve. She's not just your fucking meal ticket."

"Why don't you just go home, it's late." Steve's calm tone, as though nothing I said fazed him, only further enraged me. "David and I have this handled."

"I'm not leaving until I know Brooke is okay . . ." I attempted to rush past him but he stuck out his arm, stopping me in my tracks.

"No, I think you need to leave. *Now*."

I turned to take one last look at Brooke, who sat in the living room stiff as a corpse. Enveloped in both spiritual and spatial emptiness, her eyes remained hyperfocused on the floor below her—not a thought in her mind registering. The world as she knew it had screamed to a halt, for a moment that is. Just a few hours later she'd be expected to shake it off, cram her body —bloated and sore from the night's activities—into some kind of skimpy costume. She'd be expected to show up shimmying and shaking, smiling and winking, ready to sing her heart out— over, and over, and over again. But for now she was subdued in a sickly kind of half-sleep. I crossed right in front of her as I made my way to the door. Hoisting it open—all thick and heavy—I noticed she remained fixated on the same patch of carpet— totally unaware of the world that moved and breathed beyond her sphere.

Closing the door on the macabre scene behind me, I already felt haunted by it—certain that this moment would hang over me like a dark cloud, flashing back at me in shades of scarlet and pink.

Chapter 21

Imagine taking off your makeup and
nobody knows who you are.
–Steven Tyler

*She's got a new album that's dropping early next month
—not to mention, an Industry of Music Award. In just
a moment we'll have pop princess extraordinaire, Brooke
Parker, here in the studio, for an exclusive interview. Don't
miss it . . .*

I turned on the T.V. in time for Brooke's *Hollywood
Junket* interview. Shocked that she actually made it—
well, maybe not, since Steve clearly intended to get
her there dead or alive—I had to see how bad the train
wreck would be.

Surprisingly, she looked great. Her skin looked sun-
kissed and her hair flowed to her shoulders in shiny,
golden cascades. Somebody spent a lot of time fixing that

disaster, but I could see it in her eyes that she was still out of it and in tremendous agony. Her smile seemed forced. Several times in the past day, I picked up my phone expecting to hear her on the other end, but nothing. I needed to know what happened, how Steve was treating her; all I wanted to know was simply, is she okay? But there was no one safe to call for the answers— not David and certainly not Steve. Then, I remembered the one person I *could* count on.

"T—it's Jackie."

"Baby girl, can't talk now. But Steve's been tellin' her all this crazy stuff 'bout you having an agenda and shit."

"Ugh, you know I would never . . ."

"I know. I know—I try to stick up for y'all but you know Brooke—she believes anything anybody be tellin' her. 'An Steve's givin' that girl an earful. He's all 'Jackie's just using you to make a name for herself' 'n 'Jackie don't care none for you, she just wanna be a song writer.' I gotta protect my girl, Jackie. You know how it is."

"I know T. I know. It's so crazy. Brooke's the one who's been pushing my songs. I never even wanted to play for her in the first place. I just can't . . . Well, take care." All of this should have come as no surprise, yet each further nail in the coffin was every bit as difficult to process as the last. I'd been completely cut off from Brooke. What could I do?

Days passed rapidly, and I dreaded opening my email. I knew that, before long, billing statements would outnumber the usually endless stream of invites to the town's most fabulous events. Because my parents had been so proud of me, continuously talking about their daughter's fancy job to all of their friends, I couldn't bare to tell them the truth and risk disappointing them. I knew exactly how that conversation would go:

My mother: "What? Please tell me you didn't screw up another opportunity of a lifetime."

My father: "Well, kiddo—you gave it your best . . . there's always going to be someone just a bit better than you ready to take your place at the top."

Then they'd both sigh and exchange knowing glances that their daughter was unable to follow through once again.

My standing with the Bellezza Agency wasn't exactly great, either, and I knew my chances of getting on the roster there were slim to none at this point. Still, I had been the makeup artist to one of, if not *the*, most famous stars in the world, and that had to count for something, right? I needed a fresh start, I decided, more than a second chance, and so after a few weeks I jumped on the opportunity to take a meeting at Cicely—a competing agency, just as well known as Bellezza. I remembered how Sheryl displayed her work, and as I began preparing for the interview, I decided to do the same, only with some of my own style. Scouring the racks of a Beverly Hills photography store, I chose a sleek, satin portfolio with an aluminum finish—determined to make my book stand out among all the others agents routinely went through.

The Cicely offices were located in a concrete and glass building on a palm-fringed stretch of West Hollywood. Armed with my portfolio, I waltzed through the towering green glass doors, ready for my meeting with one of the top-level agents.

"I'm here to see Lucy McPherson," I hummed to the young female receptionist who busily juggled a stream of phone calls in the lobby.

"Cicely Agency . . . I'll transfer you to her voicemail." With the receiver cradled between her head and shoulder, she motioned to a small cluster of leather Eames-style chairs to my left. I sat, and I waited; I riffled through a *Scoop* magazine on the coffee table, then read another one cover to cover.

Nearly forty minutes passed before I was summoned from the lobby into a large office, where I was greeted by an elegantly dressed woman in her early forties. "What do you have for us?" she asked, reaching for a pair of thin tortoise-shell reading glasses. Thrusting my book down on her desk, she looked at it curiously—as if it were a foreign object—before touching it. Slipping her index finger under the heavy cover, she paused.

"Industry standard is black and leather bound . . . or if you're vegan like me, clamshell." I nodded, suddenly and unexpectedly embarrassed with my standout portfolio.

"Ahhh," she said raising an eyebrow as she scanned the first page—the *Femme* shoot. "Very nice, I love this cover, she looks so natural." At this, I let out a silent sigh to ease my tension a bit. She kept nodding her head in approval as she looked at the rest of the *Femme* pictorial.

"Ooooh, I love your range—the way you've taken her from this soft kind of seaside look to," turning the page, she pointed to another image of Brooke with winged cat-eyes and a red lip, "sultry screen siren." I could feel my confidence growing as she gingerly flipped to the fourth page.

"Hmmm." Lucy's face twisted into a state of confusion as she turned to a double-pager torn from *Scoop* magazine's "Star Wears" section. "Whose makeup did you do here?" I pointed to Brooke's image, sandwiched between five other red carpet beauties, and said, "Brooke's."

I remained hopeful. It may not have been *Vogue*, but it was a major magazine with a swelling circulation—and it showed off some of my best work. From there, however, it all went downhill. The last three remaining pages were pieced together with Polaroid snapshots and small cutouts from weekly publications, followed by a bulk of naked pages beneath. Shocked, she shuffled through them and slammed the aluminum book shut. Lucy looked up at me.

"First of all, no empty pages in your portfolio. Secondly, your book needs a lot of work. You only have photos of Brooke

Parker here. We can, of course, work on building it up." She slid her glasses down her nose. "So when is your next gig with Brooke?"

I sat there silent for a moment. The truth was I couldn't even get her on the phone. Thinking fast, I stuttered, "Well, I've decided to, you know, move on from that and work with some new clients. Um, like you said, my book needs diversity—and that's exactly why I'm here?" My voice betrayed me, trailing up as if I was asking and not telling. Lucy's face went from confusion to *Yeah, you're not for us. . .* She was a veteran agent, and she was smart enough to know something had happened—what idiot would walk away from a client like Brooke Parker who was at the height of her career?

"Look Jackie, you do have a lot of talent but this is a dog-eat-dog world and frankly, your presentation is not up to par—but if you get any bookings let us know . . ."

I sat there, shocked momentarily, while defeat sunk in yet again. *If I wasn't working with Brooke, I was worth nothing?* My chances of getting into an agency even *half* as good as Cicely were slim to none—because *all* agencies were looking for gold mines, people who could really rake in the cash. But me? I couldn't even cover my car payment.

Beneath the indigo sky, fleeced with white, fluffy clouds, I stepped out onto the pavement, slightly bewildered. *How could I have let that happen? Had I, just like everyone else, gotten caught up in myself? Had Brooke, my first and only client, and her mounting fame tricked me into thinking I possessed these overinflated powers and abilities that I did not?*

And most importantly . . . what now?

Bewildered and discomfited, I stood there on Melrose Avenue looking around as if waiting for the answers to fall out of the sky. Life per usual buzzed in and out around me: the health food fanatics toting their goods in organic cotton bags to the nearest PureGood Foods; Yoga-mat-carrying Kabalist wannabes placing orders amid maddening crowds inside a small, hip café; and iPhone-wielding, vanilla-soy-latté–fetching publicists trying to nab a spot on the terraced patio, where they would balance their organic meals by puffing on Marlboros. An eclectic blend of characters strolled lazily down the street, making their way through the menagerie of boutiques and tattoo parlors without a care in the world. Some walked pooches with matching sweaters, others pushed babies in high-end strollers, a few walked hand-in-hand with their lovers. Everyone seemed so content, and there I stood radiating misery for all to see. I then realized the truth about myself. I came in with nothing, and I was going to leave with nothing as well. I crumbled under things that were bigger than me rather than rallying against them. I felt painfully self-conscious and quickly headed back to the more isolated confines of my car until something stopped me in my tracks.

On the corner, at a small newsstand I caught a glimpse of *Guitar*. I whirled around to take a closer look, and if all the self-loathing and embarrassment weren't enough, this took care of any of my remaining sense of worth. Since Brooke's album release date was pushed back so her first single wouldn't coincide with the Emersons' "Betrayal," they held the magazine cover. I guess this meant her single would be out soon.

I examined the cover in shock—they'd perfectly executed my plan—the green fairy wings affixed to her back, the loose and wavy locks caressing her shoulders beneath a wreath of white hydrangeas and purple mascagnia, the airy pastel makeup. Another impressive addition to my portfolio—that shrine to Brooke serving as further evidence of my life's singular focus. This, I had not expected. Clearly, I hadn't suffered enough. As if moved by an invisible force, I rustled through my purse to find $5—which was no small sum in my situation. Deep in a pocket behind a crinkled dollar bill, I noticed a folded business card that looked as if it may have gone through the wash. Something compelled me to fish it out, and I almost laughed when I read: Jorge ("Rita")—The Queen Victoria. I ponied up the cash and hurried back to my car.

Settling in, I took a deep breath and pulled back the cover. Inside, Brooke posed in the middle of an ethereal wooded glen, blowing bubbles from a wand in her left hand. The ruffle trim of her panties was visible through the short whispery tulle chemise she wore that clung onto every curve of her tanned, taut body. The title of the article, which was chosen simply because Brooke appears shoeless throughout the pictorial, read in whimsical purple lettering: *Barefoot Contessa*. My stomach tightened, forcing me to grip the steering wheel. I didn't need any further humiliation. Besides, I needed to get busy finding work. Jorge's voice echoed in my mind:

Everyone knows, honey, that the real money is in cocktail waitressing. I know what you're thinking, but it really is a lot of fun. Plus . . . you can keep on doing makeup—some of the best makeup artists count drag queens as muses. Think about it.

I was out of other options.

It took me about a week to actually walk through the doors of the Queen Victoria, and I wasn't quite sure what to expect. I stood inside the doorway scanning the place and trying to decide whether or not to turn and run. Part seventies time warp with low ceilings, dim lighting, and multicolored tiles, part portside bar with anchors and captain's caps hanging on the walls, the place certainly had character even though it felt vast and dingy in the middle of the day. The drag venue offered plenty of room for dancing and sitting ringside around the immense stage. A baby grand piano off to the side gave it a small touch of class.

"Can I help you doll?" One of the "girls" asked as she flitted by in a sailor ensemble.

"I'm looking for Jorge, oh, I see him. Thanks!" At a long stretch of bar I spotted him, dressed in a shimmery gold mini and matching wedge espadrilles.

"Can I help you, honey?" He looked up from the fruity concoction he was blending, most likely for himself given the place was nearly empty. A few waiters and men in drag were getting things ready for the night's crowd.

"Remember me?" I asked tossing my hands out to the side as if to say *ta-da*—the kitschyness of this place was rubbing off on me already. I quickly put my hands down to my sides. "The red lipstick and the crème de cocoa foundation? You were doing, um, so over Jayne, uh, Mansfield I think it was?" His eyes looked upward as he tried to recall. "Oh, right! You're the makeup girl from Beverly Hills."

"Right. So, anyway, I came across your card from ages ago, and I thought I'd pop in on the off chance you'd actually be here . . . and still needed another cocktail waitress?"

"The hash brown slinging isn't going too good for you, huh? You decided to wise up and listen to ole' Rita now, huh? I told you honey, this is where the money is at."

"Yeah, well . . . I need to be in a place 'where the money's at,' that's for sure . . ." I hoisted my purse onto the counter and took a seat as a long, dark-haired drag queen in an aqua halter dress with yellow polka dots pranced by. She did a double take. "Oh, you've got the new issue with Brooke Parker! May I?"

She reached for the *Guitar* magazine sticking out of my purse and started flipping through it. "*Barefoot Contessa*? Why, that's my movie. I'm Ava you know . . ." the Ava-Gardner-incarnate screamed. Ava hugged the magazine close to her chest. "You seen it?" I shook my head.

"Oh, it's absolutely fantastic, you really must see it—it's

about this girl who's plucked from a night club by these Hollywood vultures who turn her into a star overnight and all that jazz . . ."

Quite appropriate, I thought. Hesitating because I felt so ridiculous at that point, I then mentioned that I'd been working as Brooke's makeup artist.

"Oh! My! God! I love her. You lucky, lucky girl!" She turned to the others and started yelling. "Ladies! This is Brooke Parker's makeup artist. Can you believe it?"

They gathered around me, propping themselves on the barstools as if they were makeup chairs, and began cooing over the spread. "I love her eyes, the way they . . ."

"Well *I* love her . . ."

"Oh, my God. And her hair . . ."

Sitting in this bizarre place, being fussed over by half a dozen drag queens made me chuckle, lifting the dark cloud hanging over my head. They all wanted to know if I could make them look like Brooke and asked about my training and my style secrets.

Jorge smiled slyly from behind the bar. "When can you start, sweetie?"

"Whenever—anytime. . ."

"Perfect—we'll see you tonight."

Gulp. I wasn't sure what I expected walking in, but suddenly I felt overwhelmed and oddly excited. I waved to the ladies and headed for the door as Jorge called after me.

"You're a lucky girl honey! No one's got prettier cocktail waitresses than we do. Nobody."

An hour into my first shift and I was off to a rough start. I'd already spilled two jumbo piña coladas—the drink special of the night—forgot a table's entire order, and burnt my tongue on the mozzarella stick that was my dinner. As days passed, I improved little by little, but each night the place delivered the same culture shock I'd first experienced..

While the entire place shook with a vibrating, computerized version of a Venga Boys song, my skull throbbed. The thumping of the drums on stage coupled with the tune signaled it was time for Abe to take the stage. Abe was a petite yet brawny guy who did the same shtick every weekend. With the drumbeat, he appeared in a spotlight dressed in a gorilla costume, rousing cheers from the crowd. The routine, in which he'd barrel through the audience like an ape before stripping down to nothing but a banana hammock, was funny the first couple times I'd seen it—but tonight, feeling sweaty and exhausted, I paid little attention.

"Ma'am . . ." I heard a voice call out faintly behind me. I tried to ignore it until it became louder, "Ma'am!" I turned to find an older brunette in a denim dress with stiff, platypus lips.

"Ma'am . . ." she started slowly, again. I could see the end corners of her eyebrows struggling as she attempted to raise them. The effect, I supposed, was to complement her condescending tone, but her face was so unnaturally taut that it barely moved. "I said no salt." She pointed a square-tipped French-manicured fingernail at the half-drunk margarita on her table. My first instinct was to flip her off and just walk away—but I was suddenly distracted by the scene at the next table over.

"Oh my god, it was a *harrr-ibble* film. Ew . . . it was all *Barber Shop* set in Hollywood." Throwing his head back in incontrollable laughter as Abe shook his thong-clad behind in the face of a patron at the table over, was Robert—like a queen holding court.

"Take it all off! Show her what you're working with!" his companion screamed. The object of Abe's affections shielded her face with her left hand, flashing a gigantic sparkler on her ring finger.

"A-hem . . ." Platypus coughed, growing testier by the second.

Ignoring her, I stared at Robert in shock for a few moments before quickly ducking behind a chair, causing the Bahama Mama on my tray to crash to the floor—not a smart move, but an immediate reaction. Ava, who was standing at the server station a few feet away, twisted up her face in a confused annoyance. I just shrugged and nodded.

I had hoped to sneak past them undetected, but as my lack of luck would have it I rose to my feet in the same instance that the music ended, putting an end to Abe's humping charades. I found myself in the midst of my worse nightmare come true.

"Holy shit!" Robert said in a loud, unenthused moan. "What the hell are you doing here?"

"I'm just, uh, helping out a bit," I stammered, sure that once he saw the apron tied around my hips he'd publicly ridicule me. But, five vodka and tonics deep, Robert didn't seem to care.

"This is Andres," he screamed over the din, pointing to his friend who was wrapped in a hot pink sash that read *Bride to Be* in rhinestones. "And this is Oscar," he said, pointing now to the man on his left, also wearing the very same hot pink sash.

"They're off to Connecticut tomorrow for their fairytale ceremony."

Robert's minions wore pink *Girlfriend of the Bachelorette* nametags sloppily affixed to their matching black T-shirts. Robert's said *BITCH*.

"I didn't know this was your scene," I said, realizing I didn't really *know* anything about Robert apart from his role with Brooke.

"Where else can you get a drink in this town after 1:55?" he asked smugly, adding, "And also, my roommate Jorge works here—so I'm around all the time."

Great. There was no escaping him! Was the universe punishing me? What were the chances?

"Everyone *has* to have a name tag!" One of his friends yelled, waving the small remaining stack in her hand as she struggled to yell over the din.

"Who doesn't have one?"

"I don't—but I'm working—so I don't count," I laughed.

"Ohhhhh . . . you need one too! What should we call you?" Andres nibbled on the cap of the pen, thinking hard.

"Jackie's got a nickname." The sing-song voice of Robert sounded from behind us. "Don't you know it?"

I shot him a look of death, knowing what was to come. I'd never be able to live "Calamity Jackie" down as long as I lived, and here he was beside me to make sure of it.

"What was that look?" he piped up suddenly. I'd been so used to shooting him dirty looks—sometimes hundreds of them in just one afternoon alone. But I was also used to him completely ignoring me too, which was exactly why I did it so often. He'd look over my head, to the side, at the ground—anywhere but directly at me. And now, dressed in a pink boa and what looked like a pageant queen sash affixed with silver Trojans that looked like artillery, his eyes challenged mine.

"Come on, Calamity? Would you want to be pegged with that one?" I asked him, giggling.

"Why not?" he asked, his indignation morphing into a wide, dreamy smile.

Andres chimed in, "The musical from '53— *loves it*—it's his favorite."

"Plus, I'm *obsessed* with Doris Day. *Ob-sessed*," he stressed. "When she sings 'Secret Love'?" He waited for my response, a simple shrug of the shoulders.

"*Once I had a secret love that lived within this part of me*," he sang out to give me a demonstration. I shrugged again, wincing slightly at his scratchy, high-pitched voice. "Come on! *All too soon my secret love became impassioned to be free*. No?"

"I've never seen the movie—sorry!"

"You've never seen *Calamity Jane?*" Robert was aghast. "Oh my God! Doris Day sings it in the movie. That song won an Oscar. So how—*how* could you object to that fabulous nick-name?"

"I don't know," I shrugged, staring down at the nametag em-blazoned *Calamity*, including a tiny heart to dot the *i*. "It just—it makes me feel bad. Like I'll never be good at anything—I mean, really, good."

He smiled back. What was more amazing was that he was still listening as I finished my sentence, perhaps, I thought, as seconds of silence lapsed, waiting for me to continue.

"Jackie," he said, turning to me, the seriousness of his facial expression offset by shedding pink feathers. "Obviously . . ." he paused for what seemed like an eternity, using the silence to emphasize a dramatic roll of his eyes. "There are a lot of things you're good at."

There were? Then why hadn't anyone ever told me that before? Why did I always feel like the set disaster? And most importantly, why was Robert being so nice?

"Even when you're such a hot mess, you little bitch," he teased.

"Ahhhh!" A screech out of nowhere pierced our ears. "A-dor-able!" Jorge, who'd apparently only heard snippets of our conversation, looked ecstatic.

"I had *no* idea you guys were friends!" he cooed, causing us to both turn up our noses, brushing our little moment swiftly under the rug. But oblivious to our body language, Jorge gushed on. "You two are like, total BFFs! *So* Jack and Karen!"

The next several weeks brought plenty of double shifts to rake in the necessary funds for keeping up the façade of my double life. Between my outrageous car payment and the rent I owed my father, I knew something had to give. Besides, pulling into the Queen Victoria in my Cayenne started to feel increasingly ridiculous.

A lot of the time, I went hungry. But it was my own fault, I guess. I never wanted to eat the food at the Queen Victoria—well, I *wanted* to, but in truth I was just kind of scared to try it. The Queen Victoria had many strengths as an establishment; however, the cuisine struck me as a low priority, precisely why I was sneaking into my parents' kitchen to grab food.

As I bent down to grab the spinach out of the fridge, someone flicked the light on, causing me to stumble back.

"Oh. Uh, hey Mom. Did I wake you?"

"Jackie. You've been getting home so late." She squinted as her eyes adjusted, then seemed focused on something near the table. My apron, stuffed with wads of bills, hung from a chair. *Oh shit.* I had to tell her now.

"Oh, um . . . about that." I could barely make eye contact. I felt so ashamed. It didn't matter that my intentions had been noble; I felt like a colossal failure. "Mom, I don't work for Brooke anymore." The weight left, and I sighed, "I know what you're thinking, so just go ahead and say it."

I braced for the worst, knowing that she always exceeded whatever I thought was her worst. But to my surprise, she just sighed.

"Oh Jackie. I'm sorry to hear that. I know how much you loved that job." She looked at me with a sympathy so foreign I wondered if I might be dreaming it all.

"You're not disappointed?"

"Sweetie, I've been so proud of you the last few months," she took a seat, waving me over to join her. "Listen, I never followed my dreams—you did. That's more than I can say—more than *most* people can say."

"I'm . . . I . . ." What could I say? Words felt inadequate. "I'm sorry. I know I was just awful to you through it all. I got so carried away in the nonsense. And it was all so fake. It was just Hollywood, and I chose it over you." And she just kept on with that motherly, sympathetic look. "Don't you even want to know how I lost it?" I asked her skeptically. Again, she patiently shook her head. It didn't matter to her—I was her daughter—just a girl who needed her mom.

So I did it. I cried. And honestly, it felt good—*really good*. Tears streaming down my cheeks, I embraced her. My whole life I wanted to hear her say that. We never did this mother-daughter Hallmark moment thing. We fought. She made it clear what a screw up I was, and I resented her for it. And now, when I thought she actually had a reason to be let down, she finally says it. Of course. Finally I'd been humbled; I could set my stubbornness aside to see she really loved me no matter how horribly I screwed up.

Chapter 22

Much more frequent in Hollywood than the
emergence of Cinderella is her sudden vanishing.
At our party, even in those glowing days,
the clock was always striking twelve for someone
at the height of greatness; and there was never a prince
to fetch her back to the happy scene.
–Ben Hecht

I was covered in the slush of half-frozen margaritas and
catsup and it was getting late. Hunkered down in one
of the back booths, I rolled the last of the clean silverware in oversized paper napkins faster than I ever had
before, motivated by the warm, cushy thoughts of my
comfortable bed awaiting me at home. Wriggling out of
my apron, I lugged the neatly wrapped collection of cut-
lery to the kitchen, hoping I'd be able to make a clean
break.

"Jackie?!" a voice rang out. I stopped as dread tingled

up and down my spine. The sound of six-inch stilettos clapped along the tiled floor and, as my eyes darted around searching for a place to hide, I half-considered ducking in the freezer for a moment.

"Jackie! There you are!" Channeling Kitty Collins, there stood Ava—a femme fatale in a curve-hugging black dress, long periwinkle gloves, and black sky-high heels.

"Thank the lord you're still here!" Puffing out her lip to a pout, she mock whined, "Ava *needs* her 'Ole Blue Eyes' before bed."

I made the mistake of what I considered to be "goofing around" on the stage piano for my co-workers one night, seizing the opportunity to unwind after hours. The bigger mistake was appeasing Ava's request for Frank Sinatra—among all the others that'd been hurled in my direction. *I knew I should've picked* "Wind Beneath My Wings," I scolded myself. Ava was impossible to say no to, mostly because of her tumultuous the-world-is-coming-to-an-end temper tantrums that she fondly referred to as anxiety attacks. "I'm really tire—" I started to explain. Taking note of the tenseness taking hold of her legs—the first sign of her tantrums—I stopped. "But what's one song, right?"

Full of glee, Ava scampered behind me to grab a seat. The place was almost empty and still, she looked around carefully as if trying to select the perfect one.

Clearing my throat, I placed my hands on the keys, and then stopped—remembering how much she liked it when I addressed the crowd (*her*) as if I were opening a show at the Copa Room, which, by the way, I'd only done once. Still, she hadn't failed to remind me every hour on the hour, how it had made her night.

"I used to go on many adventures," I started. Already I could see Ava squirming in excitement in her seat. "And these adventures took me far and wide from Rio de Janeiro to majestic Saratoga Springs, and yes—even back here to . . . *Las Vegas*."

At this, Ava cheered and clapped her hands for a quick moment.

"They truly were the best of times, and the—"

"Worst of times!" my lone audience member cried out, finishing my sentence for me.

"That's right. And yet that is the path we all must follow in this lonely world we call showbiz. For all you pretty little things out there in Hollywood tonight. This one's for you."

I coughed loudly, stirring my parched throat, as my hands glided over the porcelain-colored keys.

This town is a lonely town . . .

"Sinatra! Love him!" I heard one of the stragglers sidled up to the bar proclaim to his small entourage. Abandoning their posts, they suddenly gathered around me.

This town is a make you town. Or a break you town . . .

"Who knew a sister could sing Frank?" Two joiners appeared out of nowhere.

This town is a love you town. And a shove-you-down and push-you-round town . . .

"Amen! You said it g-u-r-l . . ." came a voice from the floor as I continued to sing, pounding faster on the keys.

You better believe that I am leavin' this town . . .

Stemming from those gathered around, a kaleidoscope of voices chimed together:

This town, bye-bye, bye, bye, bye. . .

Everyone started clapping—Ava letting out loud whistles of approval—as my cheeks burned and the mouth spread into a bashful grin. In front of me, eight people stood—still applauding as I rose from the bench.

"Thanks—you're a beautiful crowd," I chuckled warmly, scanning them. I was enjoying my night's warm sendoff when I spotted something—or should I say *someone*—among the small group of revelers that made my blood flip-flop from warm to cold.

I quickly sat back down on the bench, dumbfounded, wishing I could crawl into a hole beneath me. *"I'm around all the time."* Tapered jeans, a faded seafoam-green polo, last week's crumpled boa, and a tiara swiped from the head of a queen-in-training named Thursday—the most recent "newbie" at the Queen Victoria—it was none other than Robert. Expression: Smug. *Wait? Or was that . . . loopy?* I was too busy overanalyzing all the crap I'd just said: *The best of times and worst of times? In this lonely world we call show business?* All the nice things he'd said to me before were most certainly discredited by my jackass lounge lizard act. *Thanks a lot Ava!* I was too busy berating myself to even notice him climbing the steps to the stage behind me.

Becoming aware of his presence as he sauntered closer, I took a deep breath. I could only imagine the snide comments he'd be able to spout off to me now that I'd basically handed him the ammunition to do in my last shred of self-worth. Before I even knew what he was about to say, I literally winced as he opened his mouth.

"You got some talent in those hands Misssh O'Reilly . . ."

I looked up at him cautiously, still squinting one eye, prepared for any insults he was about to toss in my direction. Instead, I was surprised to find that the only thing emanating from him at that very moment was the hot mist of alcohol rising from his breath.

"What?" I asked, confused.

"You're good. You ever write anything yourself?" My new BFF slumped across the piano, nearly spilling his martini on the keys as the overstuffed olives swilled in a shallow pool of gin.

"Uh, yeah—actually," I stammered as my eyes followed his glass. "You remember that song Brooke surprised the crowd with in Rio?"

"Mmm-hmm," he said, going through a series of matches as he attempted to light the cigarette dangling from his lips. After several tries he tore it from his mouth and tossed it aside. "Ugh, I hate cigarettes, anyway." He rubbed his eyes, staring blankly for a moment before focusing again. Springing back to life, he exclaimed, "Yeah, yeah . . . the song! I mean Brooke totally butchered it, right? But the song itself, the lyrics were great. *You* wrote that?"

I nodded silently, taking Robert's stamp of approval as a good sign.

"I never did understand why they didn't put that one on the album? I mean, they could've easily doctored her voice in the studio . . ."

"We talked about it. But of course Steve made sure it never saw light of day . . ." I vented. I no longer cared if the two of them went way back. Then to my surprise, Robert tossed his head back in annoyance.

"That phony little tick . . ."

I was shocked for a moment. Was that the alcohol talking?

"Don't let that little hyena dictate your worth, you've got a lot of talent girl and if he can't see it that doesn't mean it doesn't matter . . ." He paused for a moment, getting into serious mode. "Look, I had a *vision*—a creative vision—when I first started working with Brooke. If you think Lycra NASCAR ensembles are my forte, you're sadly mistaken."

Perhaps, Robert was . . . serious? Harboring a secret contempt for Steve as someone who'd stifled the artistic talent inside of him? Looking overwhelmed, Robert rolled his eyes. He was, it appeared, in true gossip mode.

"So, I was supposed to do the shoot for Brooke's new video, right? The one that they're shooting tonight—matter of fact, probably as we speak . . . anyway, they asked me to do this little sailor bolero—with like, a striped trim collar with anchors and stars—the *works*. Hideous. I was like, are you fucking kidding me? I don't do Halloween costumes . . ." He snapped his finger just inches from my face and, yet again, rolled his eyes in exaggerated disgust. I wondered how many times his eyes made those same roundabout motions each day?

"Oh, and get *this*. The kicker?" In his drunken stupor he leaned towards me, almost a little *too* close. "They asked me to make these cuffs—you know she's still got those hideous scratches all up and down her wrists . . . and they were all like, 'Can you make these big First Mate cuffs'—you know—all decorating with piping and shit . . . to cover them up."

A sickening feeling crept into my stomach, and I tried to push out of my mind the memories of that horrible night a few months ago in Benedict Canyon. Coming to my rescue, Robert snapped loudly.

"I was like 'Hell no, honey. I'm styling for *Femme* now. I do *real* work, got it?' The nerve! And the dancers costumes?" He was aghast. "Atrocious! They were supposed to be these sexy shark costumes. Cropped silver spandex with a little fin on the back and sleeves."

From the same proud stylist who championed the child dominatrix freak ensemble for Brooke on my first day—this sounded to me like it should've been his proudest moment.

"But—you know," he continued, "I did what I could. And I made the best of what I had to work with." Robert stopped again, shuddering at the thought of the sexy shark suits, quickly moving on to the next thing that had popped into his brain.

"Ooohhh . . ." His lips gaped sloppily into an O, as if he'd just had the world's best idea. "I've got it." Watching it creep into a slow smile, I waited for something brilliant to come out of his mouth. He brought his hand to his chin, his index finger extended, forming a little dimple on his cheek—from the intensity of his stare I figured the solutions to the world's problems rested at the tip of his tongue.

"I could get you a meeting."

"A meeting?" *What on earth was he talking about?*

"A meeting!" He waved his arms, looking flustered by my nonexistent telepathic abilities. "For your *music*."

"Really?" I asked more in disbelief than in excitement.

"Darling, *all* the right people," he retorted snobbishly as he crossed his legs on the floor of the stage. "Mindy DiMarco is one of my best friends. If she likes your stuff, she can get it into the right hands."

"Yeah, I know who she is." The excitement had found its way into my vocal cords. Mindy DiMarco was *the* most in-demand songwriter in the free world. She's written her way to the top of charts countless times and was commissioned by nearly every hot musician on the market. Her list of hits read like the who's who of the recording industry.

"Thanks . . . I would really appreciate that."

I felt as though I've heard this one before. In L.A. when people say *Let's meet for coffee tomorrow*, what they're really saying is, *I-don't-care-if-I-ever-see-you-again-but-let's-have-some-*

pleasantries-so-I-don't-look-like-an-asshole. Even though I was just starting to believe drunk Robert may actually want to help me, I was skeptical that morning-after Robert would.

Besides, the very idea of Mindy DiMarco even considering my little chicken scratches seemed improbable. He must've really been drunk! Still, it was a nice gesture . . . come to think of it, a little *too* nice of a gesture.

"Why are you being so nice to me?" I couldn't help but ask. It just didn't make sense. The one person I loathed more than anyone else was now sitting in front of me, offering to help me make my dreams come true.

He didn't jump on the defense as I figured he might. Instead, he looked . . . *whimsical* . . . I guess.

"You know," he said softly. "I had dreams when I was a little girl too—I've been in your shoes." His eyes scanned down to the black Aldo flats that were a part of my required dress here. "Only, mine were Christian Louboutin's."

Cushioning his soft little blow, he raised his glass, prompting me to raise my imaginary one.

"To . . . us!" he slurred, thinking as hard as his blood alcohol level would allow. "For . . . being here tonight and *not* at an airport hangar in the Valley—*shooting* for twenty-three-plus hours!"

"Here, here . . . to . . . *us*."

Leaving the Queen Victoria, I emerged from the jovial world of cross-dressing and cocktails and stepped into a more foreboding one, the real one. The air wasn't chilly as it should have been for mid-November, yet the Santa Ana winds were heavy and ominous, fiercely shaking the serrated fronds of the arching palm trees. Meteorologists called currents like these, carrying with them a *whoosh* of positive-charged ions, "witches' winds." They were notorious among the superstitious, blamed for sudden rises in traffic accidents, riots, bizarre behavior in general, and poor-decision making in Hollywood. Superstition or not, something in the air was not right. I drove with caution.

I honestly couldn't place what exactly was making me so un-comfortable. I thought of Brooke and the video shoot I would've been a part of—the one that was filming that very moment until the wee hours of the morning. Was Robert right? Was I better off covered in sticky cocktail mix and carting home my nightly earnings of $175?

When I pulled into my driveway back home, I felt a sense of déjà vu, like paparazzi or some sort of stalker were lurking around the corner; I just felt like I was being watched. Opening my car door, my phone rang out and I screamed sharply, laughing at myself as I pulled it from my purse.

It was David. Thoughts raced through my mind—Steve . . . Oh God. Why would he call? Maybe he wanted to make amends? *Doubtful.*

"Uh, hello?" I asked cautiously. From the way my voice echoed I could tell he had me on speakerphone. Great—was Steve back for round two?

For a moment all I could hear were heavy breaths followed by a crumpled noise as he fumbled to switch on his earpiece.

"Where are you right now?" David almost shouted, heaving and sighing as if he were being chased.

"At home. . . ?" I didn't like the way his tone sounded. Something was wrong—very, very wrong. "Are you okay? What's going on?"

"Jackie—I don't have time to explain can you meet me at the E.R.?"

"What? What's happened? The E.R.? Are you okay?" I blurted.

"Just be there okay?"

"Well, where are you? Which one?"

"In the Valley right now, we're gonna head up over the hill I think . . ." The heavy wailing of a siren pierced my eardrums. "Shit . . . I'll text you when I know where we're going for sure," he said trailing off to survey whatever kind of scene they were in. Speaking back into the phone, the last thing I heard was a muffled, "I gotta go, gotta go—just please get there as soon as you can . . ." *Click!* A wave of nausea soon washed over me.

The willful downslope winds played upon my hair, tying it into copper knots while my mind tied itself in its own nexus of unrequited worries and shiftless anxiety. Running from the parking deck, a lone squad car flew up the road, and I started pumping my arms, breathlessly booking it to the E.R. doors before they finished erecting screens. The press had descended. Mobs of people swarmed, wanting to be part of the action.

"Live at the scene, this is Kit Kruz." A reporter launched into the late-breaking story along with others rapidly firing it around the world, though no one knew what the story really was quite yet. I wondered where Delia lurked in the masses.

I pushed my way through and rushed in desperately looking for David—he wasn't there yet. The fluorescent lights inside the waiting room, harshening the faces of its tired and weary visitors, seemed only to accent the evil influences of the Santa Ana winds awaiting just beyond its doors. I felt the stale white walls closing in on me as I took a seat in a sea of armless plastic chairs bolted to the ground. Across from me, a blue-haired woman with glassy hazel eyes stared catatonically back—some version of punk zombie that only further unsettled the atmosphere. The way my heart raced and how hyperaware I was made everything darkly surreal, dreamlike. This was some circle of hell—the same five elevator music tracks looped endlessly, my back ached, and all I had before me to occupy my thoughts were the blue-haired undead or the huge double doors withholding the fate of those lying behind them.

I got up to look outside as I heard the ambulance siren grow closer and closer. Bright, spotlight-like flashes blinded bystanders, and I closed my eyes to block out the light. The panicked voices grew louder. "I heard she's dead!" The speculation grew though no one had any basis for it. "Get out of the way!" "Here they come." "Move!"

I stood inside the hospital. While the elevator music chimed on, I watched legs tangle and elbows land, lights pour in and flash in and out like waves—chaos, sheer frenetic chaos to the soundtrack of an Enya wannabe. This couldn't be real. It was too organized, too orchestrated in its madness—Hollywood humanity at its very finest, where drama was the lifeblood of dramatic people. Here, in front of the hospital, was the congregated backbone of the studio system, the Hollywood extras earning thousands for photos and words worth nothing more than the sensationalist pages they were printed on, swarming an ambulance like four-year-olds on a soccer field. On its way was a damaged commodity, pure gold for the luckiest crazy in the crowd. This was Holy Mass for the syndicated soul.

Brooke's ambulance pulled up and everyone sprang into action. Immediately, security set to work sealing off the entire area. Other ambulances were diverted to different hospitals, and the police blocked several streets to keep spectators at bay. Then a police S.U.V. came to a screeching stop and David flew out. He nearly missed me as doctors and nurses ushered him back to the side entrance they were taking Brooke through to avoid the drama outside.

"What's wrong? What's wrong? Is Brooke okay? Did something happen to Brooke?" I jogged along side him. My mind flashed back to the last time we'd seen each other, that ugly scene at Brooke's. He let out a deeply troubled sigh.

They guided us past the reception desk—away from the inferior waiting room used for normal people and up to the second-floor V.I.P. waiting room—the celebrity wing. The gleaming hospital floors, scrubbed clean of any illness that may have shuffled across it, smelled strongly of disinfectant. The distance was short, but the whirling in my brain stretched it on and on and on.

The long, gloomy hallway served as a thoroughfare for doctors and patients, nurses pushing wheelchairs and custodians changing light bulbs. But it led to a surprisingly cheerful room that expanded from the hallway into a spacious sitting area with vast windows and stylish, comfortable chairs. Plasma-screen televisions adorned the walls and another area housed half a dozen iMacs. Completely separate quarters were available for those waiting for news, and the hospital staff made sure to bring them water and whatever else they needed to make the wait more comfortable. Nevertheless, the usual doctor's office cacophony of ringing phones and message taking provided the soundtrack.

Few people surrounded us in our little alcove. The ticking of a heater built against the window offered the only noise. Finally, shattering the silence, I asked once again, determined this time to hold out for an answer.

"Well, what happened exactly?" I asked. From the strange way she'd been acting the last time I'd seen her, I could only imagine. David heaved a heavy sigh, shrinking backwards in his seat. Massaging his temples in circular motions with his knuckles for a few minutes, he turned his weary head to me.

"Let's go grab some caffeine. This could take a while." He chuckled before sitting upright.

"David," I said, as we stood and started walking. "This is ridiculous—I'm kinda freaking out right now and you know something, everything that I don't! I nearly killed myself cutting lights all through Hollywood to get here, tell me what's going on?" Without stopping, he grabbed my arm—forcefully, but not aggressively—and we made our way down the carpeted hallway to the cafe.

As we walked, David told me everything about the music video shoot in the Valley that night. A lot rode on this upcoming single, "Love Tide," the first from her new album. She completely buckled, he said, forgetting every dance move she'd learned. She grew more and more self-conscious and eventually broke into tears, wailing about how she wanted her mama, and then even me. Eventually, David said, she just broke down completely.

"She kept sobbing, saying she didn't know what was going on with her life and that the only person she knew she could trust was you." David looked for my reaction, though I couldn't really put one together. "Then she stood up and walked toward the door and collapsed into a fit of hysteria. She was raving and inconsolable, so I called the hospital because I had no idea what else to do."

A vision of the night flashed through my head—Robert's sarcastic rants of the outfits matched with David's details. I could imagine Brooke in her sailor corset with underwires and boning, anchor patches and satin bows, tutu skirt and navy hat. The backdrop of the high seas, dancers surrounding her, some thirty-five crew members, cameramen, and friends gathered in a cavernous airport hangar to watch her play out the scene she'd been dreading for days.

"That must have been awful." I shook my head, wondering where Steve was when it all went to hell.

Lattes in hand we walked back to the waiting room. I watched the staff breeze by with volumes of paper charts and wondered what it might be like to work with chaos day-in, day-out. Probably not that different from working with a celebrity sensation, except, of course, lives depended on them, not livelihoods.

"Thanks for calling me, really," I told him. The awkwardness had eased a bit but remained palpable. There was so much I wanted to say, and so much time had passed that I couldn't hold back.

"I know you really believed in me—what can I say? Maybe I'm a cynic?" I laughed. "I was just trying to protect myself, I guess."

He shrugged as if he were holding something back. "Jackie," he started, "I'm no saint. I could have stopped the video production. I could see plain as day she needed a miracle to pull it off. You actually had the strength to walk away from something you knew in your heart was wrong. I admire that—it took a lot of guts."

"You're giving me too much credit—"

"No. Steve needed someone to call him out that way. Everyone else is too busy kissing his ass. You're a good person, Jackie. The best kind."

I felt sheepish and withdrew a bit. I appreciated the words and enjoyed being with David again, but I still felt uneasy.

As we made our way back inside the private waiting room, an anxious voice filled the corridor behind us. Scouring the hallway, marching forcefully against the protest of a helpless nurse he'd pushed his way past, Steve moved toward us.

"What's *she* doing here?" Reaching us, he snorted.

"I called her," David said, unwavering.

A nurse came into view up ahead. "She wants to see . . ." she looked down at the clipboard as both Steve and I hoped our own names would be called, ". . . Jackie?"

At this Steve clucked in disbelief. "I'm her manager. It's far more important that I see her than her little friend here."

"I thought he," the nurse said point a long narrow finger at David, "was her manager?"

Steve looked over at his ever-loyal employee. The look of impatience on his face seemed to say *you better hurry up and explain*. Taking a deep breath, David jumped to his feet.

"That's—that's right," he said quickly, becoming more confident with each passing second. "I am her manager. David Kagan."

"David—seriously . . ." Steve fumed.

The nurse was looking down at her clipboard. "That's right—that's what I got here. Mr. David Kagan."

"He's a junior staffer at my firm." Steve reached for a business card in his pocket—not finding one he huffed, exasperated. He dropped David his heaviest stare, as if to say he had one last chance. "Mate . . ." he snarled, "you really want to do this right now?"

"Yes—Steve. I do." David knew what this meant for him, but—wanting to do the right thing—he nodded, slow at first and then picking up the pace as Steve glared at him. "Someone's got to look out for her—you've pushed all the people who ever really cared for her—who wanted the best for her—you've pushed them all away. But not this time."

Piping up again, the nurse chimed, "I'm sorry sir. . . . Miss Parker clearly stated that a . . ." her eyes scanned the page to check again. Looking up as she nodded, she continued, "Jackie. She's the only person she asked for."

"This is absurd . . ." he stammered. A shark ready to take a bite out of anyone in his way, Steve started to push past the nurse. Sticking her hand out to stop him in his tracks, blocking to the same side he tried to dodge, she was unmoving.

"Sir, I *will* call security." She meant business. No amount of sweet talking could get Steve past this velvet rope. We were far, far away from the red carpet. And so he stood there, paralyzed. Steve scowled at me as we passed back by each other—this time, I didn't wince.

Nestled away in a private room with 600-thread-count sheets and a private-duty nurse, Brooke rested with an IV drop pumping her full of fluids. As we entered, a nurse was pricking her finger to test something or another. Like a child, she looked the other direction, wincing as the needle poked through. "They tell me I'm suffering from exhaustion—something like excessive exertion and fatigue," she said trying to recite what the doctor said to her verbatim as another nurse entered to take her blood pressure.

True to form, she seemed unusually chipper for someone in the hospital. She looked, on the other hand, like someone who'd just suffered a panic attack after a weeklong bender: ragged. The nurse smiled and optimistically chimed in, "A little bed rest is all she needs."

"I always thought 'exhaustion' was just a code word for rehab?" I joked about the celebrity-mandated euphemism, thinking really that rehab was exactly what she needed.

Exhaustion. *That was the understatement of the century.* Sure, she was overworked, twisted into knots and left a tangled mess. Brooke was rarely able to get a night of sleep without worrying about an upcoming obligation . . . 'twas the wrath of the celebrity machine. Hounded relentlessly by the press, and deliberately contained in this artificial world, she endured more stress than I could possibly fathom. I sensed her emotional turmoil was too much for one person to deal with it all, let alone with her lack of time for personal care. She'd worn her body and mind out to the point it was crazy to think she could function properly. Sure, she could afford to go to a five-star hotel or rent a villa in St. Tropez, but her fame always followed, her anonymity lost forever.

I squeezed her little hand and gave her a sympathetic smile.

"Jackie, this is gonna be real good for me—I just need to get back to being me again—and not—not be so paranoid about everything. Things will get better, I know they will."

"You're not a machine Brooke, you have to stand up for yourself." I tried, hoping to get some truth across while she appeared willing to accept it. "Believe me, you've sacrificed so much already, and if you don't, there will be no greater consequence than your happiness."

She began to ramble on in a sweet, virginal soprano voice, "I want to get back to the way it used to be. My momma could manage me again—I'll move my family out here into a big, beautiful house on the ocean."

"Shhh. Don't even worry about that right now." I wanted her to relax.

"I still feel real bad about what happened with your song too . . . you're sooo good!" The song never made her album, thanks, of course, to Steve. "You can write every single one for my next album."

I shook my head as she presented this amazing offer. Most conversations with Brooke involved grandiose visions and breathless observations about life. She pushed her plate aside and toyed instead with the glass of juice on her bedside tray, now serious. "You're the only one who was ever a true friend to me."

Though it comforted me to hear her say it, I had struggled from day one to know where our friendship began and business ended. And that was precisely the problem. Everything had just been a blur—fame, partying, love—all of it. Faster. Faster. And the faster the merry-go-round of her life spun, the less she was able to hold on. While her young body could take the hit, her emotional being was thrown to the dogs. Sooner or later this burnout was going to be inevitable. She burned the candle at both ends, all the while burned by all those around her as well—the ever-present media, Steve, her demanding schedule.

She had no concept of her limits when it came to working and playing too hard. I had learned that the hard way, been burned myself in the process.

I needed to get off the ride.

"Oh Brooke," I sighed. "I think you should just focus on resting for now. Okay? I just want to see you healthy and happy. I'm no good to you this way." I gave her a playful punch in the shoulder, followed by a hug. "You're a star, but you're still human," I said, "and me? I'm just a plain old human . . ." As I pulled away, I knew then that Brooke would never call me again. Even though we would leave as friends, she knew, somewhere, that I didn't want the chaos.

"Okay, I need to catch my stagecoach," I teased, trying not to cry.

"Gimme one more hug, Calamity," she begged. Ours wasn't a story about jealousy, for sure, and it didn't end with two happy couples riding out of town together. But it had been about overcoming something, far more than I realized then, but we did it together.

"Brooke. You are going to be just fine. Just stick to your guns. Don't let anyone walk all over you." I heard the door open, through the threshold came Mrs. Dianne clinging to Willy's arm. They looked so scared, terrified actually, but forced grins for Brooke's sake.

"Well lookatcha! Here I thought you'd be hollering like a stuck hog—all laid up in here!" Willy bellowed and slapped his knee. "You meaning to tell me ol' Steve sent a plane so you could show us all yer good looks? You know I can't stand flyin' missy."

Mrs. Dianne hugged her daughter and kissed her forehead. "Oh sweetie."

"Jackie darlin', thanks for keepin' our baby company." Willy rested his one big weathered paw on my shoulder. "That night you woke us—gave us quite a scare, but we're thankful. Famous 'er not, she's our little girl, and we're truly blessed that you're lookin' out for her."

I could hear Mrs. Dianne apologizing to Brooke through tears. "I never wanted to be one of those pushy mothers. All I ever dreamed for you was to be as successful as you could be, whether that meant gettin' a scholarship or havin' the chance to become a role model for other young girls. I wanted a life for you—a real life, one I was afraid at times we couldn't give you."

"Oh mamma." Brooke took her hand. I wanted to leave them alone so they could have their moment.

"Yer brothers are mighty worried about ya." Willy looked as stern as one could expect from a gregarious alligator man like himself. "They're just outside, and they'd love to see ya if yer feeling up to it. Didn't want to unleash those lil' hellions on ya too soon." He broke into a laugh.

"Of course I wanna see those Tweedles." Brooke actually smiled, and I knew she had everything she needed right then and there.

"Well, I better make room for the boys. I'll see you . . ." Maybe I could have, maybe, another time or place. We both knew better, but it felt easier to leave it at that. I blew a goofy kiss at her as I left. Shrouded in the Parkers' love and warmth, I battled a downpour of emotions as I plodded out through the private waiting room.

Steve hadn't calmed down at all; his face was blood red as he hopped up, trying to get back to Brooke. The twins chased around him, shouting "Wah! Wah! Wah!" and "I am a Comanche." Certainly he'd come across his own private hell, and despite all the pleading in the world, he'd been denied access to his most precious commodity.

"Sir. I'm sorry, sir," the nurse sternly told him. "You'll have to come back, and see if she'll see you tomorrow."

I tried to wipe the grin off my face, but then I let it shine. I brushed past Steve, ignoring his inquiries about her status. "Mmm. Nope. Confidential info."

Up ahead, the sight of someone barreling down the hall kept that smile shining.

"T!"

"'Sup my girl! How you do?"

"I'm . . . you know. . . ." I said shrugging. *How did I feel?* That was a good question.

"I got here as soon as I could. I got stuck fillin' in for one of the other guys this mornin'. Been at . . . Hollister? Some shit like that?" He shook his head. "Landon was there signing some promo C.D.s or somethin'—whooo—I tell you, it's *loud* as shit in there, blastin' music louder than anyone I know! I ain't even had time to wrap this up for the princess." Enfolded in his gigantic paws, a dainty fairy with butterfly wings knelt upon a small pewter box.

I held it in my hands and read the dangling tag aloud: "Make a wish and hold it true and I will help make your wish come true . . ." I smiled broadly.

"Yeah," T-Roc huffed uncomfortably, looking around, "it's a wishing fairy or some shit."

"Oh my God—*T* . . . that's so sweet!"

"You know the kind a shit I got buying *this* in my 'hood?"

"Please, don't give me that T . . . you live in Brentwood."

"*Girl*—I got my boys there too! They all callin' me Tinker-bell now—I'm not playing!" He chuckled, though there was a gentle sadness to his tone.

"Well, she's going to *love* it." I smiled warmly. "You better get in there . . . they told Steve that visiting hours were over . . . but, uh, I think that only pertains to him."

We stood there for a second, both knowing it was quite possibly the last time we'd see each other. We might've lived in the same city, but our worlds were drifting further and further apart with each passing day. He started to turn towards the waiting room and then stopped.

"Listen—I been doin' this thing for a long time, and I can tell you there's barely anybody in this business I'd call the *real* shit." He pointed a fleshy finger in my direction. "But *you* girl, you the real shit, you know. You always done me good . . . stuck by me, helped me out."

"I'm sure there were a lot of things I could've done differently . . . better . . ."

"That's fo damn sure—that goes for all of us—me too." T-Roc grinned. "Ain't nobody perfect, we all make mistakes. But you know the real important thing about you and me—about us all?" He exhaled deeply as I nodded. "We get up every day and take a chance on the things people are too scared to ever try . . . a lot of 'em want to . . . but they scared, you know? Because we're taking a risk, we're strong enough to persevere, knowin' that with the right faith and attitude, there's a good probability something *good* will happen. What I'm tryin' to say here is—no matter how you come outta this whole thing with Brooke, don't you stop taking chances. A coward dies a thousand deaths . . . a soldier dies but once." My eyes opened wide. Here T-Roc stood before me now—a wise old owl.

"I wouldn't have pegged you as a Shakespeare fan," I told him, walking slowly backwards.

"Shakesp—huh? Hell no! That ain't no Shakespeare—that was Tupac."

"I'm pretty sure it's from *Julius Caesar* . . ." I shouted back behind me now. "No wonder everyone's calling you Tinkerbell!"

"It ain't no Shakes-peare! Tu-pac Sha-kur . . . read my lips. . . !"

Laughing as I walked away, I approached the door to the

main waiting room and took a quick look down the hall. David had disappeared; maybe he went for coffee again. *Should I look for him*, the thought echoed. I headed for the main waiting room, deciding I just needed to leave.

"Hey!" a voice yelled out. I turned around to find David, two cups in his hand. "I got you tea. The rugrats were kinda cute at first, but between them and Steve my nerves were becoming a little grated," he laughed, "so I stepped away for a minute."

"Oh. Thanks." I smiled, taking the warm cup in my hand. David's character never failed. Reliable. Thoughtful. I hated the many times I questioned his worthiness.

"Everything okay?" He was sincerely concerned, unlike the schmuck hounding the nurses to gain access to Brooke's bedside.

"Yeah, you know Brooke, in good spirits it seems."

"I guess I meant, is everything okay with you?"

"Yeah. I think so . . ."

Out of the corner of my eye, I spotted a copy of *Scoop* sitting atop a nearby table, and on its cover—Brooke. I stopped and stared down at it for a moment as the buzzing of the T.V.s mounted in the corners rung in my ears.

We would ask well-wishers and other fans to respect the star and her family members at this time . . .

I peered up to see some older picture of a disheveled Brooke in a mesh trucker cap exiting a club with a crucifix in hand. The caption read: "Party Girl's Wacky Behavior Makes a Comeback."

The hospitalization came hours into the filming her new music video . . . the pop princess's publicist has cited exhaustion . . .

Inset, a headline pronounced "The Next Big Thing"—the cherubic face of a scantily clad fifteen-year-old girl stared up at me. The contrasting stories seemed to scream out the most blatant of warnings, the irony was that no one noticed, or cared.

Because there will always be a new girl, the next big thing, the next Brooke Parker, willing to shed her innocence for a shot at infamy. She waits eagerly in the wings, ready to provide us with entertainment and to satisfy our fantasies, unknowing of what really lay ahead—how could she?—but willing, nonetheless.

"Yeah," I said, with a faraway smile. "Everything is going to be just fine . . ." The sliding tempered glass double-doors swung open with a *whoosh!* as I stepped toward them.

"Hey Jackie," David called out again.

I paused, holding the doors open with my presence, and looked back.

"I hear ol' Herbie's getting a bit lonely. Maybe we ought to pay him a visit . . . it's no Ric Craia shoot, but . . ." David made some sort of peace offering.

"Sure. You know where to reach me," I said coolly, though my heart did a little somersault in my chest.

Just beyond the automatic glass doors, particles of soot and dust scattered sunlight into the darkness and the world slowly awoke. First only the sound of timer-set sprinklers spouting across the parched hospital lawn could be heard, which was soon followed by a Doppler effect of chirping birds, automobiles, and a crescendo of voices. The Santa Anas had died down, and the air caressed my face in soft currents. Watching as the glistening yellows in the east bathed everything in warmth, I felt life all around me—loud and clear. I'd spent so much time living almost exclusively in Brooke Parker's world—segregated and empty. Beyond those doors where Brooke lay vacuously, I'd stepped into the dawning of a new era. Now it was only me. I faced a future that hinged on my own desires. I remembered my childhood, and the days I was able to look into the smog-free sky and inhale deeply, feeling really happy to be alive. I love having those moments tucked away in my memory. And looked forward to all those that lay ahead.

Chapter 23

You're always writing about yourself . . .
you hide it in a variety of ways
and you meld your voice with other lives.
—Bruce Springsteen

"Where's the hairspray? Seriously! Who's got it? I'm going to *freak* out!" Ava scampered frantically backstage, turning over chairs and whimpering before seizing an abandoned can of Aqua Net from one of the vanities. "It's not my brand," she sighed, hoisting a firm calf onto a nearby stool. "But it will have to do." Pressing down with all her might, a mist coated the miniscule run in her stockings.

"Guuuurl," a Persian beauty by the name of Miz Seducktrez cried out, casting a disapproving look at Ava as she paused from dabbing clear deodorant across her hairline. "My chair better not be any kinds of sticky."

Turning back to the mirror, she continued "sweat-proofing" her face while Thursday Florentine, the novice of the group, chatted on and on to no one in particular.

". . . Can you believe it? Seventy-five pounds! All by drinking coffee and cutting out carbs—a miracle if I ever heard one. Oh, yeah—and I started doing those Rudy Reyes videos too . . ."

Though I hated to admit it, being a fly on the wall backstage at the Queen Victoria I probably learned more from the "girls" than they did from me. Standing just behind a dimple-faced blond, known to us all as Daphne Hourglass, I watched as she dipped a thin wooden stick into a mess of goo on a napkin spread across her thigh. "See? You can almost forego the liner!" she squealed.

In typical Daphne fashion, while she'd started by asking for my expertise, it had somehow turned into another one of her tutorials. More or less, she probably just liked the attention. The other girls flashed me sympathetic looks as they passed by.

They'd all come to loathe her, apparently, as she'd made a habit of asking for help, ignoring advice, then dispensing overloads of her own upon any flaws she found in the others. "She has to be the authority on every little thang, don't she?" I heard Ava snicker to someone else.

Saving me from her clutches, a semi-panicked Jorge, who'd recently hung up his Rita act for good with no other explanation other than he'd had a "revelación," grabbed my shoulders. "Any luck? Please say yes-s-s-s?" he pleaded.

We both swiveled around to the vanity behind us where Miss Jade was leaning back, admiring the thick, straight eyebrows she'd just finished painting onto the middle of her forehead.

"I haven't gotten to her yet," I admitted as I stared at my next challenge.

"Do it! We need her in that spangly cowgirl costume sans the snow white face and quick! The theme is Wild West, *not* the

Shanghai Express! Don't let me down!" Jorge pivoted, hot on his heels in the other direction, whirling off in a cloud of perfume and attitude to put out the flames of his next disaster.

"I used to do it the vintage way," Miss Jade, accompanied now by a lost-looking Thursday, rambled on, "you know, the bintsukeabura and every-thang, the whoooole kit and caboodle." I had pretty much no idea what she was talking about, and Thursday, hoping to change the subject back to her miraculous tale of weight loss—compliments of a borderline dangerous amount of caffeine—was quickly stifled before the words could even escape her mouth. "And you know," Miss Jade continued, "all that authentic stuff? *Highly* toxic."

That Miss Jade—the queen of "iki chic"—as she called it, was a tricky one. I proceeded with caution.

"Hi," I said, smiling sheepishly as I approached. Miss Jade exhaled noisily in response, before pursing her crimson lips.

"Yes? What can I do for you?"

She knew quite well what she could do for me. I waited for any sign from her—an expression perhaps?—but her skin, painted porcelain everywhere but her hairline, remained motionless, like a mask. I looked down at my watch, only a half hour to go. There was no time to beat around the bush.

"Just a little reminder," I tried, "about tonight's theme? Did you forget?"

"No." Turning back to the mirror, she swiped a large sponge from the tabletop and began patting her throat with a steady hand. "I didn't."

I was losing my patience. "Come on, Larry! Look, if you don't get that pink, sequined disaster hanging up over there on your body in five, I'm going to personally help Jorge set fire to your katsura."

Miss Jade, aka Larry, looked horrified, but rather than punching me square in the face as I half-predicted, she cowered in her chair instead. I couldn't help but grin, unashamedly amused with the absurdity of this whole scene as I sauntered off. I'd been through too much to back down now to an ex-7-11 employee from Torrance, who'd just run out on his wife and kids due to a severe identity crisis. And man, did it feel good to stick up for myself.

"He's almost here," Jorge gushed as I made my way to the bar. We'd spent the entire day transforming the Queen Victoria into Golden Garter Saloon, the backdrop for Robert's "Calamity Jane" surprise birthday party and with just minutes to go, he looked . . . tense, to say the least.

"He thinks my car broke down." Jorge smiled mischievously, easing up a bit.

"Genius! And totally believable considering you drive an antique," I joked.

"That *antique* is an MG in pristine condition, I'll have you know." He frowned. Quickly dissipating to a smile, he added, "It's a collector's item."

As the front door chimed open, momentarily casting rays of twilight into our magnificently festooned saloon, Jorge held his breath. The color drained from Robert's face.

Seeing his Doris Day dream come to life, he looked around astonished, entranced by the dozen plasma screens surrounding the bar playing his favorite musical.

"You little bitches!" Robert squealed affectionately as he rushed over and kissed my cheek while throwing an arm around Jorge.

"Hey, not so fast Miss Day," I teased as Robert clasped his hands together in delight. "This is one thing I'm gonna have to take credit for . . ."

On cue, the girls filed onstage one by one, all dressed as fast-shootin', tough talkin', sultry cowboys—er, girls. Robert's eyes darted from one to the next. The diva of the moment, he could scarcely contain his delight. Jorge, however, suddenly shot me a nervous look.

"Don't worry," I smirked. "We ended up with a, um—let's just call it a compromise." No sooner had I said the words than Miss Jade stumbled on stage—her face still ghostlike, her crimson pucker intact—but below the Geisha mug was the body of a Dixie Chick, swaying to the beat of the choreographed shootout number.

"Oh. My. *God.*" Robert squealed again; and we all erupted in laughter.

"It's not the stylings of *Robert Bernstein* we know," Jorge whined, "but we tried our best." Wiping the tears from his eyes, he turned towards me, smiling.

"We know you can outstyle any boy on the range," I laughed, tossing my hair back and joining the smiles. Whatever this was that we had pulled off—no small feat, if I might add—it was quite a sight to behold.

Robert threw me his most serious look: "Guurrl," he huffed, "I can out*style*, out*shoot* and out*sing* them all." Then as the next song commenced, he clasped his hand to his chest melodramatically. "Oh. My. Gawd. I loooooove this song!" and began humming whole-heartedly, eyes closed, as if pronouncing the words would cause him to keel over in ecstasy.

In a way, I was still reeling over the fact that the nickname Calamity, which Robert had no small part in handing over to me, actually held a place close to his heart. I followed his gaze over to one of the monitors where, on screen, Calamity Jane stood in a dressing room talking to a young singer named Katie Brown. It was the catalyst moment—the point of no return—when her entire life changes. Having watched the film at Jorge's behest more times over the past week than any healthy human being ever should, I considered for a moment that maybe, just maybe, Calamity Jane and I had more in common than I could have ever known. Take away the stagecoaches, the jilted lovers, the pistols, and the perfect harmonies—at its core, it was a story about friendship, mistaken identity, and ultimately, transformation. Destiny may not have allowed Brooke and I to ride off into the sunset together, but I truly hoped that our experiences, at the very least, had made us both stronger. And when it came to Robert, well, that was another story. The truth: he was a son of a bitch, but seeing him here with his Broadway-belting, shamelessly squealing troupe of queens, his insults pretty much amounted to compliments. Sure I was a "bitch," but so were all of his best friends.

"Hey Calamity!—uh, sorry, I mean *Jackie*," Robert said, as he leaned over toward me.

"Of all nights, Robert, tonight I'll let that one slide." I smiled, looking up at him. All sassiness aside now, he looked heartbreakingly sincere.

"I really owe you one for this."

I waved my hand bashfully. "No you don't. It was my pleasure. Besides—wasn't like I had any choice in the matter. It's my job. Literally."

He smiled again. "But seriously, if there's anything I can ever do to help you out, let me know. That is, unless you *want* to sling piña coladas in a drag bar for the rest of your life." Cocking his head back, he quickly added, "No offense, Jorge."

He'd already forgotten—that is if he'd even registered it at all in the first place—about our conversation the other night that had dissolved into a vat of Beefeater's. I knew I could've spoken up. I could've said, "Don't forget about Mindy DiMarco!" Yet even if it might've jogged his gin-logged memory, I had come to realize that speaking up in the vein of opportunity and speaking up in terms of self-respect were two very different things. And I didn't want to be the type of person, found so commonly in an industry such as ours, who ignored the obvious difference of the two. Besides, I told myself, lightning doesn't strike twice—and if it did, it certainly wouldn't for someone who bore the kind of nickname I had earned, even if it did have a silver lining. I was ready, willing, and able to take my destiny by the reins and finally make it my very own.

I could feel it starting at the corners of my mouth, a rich smile that moved up to my eyes and then spread across the apples of my cheeks. Now—using Robert's affectionate phrasing—it was my turn to be heartbreakingly sincere.

"Thanks . . . bitch."

Ending things with Brooke left me liberated and empty all at once. I'd lived almost exclusively in her world, and everything she did dictated my existence. Now it was my turn to be me for a change, as I faced a future that hinged on my own desires. Energized with a fresh start and fresh outlook, I decided, before anything else, to go to town on the tornado-swept disaster of my room, because starting there was as good a place as any.

It seemed that every nook contained my former life. Tangled up in a stack of dirty laundry, I noticed my "special" tour pass dangling from the bottom. It had, at one time, signified my own inflated self-importance; earning that privilege had informed my entire sense of accomplishment, and its exclusivity had reaffirmed my worth. I sifted through unopened stacks of mail, sorting out the bills, occasionally coming across a photo wedged somewhere it shouldn't have been. Brooke, T-Roc, and I flashing peace signs and goofy grins at some disco-themed party; Brook and I sitting on her parents' four-wheelers back in Florida. So many good times to remember. Wiping up the messes and tossing out the clutter, I collected scattered souvenirs from my rock 'n' roll days and fondly placed them in a box, and then another box—and before long, I realized, I was gonna need a bigger box. I thought back to my summers at Dodo's and the time I spent digging through the treasures of my grandfather's glamorous life, then I tucked them away in my closet.

Finally, my surroundings began to sparkle, and it was high time I dove into the mess my finances had become. I looked out the window at my beautiful car as I searched online trying to determine whether to trade it in or sell it. Who in their right mind drove a Porsche Cayenne in my situation? This was yet another moment, one in a long line of recent moments and many more to come, that signified the whole shiny, glittery facade had truly crumbled. Here was the raw, honest life beneath it. I had not only actively participated in this world of utter chaos, but I had survived it too. And in some small way, I'd been a part of modern history—even as if just a passing influence.

Once again, I had to figure out who I wanted to be.

With my room glistening, and my expenses, well, organized, I felt like I was on a roll. There was a restlessness in me that I couldn't contain. I felt great; I felt strangely calmed and clearheaded; I felt inspired. I grabbed my tote bag and ran back to the main house. Toeing the threshold of my living room, I thought about all the days and nights I'd spent criss-crossing this floor, this house: it had all amounted to something. I looked over at the old piano in the corner, my destination, and didn't pause a second longer.

Sometimes, I'll sit at the piano and play something and all of a sudden, I'll hear all these parts coming together in my head and for a brief minute, I hear the whole thing. That's when I hit record and try to at least get a general sketch of the sound, the timing, the feeling. Lyrics came in much the same way—they relied only on my ability to let go. I think the more honest you are in your lyrics, the more people will respond, but there was a period of time in my life—a long time—when I turned my feelings off. It just didn't seem to me that anyone really cared about how I felt.

Allowing my fingers to glance the keys, I just started playing. At first a few random notes, and those slowly took shape. Playing around with minor fifth and seventh chords, I touched on a dark, inner tension, and without warning, I started to cry. As I played, I began to understand how I'd not been fully conscious of all the feelings that were coming out. Then the strangest thing happened, a word fluttered into my head, and then another. They just kept on flowing. Grabbing my purse, I searched for first piece of paper I could find, and began scribbling words down on the back of a cocktail napkin. It was perfect; it was electricity. I was writing from the heart and I was no longer afraid to say what I felt. I had to strike when the idea was hot.

I leapt into the kitchen and grabbed a notebook off a shelf, pivoting and leaping right back to where I had been. I poured out full thoughts, half-thoughts, phrasings, and plays on words. I wrote big, sometimes occupying two or three ruled lines of paper with just a few words—it didn't matter how much paper I went through, just that I could keep up with my own thoughts. I'm not sure how long this went on for. It became a blur, ecstatic.

I was feeling almost winded, if not downright dazed, by this outpouring of inspiration. I looked up from the leafs of notebook paper littering the table and ground around the piano, my vision readjusting to a distance more than a foot in front of me.

"Jackie!" my mom called from somewhere in the house, startling me from my daze, "you have company!" I turned around just in time to see Lauren round the corner from the foyer into the living room. The warmth in her face surprised me.

"Hey," I said almost inquisitively. "What are you doing here?" I was happy to see her, but in all honesty, I wasn't so sure I deserved her friendship.

"Hey yourself." Lauren smiled, tucking a strand of her unruly hair behind her ear.

Walking through the house and outside the kitchen doors to the yard we made the usual small talk. *How have you been? How's the gallery? Dating anyone?*—things like that. Reaching the base of the stairs up to my little apartment, Lauren turned to me and stopped, her eyes opened wide.

"Before *anything*—"

Great, here it is, this is the part where she tells me what a shit I've been.

"Can. You. Believe it?!" Here was Lauren, right back in her joyously dramatic mode, as if nothing at all had happened.

Oh boy, I thought, *here we go. Brooke, Brooke, Brooke.* Brooke's foray into hospitalization, obviously, was the hottest topic in town. It was also just about the last thing I wanted to talk about, but there was little I could do to stop it.

"I just can't believe this happened . . ." she continued.

Ugh, let's just get this over with already . . .

"I mean, Med has a sex tape?! How wrong is that?"

Startled, as confused as I felt, I couldn't imagine what face I'd managed to conjure. "Good old Rexy Lexy's quite the exhibitionist apparently . . ."

"Wait, wait up a second . . ." I stalled, "she did *what*?"

"Oh. Come. *On.* Don't tell me you haven't heard this."

"I've kinda been in my own little bubble for the past few days," I tried, glancing around. "I'm sorry, did you say *sex tape*?"

"I sure as shit did young lady, your ears do not deceive you. Rexy Lexy and that not-at-all-sleazy Med are apparently not the brightest birds in the bush."

"I can't believe they let it out of their sight," I offered.

"I guess we shoulda seen this coming . . . they look completely hammered, must have been after some big night."

"Wait, you watched it?"

"Um . . . *yeah*. Of course I did, you kidding me? Not that it was the most pleasant thing I've seen but how could I not?" Pulling her laptop out of the bag, she feverishly opened it and started clicking through her Internet browser.

"Oh no you don't, c'mon Lauren, there's no way I want to see this," I stammered.

"Just a peek, you just have to see how ridiculous this is," she gushed. And before I could look away, there they were. *Oh my God. I know that place . . .*

"*Nooooo way!* The Monte Puchol Villa. I was with her that night!"

"Ew . . . do you think their memberships have since been revoked?" Her look of disgust seamlessly morphed into a sly grin, and we both started laughing our heads off. I couldn't believe I had ever treated this girl like I had, we had been so inseparable for so long. More than anything, laughing with Lauren brought me right back to the headspace I needed to be in.

Turning back as we hiked the stairs, quickly she grinned.

"But—there is just one more thing I have to know."

"Oh yeah?" I said. "What's that?"

She hesitated, clearly trying to put together the best articulation of what it was on her mind. "Is 'exhaustion' really a true medical diagnosis?"

"It actually is!" I said declaratively.

"Really?" She scrunched up her face—squinting one eye tightly. "I always thought it was a code word for rehab?"

We started laughing hysterically again, by this point my stomach ached. Unexpectedly, I started welling up with tears. How was it that after all I did to Lauren—the way I treated her and abandoned her—she could be there so effortlessly to lift me back up? Trying to stifle the laughs, I went over to her and just gave her a bear hug—not quite the T-Roc kind—but good enough. This was exactly what I needed, more than just her presence, but the big happy slap in the face to remember that a *true* friend is always there when you need her. When the world walks out on you, *that* friend walks right in.

"So, I have a surprise for you." Lauren clucked, as she trotted over to the couch. "I downloaded an old high school favorite of ours on Web Flix."

I knew where she was going with this. "Isn't my house classic? The columns date all the way back to 1972," I quoted with a smile. "I haven't seen . . . *Clueless?* . . . in forever."

"It doesn't matter, the dialogue is permanently etched in our brains." Lauren smiled before reciting another line: "He does dress better than I do, what would I bring to the relationship?" We laughed again as she flipped open her laptop and then silenced by what popped up on the screen as it connected her home page, which of course, was set to Delia's Dish. Brooke's image stretched across the screen with a one-word headline: "CRAZY!" I stared at it sheepishly. It was indeed *crazy*. Here I was, sitting at my own house, laughing with my best friend, embarking on a new life and leaving Brooke's behind. But would I ever truly escape her? Would her chronicled life always be a nagging, constant reminder? I knew I would just have to come to terms with the impossibility of ignoring the passing details of her life. Every time she went to the gas station or broke up with a boyfriend, I—like everyone else that ever read a newspaper, owned a T.V., or logged onto the Internet—would be made aware of it. Only a day had passed and yet new rumors surfaced hourly on almost every blog and news site one could imagine. She was either recovering from a heroin binge, suffering from schizophrenia, or recuperating from her involvement with a radical religion that a few Hollywood A-listers had hoped to make trendy, depending, of course, on which webpage you happened to land on. For those who followed the story, it was hard to keep up with her life. Her most recent exploits had achieved for her another level of stardom—that is, infamy—the kind bestowed upon Hollywood's tragic icons like Marilyn Monroe, James Dean, Elvis Presley, Michael Jackson, and Britney Spears. I had no interest in keeping up; I'd been on that insane ride and was thankful to have gotten off in one piece.

Lauren must have sensed my focus had taken a turn for the worse. "Okay, so you're probably going, 'Is this like a Noxzema commercial or what?' But seriously, I actually have a way normal life for a teenage girl," Lauren suddenly chimed in.

Forget the pain in my gut, I broke out into hysterics, she always had the ability to pull me out of a funk by making me laugh. She reached past me to yank control of her laptop and quickly opened to her Web Flix account. "I think we both could afford to lose ourselves in a little comedy right about now."

"I'm with ya." I smiled.

"So . . . all we need now is your H.D.M.I. cable . . ." she said looking every which way around her.

"My what?" I asked puzzled though not surprised. Lauren was always much more technologically advanced than me. Just as we had settled ourselves on my futon, my nagging cell phone interrupted us.

"Sorry," I groaned, "let me just get rid of whoever this is." Fumbling through my purse, I reached my Vivi on the last ring.

"You don't know what an adaptor cable is but you *do* have the cell phone with a two-year waiting list."

"What? Really?" I smirked.

"What—ever." Lauren rolled her eyes and formed a *w* with her thumbs and index fingers. I walked away, flipping her the bird . . . sarcastically of course.

"Hello?"

"I'm looking for a, uh, Jackie O'Reilly?" came the voice at the other end.

"You've found her."

"Oh, great—my name is Mindy DiMarco, I'm a friend of Robert's . . ."

Chin deep in martinis—holy shit—he'd actually remembered!

My heart fluttered a bit. I could feel Lauren's quizzical eyes upon me, surveying my face that had turned ghost white, watching now in suspense. Turning up the volume on my phone I motioned her over.

Mindy, who hadn't paused for my response, kept talking as Lauren nestled in close to listen. "I'm sure he's told you a little about me—"

"Oh, I'm a big fan of yours . . ." *Fan?! I sounded like the amateur I was!* ". . . I've followed your career a bit." I stuck out my tongue, giving Lauren an *I'm-making-an-ass-out-of-myself-aren't-I?* glance. Scrunching up her face, she shook her head in the same way a mother does when she's trying shake her third-grader out of stage fright—you know, the ultimate parenting con, instilling courage that inevitably ends up with the kid peeing his pants.

"So . . ." she continued. "You were working as a makeup artist beforehand with no real musical training, is that right?"

Shit. Right now, I was "Piss Pants O'Reilly."

"I've dabbled in songwriting all my life," I quickly responded, hopeful. From past experiences I could tell this wasn't going so good.

"Great . . . listen, I'm working with this up-and-comer called Luna, she's signed to EMI and we're looking to team up with a couple people. Why don't you come in, say, Tuesday? If we both like your stuff and think you could be a fit, great—if not, we part ways. It really is that simple."

I just kept nodding as if she could see me, jarred out of my stupid trance only when Lauren socked my playfully in the arm. "Can you *believe this?*" she mouthed to me, her eyes bulging in excitement.

"That, uh, that sounds great!"

"Well, you've done something to impress Robert and that's an accomplishment in and of itself. He said he thought you had a lot to bring to the table—said your energy for music is contagious. And your drive is inspiring . . ."

"He *said that?*" I didn't mean to sound so shocked . . . but I was.

"I know," she laughed. "Doesn't sound like Robert . . ."

"Not the slightest bit," I agreed with a grin.

I grabbed a pen as she gave me directions and other minor notes. Yes, I was completely shocked, but for some reason, I wasn't nervous. *If we like your stuff, great. If not, we part ways, it's as simple as that.* I could see how that would be intimidating to some people, but considering the hoops I've had to jump through to stay afloat, the cold, hard, no bullshit truth was all I wanted. For me, it was refreshing.

Was this my second lightning bolt? *Nah*, I assured myself, *this one I earned*.

"Are you dying right now? You must be stoked!" Lauren asked wide-eyed.

"This is all just so . . . so . . ."

"Surreal?" Lauren interjected. I shook my head. Then, without warning or a second though, the perfect word to describe the moment popped into my head.

"It's *seredipident*."

"Serendipitous?" she asked, confused.

"Yeah," I laughed to myself, "that."

Photo © Jeffrey Fiterman

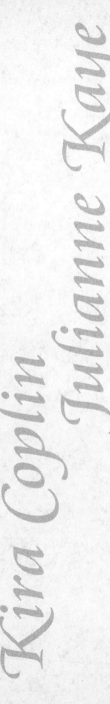
Kira Coplin   Julianne Kaye

KIRA COPLIN is a seasoned writer, filmmaker, and pop culture journalist no stranger to the glamorous and often times gritty world of Hollywood. Formerly on staff of *US Weekly*, Coplin was also the Editor at Chicago-Scene and is a contributor to CosmoGirl!, *The New York Post*, and *OK!*, as well as *CITY* magazine and 944, among others. Coplin is also producing an upcoming documentary, *Girl on Fire!*, about the life and legacy of factory girl Edie Sedgwick.

JULIANNE KAYE is a Los Angeles native and makeup artist to the stars. She has worked with some of the world's most well-known celebrities for countless red carpet events, award shows and film as well as having her work published in *Harper's Bazaar*, *Rolling Stone*, and *Vanity Fair*. Currently she is the creator of Revolutionbeauty.com, an informative take on beauty including how-to videos from an expert point of view.